"It's visionary. It's passion̲ ....-y.
It's an extraordinary jour̲ ....ind of two artists -
Remedios Varo's, and Rym Kechacha's."
Francesco Dimitri, author of *The Book of Hidden Things* and
Never the Wind

"Rym Kechacha has created an enchanting world, filled with the
magical, mysterious and mesmerising. It left me spellbound."
Elizabeth Lee, author of *Cunning Women*

"Exceptional, impossibly beautiful, important."
Anna Smith Spark, author of the *Empires of Dust* trilogy

"To say that there are owl women and witches and daughters of
the moon, seamstresses and writers and painters who can call
worlds into being, enchantments and sorrows, is to only scratch
the surface of this extraordinary new novel by Rym Kechacha.
Inspired by the work of Spanish surrealist Remedios Varo, this
is a magical, melancholy story, the kind of book that makes you
remember why you love reading in the first place"
Lynda E. Rucker, award-winning author of
The Moon Will Look Strange

"A surreal, mystical, celestial wonder of a book!
To Catch a Moon is an inspired creation."
Oliver Langmead, author of *Birds Of Paradise* and *Glitterati*

"Through Kechacha's exquisite writing, the many glamours,
both dark and light, of the world of *To Catch a Moon* will
transfer to the reader like a spell. A weird and wonderful fairy
tale that pays due homage to its inspiration."
Peter Haynes, author of *The Willow by Your Side*.

Also available from Unsung Stories

TO CATCH A MOON

RYM KECHACHA

UNSUNG STORIES

Published by Unsung Stories

3 Rosslyn Road
London E17 9EU, United Kingdom

www.unsungstories.co.uk

First edition published in 2022
First impression

Paperback ISBN: 9781912658183
ePub ISBN: 9781912658190

Edited by Dan Coxon
Proofreading by Jonathan Oliver
Cover design by Vince Haig
Text design by Cox Design Limited
Typesetting by Vince Haig

Printed in the UK by Clays Ltd, Elcograf S.p.A.

For Ed

AUTHOR'S NOTE

Remedios Varo was born in 1908 in Spain. She was exiled from Spain to Paris because of the Spanish Civil War and then fled the Nazi occupation of France. She settled in Mexico City, where she painted surrealist images charged with symbols of myth, witchcraft, astrology and dreams. Her legacy, as well as that of her contemporary female surrealists, is being rediscovered by a new generation. Remedios died suddenly in 1963.

I have invented the events of this novel; however, I cannot say for sure they didn't happen.

CHANSON

MEXICO CITY, 1955

Remedios Varo is sitting at her kitchen table and thinking about the moon; the ponderous curve of its belly as it hangs full, the tender arc of its crescent, the dark patches of shadows where surely there are mountains and lakes hidden on its surface. There should be a moon of some sort in the painting she is working on but she cannot see where it should be, or in what phase she should paint it. She thought this morning that she should paint the moon personified, a woman wearing an evening dress made of tiny shards of glass, but she cannot envision where she would put such a woman in the painting; her presence would disrupt the harmony of the composition in a way the moon never disrupts the sky. Should she paint the moon as a man? She laughs away the thought as soon as it enters her mind. The moon is female, any cursory glance at the sky will tell you that.

She eats roasted corn one kernel at a time while she waits for Leonora. The clock ticks; motes of dust drift lazily in the sludgy afternoon light; a fly lands on the soft avocados in the bowl above the sink. She feels as though the world is suspended in this sticky moment and she is glad. *If the world stops turning and this is all there will ever be*, she thinks, *I will never have to finish that painting.*

Leonora announces herself, calling out, 'Cuckoo, I'm here,' and Remedios tips more roasted corn from the pan into the bowl. Leo pushes the door to the kitchen open with her backside and it bangs against the cupboard. An apron no one ever wears falls off the hook onto the grimy tiles.

Leo's arms are laden; she carries a basket full of herbs. She looks like one of the old women pitching and rolling like sailors with their bandy legs, carrying baskets on their heads with coriander spilling from the sides. Remedios takes the bundles of green and kisses her on both cheeks.

'I went to see the *brujas* at the *mercado* Sonora,' Leonora says, her accent missing the rasp on the *jota* and the rolling of the tongue on the *erre*. After all these years, she still sounds like a duchess on a curiosity tour of Andalusian cathedrals, even though her Spanish is flawless in its grammar.

'What did they give you?'

'I asked La Flaca for something that would bring visions and she was thrilled – you know what she's like. She says she's got you in for an appointment next Thursday if you still want it?'

Remedios sets the herbs on the side and crushes one of the leaves between her fingers to release its scent. The kitchen begins to take on that earthy, witchy smell of green that she loves.

'I do,' she says. 'The new painting is going so badly, I can't see what it should be or where it's going wrong.'

Leo pats her on the shoulder sympathetically. 'I might go and see her myself. The antichrists have been at it again and it's impossible to get a moment's peace.'

Remedios nods at the leaves bundled on the table. 'Tell me what you got.'

'La Flaca gave me three herbs – I told her nothing too crazy as I have to pick the children up at four – and she assured me they won't taste like a dragon's ass, not like last time.'

Remedios makes a face. 'That was foul.'

'So, there's sage, for clarity.' Leo rubs her fingers along the green-grey leaves. 'And a bit of epazote, just to make it taste nice.'

'Thank God,' Remedios says.

'Quite. And then this, the magic ingredient.' Leo runs her finger along the spine of a dark green leaf lying innocently next to the sage. 'Toloache. Beloved of the Aztecs to guide them in their vision quests.'

'But there's only a little bit here,' Remedios says. 'She's shorted you.'

Leo shakes her head. 'La Flaca only gave me a little. She said she couldn't trust us *gringas* to get the dose right on our own.'

'Charming.'

'Well, she also said it could make you fall madly in love, so I think it's a good job she's rationing it. Apparently, if you want to make a man crazy about you, you mix it with a little chocolate and a little menstrual blood and you slip it into his food.'

'I do want to fall in love,' Remedios says. 'I want to love my work again.'

Leo rootles in her handbag while Remedios fills the kettle from the tap and lights the stove. She repeats the names of the herbs to herself, their Nahuatl cadence rolling around her ears. *Eh-pah-zo-teh*. Like a silvery cloud hanging low in the sky. *To-lo-ah-cheh*. Like a buffalo on the fringes of the desert, scraping his hoof on bare bones of rock.

Ever since she arrived in the city she's tried to learn the language of the native plants of this sprawling continent, walking in the parks of the city to greet them, asking the beggars their names. Only now, almost ten years later, are their leaves beginning to whisper secrets when she passes.

'She said to brew it up and stir it with these two owl's feathers,' Leo says, holding the feathers aloft as a yellowed piece of tissue floats to the ground. Remedios sets out a teapot and two mugs and picks the sage and the epazote from their stems to place gently inside. She drops two of the toloache leaves on top. She leans against the counter as Leo kicks off her shoes and sits at her usual spot. The two owl feathers lay on the table next to the mugs.

'What did she tell you about this toloache, then?' Remedios asks, curious. Later, she will dig out the notebook she keeps for this kind of thing and on a new page she will write the plant's name and anything Leonora tells her. The next time she goes to see La Flaca, she will ask her where she'll find the plant growing and she'll write that in too. She dreams of making a Mexican herbal, an encyclopaedia of medicinal and magical herbs. Every time she goes into one of the bookshops or a market she looks to see if something like it already exists, but she finds nothing. Kati says you must make the work you want to see in the world, and as a statement of artistic intent, Remedios finds this better than almost anything else she's heard of.

'She told me it's an ancient plant,' Leo says. 'That it was one of the first to grow from the ashes of the great fire the old gods of the Aztecs sacrificed themselves on to create the world.'

The kettle starts to sing and Remedios reaches over to turn off the stove. She loves the stories of those terrifying old gods with their throaty names and their bloodthirst.

'Really? What were the others?'

Leo shrugs. 'She didn't say anything about them.'

'It is through their stories of creation that I learn most about the Mexicans,' Remedios says. She pours boiling water into the teapot and green-smelling steam rises before she fixes the lid and brings it to the table.

'Every people's creation myth says something about them,' Leo says. 'The Bible doesn't say God had much worry about creating things, he didn't seem to suffer as we do. He separates darkness and light, then the land and water, and then he pulled the sky up to make a dome above it all. Or maybe it was the other way around. I forget.'

'I thought God began with the word?'

'What?'

'You know, it says, "In the beginning was the word and the word was God."'

'That's not the beginning of the Bible, nincompoop!' Leonora shrieks. 'All those years at convent school and you don't know your Genesis?'

Remedios throws back her head and laughs, two of her red curls escaping their barrette to dance around her face.

'If that's not the beginning of the Bible, it should be! Where's it from then, scholar?'

Leo picks up an owl feather, still chuckling, and stirs the murky liquid in the pot.

'How should I know? One of the disciples said it, I expect.'

Leo pours the tea and they both sit for a moment with their hands cupped around the hot surfaces. Remedios clutches an enamel mug, one with a daisy pattern she doesn't recognise. One of Leo's or Kati's children must have brought it round when she picked them up from school, sipping *horchata* while they told her stories about their school friends they would never tell their mothers.

She lifts the mug to her nose and sniffs. It smells sharp, like rancid oil, and Remedios wrinkles her nose. Leo smells her own mug and shrugs.

'Ah well. She said it would taste better, not nice.'

Remedios tips some water from the jug at the other end of the table into their mugs and watches the dark green colour dilute a little.

'What did your Irish grandmother say about the creation of the world?'

Leonora grins; she loves the opportunity to talk about those ancestors. *The true roots of my heart*, she calls them.

'She said that there was only water and earth for aeons, and then at the place where the sea met the land a white mare was formed from sea foam.'

'And then what?'

'She charged about the land making things, I expect. I don't know. My grandmother never said much more than that.'

Remedios pokes her tongue towards the brew to taste it. A hint of soil slides onto the tip of her tastebuds and creeps towards her throat. It is not as unpleasant as the smell but still it wrinkles the nose and puckers the lips. She takes a sip, swallows, lets the fire spread into her belly. How long will it take to work, this herb the bruja has given them? Perhaps she can get an hour of painting in after Leo leaves and Walter clatters home.

'If I knew more about creation myths this painting would be easier,' she says.

'I thought you'd decided on it.' Leonora gulps from her mug as though she is drinking wine; she can chug back hot liquids like her gullet is lead-coated. All that drinking tea on the lawn with the lords and ladies, Remedios teases her.

'I thought you had the figures of the zodiac all sketched out already.'

Remedios sighs. 'I don't think it's quite right. I need more time to think about it.'

'Drink up,' Leo says. 'The toloache will help you.'

They sip in silence for a while. The tea has turned Leo's pale cheeks pink, and when Remedios mentions it, she giggles.

'I must be falling in love with you!'

Remedios giggles too. She feels her own face has caught aflame to become the colour of her hair and now her whole head has become the beacon in a lighthouse, beckoning all the wandering fancies adrift in the city towards her stained and splintered kitchen table in the Avenida Álvaro Obregón.

'What if,' Leonora begins, 'the world was made from the shattered fragments of a turtle's egg as it hatched?'

Remedios shivers with delight and takes a swig of the tea. It is the deepest pleasure, to soar beside Leo's imagination in this way. They speak of painting together one day but there is never time; things get in the way like chickenpox and broken toilets and boring commissions, but whenever they get despondent Leo will say, 'Soon,' solemnly, like she is prophesising, and they will return to planning this canvas that contains all the animals from the English countryside Leo cannot escape from and all the wheeled machines Remedios does not want to escape from; the canvas that will one day, so they dream, will be thrown into an undiscovered Aztec temple and torment art historians with the hints of its existence in their mildewed diaries.

'What if,' Remedios replies slowly, shuffling the options around in her mind the way she might move the cards of her tarot deck. 'What if the world was made when an eagle shat it out? It landed on the water and made ripples so huge they became mountains and the shit became the mud the Mexican plant their maize and beans and squash in. Is that too crazy?'

Leo barks her own delighted laugh. 'Nothing we can come up with can be as crazy as the birth of a human, that one must be a joke.'

Remedios inclines her head to her friend softly. 'Ah, but that is the ancient contract between woman and world,' she says. 'And I have got away with breaking it.'

She does not think about the unborn babies any more. Only when one of them hangs about her head like a hangover while she's painting and directs her brush around the delicate facial features of a character who looks a little like all the men she has ever loved.

'What if,' she says, 'there is a different sort of contract, something written somewhere like a legal deed that all parties have to obey or there will be cosmic punishment? Here it is: the moon must give up her daughters and send them to the earth so they can write books that tell the story of the world and everything that happens in it, and in return the earth spirits will make sure the moon can renew herself each month, to swell and shrink.'

'And in the contract,' Leonora says, 'everything has to pick a side.'

'Yes! And the water is on the side of the moon, obviously.'

'And the rocks are clearly on the side of the earth.'

'But fire is neutral,' Remedios says with some urgency, because she adores fire and too often it is cast as the great evil in the world. 'And it never picks any side at all throughout the long wars they have all through the centuries.'

Leo takes a long sip of her tea. 'You should paint that,' she says, her voice taking on the same hushed, thick tone it does when she's recounting one of her dreams. 'Give up on the other thing that's giving you so much trouble.'

Remedios shrugs and slurps the last of the tea, even though she already feels as if her eyes have floated somewhere above her head where they're hovering and blinking, only allowing her to see her kitchen in flashes of tableaux.

'But then they'll ask for the money back, Leo, and I've already spent it.'

Leo pours herself another cup of the tea, but glances at the clock and makes that sound like a hungry fox that means she's forgotten something important.

'Jesus and Mary, I'm late for the boys.' She pushes her chair back with a shriek of wood on linoleum and grabs at the bag that lies slumped on the counter by the pile of potatoes. She kisses Remedios on the forehead and sails into the hallway. Hurried footsteps; the slam of the door. And then, nothing but the cooling teapot and the gentle hum of the electricity in the walls, ready to crackle into the light bulb whenever she flicks the switch. Magic of the everyday, ordinary kind.

She takes the full cup of tea Leo poured for herself up to her studio and sits in front of the failing, hated painting. She squints at it, trying to see it as she wishes it was, as it was in the perfect, embryonic form of her sketches. There she has zodiac signs hovering far above the earth in flying coracles, pouring alchemical liquids into mixing machines that transmute it into delicate threads that flow towards the ground to create all manner of beings. That's what she's supposed to be working on. That's what she's supposed to be making good.

Instead, she takes a sip of the lukewarm tea and pulls open a drawer where there are notepads of thin paper she keeps to entertain Kati and Leo's children, when they demand entrance among her half-finished canvases and dirty paintbrushes.

She takes a pencil from the desk and begins to write.

Section 1, clause 1
This contract shall set out, in certain terms, the foundational principles for the creation of the world. Principal signatories are: the Artist, the Moon, and the Thirteen Earth spirits.

Section 1, clause 2
Let there be thirteen spirits of the Earth to undertake the creation, preservation of all things on the land, including but not limited to: the rocks, the soil, the plants, the trees, the animals, the humans and everything they build and destroy.

She scribbles in a fury, the way she can never paint, not even when it feels as though there is quicksilver flowing from her heart through her arm and into the brush. She puts everything in creation on the page: the moon and the sun, the earth and the stars, even the thin barrier of that strange kind of oxygen the scientists say keeps life in and space out. She gives everything a side and punishments if they betray their nature. She makes the whole thing cyclical, because that is how the world really is. She writes in all kinds of her favourite characters: witches and tricksters and animals who can talk like human beings.

And when she looks up from her notepad to see that the sky is darkening and hears Walter filling the kettle downstairs, she signs the contract with a flourish and tosses the notepad into a drawer of her desk, kicking it shut when she closes the shutters and turns off the light in her studio.

The next spring, when Remedios does her annual clear-out of her study, she directs Walter to take the desk down into the cellar, as she is beginning an experiment with minimalism. She doesn't empty or check the contents of her desk before she banishes it.

So the contract stays hidden – *occult*, as Leonora would say – and unknown to everyone other than that part of its creatrix which holds all her creations as tightly as a mother holds a newborn baby; close to the heart, close to the warmth of her breast, so close she can forget its face.

MADRIGAL

Section 7, clause 4

*And the Earth spirits shall find human girls
on the cusp of menarche and bring them to the
Tower. They shall be girls with hair the colour of
flax who have no living relations. Six shall make
the day and six shall make the night and they
will live in the Tower with all their bodily needs
fulfilled until such time as they stoop a little in
the shoulder and squint a bit about the eye. Then
they will be sent out to the world with as many
coral rings as moons they have served and they
will be honoured in their villages and live long
and happy lives, and for as long as they live they
will not speak a word of the Tower or the Earth
spirits or what they have sewn to a single living
soul.*

Here are the labra trees, stitched in a thread that sparkles
green and gold when they raise their needles. Here are the
flecks of grey foam, frothing on the waves as the wind drags
them into a curl. Here are the sloping slate roofs, perfect
cones and pyramids balanced atop the boxes of houses.
Keep the hand steady, don't let the fingers slip. Not a stitch
too many, nor a snip too few. Mandoré calls out the patterns
from his book and stirs the urn with his great silvery staff
and they'd better keep up; let their fingers fly across the

silken folds of the world they're making. If they let it slip by unmade they'll feel the sting of that staff across their backs.

The six girls sit at the top of the Tower, bent over their work with their spines curved, the golden hairs on the napes of their necks settled over their collars. Alissa sits by the biggest window, pushing her needle through the silk over and over again as the night progresses. She doesn't look through the glass towards the Outside, for snatched glances of what might be out there earns you a whack on the wrist. Instead, she keeps her eyes on the silk as it tumbles over her lap and under the windowpane. She sews fields of golden wheat, dark patches of bramble in the hedgerows and bracken in the forests, and she does it all in the heavy silence that squats on the Tower, only broken by Mandoré's voice. So still is the air between the girls that her ears become as sharp as an owl's. Here is the scratch of needle tips on silk, here is the soft breathing of the other five girls who sew with her, here is the creak of her nails growing from her fingertips.

The girls who embroider the world are allowed only the faintest of sounds to prove they are still alive, but the world outside the Tower goes on with the noises they have sewn into it. *Crack rumble* goes the thunder in the night. *Whistle squeak* goes the wind in the eaves. And *hiss spit* go the words of the world as they bubble and broil in the urn, condensing into a thin thread of light. Alissa draws her needle towards the table and pricks the silk. She sews the trees and the waves and the roofs. She embroiders the world with thread spun from Mandoré's words as the silk of creation spins beneath her.

'The boat with the seven sails shall list to starboard as it docks,' Mandoré intones, clutching the heavy book he reads from with one gloved hand and stirring the glowing urn with his staff in the other.

'And the seagull shall keen as it soars away from the shore. The path from Stritina is repaired with bricks from the new kiln.'

Six sets of fingers busy themselves with tiny stitches, and after a breath the words he called into the thick silence of the Tower appear on the silk and flow out into the world.

Here is a boat with a stiff white sail, bearing treasures from the city. Here is a seagull screeching as he rides the hot air over the lakes. Here is a road made of tessellating bricks, each one a block of stitches smaller than a speck of dust. Alissa stitches it all in tandem with the other girls, sewing the word thread with her fingers moving faster than wind; never dropping her needle, never thinking about the fabric of the world once it has passed through her hands, never disobeying nor questioning the voice that makes the world.

Sometimes, as she sews, Alissa can let a part of her mind detach from Mandoré's drone and make her fingers fly over the silk, while her real self, the part of her that is more than just a sewing girl trapped in a tower, can drift to a place where she lives inside the world she sews onto the silk. Last night, she imagined that she lived in a cottage by a river with a watermill, and she helped her mother, the miller, clean the slimy weeds from the blades that sliced through the water. She has never seen a watermill other than those she has embroidered, but now she thinks she would rather live there than in a barge drifting along a canal, which was last night's fantasy home.

But here is a sound that starts quieter than Mandoré's droning voice and then grows loud. It cuts into Alissa's calm and drags her attention towards it, the sound ringing in her ears. She lets her needle pause, stills her body so she might hear it better. It comes again, there, just under Mandoré's patterns. The sweet lilt of music, a snatch of flute or pipe that trills a few notes of a song and then stops. Like a wren warbling before the rain falls. It lasts no more than a second, it is just a momentary falter in the usual hush of the tower, but it snares her completely. She lets her eyes slide off the silk. She longs to turn around, to see who or what played the music that entranced her so, but she dares not show Mandoré that she is no longer looking to the silk falling across her lap. She wonders if the others have heard it; glances quickly to her right, but the girl who sits next to her still pushes her needle through the silk as if there is nothing out of the ordinary. Perhaps there is not. Perhaps Alissa's imagination is tricking her.

Mandoré keeps chanting the patterns but now his voice sounds faded. She is listening for the music again. Her fingers stop as she squints at the wordlight flowing through the eye of her needle. The music will enter the thread, she is sure of it, the way all the sounds of the Tower become the thread and find their way onto the silk. She waits for it to show as a fray or a lump or a knot. She has stopped sewing; she will feel Mandoré's staff across the nape of her neck in a second or two if she does not move her needle again, and yet she is frozen with the anticipation of the wordlight. She holds her breath tight in her chest so that she will not miss the moment when it comes.

And yes, she is right. Here is the part of the thread that the pipe music has become, here is a lump under her fingers that feels warm to the touch, throbbing slightly as if it is already alive. She lets it flow through her needle and onto the silk but her fingers cannot shape it into a tree or a wave or a roof. Nor will the throbbing thread of wordlight become a boat or a gull or a road. It tugs at her fingers, wanting its own form, dancing away from her. She lets her hands go limp and be guided by the needle, then she leans towards the silk.

Here is a scarlet cape, a pointed hat the colour of a kingfisher, a nonchalant glance that keeps a secret tucked behind that one raised eyebrow. Here are pale balls of wispy light thrown high into the air; five, six, seven of them, more, she loses count. Here are the spectators, shrouded in their uniform grey cloaks, applauding delightedly when the man catches his skyborne balls of light and bows low to them, the tip of his hat grazing the earth.

She has a word for what the thread spun of strange music has sewn, but she cannot remember where she heard it for she has never seen anything like it before. It bubbles up on her tongue but she bites it back. She presses her lips together and forces the word back down her throat, where it fizzes in her chest. *Juggler.* That's what he is, that's what the music-spun thread has made with her needle.

The silk with the man and the spinning balls and the crowd of onlookers cloaked in grey slips through her fingers, out past the window ledge, to become the world along with the labra trees and the foaming waves and the sloping roofs and everything that the sextet of girls have sewn.

Mandoré's voice cuts through her thoughts and pulls her away from the thing she has made.

'There shall be labra trees that shelter the woodcutter from the tempest, and the storm that comes will be the break of the drought for the wheat and the barley and the root crops lying snug in the soil.'

Now there is no music, no flute, no strangely warm thread, only the usual chill of the wordlight as it slides from the urn, over her fingers and through the pointed eye of her needle onto the silk. She embroiders a road winding through a labra forest that leads to a sea with a storm threatening. Mandoré tells her to add a pair of lovers who sob as they kiss goodbye on the sand. She does not think about what that man, the juggler, might be doing in the world he should not exist in. She listens for the hint of music she heard, but there is nothing except the usual silence and Mandoré reading from his book.

Here are the stars, made of needle pricks in the black silk of the sky to let the wordlight shine through. Here is a tunnel for the wild water to flow under, rushing to the far away city. Here is a boat, struggling against the tide with its sails turned crosswind so that it might safely reach the shore.

The stars pass across the sky and then day comes with a pink hand reaching over the eastern horizon. Alissa hears the mouth of the girl next to her stretch open in a silent yawn, but she does not feel tired at all. She is fizzing; she could keep going as the sun climbs up the eastern sky if it meant she would hear that music again.

'Tie your knots, snip your thread, and smooth the silk ready for the day,' Mandoré calls, and there is a small sigh of relief and a scraping of stools on the stone floor of the Tower. Alissa links her fingers and pushes her palms away to crack her knuckle joints. She tries to pretend nothing extraordinary has happened, that she did not hear illicit music which made her embroider something out of the pattern. A juggler. Her heart is thrumming a tattoo in her chest, *ba-rum BA ba-rum BA ba-rum BA*, at the memory of those balls of light flung up to the sky. She follows the girls out of the Tower and hoists her blue robes up to her knees to walk down the steps towards the dormitory. There is no talking until they reach their room, and there is no one who wishes to speak while Mandoré can hear them. Their usual time for the girls to chatter is at dusk, when they are waking up and washing themselves and pinning up their long yellow hair. Then they discuss remedies for swollen fingers and aching backs, what will be for lunch, and who has the neatest stitches on the day shift. Sometimes, Alissa feels as though no one would notice if she began to moo or cluck or bleat, as long as she joined the line to climb the stairs to the sewing room at sunset.

But in the mornings they are too tired for any of that. They file into their room with the sunlight streaming through the gaps in the shutters. One of the girls flicks them shut as they pass on the way to their beds and the room snaps into darkness.

Alissa sinks onto her bed and pulls out the pins that contain her hair. She lets them clatter onto the nightstand; she hears the sounds of the others doing the same. The door shuts with a click, and on the other side Alissa hears the footsteps of the six girls who will embroider the day climbing the stairs to the tower. She drapes her robe over the chair at the foot of her bed and changes into her nightgown, before she slips beneath her blanket and lays her head on the lumpy pillow.

The sounds in the dormitory soon soften into sleep. Snoring and mumbling and soft sighs of cryptic dreams.

These are the sounds she knows so well, the intimate noises of the only people she has ever called any kind of friend.

But Alissa cannot sleep. She is thinking about the music and the feeling of the thread when it was warm under her fingertips. She is trying to remember how many balls of light the man threw into the air, she is trying to hold the image of his face in her mind, the way his eyebrow curved so merrily, with so much hidden behind it. She is trying to call to mind the snatch of that music she heard, trying to hum the tune very gently among the snores. Every time she thinks she could sing it to herself, her mind slips away from it like an eel but the experience is not frustrating. Instead, Alissa feels a delicious longing, like she has been shown a beautiful secret.

Under her blanket, her hand drifts to her belly and fondles the tuft of white feathers there. The other girls stared at her, all those years ago when Mandoré brought her up here. They let their eyes drop to her midriff, and when their mouths fell agape with surprise, Alissa did not understand what was wrong. It was only later, when they all shyly undressed in the light – for they did not sew the night shift then – that Alissa saw that no one else had feathers sprouting from their bellies. They had little nubs tucked away in a tiny hollow instead. They stared at her until she covered herself with one of the blue robes they all wore.

'Why, she's just like a bird!' one of the girls had exclaimed, and now Alissa cannot remember any malice in it, only wonder. But Mandoré cuffed the other girl over the head and no more was said. No one ever mentioned her feathers again. Sometimes, Alissa wonders if any of them even remember she isn't like them. It was all so long ago and they have all seen and made so many other improbable things since. True, also, that there is only one girl left embroidering the night shift from that group Mandoré brought her to that afternoon. She was young and tall then, with bright eyes and a quick smile. Now that woman stoops as she walks and her skin is lined. She gave up acknowledging the new additions to the shift some winters ago.

The first time Alissa saw Mandoré was when he arrived at the orphans' home. She had not considered herself a happy child before he arrived; she was a girl who had lost her parents and had to rely on the mercy of the matrons. She knew she was to be pitied. But now she looks back on the days before Mandoré came as light and free. She used to play on the edge of the labra forest with the other unlucky children, climbing the tall, straight trunks until they could no longer hang on and then slide down the smooth bark. Her hair would lift from her collar and her dress would billow and she would pretend she was flying. She did not recall what the other children had or did not have at their navels. One day out of five there was honey pudding after lunch, and there was always a big fire in the main hall to warm your cold hands at.

And then he came. She was perhaps eleven or twelve; she did not count birthdays then and she doesn't now, the days and nights blur. The man she would come to know as Mandoré had his cloak the colour of the earth pulled around his body and over his mouth. The girls had to line up and hold out their hands, and Mandoré walked along the line and inspected them all. He pulled her out of the line and kept her by his side as he completed his tour. She was the only one he chose. He gave her a drink of water that tasted sweet, like a bee had shaken pollen into it and lifted her into his carriage. The children crowded around her to watch it clatter away and she wanted to smile and be brave like she had seen all the others do when they had left but her eyelids began to droop before the wheels began to roll. She remembers nothing about the journey except that none of the matrons smiled to see her go. She has never tasted that bright, pollen-like taste again.

She awoke in bright sunlight, swaying groggily with the motion of the carriage. The man with the earth-coloured cloak was sitting next to her. The bottom half of his face was still covered and his eyes were so dark she could not see a pupil. There was something stern about them. She wriggled to sit up straighter on the bench.

'They call me Mandoré,' he said. 'And you are?'

For a moment she wondered if she was supposed to say her own name, or something else about her; her favourite season, perhaps. 'My name is Alissa?' she said, like a question, just in case she had got something wrong.

'Do you know where I'm taking you?' She could not hear him very well as his voice was muffled by the cloak over his mouth, but she would never hear him speak any other way. She didn't know then she would hear his voice every day of her life from that moment on, always from behind the cloak, always muffled.

She shook her head. Children often left the orphans' home, to go to work in big houses, to work on farms, to seek their fortune in Uranga. Visitors came and took the older children away all the time. They never came back, so the other children assumed they were happy.

Mandoré turned away from her. He had a staff in his hands about as long as her arm. He rubbed his thumb on its polished surface and Alissa leaned forward to see it better. It was silvery and it seemed to glow under the pressure of his fingers, as if it were purring at his attention. She is still not sure what it is made of although she sees it every day.

'You are a very lucky girl,' Mandoré said. 'I'm taking you to a place few people ever get to go.' He paused. She had the sensation he was telling her a story.

'Tell me, Alissa, do you know who makes the world?'

Alissa shook her head even before she had considered the question. What a strange thing to ask, she had thought. No one made the world, it was simply there.

'The world is written by a being far older and wiser than you,' he said softly, looking past her out of the window of the carriage. 'The words, as read by me and beings like me, become a thread made of light, which is sewn into a great silken tapestry that creates everything that has ever been and everything that will ever be. I am taking you to a special place, the centre of the world where everything is made. You will help stitch and sew all of creation.'

The carriage stopped and he opened the door to step out. She followed him, dazed, the bright taste of the pollen drink lingering on her tongue. They were in the middle of a forest with a huge tower built of moss-covered stones looming out of dusk before her. Mandoré walked towards a doorway cut into the wall, and without meaning to, her legs carried her along behind him. She climbed the stone steps that presented themselves to her as though she had always known she would end up in this place, the mud-coloured cloak dragging a few steps behind his feet so she had to gaze at it to avoid tripping. The stairs went on and on forever. She felt as if she were climbing up into the clouds.

Mandoré had brought her to the room she still sleeps in now and held out a dark blue robe for her to change into. She remembers the shame as they watched her, Mandoré and the five other girls who each had yellow hair like hers, the colour of a labra leaf in autumn. Some of them were a few years older than her and one looked about her age, but they all stared as she took off the dress and shirt and leggings everyone wore at the orphans' home and wrestled with the tight neck-hole of the robe to get it over her head. Then the gasp, the exclamation and *thwack* of Mandoré's stick. She pulled the new blue robe quickly over her body to hide her feathers and turned to look at Mandoré. His dark eyes no longer looked stern. Instead, they looked faintly troubled, his eyebrows drawn together like two halves of a broken bridge.

In the days and nights to come she would learn the rules of the Tower and the silk and the wordlight. Eventually, she learnt to be silent in the Tower in front of her silk. She learnt to hear Mandoré's muffled instructions and to let the wordlight guide her needle as she stitched. She learnt to sleep in the daytime when they started to embroider the night. And she learnt that she must always, without exception, sew only what Mandoré told her to. She knew that nothing must appear on the silk that Mandoré had not called out himself. No one ever said what would happen if one of the girls improvised or made a mistake. No one seemed to think that was possible.

And as the sun has proceeded from its summer home in the sky to its winter one, and back again, girls have left the Tower and others have joined. There have been times when Alissa and the others have awoken at sunset to find one bed empty and cold and its mistress gone without a trace, and others when Mandoré wakes them not with the usual knock, but with the name of a frightened little lass wearing blue robes that dangle over her wrists. None of them are sure why their friends disappear. Some whisper that the missing girl made a mistake in the silk or wilfully disobeyed what Mandoré called out from his book, while others say they went because their hair was beginning to turn a dull grey and their eyes were lined and tired, and when we get old we'll get to leave too. Nobody knows for sure. Alissa and the others make the world but there is so much about it that they do not know.

She rolls over onto her other side in the bed and considers what she has done. Perhaps the music can be blamed, the strange flute that warbled for only a few moments, but long enough to create a juggler. A memory drifts across her mind like one of the fluffy clouds she sews on a warm night. A man turning over and over like a wheel, his arms and legs like spokes, to a chorus of the delighted giggles of children. Red balls that sparkle like stars thrown over their heads, the thrill of it chasing her heart out of her chest and up to her teeth. A one-wheeled machine that spun in circles. She remembers turning to a matron and tugging at her sleeve. 'What's that man doing?' she said. A smile, the matron's eyes as enchanted as the children's. 'He's juggling, girl,' she had said. 'That man is a juggler.'

She thinks of her own juggler, as she has quickly come to think of him, and she imagines that he turns his gentle, inscrutable smile towards her and looks her deep in the eyes. She screws her eyes shut and she lets her inner gaze rove over the figure she made, remembering things about him she had not known she knew. The spare balls tucked away inside his cloak, trying to break free of his belt. The exquisite paleness of his hands. And the strange way his beard forked from his chin, making two points of hair heading in different directions. Oh! She stifles a gasp with her hand clasped over her mouth. She sees now that the spikes of his beard form the two legs of a star shape, the brim of his hat making the arms and the conical point completing it. The juggler has a star for a head. He is a star man.

What has she done?

Maybe it was the wordlight did it. Maybe the wordlight knew something about the whistling wren's song that she doesn't and it leapt through her needle before she could stop it. Maybe Mandoré will never notice what went out into the world from her hands. Maybe she will not disappear like those other girls, maybe the juggler will stay a secret between her and the wordlight.

But maybe she doesn't want him to be a secret. Maybe she wants to disappear.

BALLATA

Section 3, clause 1(d)
And the trickster may appear in many different
guises and forms, including those commonly
written by the star children, although he may not
always be known to the women, men, and beasts
of the land.

They find themselves on the western approach to a town
called Janat just before lunchtime, and they pull off the road
to decide what to do first. There is a scent of baking in the
air as the forest thins and cottages start to line the road, and
Lion's mouth begins to water at the thought of tearing a loaf
of bread in two, breaking the hot, hard crust of it and gouging
his claw inside to rip out the soft dough. Of all the pleasures he
can no longer enjoy, it is freshly baked bread he misses most.

Goat wants to go straight to the plaza where there will be
wool traders and shiny fat bakers and drinking dice players,
enough to start a show and make a tidy sum.

Vanna flicks her long black hair and says she is too hungry
to begin the show but she agrees they should go straight
to the plaza, as there will certainly be a stall set up there
selling pies, wizened apples and mugs of petty beer. After
all their years of travelling the land, they know every town
has one of those places.

Owl says nothing. She rarely says anything before dusk
and today is no exception.

Lion sighs. There is no point in asking them to follow the delicious smell of the bakery. They know he cannot eat it. They will only fall silent in pity. Vanna will look at him sadly with her limpid eyes and Goat will paw at the ground awkwardly. Owl will blink. Their sympathy seems bottomless. It has been almost a year now since the spell, and not once have they told him they are fed up of hearing him complain. He is beginning to wish they would tell him to stop moping. He has a feeling their tender compassion for his circumstance is hindering his acceptance of his new form.

'Lion?' says Goat. 'What do you want to do?'

He swallows the saliva the baking smell has conjured and shrugs lightly as he turns away. What he really wants to do is sink his teeth into that soft throat and feel the blood rush over his tongue. But Goat is his oldest friend. Whatever disgusting urges his new form forces on him, he must never, ever sink to that.

'Let's get something to eat,' Lion says, trying to keep the misery out of his voice. 'I'm hungry too.'

Goat touches his hoof to Vanna's thigh to nudge her. 'Your turn to drive,' he says.

Vanna sighs and clambers past him to sit in the front bay for the driver. She leans far to her right to check that the road is clear, then tugs at the string to pull the sails taut. She waits a moment while the sails catch the wind, and when the wheels begin to creak she gently guides the carriage back onto the western road, heading towards the baking smell, towards the centre of Janat.

'Do you know, I don't recognise this place at all,' Goat says as he watches the houses gather closer and closer together as the carriage rumbles along the road. 'I feel as though this is my first time here.'

Vanna steers slightly to the left to move the carriage out of the way of a branch fallen across the road.

'We came here once, years ago,' she says, readjusting the wheel. 'I think you liked it well enough, Goat. There was a fountain with a fish mouth in the plaza, remember? And Lion did a huge flip off it that all the little boys hassled him to learn until we left.'

Goat frowns and leans out of the window to watch the houses going by. Lion thinks of that flip and his heart sinks to his rumbling stomach. Even though a cat's body is far more agile than a man's, he can no longer do that kind of showstopping trick, and their takings are suffering for it.

Their carriage attracts a few stares and nudges from the locals as its wheels clatter along the bricks. Its sails are clean and well-mended, the ropes that hold the sails in place made of strong birchbark twine, its wheels worn but strong enough. Its windows thickly curtained with pink velvet Vanna bought at auction last winter, the shutters lined with felt to keep out the night chills. For this season, its six beechwood walls are painted the colour of lichen on an oak, to better to blend in when they stop in forests. They bought it several years ago from a woman who lived alone in the woods and created fabulous wheeled machines out of scraps she found. All the best circus troupes have a sailed carriage, it's considered a mark of quality. Goat, Vanna and Lion had travelled on a common cart and carefully saved their coral rings until they could afford it.

They pass a group of young boys with wicker baskets loaded with acorns and mushrooms and chestnuts, their cheeks rosy with autumn winds. They pass a woodcutter sitting on a freshly sawn ash stump, drinking from a mug his wife has just handed him, and a harassed-looking young father trying to calm the mewling baby he holds in a worsted sling on his chest. Lion watches the scenes of everyday life pass by and mourns all he has lost.

The road becomes narrower and Vanna slows the carriage so it might pass the other vehicles. She steers it towards what she thinks must be the town plaza, even though she cannot navigate there by memory alone. She follows that compass which directs a wanderer towards hospitality and gaiety, a hot meal and a warm bed, that seventh sense all circus folk have; an unfailing knowledge of where the audience is, where the dreamers wait, where the people are who need to float out of their humdrum existence to stand and stare at the clouds awhile.

She steers the carriage around corner after corner, following the flow of people with their best hats and their baskets, all heading towards the plaza. The smell of baking bread grows stronger and stronger and Lion swallows a moan.

'Yes!' Goat cries, so loudly that Owl turns her head languidly towards him and blinks in that way she has of letting them all know she is annoyed. 'I remember this town now! There were treacle tarts in the bakery and they were warm, and we ate them with fresh cream. Lion, do you remember?'

In his excitement he has forgotten to be sensitive to Lion's new, reluctant digestive requirements. Lion tries to smile but now he has a memory of the thick, sweet treacle sliding down his throat, flavoured with a hint of ginger and cinnamon, and he turns his face away so that neither Vanna nor Goat will see the tears leaking into his whiskers.

But they are not watching him. Instead, they are hanging out of the front window, their shoulders pressed tightly together inside the frame so they might both see out. The carriage slows and then halts, and there is a slow grind of brakes as Vanna manoeuvres the carriage into a space between two dairy carts.

The plaza is humming with busyness. Lion can hear footsteps and chatter and the clink of coral rings as the commerce of the town hurries on. Goat's hooves patter on the floor of the carriage as he scrambles towards the driver's bay to squeeze next to Vanna and look out the front window. Lion pays none of it any attention. He is trying to regain control of himself and forget that he ever tasted treacle or pastry or the sweet tang of cinnamon.

'Well,' he hears Vanna say quietly. 'That's never happened before.' He wipes the tears from his snout with the soft pads under his claws and sniffs. He hears faint applause and gasps of pleasure from the plaza, then the drumming of Goat's hooves on the ledge of the driver's bay and a high-pitched bleat.

'You're never clapping for him!' Vanna says indignantly. 'He's on our patch! He's taking the food right out of our mouths, slinging those sparkly things around like that.'

Lion hears Goat sigh, and he turns to see what's happening. 'Oh, but he's so good!' Goat breathes. 'Just watch him.'

And watch him Lion does.

With his snout resting on Vanna's shoulder, he counts the balls as they fly high in the air, seeming to defy the rules that keep everything else invisibly tethered to the earth. Five, six, seven of them; more, he loses count. They're sparkling, glowing with a white light that seems neither hot nor cold, and they leave a little trail of light behind them like a comet trailing through the night sky. Lion sees the man's eyes flick towards their carriage. It is only a moment and then the man's attention is back on his airborne tricks, but in that second Lion has the feeling that he's been waiting for them.

The man catches all the balls he sent soaring among the rooftops and applause shatters the silence. It comes from the ordinary folk of the town, the milkmaids and the beer sellers and the meat merchants who have dropped their busy work and let their jaws slacken in amazement. They've all seen a few travelling circus folk in the past few years, but never anything quite so enchanting as this.

'More, more and more!' some of the goodwives shout, snapping their fingers at their daughters-in-law and nieces to get them a stool from inside the house, and be nimble about it.

'Show us another trick!' call the little boys who sit on the cobblestones of the plaza with their legs tucked neatly beneath them, the way they never do when their schoolmistress asks them to.

'Don't be shy!' giggle the young maids who have left their work in the hot, airless kitchens to follow the noise of the plaza to watch the strange man in delight.

But it is the group of grey-cloaked burghers that fascinates Lion. With their bare heads and their silken grey cloak that ripples like water when one of them moves their shoulders, he watches as they stand with slack lips, watching the juggling man in their square. They must have been in session, Lion realises, to be still joined inside the one cloak like this and out among the townspeople. They must have streamed out of the door to the burghers' hall like an octopus squeezing into a tiny cave, all the bodies inside the Cloak of Council independent, but united in their desire to see the man performing these ball tricks.

'They didn't even remove their debating cloak before they came outside to watch him,' sighs Goat. Vanna makes a harrumphing sound.

'It's deathly boring here, what do you expect? They were probably talking about those shocking potholes on that road we've just skidded around on, and thought that even watching that man play with stupid balls was more interesting than that.'

It is rare that Lion hears the taint of jealousy in Vanna's voice. He thinks of her as such a kind, even-tempered person, even if she does hold a certain amount of pride in her singing voice.

The man has begun to juggle again, for that is what he's been doing, Lion sees that now. He follows the balls as they arc in a new pattern, moving out of Goat's way as he ducks under his paw.

'Where are you going?' Vanna hisses after him.

'I want to see how he does that,' Goat says as he darts out the back of the carriage and jumps down into the street. 'I want to learn!'

Vanna makes a noise of disapproval but she keeps watching the juggler. It is hard not to watch him; the crowd in the plaza grows thicker and thicker with each throw and there are shouts at the back to mind out of the way, let us poor fellows have a look.

Lion watches the burghers' faces as the balls tumble over their heads. He thinks of that moment when the juggler looked towards their carriage. Maybe he imagined it. It is so easy to be paranoid in his new shape; the senses of the lion are so much more refined than those of a man. His whiskers quiver at every change in the air and his nose is the delicate, probing organ his tongue used to be. But no, he knows what he saw. The juggler is a strange apparition and the juggler is there for them.

He catches all his balls with a flourish and the plaza erupts with a roar of applause. Goat is there at the front, drumming his hooves on the cobbles. The juggler sweeps his bright blue hat off his head and bows low. When he stands he pulls the hat onto his head by the wide brim and turns again to the carriage. He winks. Lion sees how his double-pointed beard, the opposite edges of the brim of his hat, and its conical point facing up to the heavens make up a five-pointed star. It must be on purpose. Do the burghers know? Have they seen it too? Lion watches as they drift away from the plaza, the spell that had drawn them outside with the silvery cloak of debate still holding them together. They glide back into the burghers' hall the way they must have come in, quietly slipping their heads out of the holes in the cloak and queueing to get back through the door. The others in the crowd drift away too. Some would like to try to speak to the juggler, Lion can see them craning their necks to judge how many excited well-wishers there are around him, how long they will wait to have their own chance to touch his hand, deciding it is too long and too public. Only those who do not know that circus folk are for seeing and not hearing, or those who no longer care, remain in a circle around the man, their fingers itching to grasp those shiny orbs of light, questions bubbling on their tongues.

Goat is one of those skipping around the juggler, waiting for his turn to speak to him, ignoring Vanna's frantic signals to return to the carriage.

'I'd leave him, if I were you,' Lion says. 'Get yourself something to eat. He'll come back soon enough.' There is a world-weary tone to his voice he hardly recognises. He was thrilled by the juggler too. Why pretend to Vanna that Goat was the only one?

Vanna flubbers her lips as she always does when annoyed. 'Fine,' she says, standing up from the driver's bay and smoothing down her skirt. 'But I'll not get him anything. He can sort himself out when he's finished licking the boots of the competition.'

Lion can tell the juggler will not be their competition for long, his cat's senses have told him that, but he lets Vanna go stamping across the square with a few coral rings clattering in her pocket, off to the inn selling turnip pies and frothy beer.

He is hungry too but he can't bring himself to eat what he knows he must. He'll wait for Vanna to return to the carriage with a leg of raw mutton or a side of beef wrapped in brown paper. She'll tactfully turn her back while he tears into the pink flesh, gnawing right down to the bone, letting the points of his teeth slice through to the marrow. Lion feels his eyes tear up at the thought of it.

He had never eaten the flesh of another animal before his transformation, not even a fish. He remembers his mother squatting on her haunches by the cooking pot suspended from a hook in the fireplace, stirring a stew thick with beans and carrots and parsnips, flavoured with lovage and sweet cicely picked straight from the garden. His parents couldn't afford meat but they wouldn't have eaten it if they were the richest merchants in the land. They thought it dulled the heart and made a person blind to the suffering of other beings. A tear trickles down Lion's snout and slides towards those sharp, saliva-coated teeth. What would his mother and father say if they could see him now? Their son a flesh eater, not even a hunter, the victim of a cruel passion which has left him scarred and damaged and now living inside this alien form forever.

The gaggle of well-wishers surrounding the juggler has thinned to the point where there are only a couple of shy little boys, who don't do anything more than stare at the man's fancy red cloak and tuck their fingers inside their baggy waistbands so that they don't absently reach for one of the glowing balls, piled temptingly at the juggler's feet; and Goat. Goat ignores the boys and begins to chatter enthusiastically at the juggler, his horns bobbing up and down as he talks. He watches Goat extend his hoof towards the balls and the juggler flicks one of them up into the air and deftly catches it. He hands it to Goat, who tries to take the ball with one of his hooves but fails to balance it in the groove. The ball falls to the juggler's feet, and he picks it up and hands it to Goat again. They repeat this a few more times, until finally Goat steps back and shakes his head. It would be funny to watch, for anyone else who was not Lion. He understands only too well what it means to be trapped in a body that cannot do the things you wish it to.

But Goat does not seem too downhearted. Instead, he gestures to the carriage, still stationary between the two dairy carts, and jerks his head. Lion can't hear Goat, but he knows he is inviting the juggler into their carriage, perhaps even to eat with them. Lion doesn't mind, but he knows Vanna will be annoyed. The juggler tucks the glowing balls away inside his cloak and picks up a small blue trunk before following Goat across the square. Lion has the feeling that the juggler is pleased about this, as if this is what he has wanted from the moment he started performing his tricks in the plaza.

Goat, the juggler and Vanna all reach the door to the carriage at the same time. Vanna stares at the juggler, a curl of dismay on her lip.

Lion clears his throat. 'Welcome to our little moving home,' he says, extending his paw to brush the juggler's hand. The juggler reaches out with his own hand and the backs of their fingers brush politely.

'Nice to meet you,' he says. Lion moves back into the carriage, his tail sensing behind him for the wall. He settles down on the floor, his two paws extended behind him, his flanks nestled underneath the seat in the driver's bay. This way, he doesn't take up too much space.

Goat hops up into the carriage and turns back to the two at the door.

'And this is Vanna,' Goat says, cheerily, but with a warning tone in his voice. 'Our fiddler and singer. You're just in time, juggler, she's brought us all lunch.'

The juggler holds out his hand to brush Vanna's, but she has two armfuls of brown paper packages with everyone's lunch inside, and if she meets his hand with hers she'll drop them. Even still, Lion thinks, she should say something. Hello, you had them enchanted out there, do you come here often, whatever.

Instead, Vanna lets her eyes slip down from the juggler's face past the bulges of the glowing balls under his cloak, right down to his muddy brown boots.

'Hello,' she says, as rudely as she can, and steps inside the carriage.

The juggler shrugs, a private smile that makes Lion think again that he knows more about them than they can possible know about him. Goat makes a little mewling sound and scowls at Vanna, but she ignores him to sit down on the bench. She lets the packages tumble into her lap and unwraps all the different foodstuffs that this odd little family require.

Goat gets a small bale of hay and Lion gets a rump of mutton, just as he had feared. The juggler sits opposite Vanna in the carriage and tucks his small blue trunk under the bench. Vanna opens her mouth wide to eat her pie, then tears off a crust of pastry and hands it to the juggler without looking at him.

Silence, while they eat, only the chomping and chewing and smacking sounds of mouths at work. Silence inside the carriage, but outside in the plaza life carries on. A baby shrieks and wheels go *clack clack* on the cobbles.

Then, a quiet rustling of feathers, a soft *churr* sound from somewhere above their heads.

'Oh,' says Goat, strands of yellow grass poking out of his mouth. 'And this is Owl.' He waves one hoof towards the perch hanging from the ceiling where Owl spends her days. The juggler bows to her and Owl regards him coolly.

'Lovely to meet you, Owl,' the juggler says.

'Likewise,' says Owl, and there is something in her manner and the slight curve on the juggler's lips that makes

Lion wonder if they have met before. But Goat is talking again before he can interrogate his suspicion, and then the thought fades into nothing and is gone like a dandelion seed in a storm.

The juggler finishes the crust Vanna gave him with gurgling, spluttering noises of pleasure. At first, Vanna stares at him, as though in disbelief that anyone would make such sounds while eating, especially in the company of strangers, especially in the company of strangers who have shown they think you unwelcome.

But the juggler doesn't seem to notice or care. He licks the pastry flakes from the pads of his fingers and thumbs.

'Thank you,' he says to Vanna. 'I have been so hungry and you have shared what you have with me so willingly. I will not forget it.'

Vanna doesn't reply, but Lion can see her thawing. The juggler continues in this vein, talking about the kindnesses of strangers on the road, particularly fellow travelling circus folk like her. Soon, there is a damp puddle of resentment at Vanna's feet, trickling away out of the door and dripping onto the cobbles of the plaza.

Now, with a stranger inside their carriage glancing around their home, Lion follows his gaze and sees it anew, the way the juggler is surely seeing it. He notices the scuff marks on the floorboards, the chipped and peeling paint around the doorway. He sees the loose handles on the drawers above their heads, where Vanna keeps her clothes and soap and matches and pots and spoons and bottles, and he feels a wave of shame. He would have fixed such a weakness in their home, before, when he stood on two legs and could reach up with both arms and hold a tool in his hands with four fingers and a thumb. He can do nothing about the loose handles now. He notices that Owl's perch is speckled with woodworm; and when he taps the rolled-up sleeping mats stowed under the benches, little puffs of dust billow towards him. He settles his chin on his paws with a whimper he cannot control.

The juggler turns back to Goat. 'So, when does your show start?' he asks. Vanna looks at Goat too. Her look says, as surely as if she has spoken, go on, tell him exactly what he's done, say he's taken our spot and no one's going to want to watch us now they've seen him.

Goat clears his throat, uses his long pink tongue to catch the hay dust straggling in his beard.

'We probably won't do a show here.'

'Why not?'

'Well.' Goat looks nervous, rolling his front hoofs around each other in that worried way of his. He doesn't want to be rude to his guest.

'Well, we've found, over the years of travelling around, that it doesn't do to put on two shows in a day. It bores the people, see, or even worse, it makes them worried they're having an invasion of circus folk. Acrobats or fire breathers, stilt walkers or play actors; most towns want us in for a day, maybe a night, and then they want to wave goodbye as we leave on the fastest highway in the morning. If we were to set up a show now, we'd be looking at rotten fruit instead of corals. We'd be stupid to waste our time.'

The juggler looks at the floor and scuffs the toe of one brown shoe. 'I didn't know that. I'm sorry.'

Lion sees the puddle at Vanna's feet grow. Now she seems to almost like him.

'But don't feel bad!' Goat scrambles to his feet. 'It was a pleasure to watch you. We've never seen a juggler like you before. Where did you learn?'

The juggler shrugs. 'I think I've always been able to do it.'

Goat's eyes are teacup-round. 'Really? And do you perform on the circuit often? I have friends in troupes all over, maybe you've met them. There's Calleen and Rosey with the trapeze fellows, they travel about a bit; maybe you know Ellan? Gets around on an elephant that tells fortunes?'

The juggler shrugs again. Lion wonders if he's keeping something from them. 'I'm not sure really. I meet other circus folk all the time, and I never know the names of the towns I'm in. I just juggle and move on.' He holds out his hands in an innocent way.

'You're all the first who've taken me in,' he says.

Goat grins proudly and even Vanna musters a weak smile, but Lion begins to lick at his paw, a compulsion he found disgusting at first, but which these days comforts him and allows him time to think. This man seems tied to nothing else in the world. He seems to have come from nowhere.

'And you must certainly stay!' cries Goat.

A broad smile spreads across the juggler's face. 'Do you mean it?'

'Of course!' Goat trots the two steps to the juggler and nudges him with his hoof affectionately. 'Lion? What do you say?'

Lion hesitates in licking his paw and nods a yes. It is a sound and shrewd business proposition. The juggler is a master of his art and he'll add depth and excitement to their show. They can't carry on doing the same thing forever, they have to adapt.

'Good fellow, you know it makes sense!' Goat turns to Vanna. 'And you'll say yes, I know you will. Imagine it: a choreographed juggling show, set to your fiddle music, with a song or two and a bit of acrobatics from Lion. It'll bring them to their knees.'

And fill my hat with corals, Goat doesn't say.

'A trial period of a year and a day,' Vanna says. Lion knows she has thought about the advantages of adding the juggler to their menage just as he has, but she values the precious balance of their friendships too much to endanger it with a thoughtless invitation. 'After that we can see about making it permanent.'

The juggler nods seriously, but there is an odd light in his eyes. Lion sits up to better see his face, but he has turned towards Goat and extended his hand to brush his fingers against Goat's hooves.

'Thank you,' the juggler says. 'I feel as though this is a new beginning. To be here, with such fine people. I will not let you down.'

Goat giggles shrilly, thinking of the way the crowd cooed at the sight of the juggler performing his tricks, and Vanna smiles weakly, stamping her jealousy right down to her toes where it might remain dormant and passive until it disappears completely. But Lion shivers as he hears these words; there seems to be some trick in them he can't quite make out. He watches the juggler for a long time, chatting with Vanna and Goat. He is all innocence, he knows nothing of this town or the next, he still knows none of Goat's friends in the circus troupes, he appears to understand nothing of the ways of travelling. A year and a day is a long time, Lion thinks. A year and a day ago he was still a man.

Outside the carriage the burghers leave their debates and spill across the cobbles towards their homes. Their silvery cloak with many heads lies folded in a box lined with grey silk and locked with a key held by the oldest member of the council. It will not be worn again until the burghers return to the meeting hall to discuss some new problem facing their community. A skinny fox creeps through the long shadows to rootle in the rubbish bins set outside the houses, and the pigeons veer around their trails, eager to stay alive. Two lizards mate in a warm patch on a sunny rooftop. Lion catches the scent of these animals and does nothing. He refuses to feel kinship with them.

Later, after Vanna has washed her clothes in the stone fountain in the plaza and stocked up on oats, dried fruit and the long strips of dried beef Lion has to nibble on when there is no fresh meat, they roll out of Janat's plaza and out onto the road that winds eastwards like a stray thread through the labra forest. The stars are bright and scattered in the usual places but there is hardly any wind, so Goat asks Owl for her help. She submits to Vanna tying the two sail strings around her claws and extends her wings, dragging the carriage behind her. They travel the whole night long in this way, through the darkness, steered only by Owl's long wings and her keen eyes.

Inside the carriage, Vanna rolls out the sleeping mats on the gently rocking floor and they all lie down. It takes Lion a while to fall asleep; he is too distracted by the unfamiliar noise of the juggler's breathing, raspy and short, as though he has been running up a mountain. A year and a day, Lion thinks again. Thirteen moons. Things will certainly be different by then.

TOCCATA

Section 2, clause 4(n)
And the star child will never again seek to know
or be with her companion, leaving her to enjoy
her retirement in peace and seclusion.

Section 2, clause 4(o)
When the companion is in her retirement, let her
never venture to Uranga, the navel of the world,
lest the power of the Moon becomes too much and
overwhelms her.

The machines are made from anything she can find on her wandering forage. She picks up fallen birch branches and elm twigs, acorn cups and conkers. She collects feathers and furs and each spring she gathers the antlers the stags shed. Wood is good for her machines but bone is best. When she finds the carcass of a wolf or a lynx she stays nearby, sometimes for days, waiting for the animals of the wood to come and feast and strip the bones for her. Then she drags the skeleton home and cleans it, bone by bone. She leaves what she has not yet used in a heap outside the front door. To deter visitors.

Once, she found the axle of a cart lying half submerged in a bog. It was beginning to rust and the oak was almost completely rotted away but she dragged the iron bar back to the cottage, scraped off the light orange blooms of rust, and used it for a flying machine that she still hasn't finished.

She does not make anything from labra wood. Labra wood is never dead, even when it is detached from its mother tree, and it interferes with the functioning of the machine. Labra has its own ideas; it makes mixing machines walk on the legs that are supposed to keep them still and it makes wheeled carriages grow stubborn roots. Once, it made one of her coracles grow wings and fly across the treetops. She has never seen that one again.

Her cottage has a big room and a small room. The small one is her living room, where she cooks stews in a cast-iron pot at the fireplace. She no longer makes bread. Too time-consuming, both to make and to eat. She brews beer from wild barley and hops and keeps it in a barrel in the corner. She likes to lie in her bed under her blankets and have a mug when the wind gusts the wrong way down the chimney.

The big room is her workshop, the dearest place of her heart. Here live all her babies, all her machines in different stages of becoming. Here are all her experiments with wheels; all the vehicles she has made, trying to mimic the smooth rolling motion of the Thirteen as they used to move along the underground corridors of the Tower. Here are all her flying machines, some half covered with feathers, others sleek and sharp so as to slice through the air. Here are her levers and her pulleys, her chains and her cogs, all waiting to be placed inside some kind of machine. It seems as though nothing in this room works properly, but that is only because as soon as one of her inventions works precisely how it is supposed to, either someone comes to buy it or she installs it in her home.

Like the water system. The pump and its spider's web of attendant pipes is her pride and joy; she tinkers with it each summer, trying to find little improvements here and there. She collects rainwater in tanks behind her home, gathering runoff from the sloping roof and the nearby trees, and then filters it through stones and gravel to make it clean. Ten years ago she fashioned a wide pipe to bring some of the water past the fireplace to heat it. Ever since, she's been able to have a bath when the weather is not too cold. She lies by the fireplace in the wooden tub she lined with otter hides and sings to herself.

She is in her bath when she hears the pipe music. For a moment she thinks she has fallen asleep, as she hears pipe music all the time in her dreams, particularly the ones where it's snowing and she runs out of a dark tunnel into a blinding white swirl of frost, but then she hears the door click open and feels a gust of cold air on her neck.

She turns and water slops over the edge of the bathtub. A slow smile spreads across her face.

'Well,' she says, and the pipe music fades. 'I didn't think I'd ever see you again.'

The figure standing by the table is tall, so tall the flat platform of their grey hat scrapes the ceiling. They're swathed in a grey cloak with deep folds that ripple with every breath. Gloves on the hands, mud-encrusted boots on the feet, and a dark hood pulled tight over their head to cover the space between the shoulders and their hat.

'Your water pump is very fancy,' the tall figure says. They move the inventor's pyjamas off the stool by the bath and sit on it.

'I like doing water systems. You can keep re-making them until you get bored of them, there's no such thing as too much modification with pumps.'

There is a pause and the inventor woman reaches out for the sponge balancing on the rim of the tub. 'Do you want to come in after me?'

The tall figure chuckles and shakes their head.

'Leira, do you know the story of the Minstrel?'

The inventor, whose name is certainly Leira, although no one has called her that for many years, dips her sponge in the bathwater and squeezes it over her shoulder.

'So there's no hello, how are you, what have you been up to all these years, sorry about the chaos I left behind?' Leira asks. She can't decide if she's upset or thrilled to see her old friend, her only friend. Her skin erupts into gooseflesh despite the steaming water. 'Aren't you going to tell me where you've been?'

The tall figure frowns. 'Sorry. I don't do much talking any more. How are you, Leira?'

'Fine, thank you.'

'And I know what you've been up to, I wrote it, and I'm not really sorry about the chaos, and no, I'm not going to tell you where I've been.'

Leira sighs. 'Fair enough.' She sits back in her bath. 'So, you want to tell me the story of the Minstrel. Why?'

The tall figure is quiet, and for a while it is like the pair of them are girls again, trapped in a cellar with silence stretching between them like spider's silk, one waiting with a towel-warming iron while the other splashes in the bath.

'Do you think you could make something a bit like a plug? Lots of plugs, actually.'

'Like a plug for this bath?'

'Yes. Except they need to be adjustable and completely watertight, even under pressure.'

'What does this have to do with that old story?' Leira cocks her head. 'Aren't you going to tell me anything more than that?'

The tall figure grins. 'I've always given you just the right amount of information to keep you alive, Leira. You wouldn't want me to stop now, would you?'

She laughs. 'Alright then. Say I manage to make these plug things, then what?'

'Bring them to Uranga for Midsummer.'

Leira raises an eyebrow. 'I'm not allowed to go to Uranga, as I think you know.'

The tall figure smiles again. 'Don't worry about that.'

Leira sits up in the cooling water. 'Can you pass me that towel?'

The tall, masked figure takes the towel hanging on the back of one of the chairs and holds it up for Leira to wrap herself in.

'What do you want me to use to make them?'

The visitor sits back down on the bath stool and picks up the pyjamas from the floor. When Leira is dry they hold the flannel out and Leira grins.

'There's a pile of seasoned labra wood in your woodshed, I think that'll be best. I trust your judgement as to the connections and seals and all that kind of thing.'

Leira starts to button up her pyjama shirt. 'Do you want to stay, Luna? I can put the kettle on, make some supper if you're hungry.'

The tall figure looks to their hands. 'I don't call myself Luna any more. Not for a long time.'

Leira shrugs. 'Alright. But you can have a cup of tea, whatever your name is.'

The tall figure sighs. 'I can't. Something here is sure to betray me if I stay too long.'

'We're a long way from the Tower now,' Leira says, pulling a woollen jumper over her head. 'They won't find you.' But still, she looks around her cottage guiltily, as though she should burn the wood and dismantle the stones so they don't rush, whispering secrets of hooded star children, straight to the Thirteen.

The tall figure stands up and crosses the little room. 'I'll see you in Uranga,' the person known as Luna says, their hand already on the front door handle. They pause.

'Did you knit that jumper yourself?'

Leira looks down at the thick green and orange stripes and gives a short bark of laughter. 'Oh no! I've got better things to do than sew.'

'Of course.' The tall figure looks down, as if chastened. 'Midsummer, then.'

And before Leira can say anything else, the door is open with a burst of cold air and the tall figure has disappeared through it, leaving nothing but shock in their wake.

The inventor woman, whose name is and has always been Leira, stands by her still-full bath watching the door to her cottage. She wants to hear that music again, for her friend to come back through the door and sit at her kitchen table with a steaming cup of tea between her palms, the way they used to in an underground cellar. She feels windblown, like a hurricane has swept through her house and left her and everything in it whirled and shaken. She wants her friend to come back, hang whatever might betray them. She wants to hear about what the person she used to know as Luna has been doing for the past twenty-two years.

Leira has lived in this cottage, alone, for all that time. Occasionally someone drops by to buy one of her machines, and they leave her a few sacks of barley and oats and sometimes some wool in exchange, but there has never been a friend in her kitchen in all that time.

Leira drains the bath, putting the plug on the table to study it later. She pulls a pair of red socks onto her cold feet and studies the wool. She remembers who brought her this; a young mother of triplets who took away a kind of cart to transport her babies around in. But Leira didn't knit these socks herself either, she never does. She always takes the wool to the village and swaps it for ready-made jumpers and socks and hats. She doesn't sew, not any more. Even after thirty years her fingers are still calloused and lumped from the needle, her back prematurely hunched from leaning over the silk, her eyes short-sighted from squinting at the details of the world the wordlight revealed to her. No, she will not sew, even if she has a hole in her breeches a foot wide in a scandalous place, and she wishes the old friend she used to know as Luna could have stayed, so they could talk about why she won't.

She sewed the world, once, and look what happened to it.

TIENTO

Section 1, clause 14(a)
And the Thirteen Earth spirits shall be known by
a number in the first instance. They may make
their true names known at their own discretion
and may use them among their brotherhood
while they are in council or at leisure.

Section 1, clause 14(b)
Wheel care shall be conducted as needed. First
the beard shall be oiled with the juice of obsidian
and the connecting vertebra massaged. Second
the weight-bearing vertebra shall be smoothed by
hawthorn leaves and the spokes kept in tune with
a yearly poultice of pig's blood.

Section 1, clause 14(c)
No brother shall suffer a mortal being to see
him transported by wheel, the enchantments
of legs, feet, trousers, shoes, cloaks and all
such accoutrements shall be constantly and
consistently applied.

They meet far beneath the Tower, in a room filled from
floor to ceiling with shelves. The shelves are mostly empty,
but here and there are scattered some thick old books, as
long as a forearm from elbow crease to fingertip. The books

are leather-bound, with cracked spines and pages that poke out of the covers and fray at the edges. They are labelled only with signs, embossed with gold leaf on the back cover, each symbol unique to each book.

Some of the symbols are intricate and curl with triumphant flourishes, like vines of sly ivy creeping over a ruined wall. Others are solid blocks of rectangles and squares that stack on top of each other in formal, tessellating patterns that do not betray much imagination. Some of the signs are made of staccato dots and dashes, made as if someone was interrupting them as they tried to speak.

The beings who can read the strange language of these symbols come to this library, as they call it, although it is not strictly a library as once books leave this room beneath the Tower they never come back. Books have been leaving this place for a long time, and so the ones that remain on the shelves have a lonely, despondent air. Most of them lie on their sides, reclining with their spines sagging against the shelves, no cousins to hold them upright, shoulder to shoulder. If books have a memory, which those who can read the symbols believe they do, then these books remember when the room was filled with their family, every shelf creaking under the weight of paper and ink, every gold symbol pressed happily against its neighbour, and they feel sad. That was a long time ago, now.

The room is lit by lanterns bearing a yellow light, hanging from the ceiling. The floor is stone and cold. From that stone floor a huge mushroom-like object protrudes in the centre of the room, a thick trunk as high as a waist that swells outwards in a vague circle. It makes the shape of a table, although its surface is not flat enough to balance anything on top. The only thing on the stone mushroom table is a silvery mass of silk.

Thirteen men with the lower halves of their faces covered enter the room and surround the table. They all have dark eyes that catch the yellow light and twinkle, making them look kinder than they really are. One by one they pick up the silk and run their hands along it to find the holes, before pulling their heads through and settling the silk comfortably around their shoulders. All thirteen men stare at the others.

There is silence for a moment. There are no leaders here, but no one would call themselves a follower, so it takes a quiet wrestling of wills to determine who will speak first.

'The books have been counted and there are fifty-seven left,' the man known as Eleven says. 'We have counted over and over again. We are not mistaken.'

Silence again.

'That will take us just to Midsummer,' Three says.

'Those are my calculations too,' agrees Seven. 'We have nothing beyond that.'

'Can we slow the girls?' says Nine. 'Can we make them repeat or get them to spread out the stitches?'

'You know we can't,' says Five, who is also known as Mandoré. 'We have tried it before and we've found it to be dangerous. The world becomes thin and the people start to fray. The last time there were rebellions and revolutions and we cannot have it again.'

Silence. The voices of the thirteen men are muffled under their face coverings but they are used to speaking and listening to each other in this way. The cellar room dampens all other sounds and amplifies their voices in the turgid air.

'We need her back,' says Eight, and there is an inaudible sigh of frustration in the room, a shudder from the shared silk of the cloak that is quickly suppressed. It is nobody's fault, this problem. They wear the cloak to remind them all of this.

All thirteen can remember the time when this room was not their meeting room, when instead of a mushroom-shaped stone table there was a bed and a washstand and trunks filled with the kinds of toys a young girl might like; dolls and buttons and brightly coloured scraps of silk. In those days they didn't enter unless invited, and then only to collect a book, perhaps with the ink still damp and smudging a little on the last page, to carry up the spiral staircase to the very top of the tower.

'You know she's been toying with us,' One says, his voice tight with anger. 'She knows we're about to run out, she's been appearing more and more in the tapestry.'

Twelve tightens his lips. One's been obsessed with the mistakes in the patterns for years now and the others never know what to say to him. He's right, he's always been right, but they don't know what to do. They meet down here in the darkness of every new moon, and still they cannot solve this problem.

'Has anyone seen anything in particular?' Twelve asks. 'Something, anything we can use. We need a plan, we need to do something.' He lifts his hand over the silken cloak and gestures to the empty shelves. The absence of the books is more eloquent than him.

Five, or Mandoré, puts his head to one side. 'There was something on the night shift, a few days ago,' he begins. There is a ponderous quality to his words that the others pay attention to. They have known him for a very long time, and they have come to realise when Mandoré is having the glimmer of an idea worth listening to.

'There was a glitch in the pattern – I've seen them becoming more frequent, as you have, One – but this was big. It was a man throwing balls over his head, a juggler. He appeared near Janat.'

This is only mildly interesting. Normally the glitches in the pattern are on the land itself: trees come down across the roads, corn sprouts where barley was sewn, an oak blooms with may blossom in winter. It is unusual for the glitches to take the form of people, but not unknown. They have all seen a juggler before. It isn't so mad.

'But,' Mandoré continues, 'the girl who stitched the juggler is the daughter of the owl woman.'

This is more interesting. These men look for coincidences and correspondences, this is how they have kept the seams of the world aligned for so long.

'How long has that girl been here now?' asks Seven.

'She is sixteen,' Mandoré says. 'It has been four and a half years.'

'The star child is trying to communicate with her,' Eight says, and the others all hear it, a hint of excitement behind his careful words.

Mandoré nods. 'I think that's so.'

'Do you think she knows who the girl is?' asks Eleven.

'She must,' says Nine.

'She wrote her!' says Six.

'She wants to parley,' says Three. 'She's trying to get at us, there's something that she wants.'

A long, absorbed silence. This may not be true, but if it is then it is important and it changes everything.

'Do we think the juggler is the Trickster?' Nine asks. He is careful; that form is not one that is mentioned casually here in their council.

One makes a humming sound. He, of all of them, is particularly averse to hearing that being spoken of in their home. 'And if he is,' he says, 'there is nothing to say she is in league with him. The... *rogue one* might be working alone, for their own ends.'

There is contemplative silence in the room. Each of the earth spirits is thinking of the symbols of the Trickster, the signs that they are abroad again in the world they all love. There have been no infestations of hare nests in the barley fields, and an ordinary number of crows cawing disdainfully at the travellers on the roads.

'We should send the girl out into the world,' Thirteen says, and although there is no real hierarchy within this group, if they had any senior member it would be Thirteen, who is oldest. 'We should let the owl woman's daughter find her as we have never been able to. And if the juggling man is a sign of something else, then so be it.'

Four frowns. 'But if it isn't written? How can we—'

'Let her handle that,' Thirteen says. 'She is disrupting the patterns. She may well be writing new ones.'

Mandoré clears his throat. 'All those in favour of sending the girl Alissa into the world?' He raises his hand, and one by one, all the others do too. Some immediately, with a sense of relief that finally they are doing something about the depleting shelves; some raise them reluctantly, after a pause to show those they share the cloak with their doubts.

Mandoré brings his hand down onto the mushroom table with a thud, and a second later twelve other palms land too and there is a reverberation throughout the room of the impact, a shadow of the sound of their agreement.

One by one, they slip the neck holes of the silken cloak over their heads and leave it lying in watery folds on the table. Deftly, each man reaches behind his head to untie the fabric that covers his mouth, removes it and stuffs it into a pocket of his cloak. Instantly the room is filled with long, luxuriant beards that fall to the floor and curl into a perfect circle at their feet, strong and vertical, a perfect wheel ready to take its owner whither it wishes. The subtle scent of oil fills the air; all thirteen know it to be the best thing for smooth, silent motion. Each man looks to the stone floor to check his wheel is rolling as it should; no bumps or squeaks or cracks in the bones.

Thirteen leaves first, a small sound of relief in his throat as the pressure on his spine eases and he can rest on his hair wheel for a while. The others wait until he has passed, then they stroke the hair that flows into their wheels, roll towards the door and queue patiently.

As he waits behind Three to pass through the door to leave the cellar room, Seven reaches up to a shelf and takes a book bearing a sign that resembles a bare tree in the winter and tucks it under his robe.

'Fifty-six, then,' says Mandoré, as he rolls up beside his brother. Seven grimaces.

'I know. But there's nothing to do be done.'

'Let's hope the girl can find her,' Mandoré says. 'Everything rests on her, now.'

CACCIA

Section 3, clause 2

*And the following spirits shall belong to the
Moon: the rivers; the canals; the sea; the springs
and wells; the clouds; the rain; the coral rings; the
thunder; the fishes and sea mammals; all manner
of birds of land and water excepting corvids; the
witches; the frogs and other creatures that live
between land and water; the ferns; roses and their
cousins; the wolves; the snakes, lizards, and their
fellow reptiles.*

*And the following spirits shall belong to the
Earth: all manner of trees both humble and great;
all manner of metals both common and precious;
all manner of rocks; bees and insects of all kinds;
all manner of plants excepting the rose family
and all other animals that have not expressed a
distinct allegiance for the Moon or for neutrality.
And the following spirits shall not belong to one
nor the other, but shall remain neutral in all
their dealings for as long as this contract shall be
suffered to exist: the hares; the foxes; the ravens;
crows and other corvids; music both soothing
and turbulent; the Trickster; the Sun; fire and the
lightning that blazes in the storms.*

The juggler has been travelling with them for almost a moon now, and while Vanna is completely won over, thinks he could juggle with the stars if he chose and denies she ever thought differently, Lion has come to rue the morning they rolled into Janat and set eyes on that man in the red cloak.

There is nothing Lion can find to complain about. The juggler has been nothing but a considerate travelling companion, never sleeping last in the morning and taking more than his fair share of long, boring days in the driving bay. But Lion is unsettled by his presence and he cannot explain why.

Perhaps it's to do with the box that now lives under the bench on the port side of the carriage. Every time the juggler opens it, Lion – who tries not to look, but nevertheless finds his eyes drawn towards it like a bee to a rose – sees neat little rows of cork-stoppered bottles and a strange, formless mist that begins to swirl inside them. Lion has the irrepressible feeling that the mist is trying to tell him something, but every time the juggler opens the box and the mist starts to rise, he slams it shut again before it can take shape. Lion doesn't know if the juggler has seen him glance to the mist or if he considers it a secret. *There are no little secrets on the road*, Lion wants to tell him when he shuts the lid of his box on the mist. *We live our lives before each other as if our hearts beat in time.*

Really, if he thinks about it, it's the water that irritates him most. Every morning the juggler rummages around inside his stupid box and pulls out his empty carafe. Lion has looked at it from every angle every day since the juggler arrived and still he can't make out what the thing's made of. It's clear, like the best quality glass, but it's much lighter than glass, and much stronger too. It swings and sways and jolts with the movement of the carriage like everything else but it's not got so much as a crack on it. The juggler goes with Vanna every day to fill it with water, and this is all he sips on until evening, when the thing is empty and he tucks it away again in his blue box under the bench. He drinks nothing else, from no other receptacle. He refuses petty beer when they pass through towns, he will not drink the tea Vanna offers him every morning from her copper kettle, he will not touch his lips to the clay jug of water that stands under the seat in the driver's bay, he will not touch his lips to anything but his otherworldly glass carafe. To Lion it seems to be a rejection of the communal life of the road; to share and share alike until there is nothing but your own skin – and sometimes not even that, as Lion knows too well – that you call yours.

Lion says nothing of his antipathy to the others, not even to Owl, although he thinks she knows anyway. Owl knows most things. When Goat gleefully sits down with the hat to count the corals and shuffle them into piles, Lion makes appreciative noises and turns away to groom before he is called upon to celebrate how much richer they all are now the juggler performs with them. When they stop the carriage by the side of the road and Vanna and the juggler go off into a clearing to coordinate her music with his tricks and rehearse their part of the show without inviting him, Lion stays morosely in the carriage with his memories. He remembers when he and Vanna would rehearse together; she playing the same snatch of fiddle music over and over again, he practising the flip that corresponded to the notes until it was perfect. Now he is not invited to their rehearsals, he performs in a separate part of the show. As a lion he no longer elicits the same excited gasps and held breaths that he used to. A cat's body cannot do the contortions he spent his youth training his human body for. Now he does the tricks he can, leaping from rooftops and over children's heads, twisting his legs to an improbable place under his chin, bending backwards to make an arch with his tail. That kind of thing. It doesn't fill Goat's hat, but it gets a smattering of applause, and a coral ring or two. He's the warm-up, the sympathy act, and in his kinder moments he wonders if this is what he really holds against the juggler: that the newcomer has exposed his new act as nothing but a tattered curtain over his pride.

Goat told the juggler the story of Lion's transformation one afternoon as it rained fat drops of cold water. Vanna steered the carriage into the shelter of a labra grove and they played the exquisite corpse game with a sheet of paper and a stick of charcoal until it got too dark to see. It was his own fault; Goat drew something that looked at bit like one of the towers of Settran, although of course it could have been anything; Goat's drawings were never clear, as he had very poor control of the charcoal wedged between the cleft in his hoof. Vanna asked if they remembered going to Settran, and Lion, goaded by the memory of better times, began to talk about the show they performed there.

'Do you remember, Van, how the baker burst into tears as you sang the one about the sailor and the mermaid, and then he insisted on taking you in his arms and dancing with you round the square?'

Vanna laughed. 'And then the milkmaids came to you and swept you into the dancing too.'

'And then they invited us to the wedding of the burgher's daughter,' Goat said, joining in. 'And we slept inside, with straw mattresses and porridge with clover honey for breakfast, and they paid us ten coral rings and two sacks of oats.' Goat sighs dreamily. 'You know, I dream of Sattran when my belly's empty and my heart full.'

They smiled wistfully to themselves for a few moments, recalling the warmth of the hall where the wedding guests danced and thumped their tankards of wine on the scarred tables. Of course the juggler had felt left out, of course he wanted to try to take part in their chatter. Lion knows it was his own fault for excluding him by sharing a memory from before he came.

The juggler said, 'I didn't know you dance, Lion.'

'I don't,' Lion said shortly. He knew he should say something more, be polite, change the subject, but he wanted to be left to his thoughts. Vanna had the sheet of paper in play, folded twice at the top, and she was bent over it, the charcoal stick scratching at the paper. Outside, the rain smattered against the window.

'But you used to, is that right?' He's determined to make conversation, Lion thought. He can't just sit here in blessed silence like the rest of us until the paper comes around again.

'I used to, yes.'

'So what happened?'

Lion felt the air in the carriage become tight. He wondered if Goat or Vanna would say anything, rescue him, talk about the show in the next town. He heard Owl rearrange her wings and turn around on her perch so she was facing away from them. He fancied she was disapproving of the juggler's lack of tact, but you never really knew, with Owl.

He knew Goat was staring at him, willing him to tell the juggler the story and get it over with. He knew Goat thought it a good idea in general to talk about what had happened, he said it would 'release the trauma' and 'make you look forward to the positives in your new life'.

'You can tell him,' Goat said, encouragingly. 'He's one of us, now.'

Lion waited for Vanna to say something and defend him, but she was absorbed in her drawing. He turned to the juggler and felt his tail thicken and tense behind him.

'I used to be a man,' he began, the words thick and reluctant on his tongue. 'And like men do, I fell in love.'

Lion stopped and swallowed. Vanna was no longer drawing but she stayed hunched over the paper, listening.

'I fell in love with a woman who happened to be a witch, and she didn't love me back. I scared her. I made her think she was in danger because I loved her, and she used her magic to protect herself. She made a spell to turn me into this, something that looks like a lion at first glance, and feels like a lion to me, but is actually nothing more than a pile of dead autumn leaves.'

The juggler cocked his head and leaned towards Lion, sweeping his eyes over his fur, the burnished golden colour of autumn beeches. Lion shivered under his gaze, and as he moved, the fur that looked so sleek fractured, and there was a faint rustling sound like footsteps over winter leaf-fall.

'Were you a danger to her?' asked the juggler.

'No!' Lion's tail curled and his muscles tightened to prepare to pounce. 'I wasn't! I loved her. I still love her.'

The juggler's eyebrows were raised in an expression of amused disbelief. *You can't mean to say you might still feel something for the woman who did that to you*, he doesn't say. *Fool and idiot and lovelorn loon.*

Vanna looked up from the paper. 'It doesn't matter if you were a danger to her or not, she says. She thought you were, and she did what she thought she had to.' She shrugged, bit her lip. 'I'm sorry, Lion. You know I am. But you knew she was a witch. You shouldn't have baited her.'

Lion turned away from them all. He felt naked in the face of the juggler's attention, for it wasn't like the well-meaning pity of his friends, it was a mocking of his loss, a kind of joke. He felt as though the juggler could see right through to his shamed heart and he wasn't sure if he liked the feeling of it.

The folded paper came to him, and there was only space for one picture more. Lion drew a pair of feet encased in boots that pointed towards the toes, one slightly in front of the other. He patterned the boots with little stars, then folded the paper over and handed it to Goat. He always draws the first thing that comes to him in this game, that's the point of it. To expose the mind to itself, to dip a light net into the pool of the unconscious and skim off what's floating on the surface.

Goat unfolded the paper and held it up for all to see. A hard gust of wind made the carriage quiver and the lantern swung on its hook, making the shadows dance across the paper.

Lion's whiskers bristled at the sight of what they'd drawn. For a head, which the juggler had drawn, the figure had a unique ovular shape, like an egg turned sideways. He'd drawn huge masses of wavy hair, parted at the centre around it in a way that made Lion's heart tumble over itself. For a chest, which Goat had drawn, there was a bird trailing two long tail feathers from a dark hole where the heart should be, and the bird wore the same kind of face as the woman, for it was a woman, egg-like, wry and completely self-possessed. For an abdomen, which Vanna had drawn, a fur cloak of light and dark stripes that seemed to be breathing like a hunting wolf, and a white hand clutching at a lantern. And then, to finish the figure off, Lion's boots at the bottom of it all.

He shut his eyes. There was no mistaking who it was, the figure swam in his mind all day and every day, waltzing through his dreams sowing discord and chaos, casting the spell upon him that has made him what he is now.

Vanna gasped. 'But it looks like—'

Goat grabbed the paper between his two front hooves before she could finish and crumpled it to his chest. 'Well, that's the fun of the game, isn't it?' he said, conciliatory over his panic for what Lion might say about it all, slipping the paper behind him where it fell to the floor on its face, almost sheepishly.

The juggler sat puzzled, looking from Vanna to Goat to Lion and back again.

'You can say it, you know,' Lion said quietly. 'You can say who it is. You can even say her name, if you want.'

'Lion—' Vanna said.

'I think I'd like a bit of a walk,' Lion said, turning to prod at the door with his paw. Even though it opened only a crack, splatters of rain hit the floor and a smell of the damp wood of the forest began to seep inside the carriage.

'Don't go out in that,' Goat said. 'Stay. We'll play something else.'

Lion shook his head and hopped down from the carriage, kicking the door shut. It made more of a slam than he had wanted, making it seem as though he was angry. Well. Let them think he was. He stalked off under the trees towards the shelter of a labra grove, trying not to look as though he was hunting anything, but still he heard the squeak of a frightened vole as it fled him. Let them think he roared for fury with them and with *her*, the one who did this to him. Better than letting them know his grief and his shame, and his feeling that the best part of his life is already gone.

They have not played the drawing game since.

Instead, when it is raining and the roads turn to sludge and not even Owl can help them move on, they play one of the juggler's games. He is a seemingly bottomless well of games and frolics and jests, and it is almost impossible to escape them all, especially in this season of endless autumn rains and mud churned to black butter by the cartwheels that groan along the unpaved roads.

The juggler produces packs of cards from a compartment inside his blue trunk and teaches them how to play canasta and whist and rummy and mazurka. He buys a pack of tarocchi cards at a fair near Fara and uses them to tell fortunes and predict the weather. Vanna begs him to teach her what each card means, and Goat approves. She can still tell fortunes when she's got a cold and her voice is too hoarse to sing, Lion can see him thinking, and then the takings won't suffer.

When it's not raining, the juggler strings up a rope between two labra trees and walks across it and back, giggling when he falls off into the gathering piles of shed leaves. He teaches

Goat and Vanna infinite games of throwing sticks against other sticks, and other guessing games with pieces of paper stuck to their heads and secrets they must keep and all kinds of lies and bluffs and jests.

Owl declines to play, but then she always does. Lion is not so lucky. They call him 'spoilsport' and 'sore loser' when he sits inside the carriage and outside the games, and he has taken to pretending to sleep in order to avoid them, letting snores rumble in his throat for extra realism.

Then, on a day when the wind is high enough to have them moving faster than a horse and oak leaves are rustling happily in the sunlit dells of the woods, the juggler lays out his most audacious game yet, the one, Lion soon realises, he has really come to teach them.

'Do you ever do plays, Goat?' he asks in the middle of stirring honey into his steaming bowl of porridge.

'Plays?' Goat says. 'Pretending and declaiming poetry and lying down dead, that sort of thing?'

The juggler laughs. 'Exactly. Telling a story, with actions and songs.'

Goat looks doubtful, but Lion knows it will happen, the juggler will have his way as he has since he came. They will be doing a play before the summer comes, that is what Lion has learnt about how the juggler works.

'But where would we do a play?' Goat says carefully. 'Even if we knew how to do one. They don't want that kind of thing round these parts, they want a spectacle and a nice sing-song and that's about it.'

'People want to see plays in Uranga,' the juggler says, and to Lion's mind there is something sly in his voice, as if he know precisely how to manipulate them all.

Goat shakes his head quickly. 'Oh no oh no oh no, we don't go there. There's other circuses in the city, we can't compete. We're not allowed, see. We've got our patches, we've got our places.'

'But that's for circus,' the juggler says. 'Not for plays. We could go there if we do a play.'

'I've seen a play,' Vanna says unexpectedly from the door, where she stands with a pitcher of river water cradled in her arms. 'When I was a girl. The players acted out the story of the Minstrel and it was beautiful. I cried.'

Goat's eyes mist over and he claps his front hooves together. 'Oh, the Minstrel! What a story that is, what fine love songs! We could do a play of the Minstrel, couldn't we, Juggler?'

The juggler sits back on the bench and sips at his spoon of porridge.

Lion suppresses a sigh.

'We don't have the people to act out that story, Goat. We'd need at least three of us – well, three *human bodies*—' it hurts him to say '—and I really don't know what we'd do about all the water, we can't actually perform inside a river.'

The juggler cuts in. 'Nonsense. I can be the Minstrel and Vanna can be both the water fairy and the forest fairy. Then you, Lion, can do a huge finale for the flooding river, all flips and growls and fierce eyes. Imagination will take care of the rest. It'll be magic, trust me.'

And Goat is sold, just like that, as Lion sees with a sinking feeling in his throat. Vanna nods enthusiastically; he can see she is already thinking of making herself two new dresses for costumes, one green and embroidered with leaves and bark, and the other a pale, shimmering blue with waves and ripples dyed into it.

'It's the perfect play for the Midsummer carnival in Uranga,' the juggler says casually.

Vanna squeals, a wordless sound of glee. 'Go to Uranga for Midsummer? Oh, I think I'll die.' She places the water pitcher on the floor of the carriage and slumps on the bench next to the juggler. 'I've never been and I've always wanted to. Do you mean it, Juggler? Do you really think we can?'

He beams at her. 'Of course we can. We'll perform for the crowds there, they'll love us and shower us with enough corals to have a holiday for a year!'

Rehearsals start that very same afternoon in a beech grove just outside a cabbage-growing village in the western valleys. Lion doesn't attend. He stalks off into the forest, looking for deer to chase. He doesn't mean to hurt them, he just wants to feel the scent of quivering animal trembling in his nose and hear a heartbeat skitter at his approach. He doesn't find any deer. Instead, he pounces on a leaf drift with his claws outstretched, tearing at the dark earth beneath in a way he will never tear at anything that will bleed, no matter how much he wants to. He doesn't come back until it is already dark, and no one says they missed him.

RICERCAR

Section 2, clause 8(b)
The star child will never write anything that
shall cause the underground rivers into which
the spiral canals of Uranga flow to be blocked or
diverted from their proper course back to the sea.

Sunset comes, and with it the bodies of the girls who sew the night shift stir in their beds. Mandoré's call is only a few moments away and something in their dreams knows it. Castles begin to melt, seas start to drain away, and whatever the hand was grasping for either moves out of sight completely or finally comes within reach.

Alissa opens her eyes, and when she realises she is awake before the alarm she smiles slowly, savouring the precious moments of freedom in her mind before it is filled with the jumbled roar of the world's desires when she starts to sew. Times like these are the balm for her careening mind, a quiet instant of privacy when she can think and feel what she likes.

A shadow moves on the wall beside her bed and she turns to it, stifling a startled scream when she sees the unmistakeable shape of Mandoré looming from the blackness.

His mouth and head are covered, as always, and his staff is tucked under his arm. He beckons to her.

'Get dressed and wait outside this room,' he says. He does not whisper – he would never whisper – but his voice is too quiet to disturb anyone else. 'Do not wake the others.'

Alissa sits up in bed and watches him stalk the length of the dormitory and shut the door behind him. This is about the juggler. It can only be about him.

She pulls the blue dress of her uniform over her head and fastens it about the waist. She ties her hair at the nape of her neck; she will annoy Mandoré even more if she does not appear neat and tidy. Her heart is skittering, the way it always does before a beating. The skin between her shoulder blades itches as if getting ready to heal before it is flayed.

She follows his path out of the dormitory, between the sleeping bodies of her friends. She does not look at their still, huddled forms. They will be sympathetic to her today, sitting down all day with the open wounds of her beating written across her back.

She opens and shuts the dormitory door with a creak – it's only Mandoré who can make it move silently – and finds him waiting for her a few doors along. When he sees her he opens the door, a door Alissa has always found to be locked whenever she has idly tried the handles as they walk along this part of the corridor.

The room is the same size as her dormitory but completely empty. Mandoré stands in the middle with one hand holding his staff still on the flagstones and his other hand folded deep inside his cloak. Alissa stares at him for a moment. She wants it to be the kind of stare that tells him she is not afraid of him, although her stomach is churning with fear.

'Tell me about the man you made,' he says.

He knows. Of course he knows, he is of the Thirteen and they know everything there is to know in the world. She had thought she wouldn't care if this happened, she had thought she would be glad to leave the Tower and be free from all this, but making something deliberately out of the pattern is worse than just making a mistake, she knows it, she knows the consequences for the world, how could she be so selfish, how could she do something so wrong?

Tears tumble from Alissa's eyes and flow downwards, where the two streams converge and drip from the tip of her nose.

'I didn't choose to make him! I promise. I heard music and it came into the thread and into my needle before I could stop it. It made the man by itself! I did nothing but watch it move.'

Mandoré cocks his head. 'What kind of music?'

Alissa shakes her head helplessly. She has barely heard anything but Mandoré's voice for years, she knows nothing of the subtle sounds of the world.

'I don't know. Like a whistle or a flute. A kind of pipe, I think.'

Mandoré is completely still and silent. She is not scared of his staff now, she hardly thinks of the familiar pain across her shoulders to shrink from it. Now she knows she has erred far more seriously than anything that deserved a small beating, she knows that something entirely new and wrong has happened in the world, and she has let it happen. Her legs flutter. She wants to run back to her dormitory, sink into her bed and pull her sheet over her head so that all she can see of the world she has made is a vague light through the pale wool.

'What did the man look like?'

Alissa swallows and lets her eyes shut. She has treasured the memory of the man these past seven nights, thinking of him as she obeyed Mandoré's instructions, calling the wry twist of his face to her mind every sunrise as she went to sleep. It feels wrong to describe him now, but she has no choice. She knows Mandoré has other ways of finding out what she knows. To tell him is the easiest one.

'He had a red cloak and the balls he juggled with glowed, like they were made of light. He had a pointed blue hat and his beard forked, so he looked like he had a star for a head.'

'A star.' He narrows his eyes.

Alissa nods slowly. She doesn't know if she has saved herself or handed him the axe. Mandoré's eyes are grimly satisfied, as though she has confirmed something he had suspected.

There is a long silence in which Alissa feels dizzy. She puts out a hand to steady herself against the wall, but there is nothing there but a shadow and she stumbles. Mandoré watches her calmly.

'You'll leave in a few moments, after the girls go to the tower to start their shift,' Mandoré says. 'No goodbyes, no telling the others about pipe music or stars for faces or needles that didn't behave themselves or all the ways you've betrayed yourself. You'll have a change of clothes, a water bag, and a loaf of bread, and that will be all you will take from us.'

Alissa's heart crumples.

'But where will I go?' Her voice is stuck in a whisper behind her tongue.

'I do not care. You were privileged here and you knew the rules. Now you can take your chances in the world like everybody else.'

He turns and walks out of the room, and Alissa listens to his steps as he walks into the dormitory she used to sleep in to give the wake-up. Fingertips of dread creep over her, a disbelieving panic. Where will she go? What is there in the world for her to do? Dimly she tries to think of something she has sewn, some place she could go now. Her longing had only ever been to not be here, never to be anywhere else in particular. She would like not to have a body at all, to be only a spirit floating on breaths and puffs of cloud. She very nearly feels like that now, her heart is lifting out of her chest until it is hovering somewhere above her head; but what exact feeling has it drifting there she can't quite tell.

She hears the day shift walking down the other spiral steps on the other side of the tower, their tread heavy and tired, and then she begins to hear the sounds of her own shift getting dressed: the squeak of the water pump, the shuffle of the drawers, the banging of the door to the long drop. She wonders if they have noticed that she's not in her bed, if they're thinking about her absence with puzzlement or indifference, if they have looked at Mandoré with questions. No goodbyes and no telling them how you betrayed yourself, he said. *I have not betrayed anything*, Alissa thinks with the first surge of anger. *You don't love anything, you can't know what that word means.*

When the night shift has trudged up the stairs to the sewing room – is that hesitance she can hear in their steps? – Are they feeling uneasy about where she might be? – the door opens and another masked man, dressed in the same kind of cloak as Mandoré, comes in to hand her a pack she can attach to her shoulders with two long straps. She recognises him as another of the Thirteen, but she doesn't know his name.

He jerks his head to follow him and leads her along the corridor and down a set of stairs she has never walked before, dark and narrow, lit only by occasional lanterns set into the central pillar. This staircase smells of damp stone and mould.

Down, down, down Alissa walks, following the masked man until they're both underground. She follows him along a dark corridor that is more like a tunnel, still lit with the glow of occasional lanterns. She can feel the weight of the earth and stone above her head and she struggles to keep her breathing even. She has never been underground before. Since Mandoré came to the lost children's home, she has lived like a bird in a nest high above the earth and never below it. She swallows to try to moisten her dry mouth and keeps as close as she dares to the folds of the masked man's cloak. She tries to remember that rush of rebellion that burst through her as she lay in bed the morning after she created the juggler. Exile is freedom too.

Her legs start to ache – it's been many years since she walked this far – when the masked man stops in the middle of the tunnel and presses his back to the wall to let her pass. He says nothing. She wants to stop and stare him in the eyes, to ask him where to go or who will sleep in her bed when the others come back from the night shift, or even just to see if his eyes are as stern and unforgiving as Mandoré's. But she keeps her eyes down and her lips still, the habits of the Tower, even now, too strong to break.

He points in the direction they have been walking and turns back. Alissa listens to his fading steps until there is nothing but dead, still air in the tunnel and the sound of her own breathing.

After a long time walking – which she cannot measure because the light does not change and there is no sound other than her footsteps, the usual markers by which she watches time slip by – the tunnel floor begins to slope upwards. A while after that the air becomes fresher and drier and the stone walls are no longer dripping to the touch.

Soon, Alissa emerges into a forest and when she looks back at the entrance to the tunnel she walked through she finds it nothing more than an unassuming cave mouth set into a gentle hill, scattered with fresh bear droppings all around. She climbs to the top of that small hill and turns a full circle to look in all directions, but she cannot see the Tower. This does not, to her surprise, make her feel sad.

It is still night and the air is cold. The darkness is illuminated by a moon, but she can't see it yet. There are only a few, rusty leaves left on the bare trees and the branches glisten with a little frost. Mandoré did not see fit to give her a warm cloak or fur to leave with, so she wraps her arms tightly around her chest and walks quickly, her breath misting the air before her face. She is not sleepy; she is always awake at night.

She finds a path and follows it through trees she cannot name until it widens and joins a muddy road. She could walk in either direction, she does not know what lies at either end. She doesn't know which way is north or south, she does not know where the nearest village is, she does not know which way she should go. She looks one way, then the other. There seems to be less mud to the left, so she starts walking that way.

She listens to the scuffles of mice in the dead leaves that coat the road and the hoots of the owls hunting them. She wonders who among the girls in the Tower is sewing those owls and mice and what patterns Mandoré is calling. She looks up to the sky to see the waxing half-moon perfectly framed in the space between the crowns of two trees. She thinks she sees the moon smiling at her and she stops, blinks, stares again. Yes, the moon is smiling at her, she is sure of it, although she cannot say how she knows as there is nothing different about the shape or the features. Alissa begins to walk again, keeping her gaze turned up to the sky, wondering if she should smile back. Already, she has forgotten to wonder exactly how Mandoré knew about the juggler, she has even forgotten the feel of a needle in her fingers. She watches the smiling moon and walks, and that is the way she spends her first night of exiled freedom.

PRELUDE

Section 2, clause 3(b)
Both the Moon and the Thirteen Earth spirits
shall obey the laws of fortune, chance and
happenstance and shall not seek to question their
movements. They are governed by a separate
agreement that is beyond the bounds of this
contract.

When Moon gave birth to her daughter, Sun graciously slid in front of her to hide her from the Earth's gaze. A few blessed moments of darkness was all it took for Moon to birth her child and swaddle it. When Sun began to reveal her again, offering his congratulations as he moved away, Earth rejoiced to see the night lit.

Moon suckled her daughter as she waned, first to a crescent and then to darkness. When she rose from the darkness as a sliver of waxing crescent for the first time, she brought her daughter trailing along behind her, a bright spot of light to the west.

More than fifty days' walk from Uranga, at the northern tip of a wet, forested land, the Thirteen met in the cellar of their tower, grey worsted wrapped around the lower half of their faces. They came into the cellar one by one, greeting each other with silent nods. The dank air of the cellar fizzed with the good news; there was excitement on each man's tongue. In the middle of the room there was a table chiselled out of stone, shaped like a mushroom. On it lay a silvery mass of cloth. One by one, the masked men entered the room and pulled their heads through the holes in the cloth, arranging it around their necks so its tiny fibres didn't itch the exposed places on their necks. Soon, they stood in a silent circle, linked by the tether of their council cloak.

'Moon has birthed,' Two said; unnecessarily, as each of them had seen the sky. 'And not a moment too soon.'

He gestured to the shelves, which were thinly stacked with books. There were patches where the dust was thin, where other books had recently stood.

Thirteen sighed. As the oldest among them, he whispered something inaudible, and each of the men in the room felt a weight drop into their pocket. There was a quiver of dread in each of their hearts. A lottery is a fine thing when it makes fairness from fancy, but there can be a price to pay.

Slowly, each of the Thirteen placed a hand inside their pocket and felt for the stones. Three hoped to find the number nine or twelve on his stone; Seven hoped for four or ten. None of the half-masked men hoped to find their own number name inscribed on the stone in their pocket. None of them wanted to do what luck would have them do.

Thirteen pulled out his stone first and held it above the silvery cloak to show the others. The number was four, and although he tried to control his relief the others knew of it and felt their own hearts contract in response.

One by one, the half-masked men held up their stones. If the number written on the stone was not the number of their name, they were safe from the spirits of fortune and luck. Seven's didn't match, neither did Eleven's, nor Nine's.

Eight could not stop his sharp exhale when he showed the number one on his stone, nor could Three when he saw his stone was marked with a seven. Two said, 'Number six,' when he pulled out his stone and that irritated some of the others; it seemed to them to be a sign of disrespectful levity. The lottery was traditionally performed in silence.

Five pulled out his stone next, and when he saw that the number written there was also a five, he closed his eyes. A deeper silence spread around the table as they looked at his stone, a silence that made them remember other lotteries on other nights. For a long time the masked men stood and looked at Five's stone, while Five kept his eyes screwed tightly shut.

It was Twelve who broke the solemn stillness by slipping his head out of the silvery cloak and untying the green neckerchief that held in his beard. The hair tumbled to the stone floor, curled over the exposed bone of his wheel, and his feet faded until they were no longer there. Twelve clicked his tongue against his teeth and the wheel began to turn to take him out of the room.

The Thirteen waited. Fortune was not finished with them yet.

Twelve came rolling back, dragging a basket behind him, and when he heard its clatter Five opened his eyes to look at Twelve. There was a new hardness in him now, a new sense that to be chosen changed him and his place in the world. He had been to the sky twice before, he knew that much, but it was so long ago that he cannot remember anything but blackness and freezing ice crystals stuck in his wheel. There were new constellations in the night now, new rocks peppering the earth, new life forms written into the world.

He didn't know what this next journey to the sky would bring.

Twelve rolled over to Five, who turned to face him. Quietly, he opened the basket and reached inside. He pulled out a long stick which only revealed the net attached to the bottom end at the very last moment. Five let his gaze rest on the net itself, a glowing, writhing tangle of wordlight thread. That was all he had to capture the moon's daughter. He held out his hand to pick it up by the handle. It was not heavy.

Thirteen cleared his throat. 'You know your sacred charge, you know the consequences should you fail. Moon is waxing, with only one night to go until she is half. Five, you have exactly one of Moon's cycles to capture the star child and bring her here. You have the net, you know what to do. We send you on your way with our luck and good wishes.'

And as one, the Thirteen bowed to their brother charged with travelling to the sky and back so that the world could be made and remade. Five was still for a moment, feeling the cloth that covered his wheeled beard heavy on his face, making it difficult to breathe. Then he pulled his mask down to his neck as his feet faded to reveal his spine curved into a wheel, let the luxuriant grey beard fall to the flagstone floor of the cellar and curl underneath the bone. He rolled out of the cellar room and along the corridor, towards the dying emerald light of the forest beyond the Tower. He shivered already with the unbidden memory of the chill in the place beyond the clouds.

> • <

Here is a wheeled man, soaring through a sky lit violet and indigo by the setting sun. The spirits of the air recognise him and his task. He trespasses in their realm but they may say nothing, for the contract allows one of the Earth spirits safe passage when the moon births. Here are wisps of icy mist sinking low to the hills, here are clouds flushing grey with apprehension, letting a fizz of lightning escape. 'The earth has come for the star child,' the thunder whispers and all the air spirits cower near the border of earth and sky, trying not to hear the battle that will come.

Here are the motes of ice stabbing at the skin under his beard, chilling him to the bone. The joint where his wheel meets his back aches. Yes, he remembers this. His brothers have spoken of it too.

Here are Lyra, Auriga, Ursa and the others, blazing mutely above their mother. They remember when they were taken. They remember the damp cellar and the endless scratching of the quill on the books and the silent, scurrying fingers of the yellow-haired girls. They dip their heads and turn their faces away from their mother and little sister. She will forgive them if they can't watch.

Here is the wheeled man, gripping his net so tightly the knuckles of his hands turn the same colour as the moon. *Maybe I won't have to fight,* he thinks. *She must know she's got no choice by now. Maybe she'll kiss her daughter goodbye and send her off peacefully, to be returned one day as a shimmering clutch of stars, like her sisters.*

Here is the scream of Mother Moon, round and bright in her fullness, as her child is ripped from her breast. She has lost all her daughters this way, too many to count now, but still she screams. The child fights; here are her teeth, pointed like shards of ice crystals that sink into the hand of the wheeled man; here are her flares of light to burn at his eyes and send him reeling away into the blackness of space. But the contract is written in stardust older than time and nothing can stop it.

Here is the net, woven of some kind of earth fire that scalds her before it saps her power and dims her light. The child cannot feel her mother's body pressed to her any more. Her cries choke her, she hiccups as she wails, reaching out for her mother who is now just beyond her grasp.

Here is her mother's voice, hushing her with that special song that is all the sound she has ever known. The moon tells her daughter that the earth has come for her now, and she must leave the sky to go and write the world below. She tells her of the rules written so long ago, whispering them so quietly the masked man will not hear but her words will be seared into her child's mind forever; they will be the foundational songs of her life. Then she lets her daughter go and the child falls into the net.

Here is the wheeled man and the shining light in his net, falling to earth in the darkness of night, a contemptuous whistle of air through his beard as he falls. Here is the moon, weeping. Here is the masked man, gulping a breath as he falls home.

And far below on the earth, here is a turnip farmer looking up into the sky as he slips out of his back door to pad down to the privy in his slippers. He sees a tumbling light soar across the dark sky, but when he finishes in the privy and climbs the creaking stairs to bed again he is sleepy and has half-forgotten that strange white fire. He doesn't mention it to his sons in the morning.

And this is how it goes, every time, the way it has since the contract was first signed in the days when there was nothing but sour sea water and the jagged rocks beneath.

> • <

Eleven nights later, when the moon was waning gibbous, battered and bruised from her fight with the earth, Five appeared again in the tower's cellar, covered in chalky white dust that smoked a little in the air and would burn a finger with cold if it were touched. He held the net in one hand and a cage with the other, and he panted slightly as he walked through the doorway into the room that had once contained only a stone table shaped like a mushroom and a mass of silky cloak lying on top of it.

Seven and Eleven, who were busy in the cellar with hammers and nails and long planks of wood, making a bed for the guest they were shortly to receive, dropped their tools. They threw their arms open and rushed towards Five, slapping him on the back and shouting their congratulations. The mood in the Tower had been tense since the lottery and every night the twelve masked men had gathered in the courtyard at moonrise to gaze at the sky and speculate on Five's progress.

'You didn't need to rush!' said Seven, squeezing Five's shoulder. 'We're not even ready for her here.'

Five swayed backwards and forwards on his heels, willing the roaring in his ears to abate. 'I was lucky,' he said, and placed the cage on the floor.

In an instant, the room was filling with the Thirteen either rolling through the doorway or running on their own feet like everything else in the world, anxiety and hope building as they rounded the corner and tumbled into the room, eager to catch their first glimpse of the new star child.

'Shut the door,' Thirteen said, not taking his eyes off the glowing light in the cage.

Eight moved to the door, bolted it, and took his place in the circle of the Thirteen around the glowing cage and Five, who still stood beside it.

Thirteen gave a small nod to Five, who bent down to unlock the cage. He still held the net in the other hand, just in case.

'Come out, child, let us see you,' Three said, not unkindly.

All the men watched the light in the cage as it shrank into itself and became even brighter. The Thirteen had to squint to keep watching. The light shrank further, until it was diamond-hard and fixed in its true shape of a waxing crescent. In the moments before it moved out of the cage, they all saw the face etched on the surface of the light, contorted with sorrow. Later, they would all remember how the moon's daughter looked when she first came to them and they would wonder how they missed the signs of what she would do.

A flash of unbearable heat, like a blast of fire heaving from a smith's forge, and then the cage door clanged, iron on iron, and there was a smell of singed hair in the room from all the uncovered beards.

When the heat had faded and the light was dim again, the Thirteen looked to the centre of the circle. In between Five and the empty cage, there was a little girl with long dark hair that reached to her waist dressed in a pale grey smock dress which was frayed around the hem. She looked around the room, glanced up at Five, her captor, and burst into tears.

> • <

In the first year of her life with the Earth spirits, every day followed the same quiet pattern. Three woke the star child each morning with a knock at the door and her breakfast porridge on a tray, and checked she had everything she needed for her day's work. She would eat, bathe, dress herself, and then spend a while at her desk, writing in one of the books brought to her. Normally, one of the Thirteen would sit with her in companionable silence while she worked, but not always. Sometimes they would just check in on her now and then, if things were busy.

She worked at her writing until around lunchtime, although of course it was only her stomach that told her time was passing, as the cellar was deep underground and the moon's daughter was not allowed outside. The Thirteen felt it would be too upsetting for her to see the sky.

After her lunch was brought to her – usually by Three, who liked to bring a bowl of soup for himself and chat to her as they ate – she worked at her writing for a little while longer, just to wrap up the thoughts of the morning. Then it was playtime for the rest of the day, when the moon's daughter could spend her time amusing herself with any of the things in her bedroom. The Thirteen were always bringing her new things, toys they thought little girls liked to play with, and she was careful to play with them all equally, in rotation. She would spend a while on her rocking horse, then move the furniture around her doll's house, then build a house out of blocks and then set up a tea party for her rag dolls. The masked men were sure that was what little girls did, and the moon's daughter did not want to disappoint them. Not yet.

> • <

In the second year of her life in the cellar, the moon's daughter began to play less with the toys the Thirteen brought her, leaving them to gather dust in the darkest corners of her cellar room. Every month she grew a little taller, and every month Three would wag his finger and pretend to tell her off when he saw the ragged hem of her dress dangling a handspan above her ankles.

'You're eating us out of house and home!' he'd say, putting his hands on his hips in an impression of a fishwife in the market.

She would stand very still, determined not to flinch, roll her eyes, or give him any sign of her contempt. Sometimes she would smile tightly, to acknowledge the joke.

'I'll bring you some more clothes tomorrow,' he would say, and the next day he would appear with plain spun grey dresses that were a little too big and dragged on the floor as she paced around her room.

Soon the moon's daughter was as tall as the masked men and could look them in the eye whenever they came into her cellar room, but her face was still as round and smooth as a little girl's. She started to be able to tell them apart by their smell. There was the dank, soil smell of their hair and breath that made her gag whenever there were more than four of them in her room at once, but beneath that she began to perceive that Three smelt of burnt milk, like the bottom of the pan he used to make her porridge in the morning. Nine and Eleven both smelt like the ink and leather and parchment they presented to her with great ceremony every now and then, as if she was supposed to be grateful. Thirteen smelt of sun-warmed stone on a summer's afternoon, and One smelt of blood, like an abattoir or a battlefield. She wrote those smells into her books and no one ever questioned how a star child who had been born in the heavens could know the exact texture and memory of these earthly scents, and write them so precisely into the world.

> • <

At Midsummer in the third year, the Thirteen gathered in council in another room of their Tower. They slipped their masked faces through the neck holes of the silvery council cloak and settled their wheels into stillness. Thirteen asked them each for a progress report on the star child, then looked at One expectantly.

One, who became restless if he spent too much time in the Tower and liked to roam around the world, told his brothers that everything was proceeding well. 'The harvests are good, the fish stocks in the rivers are healthy, and the orchards will give a bountiful harvest in the autumn,' he said. 'Can't ask for more.'

Two said that the moon's daughter was quiet and still and he appreciated that in a young girl.

Three smiled soppily under his mask and said that the moon's daughter was an intelligent and sensitive person who had given him no trouble at all, indeed, he found her company enlivening. He wanted to say more but he stopped himself, biting his lip under his mask in case any of his brothers started to think he was growing too attached to the star child, and they decided to take him off care duties until his objectivity returned.

Four said you never can tell until they ask for their privileges. 'That's when they show their true colours,' he muttered, 'and we all know it.' There was a short silence in the room as the Thirteen remembered other star children of other ages, other councils where they had felt the silky caress of their cloak about their necks and discussed their charge in the cellar.

'Thank you, brother Four,' Thirteen said firmly, and turned away from him to the next to speak.

Five, who was at that time calling the patterns for the day shift at the top of the Tower, told his brothers that the wordlight was appearing true on the needles of the sewing girls and there was not a hitch or dropped stitch in the fabric of the world.

Six said, 'I think she's a proud sort, but there's nothing wrong with that.'

Seven said he was about to open another chamber for the storage of the books the star child had been writing, and as far as he was concerned, a large library of books to call the world from was all that mattered.

Eight said he thought they should get her more toys to play with, and Three murmured his assent.

Nine chewed on his lip under his mask. 'I like her time signatures,' he said after a pause. 'She's got a flair for them. Always surprising, yet they make sense. Not a ripple in the fabric yet, as brother Five said.'

Ten, who was at that time supervising the night shift of sewing girls, said there had been no disturbance in the moon's cycles and everything was quiet and well-adjusted in the heavens.

Eleven, who mostly spent his days alone, in his workshop with different-sized frames bearing taut goat and sheep skins in varying stages of drying, shrugged. 'She seems alright to me,' he said. 'Always accepts the parchment I bring her.'

Twelve said, 'Yes, I agree with my brothers, I think she's highly satisfactory,' and Thirteen's eyes crinkled for a moment as he had a private chuckle at his brother's reluctance to commit himself to praise.

Then he nodded, and began to pull the council cloak over his head.

'I'm glad it all appears to be going well,' he said. 'Let's keep an eye on her as usual.'

And that was the end of the council. Each of them slipped the silvery cloak over their heads and rolled out of the room, heading back to the tasks they had been engaged in before their brother had called them.

> • <

And so it was that the Thirteen were happy. They went about their duties, ensuring the creation of their beloved earth and everything on it, keeping the wordlight flowing onto the silk and Time progressing in its usual, placid way.

The moon's daughter was also becoming happier. Every night before she went to sleep she lay swaddled in her bed blankets and recited the contract silently. She found she could hear her mother's voice faintly if she stilled her skin enough, and she listened to what it had to tell her.

She recited the contract that bound her and all the other spirits of creation, and slowly ideas came to her. She rejected most of them for being impractical, too violent, too obviously against the laws. *They will never say I broke the rules*, she would think as she puzzled out one of the more obscure clauses, *I will not give them an excuse to ruin me for good*.

As the year went on and Seven opened yet another chamber underground to store her books, the moon's daughter thought only of her mother's last words. They echoed in her mind even as she wrote, and slowly, in the stillness of her bed with her mother's singing voice whispering in her ear, a plan began to form.

> • <

In the fourth year of her life with the Earth spirits, around the time when the May blossom spilled from the hedgerows and the moon's daughter resembled a girl around the age of nine, Three brought her usual breakfast. She was already awake, sitting on the edge of her already made bed.

'I'm ready for my privileges now,' she said, without so much as a hello. Sometimes the girl was abrupt like that, but the Thirteen did not rebuke her or try to improve her conversational skills. There was no need. She only ever spoke with them, and they required her only to write.

Three placed the porridge tray beside the desk and folded his arms inside his cloak. He did not ask her how she came to know about the convention of privileges. She was a star child, and there are things known to the heavens that no one on earth, not even one of the masked men, could know.

'You know there are only three?' he asked.

She nodded. 'The first is for a window. I want to see my mother.'

Three looked down at the rug beneath his feet. Ten had brought it from Uranga some years ago, it was woven with the images of the animals of the forests, and he knew the girl liked looking at it and imagining the animals in full flight, leap or canter between the trees.

He sighed. 'You know there is only one request we are forbidden from honouring. You will have a window, but it will not open to the outside world. It will instead show you an image of the sky at that moment.'

The moon's daughter nodded impatiently. 'When will I get it?'

Three moved towards the door. 'Tomorrow.' He was uneasy, but there was nothing he could do. He did not even need to consult with the others before agreeing, the rules were clear.

The next day, Six installed a wooden frame above the girl's bed. He told her she only needed to tap the frame to see what the sky showed at that moment. He told her the frame faced east and so she would see her mother every night except the dark ones, when no one in the world saw her.

From that moment the window was always on, showing patches of blue sky or grey cloud or indigo night. The Thirteen never looked at it and they never saw the moon's daughter look at it either. Any time Three brought her food or clothes or some interesting trinket he had found in the woods, he found her engaged in some other task.

〉•〈

Over the next few years, the moon's daughter wrote so many books they had to open more cellar rooms so they could store them all. Twelve spent many happy days cataloguing the new books, and Nine dedicated himself to copying and embossing the time signature symbols the moon's daughter had invented on the heavy leather covers.

When she resembled a girl of about twelve years old, she asked for the next privilege.

'I want someone to talk to,' she told Three one afternoon as he brought in her lunch. She was sitting on the headboard of her bed, balancing on the plank that supported the magic window. She wriggled her feet inside her woollen stockings.

'And I don't want these toys in here any more.'

Three set down the tray and wiped his hands on his mask to give him time to think of an answer. He tried to keep his face expressionless. His brothers would scoff at the tiny bloom of hurt in his heart, tell him he was a fool for thinking the girl had any fondness for him at all.

'You talk to us,' he said as he fussed with the tablecloth. 'You have lots of different people to talk to if you wish to, we can discuss anything you like.'

The moon's daughter said nothing. She stared at the back of Three's head as he moved around the room. She knew he would give her what she wanted, the rules bound him.

'A companion of your own age, then? Is that what you want?' He turned to face her, the corners of his eyes dragging downwards as if he was about to cry. If he hadn't been one of the most powerful beings in the whole world, she might have felt sorry for him.

She nodded.

'It'll be one of the girls from upstairs, you know that? One of the girls from the sewing tower.'

'I know. I don't mind.'

Three forced himself to shrug, as if it were nothing to him. He had wanted to stay and tell her about the pink and yellow butterflies she had written that he had seen out in the stream by the Tower, but now he felt too sad.

'She'll come tomorrow,' he said, turning towards the door. 'Only in the afternoons, though. We don't want anything to distract you from your work.'

> • <

Leira arrived in the cellar room the next day, just as the moon's daughter was finishing her morning's writing. Another girl with corn-yellow hair and new blue robes had arrived in the sewing tower during her day shift, and Mandoré had told her to leave, she had a new job now. Leira had not been aware that there were any other jobs in the Tower, and as she followed another half-masked man down the spiral steps, past the line of the earth and deep below the ground, she began to suspect that there was no other job, that she was being led into some dungeon or pit where the monsters that were rumoured to live at the bottom of the Tower would feed on her, slowly and painfully, keeping her alive to eat her beating heart last. Terror swelled in her, she bit her lip to suppress a whimper until she could bear it no longer and opened her mouth to scream, when the masked man stopped, picked up a tray from a ledge, and turned to her.

'We house a very important guest in this room,' he said, gesturing to a wooden door with heavy black bolts set into the stone. 'You have been chosen to be her companion. You will come here every afternoon to keep her company and you will sleep in a new room, alone, just along this corridor. Your things will be moved shortly. You may talk to her about anything and tell her anything you like about yourself, but you must never, ever share anything the guest tells you with anyone else.'

Leira saw the man's mouth move under the cloth that masked the bottom half of his face. 'Not even Mandoré, or any man who wears this mask, you understand? The prohibition on sharing the guest's confidences is total.'

Leira nodded and let her breath hiss out of the corner of her mouth. She resisted the urge to press a hand to her pounding heart. She thought about the friends she had left upstairs and how she would likely never see them again, and how this had happened some time ago when one of the girls in their dormitory had disappeared in the night and no one could say where she had gone, and Mandoré's eyes were hard and forbidding until it was clear no one was going to brave his stick and ask after the lost girl. Had that girl come down to this cellar to this guest? Or had she been released out into the world? Leira had always thought those rumours were more like hopeful prayers.

The masked man slid the bolt back and pushed the door. In the moments before the door was fully open, Leira saw a flash of light so bright it seemed like an eruption and left a tenderness behind her eyelids as she blinked. Then the masked man stepped into the room and Leira saw an ordinary room with a bed and a desk and a chest of drawers with one drawer open and a scrap of black worsted hanging out of it. She followed him, her curiosity drowning out her fear.

'Good afternoon!' the masked man called in a babying voice that took Leira by surprise. It didn't sound like the same, stern man who had been threatening her just outside the door. 'This is Leira, she's come to keep you company, she'll be here every day that you want her.'

The moon's daughter stared at the girl standing on the threshold. She noted the yellow hair that wisped around her face and fell down her back in a long curtain. She saw her threadbare cuffs and the slim, exposed ankles that peeked out from the too-short blue robe. She knew all the sewing girls had that hair and a skinny, coltish look that was bred into them by many long hours listening for the thump of Five's stick. She stared and stared and stared, until Leira began to squirm under her gaze and Three decided he had done his duty by the privilege that had been requested of him.

'And this is the moon's daughter,' he said to Leira, placing the tray on a table. 'You'll get along fine, the pair of you.' He passed by Leira, still standing only one pace inside the door. 'I'll be back when I bring your dinner,' he said quietly, and although he was still using that friendly voice, it made Leira shiver.

He shut the door behind her and they listened to the creak of iron on iron as the bolt slid across, shutting them inside the cellar room from the outside.

Leira had heard of the moon's daughter before. Before her mother had passed and she had gone to live at the orphans' home, her mother used to tell her the moon's daughter would come and breathe ice into her mouth and freeze her insides if she wasn't asleep by the time the moon rose. Leira told all the children in her dormitory on her first night at the orphans' home, and the little ones screamed and screamed until the matrons came running, holding their nightgowns around their knees.

'What's the matter with you all?' they had whispered furiously. 'Why all that carry-on at this time of night?' Leira had shrunk into her blankets, trying to make herself invisible. It was long past dark and she was still awake. The moon's daughter was probably on her way now.

'*She* said the moon's daughter was going to come and ice us,' one child had whimpered, pointing at Leira. 'She said we'd get our hearts eaten.'

One of the matrons huffed and clapped her hands together in that way adults do to tell children they are really in charge.

'Nonsense!' she'd said. 'The moon's daughter is far away from all of us, and besides, she looks after us and means us well. She certainly does not make us cold or eat anyone's heart. And if anyone gets out of their bed or makes a single sound between now and sun-up, they won't have any pudding for a month. Do you all understand?'

There had been silence, then a slow rustle of blankets as the children in the dormitory shuffled under their blankets. Leira had determinedly forgotten about the moon's daughter, along with all the other things her mother had said.

Now, as she looked at the girl who sat on the edge of bed, the memory of that night came flooding back to her. She remembered that as a little girl she had imagined the creature to be a ghostly spirit, perhaps a woman dressed in a long, silken nightgown that billowed in the night as she floated across the sky. Staring at the mythical maker of the world, she saw only a girl the same age as her, skinny and pale, with a sharp, angular face topped with hair so black it almost shone indigo when the light from the lantern streaked across it, cropped close to her skull so Leira could see the pale skin beneath. She had grey eyes that hardly ever blinked and that unshifting gaze made Leira feel uncomfortable, but there was nothing malicious about it. Instinctively, she understood this girl to be a friend, the kind of friend she had not had since she had left the orphanage. That this friend was going to be a creature she had once been afraid of, and that she still had to live in this forsaken Tower with the masked men, did not seem to her the most important thing. Something unknotted inside Leira's heart. No more sewing, no more bleeding fingers, no more aching, hunched shoulders. No more whistle of Mandoré's silver stick through the air, cringing in the moments before she knew whether it was heading for her or not.

'What's your real name?' Leira asked.

'I don't have one.'

Leira tried to look patient. 'But I'd like to give you one, all the same. I don't want to call you "Moon's daughter".'

'Why not?'

Leira hesitated. 'Outside—' she waved her arm vaguely in the direction of the door '—people think you're scary. They think you come and eat children. I'd rather not call you "Moon's daughter", if you don't mind.'

The girl blinked. She had not considered others might know of her.

'Yes, alright. Give me a name.' She fell silent, trying to think of what the Thirteen called her when they came, but nothing occurred to her. Did they ever call her by name or did they just speak, expecting her to listen and respond?

'I can't think of anything,' the moon's daughter said quietly. 'You choose my name.'

Leira smiled nervously. 'I'll call you Luna,' she said. 'That's what Mandoré sometimes calls the moon when he's calling out the patterns.'

Luna was very still for a moment. 'Yes,' she said eventually. For a moment it seemed as though she was going to say more and Leira waited for her politely, but it never came.

There was a long silence. Luna still sat on her bed. Leira wondered why she had ever wanted a companion.

'Aren't you hungry?' Leira asked, gesturing to the tray the masked man had brought.

Luna shrugged. 'I don't need to eat as much as they think I do.'

More silence. Leira shifted from foot to foot. She let her gaze shift to the shelves that lined the room, packed with the spines of so many books there was not space to slide a single piece of parchment between them. Leira drifted towards the shelves and ran her hands over the black leather; they couldn't be too private, she thought, or they wouldn't be on display like this. The sight of their spines, each embossed with a curving, twisting symbol that was different to all the others, itched something in Leira's memory.

'These are Mandoré's books!' Leira gasped, spinning around to look at Luna. 'These are the ones he reads the patterns from! Do you read them too?'

Luna's mouth twisted in contempt, but Leira understood immediately that the expression wasn't meant for her. 'I write them,' she said quietly, and there was something so sad and defeated in her voice that Leira shivered all over, as though there was a fierce draught in the room.

'Were you writing today?' Leira asked.

Luna nodded. 'Every day. My back aches no end from sitting in that chair.'

Leira nodded sympathetically. What Luna did down here, she and the other embroidering girls did upstairs, endlessly, returning each shift with fingers sore and bleeding and backs cracking from hunching over the silk.

She crossed the room to the desk and ran her hands over the hard chair tucked under it, making a tutting sound.

'No wonder, this is a chair for a punishment.' She turned to Luna, a shy look in her eyes. 'I can make you something more comfortable, if you want.' She looked around the room. 'There's plenty here we can take apart and use.'

'Do you know how to make things?'

Leira shrugged. 'I used to live in an orphans' home.' She called to mind the sounds of the whispering aspens in the front garden of the orphans' home, the long queue to play on the swing and the matron's exasperated counting to ensure everyone had a fair go on it, not a moment too long or too short. She looked back at Luna.

'I used to fix things there,' she said. 'Sometimes the water pump would break and they would ask me to have a go at it before they called out the water engineer, and I used to take things apart and put them back together, you know, just playing. The matrons were going to apprentice me to a woman they knew who could fix all kinds of machines when Mandoré turned up and brought me here.'

Leira hesitated. 'But I still make things when I get a moment. I made adjustable seats for all the girls in my shift last year, and I can do the same thing for you.'

Luna pursed her lips. 'Mandoré likes to take people from where they belong.'

Leira said nothing. She understood exactly what Luna meant.

'What do you do when you're not writing?' Leira asked.

Luna sat heavily on her bed and waved her arm vaguely around the room. 'I stay in here. I think about things.'

'You don't go out for a walk or anything?' Leira was shocked. She had not been outside the Tower since the day Mandoré brought her here in the carriage, and neither had any of the girls she knew, but surely it was different for this girl, the most powerful creature in the world?

Luna made a face. 'Do they let you out?'

'No,' she admitted. She came to sit on the bed next to the moon's daughter. She was as close to the moon's daughter as she would be to one of the other sewing girls up the spiral stairs in the Tower, close enough to feel heat from her back, hear the whisper of her breath and the rustling of her dress as she moved. But there was nothing like that from Luna. She was a yawning silence like the empty night sky.

Leira looked around the room. The dark stone walls, with damp springing from wet patches near the ceiling; the rug with animals she recognised from stitching the silk woven into it; the strange wooden frame nailed to the headboard of the bed. She understood she had swapped one prison for another, and that this prison was the only one Luna had

ever known. What she did not understand – yet – was what
either of them had to do to be released.

> • <

Luna's third and final request for a privilege was a musical
instrument. She looked seventeen, and Leira thought she
was eighteen, although she couldn't be sure as they didn't
celebrate birthdays in either the orphans' home or the Tower.

Three's eyes narrowed. 'What kind of musical instrument?'

Luna shrugged. She found it easier to talk to Three
whenever Leira was in the room, listening and willing her
on. She felt as though her friend was helping her choose her
words and silently sending the right ones to her.

'I don't mind. Anything easy enough to play.'

'Can't you get your friend to invent you something?'
Three joked, gesturing to Leira, who sat sprawled on the
floor, the stretched cloth of her robe across her lap holding
a mass of cogs, screws and bolts. Leira watched him with an
inscrutable look on her face.

'She does machines, not music,' Luna said, and Three felt
chastened by the coldness of her tone.

Three nodded and turned to leave, but he hovered for a
moment, pretending to brush dust from a shelf. He could
feel both girls' eyes on his back and it made him feel uneasy,
as if there was some conspiracy afoot.

In the morning, before Leira came along the corridor
to Luna's room to do whatever it was they did together, he
brought her usual porridge and mugwort tea on a tray. Then
he turned to her, holding up a pipe made of labra wood with
eight holes carved into it and a reed at the mouth.

'Is this the kind of thing you wanted?'

She looked up from the desk, where she was already scratching away at a piece of parchment. A secret smile spread across her pale lips.

'Yes. Thanks. That's exactly right.'

Three bowed his head and happily left the room. He didn't think he had ever heard the girl say 'thank you' to him before. It had taken many years, and Three knew it often did, but he felt that finally the moon's daughter was becoming used to her life in the Tower, and perhaps even looked upon him as a friend.

> • <

It was winter, and the girls who embroidered the world were busily sewing rotting carpets of leaves and snowy storm clouds and deep, warm holes in the earth for badgers and bears and all kinds of furred creatures to hibernate in.

Deep in the cellar, Luna the moon's daughter sat on the floor opposite Leira. Luna wore only a thin cotton nightgown that barely covered her knees. Her hands and feet were painted with blue patterns; scales like a fish and spirals like a snail and tiny little ribbed lines, like an eel.

'There'll only be a few moments, at most, before they come,' Luna said. 'Do you understand? It'll be almost instant.'

Leira nodded. They had talked endlessly about this day, every fraction of a second was planned. Luna chewed on her bottom lip, and Leira recognised it as something she did that Luna had caught from her. It made her feel oddly proud, that she had passed on this gesture to her friend.

'You remember what you have to say?'

Leira nodded again. She had said it like a prayer every night before she went to bed for many moons.

Luna stood and pulled Leira up too. Hand in hand, they crossed the cellar room to Luna's bed, where the wooden frame she had asked for so many years ago still stood, attached firmly to the bedframe. The space inside it was nothing special, only the rough black stone of the cellar that formed the wall behind the bed.

Luna climbed onto the bed, her feet sinking into the piles of blankets, keeping her fingers entwined with Leira's, who moved along the side of the bed with her. She held in her other hand the labra wood pipe, and as Luna tapped on the window to bring the sky to life within its frame, Leira passed her the instrument.

The frame showed the sky, white in a way neither Luna nor Leira could ever remember seeing, thick with ice tumbling on the invisible breath of the wind. Leira whistled.

'You really did it,' she said quietly.

Luna let go of Leira's hand and held the pipe between all her fingers.

'You remember when you have to push?'

'Yes! Come on, play.'

Luna put her mouth to the reed of the pipe and blew. A long, sweet note emerged from the instrument, soaring towards the ceiling. Leira had listened to her friend play that pipe every day for the past three years, but now she was conjuring sounds from the labra that she had never done before. Leira wanted to shut her eyes and sway to the tune, but Luna had warned her about that.

Luna kept playing, and the music got louder. Leira leaned forwards, putting her hands at Luna's back, ready to heave.

There was a thump above them and Leira faltered for a moment, looking above her, but Luna made a strangled noise in her throat and her attention snapped back. She watched as Luna leant further forwards, her blue-painted fingers dancing up and down the pipe, her face almost within the frame now, her nose disappeared into the blankness of the snow.

Leira began to push now, her hands spread on Luna's back as she climbed up behind her on the bed. The music became muffled as Luna's head disappeared inside the frame, but Leira could still hear it, faintly, urging her on. A heave, a shove, and then Luna disappeared up to her shoulders. The heavy shoes Leira wore slipped on the blankets and she almost lost her grip on Luna's back, but she pushed her heels into the mattress and shoved Luna inside the frame up to her waist. She would pull the blankets straight again when Luna was gone. The seconds it would take to do so were accounted for in the plan.

The legs will be the easiest, Luna had said, *just take my feet and slide them in*. Leira could hardly hear the pipe now, just a ringing in her ears. She wrapped her fingers around the painted arch of each of Luna's feet and pushed once more. She held her breath until her toes had disappeared into the snow with the rest of her. A second after the toes went, the space inside the frame went blank and showed only the dark stone of the cellar wall behind the bed. It was done, and it looked to be a success, but they had not even had a chance to say goodbye.

Moments later, the cellar was filled with yells and shouts. The corridor buzzed with the vibrations of pounding feet and clattering wheels as the Thirteen burst into the room, their eyes wild, their masks hurriedly slipped over their mouths, their faces white and pinched with panic. Leira stood by the desk, waiting calmly for them.

'Where is she?' one of the masked men shouted, his voice booming all around the walls, echoing as if they were in a cave. If Luna hadn't told her exactly what to do and say, Leira would have been terrified. She tightened her belly and stood still.

'Tell us where she's gone, you stupid girl!' Thirteen pairs of wild eyes advanced on her, but she did not move.

She stood by Luna's old desk, wrapped in a woollen coat with a fleece-lined cap on her head. Her shoes were clunky things with iron sheets underneath the soles. She had been making them for months, for the snow Luna had told her to expect.

'I am bound by the confidences of the star child and I request my right to go free.' She spoke in a quiet, confident voice. She kept her hands tucked inside the pockets she had sewn into her coat so they didn't see her shaking. Not from fear, but from excitement. Soon, she would see the sky again.

Another of the masked men looked to her feet and howled, a pure sound of animal frustration.

'She planned it! Look at her shoes. She expects to leave, she knows of the snow!'

There were shouts and grunts Leira could not understand, then one of the masked men put out his hands to hush the others and stepped towards her. She recognised him instantly, although she had not seen him for years. It was Mandoré.

'You don't understand, Leira. You are being loyal, we know that, but it is very important you tell us where the moon's daughter went. The world depends on it.'

Leira met his gaze directly, in a way she had never been able to do as a girl. She remembered how his stick would swish through the air just a moment before it *thwack*ed against her back, and the pain would come a few moments after that, as if the skin couldn't decide what had happened to it.

She waited for a moment, holding his gaze. She had never expected to be able to have this kind of revenge on him, and it was delicious.

'I am bound by the confidences of the star child,' she said again, 'and I request my right to go free.'

Mandoré's hands jerked towards her as if his hands wanted to strangle her, but Leira looked at him calmly until her stare weakened his hands and made them drop to his sides. Luna had warned her this would happen, and she had told her what to say to save herself.

'You realise this will end the world?' one of the masked men said. 'Not today, or tomorrow, but probably in your lifetime. You're young enough to see what havoc this will wreak, you'll see it all before you die.'

Leira clenched her teeth until a pain shot up her jaw and into her temple.

'A world that relies on slaves and secrets and mysteries only you people know is no kind of world at all,' Leira said. She enjoyed the look on Mandoré's face, as though he had been smacked over the head with one of Luna's books. 'Better that it ends, painful as that may be, than stay cruel.'

Then, remembering the script Luna had insisted she follow, she swallowed to moisten her dry mouth and said, 'I am bound by the confidences of the star child and I request my right to go free.'

Three times she had said it now, and as the last word of the incantation Luna had given her rang out into the cellar, every one of the masked men slumped.

'Foolish girl!' one of them whispered, but only to himself. They all knew they were defeated.

Mandoré sighed, and Leira was surprised to see that his eyes glistened with tears.

'So, you have made your choice,' he said, and the cellar was still and silent. 'Here is ours. You will leave here with nothing but that which touches your skin. You will live far from all other people and they will shun your society. You will tell not a single living soul about your life here, neither up in the Tower nor here with the moon's daughter. You will never return.'

Leira nodded. She knew the terms, Luna had explained them to her over and over again, making sure she would be willing. 'I don't take slaves,' she had said, her face dark. She knew what kind of life she would build for herself when she left the Tower, she had been daydreaming about it ever since Luna had first began to describe her plan, falteringly, distrustfully, having to digress to explain this archaic rule or that ancient treaty. She would find a quiet place, the kind of place others would call desolate, and she would build herself a cottage. One room would be for her to live in, warm and cosy and filled with blankets someone else had knitted; and the other would be her workshop, where she would make real all the machines that lumbered through her dreams. She would not mind the solitude. She was used to it.

'Very well,' Mandoré said. He stepped aside and opened the cellar door. Beyond, on the other side of the corridor, there was a door that opened to a tunnel, lit with bright orange light from sconces bolted to the walls.

'Follow the lanterns and they will lead you to the Outside. It is the last thing you can expect from us.'

Leira felt her heart leap into her mouth at the sight of it. She could feel cold air whistling through the passage, air she knew must come from the snow Luna had written, and she walked towards it without another glance at the masked men. She followed the lanterns, drinking in the air that cooled with every turn of the tunnel. As she walked, she thought of designs for hare and rabbit traps she could spring in the woods so she could eat, fingering the box of matches Luna had given her a long time ago. She could see her breath whenever she exhaled, and her nose was beginning to turn numb.

Soon, she stumbled out of the tunnel into a world become white. Unmarked snow coated the ground and lay a fist deep on the bare boughs of the trees. She had not seen trees in so long. She ran to the nearest one, clumsy in her awkward snow shoes, and brushed the snow from a branch to look closely at it.

'Beech,' she whispered to herself. It was hard to tell, in the winter when they had no leaves. She would have to teach herself to recognise them all over again, she had forgotten so much since she was a little girl running in the forest. 'Hello again,' she said.

She looked up to the sky. It was daytime, and the sky was a hazy white, but she knew the moon was up there somewhere, watching and listening.

'I helped her,' Leira told the invisible moon, letting a smile spread across her face. 'I helped her and now we're both free. I won't see her again but I don't mind. Tell her she was my only friend.'

Then it began to snow afresh, and snowflakes settled on Leira's eyelashes. She began to walk slowly, her snowshoes sinking into the powder; the whole world still and silent and absolutely free at last.

> • <

The Thirteen needed the moon's daughter back. The first few days after an escape were the most important, before the star child could cover her tracks. They chose Eleven and Nine by lottery to go out to look for her. They returned within days, their clothes dirty from the road and breathless with urgency.

'It's not right out there,' they told the others as they climbed the stairs to the Tower, to look at what was becoming of the silk. 'She's left something in the books, the world is coming apart. We can find her later, we have to see to the patterns first.'

They were right. The Thirteen watched the tapestry for hours, searching for the tiny little faults they knew would mutate and spread across the world like a cancer, and within days they found themselves looking helplessly upon the silken tapestry of the world as it heaved upon itself, fizzing with chaos and destruction. They tried the little fixes they knew, extra stitches here and there to delay the onslaught, but in the end they knew they were powerless.

First there was a poor harvest in the south, which led to riots in Uranga; then two members of the government were assassinated when they made speeches to try to calm the city. The witches let their sabbat fires get out of control and destroyed vast areas of forest. The Thirteen could do nothing, for the witches were allied with the moon and did not consider the good of the world as they did. Bandits proliferated on the western roads between Ostar and Err, gangs of hungry young men who had been driven out of their forested homesteads by the fires. They fought for control of the western salt mines, which made it impossible for the salt tinkers to trade, and their families built shanty houses on the outskirts of towns and fought with the locals.

Then the plague of drinda bugs began, which feasted on any green leafy thing and left first disease and then famine in their wake. A year later, there was not a single region in the land that wasn't deep in civil war, and Six kept a ledger noting the numbers of those who had died. Seven thousand, twelve thousand, nineteen thousand. All over the land, people perished, and the Thirteen could do nothing about it.

Five, Twelve and Four, who were calling out the patterns up in the Tower, read the text of the books Luna once wrote through clenched teeth. When they read the patterns they became responsible for the darkness that consumed their world, but they had no choice, the alternative was to let the world end entirely. So they kept reading, closing their eyes to all the misery the wordlight made, and hoped every day that soon the chaos would end and the moon's daughter would take pity on her world and let it bloom into happiness again.

Two years later, it did. The first sign was when one of the girls sewed a machine that captured drinda bugs by the thousand and killed them and all their eggs. It appeared suddenly in one of the western cities and then the wordlight copied it for every other city, and the drinda bugs became rarer and rarer until they were gone entirely, back to the myth and farmer's fear they had once been. The Thirteen knew who had made the machine, and when they saw it, they knew the darkness was ending.

'Blasted privileges,' Three said when he saw the drinda machine. 'She had it planned all along.'

Then there was a good winter wheat harvest, followed by a warm, wet spring that made all the dormant vegetable gardens ripen and swell with food that hadn't been seen in years. There was a baby boom, and almost all the little ones were born fat and healthy, despite their mothers' recent hunger. The towns and cities began to talk about how to rebuild their peace. The scholars wanted to start a new age from the time of the first good harvest, and no one disagreed, they wanted the past few years relegated to history too. It was decided, too, that from now on all the towns would adopt a lottery system for choosing their representatives on the councils, to be replaced every four years. The wordlight flowed into a needle and made a huge silvery cloak with many holes to hold people close together as they talked, one for each village, town and city.

'She knew about our council cloak!' Ten exclaimed, watching copies of the many-headed cloak bloom across the silken tapestry. 'She's given it to them!'

'It is probably fair to assume,' said One drily, watching the newly chosen burghers of the towns struggle to put their heads through one of the neck openings, 'that she knew a lot more than we thought she did.'

> • <

So now the moon's daughter is gone and no one knows where. Yes, there was that time when Two and Eight almost succeeding in capturing her again, tracing her to a small village on the edges of the eastern swamp, but the star child had slipped from their clutches, writhing like an adder into the long grass. They tortured the owl woman she had been living with but she had said nothing, only gibberish about drawing birds with the moon's light. They had left her where they'd found her as worse than useless.

So now the Thirteen look for the moon's daughter in the tapestry of the world. They think that's their only hope of getting her back. Sometimes they think they find glimmers of her particular magic, but every time they chase her along the stitches they lose her; that star magic is no match for what they can do. She left behind the books that told the world and not much more, and the world will end when the books are done unless they find her.

None of the people living in the world know how close they are coming to the end; they are still stitching up the tears in their lives from all that tumult a few years ago. No one likes to think of those times, no one likes to remember what they did to survive when the fabric of all they thought was solid and good began to fray under their feet. If, on a warm night as a bottle of mead is passed around friends, talk turns to something that happened back then, most people shrug and turn away. They say how would they know, they are only a miller or an apothecary or a simple hog farmer. It was a long time ago, and getting longer. Best left forgotten.

No one thinks the trouble times, as they call them, had anything to do with the moon's daughter. Why would they? No one has ever seen her and no one knows anyone who has, and so she remains a legend, someone to scare the children into staying in their beds at night, and think of only when the moon is at her fullest and a tear seems to escape from her face, when one of the old women who knows all the old stories will say: 'There she goes again, the moon's crying. Mourning all the daughters she has lost.'

LAUDE

Section 5, clause 2
And once a star child has passed into the sky to
wear the glittering crown of her constellation, no
subsequent sister may interfere with anything she
once created, allowing the artefacts of the bygone
time to exist gracefully alongside that which she
writes.

She always began at the belly button. She knew that birds weren't the same as mammals, that they had no need of a pulsing blue cord and did not curl around it in the darkness of their mother's womb, but that was where it felt most right for her to start. She's drawn all kinds of birds, from owls to sparrows to swans, and for each one she has always started with the cord first. Then she sketched in the rest of them, their feathers and their claws and their beaks, and at the very end of it all she drew the smooth oval orb to incubate it and set it aside to hatch. Days later, when she could see the egg start to quiver with life, she sang her special birthing song and watched as her shells cracked and a small wet thing climbed out and shook off that pale fluid all baby things seem to be born in.

Yes, she knew birds did not have buttons on their bellies to remind them of the womb they came from, but still she started with the cord.

The children in the village used to come and stare at her through the window. Sometimes one of them would ask her if she was more bird or more woman, and she would smile at the curious soul and say that she supposed she was exactly half of each, and then the children would shriek in delighted terror and run from her cottage all the way home, gulping for breath as they told those who had stayed playing by the fountain in the square that they had spoken to the owl woman who lived in the woods and she had a voice, yes, a voice just like you and me.

But later she had time to think about it and she came to realise this wasn't true. She started her creations with an umbilical cord, and then she made the feathers, the wings, the tiny, sharp beaks. At the beginning of things she was a woman, and long after they had gone she had the urge to call back those shrieking children and tell them that.

But those children were grown and dead by then, and the village was just a scattered collection of those who had been pushed off their lands in other provinces, and no one came anywhere near her cottage in the beech forest. It was dark, midnight, the time her aunt used to call the witch's bit, and Ula sat in her study with her desk positioned perfectly to catch the moon's light through the open window. It was waxing gibbous that night, four nights until full, so there was plenty of power for her to draw, maybe even until dawn.

She held her prism glass ready. After so many years she didn't need to turn to check when the light would join her; she knew when the moon would rise and set, when it would be full and dark, where it would wander to in the sky the way she knew her own feathers and skin. The moon had been her constant companion all those years. Even her babies, the little birds she drew each night, weaned and left her in the end. The moon never did.

With her other hand, she stroked the smooth labra wood of the tiny fiddle around her neck and picked up the string. She angled the glass. She let her shoulders relax. She breathed deeply. She waited for the moon to meet her.

When the white light connected with her prism glass it became warm in her hand and hummed gently, as if it were being massaged. Ula held it still, and the light split into divergent streams of colour that splashed onto the paper.

She started where she always did, with the umbilical cord. She let the moon's light pour onto the paper through her prism glass, and with the pen that carried black ink from the little fiddle at her heart, she began to sketch a body.

She drew feathers, a little tuft of them sprouting from the umbilical cord that she would later cut off to let the bird fly. She didn't know what kind of bird it would be yet, the moon had not shared the secret with her. Maybe a crane or a heron, she would guess. Fullish moon normally made water birds.

She had not drawn anything more than a tuft of feathers when a sound interrupted the flow of the moon's light. Ula stopped drawing, put down her pen. Pipe music wafted in through the window, not playing any tune but aimlessly meandering around a theme. She put her prism glass down on the desk and listened. Nothing human ever stirred at night when she was working, even the sad people who washed up in the village kept away from her. There were only the scuffles of hedgehogs, lizards and mice, the calls of her sister owls, the flicking of the badgers' tails as they scuttled into their setts. And then, pipe music, again, a tune that lilted and swayed like a river tumbling down a gulley. She knew who it was. There was only one person she had ever met who played like that. She bit her lip gently between her teeth to stop herself from humming along.

It had been so long since she had heard music. Her heart flipped over and the tiny fiddle shivered with it. There was never any warning, never any sign of it coming. She had learnt to expect that.

She put the prism and the pen on the paper and hid her hands. She couldn't let the pipe player see how she trembled.

The door to her study opened and a tall figure came to stand in front of Ula's desk. Wrapped in a cloak the colour of mud that draped in endless folds around the body, Ula found herself staring at the fabric, not the face of the figure. She remembered when that same cloak had been piled in a puddle on the floor of her bedroom, just above this room. She remembered how it had rippled like quicksand in the moments before the masked men had arrived.

The pipes stopped and left the air throbbing in the silence behind it. Ula looked up into the eyes of the woman in front of her. The lower part of her face was covered with the cloak but her eyes were just the same: grey like a bleaching bone, the skin around them so smooth it looked like marble. The eyes narrowed, and Ula realised the figure was smiling at her.

'You're still drawing,' the person said.

'The world goes on,' Ula said. 'Nothing stops until everything does. You should know that better than anyone.'

The figure inclined her head to one side, but Ula couldn't tell if that meant she agreed or not. She wanted to stand and meet her as an equal but her legs would not respond. She knew she looked upset; her feathers were standing on end, ruffled and puffed. She hadn't wanted the cloaked person to see her distress, but it was too late now. She'd always been able to tell, anyway.

'What do I call you now?' Ula asked. She tried to make her voice curt but there was a softness to the question she couldn't rid herself of. She was too used to speaking to this woman with love, even in her mind. It was hard to break the habit.

'You can still call me Luna.' Her voice was low and hoarse, as if she were not used to using it. Ula felt her fear melt away and in its place there was a broiling rage in her belly, kept fed and snug by the scars under her feathers there.

'You said you'd come back for me,' Ula whispered. 'I was waiting for you. I could only endure it all because you said you were coming back.'

Luna let her eyes drop to the desk. Silence spread from her like a stain until it enveloped the whole cottage. Ula wanted to think it was shame that stilled Luna's voice, but she knew there was little capacity for shame in her. She never considered herself wrong. She knew how the world was supposed to be for she had made most of it.

The beetles roamed the roots of the beeches outside the cottage and they made rustling sounds as they went scrambling across the soil.

Ula let out her breath noisily and looked out of the window, where the moon had moved a fraction to the west. In the long nights beneath the moon's gaze she had practised what she would say if she ever saw this woman again; how she would forgive her, how she would beg her to stay, how she would keep her safe this time. But now those speeches did not come, all Ula could think of was the night Luna left.

'They brought the book I was called and sewn from,' Ula said. 'Did you know they could do that? They ripped through the words that made me. I can't describe how much it hurt. Then they smashed my prism glass. They took an axe to the old fiddle.'

'I know,' Luna said, and because her voice was curdled with an old anger, a little of Ula's own rage cooled.

'It was a moon before I could draw again,' Ula said.

Luna closed her eyes briefly. 'But you were stronger than them,' she said. 'Now you birth your birds again and the Thirteen leave you to it.'

'I don't know why.'

'Because they fear me.' Luna reached over the desk and caught Ula's chin in her gloved hand, pulling it towards her. They stared at each other for a long moment, Luna's grey eyes never blinking, never wavering, only piercing through Ula the way they always had.

She pulled her hand away when Ula felt tears spring. They weren't tears of sadness or joy, it was the kind of weeping an eye does when it has been injured by a light too bright to look at.

Luna put one finger on the paper with only an umbilical cord and a tuft of feathers.

'Draw,' she said softly. 'Moon has something different for you to birth tonight.'

Ula picked up her prism glass and pen, and she felt the fiddle hanging against her chest thrum a little. She looked up at her old lover.

'Is that why you came?'

Luna didn't answer.

She had to shift her desk to catch the moon's light in her new position, and when the light connected she felt a strange charge in it she did not recognise. The pen sculpted the moonlight as it did each night, but the form it drew was quite different to what it usually made.

First, it sketched the curve of a belly, then a pair of soft shoulders. Two arms, creased at the elbows, two fleshy hands, each with five dimpled fingers and soft nails that shone white in the sliver that protruded from the fingertip. A rounded bottom, two thighs drawn up to the cord where the flesh sat baggy and plump around the soft bones inside. Ten toes extending from the unlined feet, packed snugly together.

She knew what this was, she'd seen them on her infrequent visits to the village. Tucked up in leather slings against their mothers' chests, puckered mouths rooting for a breast, downy hair curling around their crowns, the soft indentation atop their skulls where the angels flew in to share their sweet dreams.

She dropped the pen and the prism glass and looked up at Luna, who had a strange, almost wistful look on her face.

'I'm a mother of birds, Luna. Not babies.'

Luna smiled, and for a moment Ula saw a tenderness in her eyes. She had forgotten how tender Luna could be, the sipping kisses, the caresses in hurt places. She almost looked like a mother.

'You are Creatrix, Ula. This is what you're making tonight.'

Ula glanced up at the moon but there was nothing in the sky to tell her what to do.

'Pick up your pen, Ula. Give your daughter a face.'

Ula dipped the pen strung from the fiddle around her neck into her paint palette and sketched a nose. It was too small even for a baby's face; Ula had never drawn a human before, she did not even have a nose of her own, and her hand was unsteady. For the mouth she shut her eyes to consider the humans she had known, thought about the beautiful women she sometimes saw at the village with mouths that looked like apple blossom. She drew one of those mouths for her baby.

She already thought of it as her baby.

She drew quiet eyes closed in repose and short but curled lashes that would brush the eyelid when the eyes were open.

She dipped her pen in the red paint and began the invisible but exhausting work of creating the inside of the being. She drew a heart and lungs and a stomach and a liver, and she created the intelligent network of blood vessels and nerves that connected it all. She made bones and muscles and ligaments and cartilage that would serve her for eighty years or more, and she whispered a prayer that it would go gently into the earth when it was finished with. She drew a womb and two little sacs filled with cells that might one day make a new baby. When an image slid into her head of herself as a grandmother, her bones aching and her feathers greying at the tips, she forced it out of her mind.

Ula made a brain designed to grow inside its soft skull, a brain made like a sponge ready to learn things like language and movement and love and pain, and then she put her prism glass and her pen down and leaned back in her chair with a quiet moan. Luna waited a moment before she leaned over the desk.

Ula looked at the baby, the perfect little girl, curled up and sleeping as if she were lying quietly in a mother's dark womb. The baby breathed, softly, her back expanding with each tiny pant.

'She's so small,' Luna whispered, as if she thought she would wake her. 'She's only got tiny lungs, she has to breathe like that.'

Ula did not respond. She knew this baby was Luna's too, in a way, but she did not understand how or when she might claim those rights. She watched the tiny creature breathing on the paper and wondered how she could be falling in love with something she did not yet know. Occasionally, she glanced up at Luna, who stood quietly over the desk, guarding them both. The owls were silent, hunting elsewhere out of respect for their sister.

When the moon dipped below the shadows of the trees Luna turned to go, sweeping her mud-coloured cloak off the floor. She moved towards the door and Ula had a waft of burning metal, that bright burning hot smell that she always gave off when her heart was glad.

'I'll see you again soon,' she said. 'I'll come back in a year and a day. I promise.'

Ula didn't look up from her desk. She did not want to watch Luna leaving twice. She stared at her baby on the paper, counting the breaths. It did not seem like a promise to Ula. It seemed like a threat.

When dawn came Ula lifted the baby from the paper and let the soft weight of her rest in her arms. The baby mewed a little, and Ula rooted under her feathers for her breast and pressed the nipple into the baby's mouth. They stayed that way until noon, the baby sucking at whatever dribbles of milk came, both of them falling in and out of sleep, dreaming of a masked stranger and feathers raining from the sky.

> • ‹

When Luna came back, Ula was waiting for her in her study, holding her daughter on her lap. The moon was dark and the night was fogged with clouds. The baby girl stroked her mother's feathers with chubby fingers, dressed in a simple brown dress and baby napkin.

The door to the study opened but Ula didn't turn around. The pipe music began, announcing her presence. Ula wondered bitterly if Luna kept those flutes swirling around her to drown out everybody else's thoughts. She swallowed her tears.

Luna came to kneel at Ula's feet. She was swathed in that mud-brown cloak, the colour of swamps and piles of rotting leaves. Her mouth was covered. She looked like one of the Thirteen, and Ula supposed that was the point. The baby ignored her, absorbed in the fiddle around her mother's neck, plucking at the strings to make a gleefully distorted sound. It was her favourite game and she didn't yet know she would not play it for much longer.

'It's time, Ula,' Luna said gently.

Ula ran her thumb over the back of her daughter's hand, letting her finger press into the dimple on each knuckle. 'Where will you take her to? Will you keep her with you?'

Luna shook her head. 'It's no place for a baby, where I'm going. I'm taking her to a lost children's home. She'll be safe there.'

Ula opened her mouth to agree but a hideous wail came out. The baby stared at Ula, her fingers fast around a clump of feathers, unsure if she should start to cry too.

'You're taking her from me to put her in an orphanage? But she's not an orphan! She's my child.'

Luna did not answer. She held her arms out for the little girl, but Ula wrapped her arms around her daughter and turned her body away.

'Don't take her. She's the only real child I ever had.'

'It's not up to you,' Luna said. 'There are things for her to do in the world.'

'Things that you've written for her.'

Luna was silent, which meant she was thinking about the particular verse in the heavily bound book in which she had written that a girl with a tuft of feathers for a belly button would go to the Tower to sew the world. Ula shut her eyes. She had always hated that sense of vertigo she got when Luna spoke of things that would be, the sense of time slipping away from her to merge into the past and future so that everything that had ever happened or will ever happen slid into one, devastating image.

'Why not just take her to the Thirteen now? You should sacrifice our daughter to them before she even knows what's happening, that would be the kinder thing to do. Why wait to commit that kind of cruelty, what's wrong with now?'

Ula's voice was loud, cracking with grief, and the baby started to whimper. Luna was calm, so calm it stirred Ula's anger further.

'She won't be sacrificed.' Luna knelt in front of Ula and placed a hand on her knee. The feathers there became warm and she felt an answering tug low in her belly. Even now, even after torture and terror, still her body pulled towards this woman.

'She'll help stop it all,' Luna whispered, as if there were someone lurking outside listening. 'She's the best hope for a future without the Thirteen.'

She held out her hands and Ula shifted the baby's warm weight off her lap and into Luna's waiting arms. She stood and readjusted the little girl so she was straddling one hip.

Luna looked easy with the child, as if giving maternal solace was normal to her. Ula clenched her fists to stop herself from reaching out for the baby.

She felt cold and naked without the child in her lap, and something was cracking behind her ribs, she could hear it snapping like the boughs of a beech in a storm, falling away from the trunk with a great gash in the side, leaving the heartwood exposed to the wind, leaking sap.

'Will you stay until morning?' she asked, but Luna's eyes were on the child and her feet were turning towards the door, and Ula knew it was hopeless already, that in a few moments these two beings she adored would be carved from her life like a surgeon slicing off a limb; but she couldn't help but ask. She couldn't help but lower herself to the level of a worm and beg for them to stay with her in the darkness.

'We can't,' said Luna, and the crack in her ribs was so loud then that Luna tightened her grip on the baby. *How quickly* they *became* we, Ula thought. *How quickly she separated me from the baby.* Ula remembered the swamp-coloured cloak lying in a puddle on the floor of her bedroom, remembered how they used to lie in the hollows of oaks wrapped up in it, skin to naked skin, Luna's translucent light that she tried to hide glowing between them. *How quickly she separated me from her, too.*

Luna left the room, and Ula jumped up from her chair and followed her out of the cottage.

'She has sensitive skin,' Ula called after her as she moved as easily through the kitchen as if it was her own home. 'You have to use very soft soap when you wash her and don't leave her in a wet napkin too long, she gets an awful rash.'

Luna opened the front door with one hand and stepped out into the night. The baby lay with her head on her shoulder, a fragment of the brown cloak snatched in her chubby little fists and her eyes drooping.

'She has feathers at her navel, you know that. Make sure no one teases her about it. I've been telling her she's special and blessed for it, and I know she's too young to understand but if you keep telling her she'll know.'

Luna walked down the path, past the cabbages and cauliflowers in the vegetable patch. Ula followed her over the threshold of her cottage and towards the forest.

'She sleeps after her lunch, that's her main sleep,' she called, a little louder this time. 'Tell them that she's been nocturnal, tell them she'll need a little help to sleep in the dark.'

Luna had reached the beeches and did not turn around. Ula could still see the cloak, winding through the trees. She could still see her baby, her breath slowed to a sleeping hum, her heartbeat soft and even and moving further away all the time.

'Tell them to rock her,' Ula shouted, 'she likes that. They need to rock her from side to side, she doesn't like being bounced up and down, it interferes with her digestion.'

But she could tell that Luna had not heard her, she had disappeared to the place she went where no one could find a single trace of her in all the tapestry of the world. Ula sank to her knees among the old beech leaves and a racking sob fought its way out of her lungs and choked her mouth. The smell of damp soil rose from the dark earth and filled her nostrils. Rotting leaves, mice and vole droppings, the musty smell of mushrooms; there was only death in this forest for her now.

Above her, the waning crescent moon watched from behind a wisp of cirrus cloud. She cried too, although Ula didn't know it. That night, the moon cried so much that she was glad to go into darkness five nights later and wipe her tears from her bright face.

ALLEGRO

Here are the bare boughs of the labra trees that shiver in the winter wind, stitched like black spider's legs across the silk. Here are the towers of Uranga, the roofers clinging to their ladders as they replace the dark slates torn off by the wind. Here are the coracles gliding on the canals, dodging the cracked patches of ice that lie entangled like lovers with the reeds; here is the dark water lapping at the bricks as the grain boat slopes by. Here is the world, still swirling from silk, still taking shape under the hands of the seamstresses in the Tower. Here are all its corners and cracks and cubbies, nowhere for anyone to hide.

Alissa's seat in the Tower has been filled by a plump girl from the coast who giggles nervously whenever sunset comes and they ascend the steps. It grates on the other five, so when Mandoré turns one evening on the stairs, raises his silvery stick to her face and threatens to cut out her tongue if she doesn't halt that infernal noise, none of them sneak her glances of sympathy or support. They avoid her eyes and ignore the sleepy, muffled sobs that leak from her bed each morning as they drift off. Eventually, when the new girl seems to have accustomed herself to her new life, they will cautiously offer her their friendship, although with a warning. None of that here, they tell her silently. Keep your sorrows to yourself. You'll see that we all do.

The girls who embroider the night don't know what happened to Alissa, but her disappearance is enough to raise a bubble of fear to their throats and keep them choking on it all throughout the dark of their shift. They listen closely to the patterns Mandoré calls out and try to stop their anxious minds sifting through the various tones of his voice for clues to what she did and where she went. They let the wordlight flow along their hands and onto the silk, and they let their eyes glaze over; it's the best way to concentrate and see that they're only sewing the forms the wordlight wants to take.

There is no time in the Tower, only the progress of the sun across the sky or under the belly of the earth to signal the change of shift and the gradual carving of fine lines around the eyes of the girls who sew. The legends say that the moon's daughter sat at her desk to write the world from beginning to end, and the girls in the Tower sew it as they hear it, each word a stitch on the silk, each sentence an inch, each paragraph a yard. But those women who have sat out their yellow-haired youth in that tower know that this is not so. They know that it is the unique symbol embossed on the front of all the books that dictates the time formula; whether the events spoken from that book will happen forwards, backwards, or will skip around in any old way like a robin on frosty soil. They know that what the wordlight stitches onto the silk might happen shortly after the next dawn rises, or next year, or it might happen long after they have left the Tower, when they are old women sitting in rocking chairs by the windows of their nephew's houses, silent with the weight of the knowledge that one of their friends may have embroidered their death, which might come at any moment.

So the girls in the Tower sew and sew and sew and they measure time only by the passing of their own lives, not the world.

But out in the world it is midwinter, the longest night of the year. The sun rests deep below the horizon, gathering his strength for the coming year while darkness blankets the earth. Everything is sleeping: the seeds in the soil, the hedgehogs in their dens, the buds poking through the greenwood of the bare winter trees. Ice creeps over the rivers and canals, and all across the land dreamers shiver in their beds.

Up in the Tower on this long night, the seventh since Alissa was last seen – although no one is counting – two of the girls who sit to Mandoré's right are stitching a storm. It has been written so huge and destructive the wordlight needs to flow through both their needles to make it, but they don't mind, it makes a break from the monotony. They watch each other's fingers to get the tension of the clouds right, black with rain and crackling with the eager force that will make the thunder and lightning. They work hurriedly, for there is a lot to sew; like the sucking, whirling wind as it pours across the land, gaining in power until the air is swirling frantically, dragging everything not tied down with it. They sew the rain, falling in sheets from the filthy clouds, the heavy droplets buffeted by the gale so they don't always fall straight downwards but sometimes slide horizontally or jump upwards. They sew the water in the canals rising and rising until the banks are flooded in some places in the west, the runoff from the boggy fields draining into them and bringing with it all the good silt that keeps the crops fed. Mandoré keeps calling: 'Thunder, lightning, rain like a spatter, rain like a shower, rain like bullets, thunder, lightning, wind like scissors at the skin.' The girls keep stitching.

But the storm is not all that is made this midwinter night.

The new girl from the coast found the wordlight insistently creating an embrace between lovers. Because she was so new, she did not recognise the yellow hair of the girl she stitched, and because she was so young, she did not understand the urgent hands of the boy who held her about the waist; but she did notice the boy's feet, which ended in lion's paws. It was not one of the moon's daughter's tricks; there was no strange pipe music nor manipulation of the glowing thread to unmake reality, just a quiet embrace, two foreheads pressed together as though their minds are trying to pour out of their skulls and into the other's.

The girls embroider such embraces a thousand times a night. They embroider all the kisses and caresses and yearning glances of all the world, this pair are not special. But the new girl does not quite know that yet, and before the silk slips past her she sighs gently with a sweet longing she cannot articulate. She is lucky Mandoré does not hear her, occupied as he is with calling the storm.

The girl who sits to Mandoré's left is not feeling very well. Her nose is blocked with green phlegm and she has a pile of handkerchiefs in a basket beside her to wipe her nostrils when the mucus leaks from her, for she mustn't sneeze or cough or make a big to-do with a snorting blow of her nose. She is hardly paying attention to the wordlight when it flows into her needle and begins to make a bright shiny round thing, like a silver coral ring polished to shining. It seems to float in the sky for a moment, then drifts away. The girl sniffs back a sneeze and sews the creature who comes after the silver coral: a man riding a single-wheeled vehicle. It seems like he is holding onto the giant, shining ring, and they float away into the sky together. *Balloon accident*, thinks the girl as she puts down her needle and reaches for a soiled handkerchief. *It happens.*

None of them know, nor do they care to know, when these things and a thousand others will take place. They let the silk slip past them in the trance that lets their needles direct the flow of sound become word become light become thread.

Here are the clouds that obscure the moon, making the shadows darker than the night itself. Here is a carriage with still wheels, pulled over at the side of the road in the leeward side of a massive beech, with four sleeping bodies within. Here is an owl who swoops for a fresh mouse among the storm-proof beeches and ducks inside the carriage to crack its bones in her beak when she feels the first breaths of wind stir.

The stitches of the storm move out of the Tower and into the sky, and across the land eyes turn upwards to the rolling clouds that gather blackness as they move across the stars. The skippers of the canal barges check their moorings. The stable lads plug the ears of their horses with uncarded wool. All across the land, mothers pull their children into the safety of the warm parental bed and fathers check the shutters; badgers roll over in their setts, their deep hibernations disturbed by the heaving sky; and the roots of an old, sickly oak loosen in the damp soil, ready to be wrenched from the earth and topple as the winds begin.

But the girls who embroider the world are safe. The Tower is protected from the coming winds and rains by words spoken by the Thirteen long ago. No, there is no thunder and lightning in there, everything is silent apart from the incessant drone of Mandoré's instructions, and the soft rustle of his fingers as he turns to the next page of the book.

SALTARELLO

Section 2, clause 3(d)
The star children shall never permit themselves
to be seen by any mortals, even if those mortals
appear to know of, or worship, them as 'The
Moon's Daughter' or any other name.

Alissa sees the beginnings of the storm arrive with a flutter of panic in her belly. Most nights she has nowhere to sleep, and has just curled up at the feet of the biggest tree she can find. She has only spent two nights inside since she left the Tower. Once she did a day's sewing for an old couple who lived on the edge of a village, because the old woman was almost blind and could no longer see a needle or thread. Alissa mended every rent in every garment she could lay her hands on, and in return the old woman gave her a water flask, a hearty dinner and a coral ring as payment. Another night she crept inside a farm's cowshed after dark and made a burrow for herself in the straw. She left at dawn, reluctantly, before the milkmaid saw her. She had climbed over the fence as a lantern was lit in the window of the house and hastened along the lane back towards the road. She kept walking south-west, as she had been the day before, but she had no idea where she was walking to.

Now she is walking along a wide road with fields of the stubble of harvested oats lying on either side. The road tracks the flat bottom of a rocky valley, and every so often a cart comes rumbling past her, forcing her to clamber down the bank and wait among the muddy oat stalks for it to pass. Lightning illuminates the sky ahead of her. For a fraction of a second she can see the line of the hills against the clouds, the rocks jagged as if they will slice at the flesh of anyone who dares climb them. Thunder follows it, snorting its song behind her. She starts to trot, holding her cloak tightly around her. Lights waver like fireflies atop the hill to the south and she keeps her eyes there, perhaps she will make it before the rain comes and washes down the steep green pasture where sheep graze, unfazed by the darkening sky. She is not cold but she shivers. It is a warning. The sun has dropped behind the western horizon, leaving the night to its mischief, although it leaves behind it a red glow that makes the clouds look like coals alight in a forge.

She hears the footsteps but her ears trick her, she thinks it is the beginning of the rain and she quickens her pace, although she still doesn't know where she might be hastening to. Then she hears the *pitter-patter* speed up with her own feet, and her belly flips over like a drowning fish. She is being followed.

Clutching her cloak around her like armour, fists clenched and her jaw hard, she stops and listens for the silence of the feet behind her. Thunder rumbles in the still-dry sky and swallows the sound of the footsteps coming closer on the path only enough to make her heart thump. Alissa turns, dread seeping up her body from her freezing toes. When she sees who approaches her, teeth gleaming in the dusk, Alissa feels her knees tremble.

The follower has scarlet hair the colour of blood that falls to her ankles in shimmering waves, and a face the shape of an egg turned on its side. Her skin is the colour of the sky on a soft summer dawn and her dress matches. Her black boots are strangely clean of the mud that coats Alissa's up to the ankles, and although the light is fading fast, the woman is lit by the glow of her cloak, a glistening fur of blue and gold stripes. Briefly, Alissa wonders what animal it could have come from. In her upturned palm she holds a small blue bird with long, bronze tail feathers that crackle with tension, sparking like the lightning above them.

A witch. A moon-hag, a hexer, a poison-stewing harridan. Alissa fights to stay on her feet as she watches those violet eyes look her up and down with some amusement. Not all witches are dangerous all the time, but she's sewn enough of them and their blinding flashes of spells in her life to know that if you aren't sure if they mean to harm or help you, you'd better get sure quickly.

The witch and the bird hiss as one, and the bird raises its wings to hover above the woman's hand, awaiting its mistress's signal. The space between the witch's palm and the bird's feet fizzes.

'Hello Alissa,' the witch says. Her voice is low and oozing. 'I thought you'd get here earlier.'

Alissa swallows, trying to moisten her dry mouth. She is not surprised that the witch knows her name but it prickles at her, like tiny eyes have opened into the puddles on the road, only blinking shut when she passes.

'I'm sorry. I didn't know you were expecting me.' Alissa knows to be polite to witches. They offend quickly, their pride easily torn with careless words.

The witch shrugs and turns her attention to her bird, stroking its feathers with the backs of her fingers. The bird watches Alissa with interest, those bronze tail feathers twitching.

'How long have you been walking now, then?'

Alissa shuts her eyes. She sees the Tower in her mind, smells the sharp, singed smell the wordlight would leave on her fingers. She feels an unexpected pang. She left the Tower and now she has no place in the world to call her own. She is wandering without a direction, without a home.

'Seven nights,' she says quietly, and when she opens her eyes again the witch is watching her with bared teeth, the ends slightly pointed like a cat's. She realises with a small shock that the witch is smiling at her.

'Anyone who is in exile from the Thirteen is a friend of mine,' she croaks, and tucks the bronze bird away inside her cloak. 'I thought I'd come and get you, as you'd never find my place on your own. You can wait out the storm with me.'

Alissa feels the first droplets of rain splatter on her head and the witch turns her face to the sky and sniffs, her eyelids heavy as if the scent of the air makes her drunk. She draws the strange blue and gold cloak over her head and turns away, back the way they both came, letting her hand drift behind her as if she were leaving it for a child to slip their own hand into.

Alissa is still for a moment, her disbelief turning her legs to lead. But then the wind gusts around her head, finding its way inside her cloak and into the tiny spaces between the weave of her clothes to chill her, and she takes two faltering steps towards the retreating figure.

'Come on,' the witch shouts without turning around. 'I don't want to be out here when the rain really gets going.'

Maybe there was a spell of command in her shout, because Alissa feels her feet move as if she no longer controls them and runs to catch up. She doesn't take the witch's trailing hand but watches the gathering raindrops pool on her periwinkle skin as she follows a step behind. They hurry along the road that traces the bottom of the valley and then up the northern slope. She treads where the witch treads as they climb a rocky path between boulders covered in springy moss, but she still slips and stumbles, scrambling across the damp stone. When she puts out a hand to steady herself and push on the mossy rock to lever herself up the almost sheer hill, a fierce hiss comes from the witch ahead.

'Don't touch it,' she tuts, without slowing her steps or turning back. 'It has no power if there's been grubby hands all over it.' Alissa snatches her hand back and shoves it inside her cloak. She looks back at the innocent-seeming tufts of green and examines them for signs of power. She sees nothing, just glistening drops of rain.

They reach the top of the valley just as the raindrops thicken to a stream of continuous water, and Alissa pulls her hood tighter around her face. Then the witch turns, grabs her hand, and drags her under a jutting, lichen-covered rock in the hill face. Alissa cries out as blackness clamps upon her eyes and earns a pinch from the witch's sharp nails.

'Ssshh!' she hisses. 'You'll frighten them!'

Alissa bites her lip to stop herself from crying out again at the thought of what twisty-turny monsters there might be in this darkness, and forces her feet to carry her forwards, following the witch into the blackness, their feet moving together over a smooth floor that smells of earth and mushrooms and rain. They are moving further and further underground. The air becomes close and still and there are no longer any sounds of the outside, of rain, of thunder.

And then, just as Alissa's wide eyes are starting to discern patches of shadow darker than the rest, and the flurries of movement that tell her she is not alone with the witch in this cave-like place become faster and louder and come towards her head, the witch drops her hand and calls out a word that sounds like the bark of a wolf. Light floods Alissa's vision.

It takes her a few moments to adjust to the yellow glow inside the cave as the witch bustles around her, unwrapping herself from her blue and gold fur, wrenching her boots from her feet. The bird with the bronze tail feathers hops onto a perch in a corner with a soft chirp and turns its back on its mistress's guest. Soon, it begins to snore softly.

'Shoes off,' the witch says as she strides across the cave and throws her cloak into a basket. 'Please.'

Alissa unlaces her boots and steps out of them, leaving them in a neat pair by the low wooden door to the cave, which has swung snugly shut behind them.

'Have a seat,' the witch says, pushing a pile of labra sticks from a chair and dragging it to the round table in the middle of the cave. 'And then you can help me get some grub together.'

She digs inside a nearby basket and throws a turnip and a swede onto the table. Alissa jumps when they land with a *crack*.

'Chop them,' the witch says. She doesn't seem to do anything gently.

Alissa sits gingerly on the chair. She hangs her wet cloak over the back of it and it begins to release a scent of damp wool in the warmth of the cave. The floor is of polished stone with fleeces and furs laid out in a tessellating patchwork, and the walls are solid and dry, hung with tapestries woven with intricate swirling patterns of green and blue thread. The witch strides around her home in her stockings, gathering firewood, and Alissa picks up the knife and turns it around in her hands, watching the witch move. She wonders where on earth or in heaven smoke will escape from this snug cave deep in the ground, or if there's some magic the witch does to keep the air clear.

The witch hauls the cauldron from the fireplace and lays a pyramid of kindling with deft, practised movements, then sets the wood alight with stroking movements of her fingers. She looks up and sees Alissa watching intently.

'The smoke comes out of a hole up on the hillside,' the witch says with a shrug, pointing to her fireplace. 'The people roundabouts know not to go near it.'

Alissa looks away, picks up a turnip and slices off its tail. She's used to the chatter of her mind being overheard, the same way Mandoré and the other masked men can see into all the dark corners of the world. She begins to peel and dice the parsnips, trying to keep her mind on the *thunk* of the knife and the pale flesh of the roots. In between slices, she sneaks glances around her at the witch's home.

The room is packed full of curiosities and quirks and tools of the witch's trade. There is only one bed, piled high with blankets and furs, and Alissa wonders with a strange heat rising in her neck if she will sleep in it alongside the witch tonight or if she will conjure somewhere else for her to lie. Alissa watches as the witch squats by a huge copper barrel with a small tap poking out the side and listens to the water as it pours out of the barrel and into the iron cauldron the vegetables will cook in. The table she sits at doesn't appear to have any legs and instead floats around the room to wherever it is needed. When she has finished with the vegetables, she puts the knife down and lets the table float away towards the fireplace, where the witch grabs handfuls of the parsnips and throws them into the water with a plop. Alissa turns her attention to the shelves that line the walls in between the tapestries, filled with a collection of random things the witch must use for her witching.

There, up on the highest shelves, are the broken eggshells, their two halves stacked neatly in giant acorn cups that the witch enchants and uses for coracles when she goes on long journeys on the canals to the south. There, dangling at head height above the witch's bed, is a tangled mass of silken threads woven in a web, like a spider gone mad. Perhaps the witch uses this to entrap her enemies and protect her dwelling. There, hanging in squat little bunches over the copper water barrel, are fistfuls of drying herbs tied neatly with string: thyme and chervil and lavender and dill. The witch reaches up, grabs a handful of leaves, and crumbles them into the cauldron.

There, slung on a hook by the door, is her broomstick, the besom end still black with mud. There, tucked away behind the bed, is a tall stack of cow bones and skulls the witch uses to tell the future; and there, on the low shelves by Alissa's right foot, is a shard of mirror as long as her leg, curved and pointed like a sword. When Alissa leans over it to see her reflection, all she sees is swirling mist.

The witch stirs the vegetables in their steaming water and she mutters something under her breath. A pungent scent of spiced stew seeps into the cave and Alissa's mouth waters. She knows she will need to learn to cook. She knows little of the world, but it's obvious there aren't many places for a girl who cannot bake bread, brew beer, and make a competent stew. Perhaps the witch is not the best person to learn these skills from, but nonetheless, Alissa watches the witch conjure flavour from her pot, humming to herself tunelessly. At first Alissa thinks it is just a pretty sound the witch enjoys making, but then she stops humming, stands up and takes a ladle from the side of the fireplace. She dumps two big spoonfuls into the two bowls waiting on the table, which has gone to hover by her side, and brings one to Alissa.

The table follows her, and the witch pulls up a chair to its opposite side. Although Alissa has never sat down to eat in this way since she was a girl at the orphans' home, this is how she's sewn countless people eating, facing each other, each settled on a chair, a spoon in one hand and a full, steaming bowl in the other. Although the table always had legs, before.

Alissa eats in silence for a few moments. She can taste the spice of the witch's magic at the back of her tongue, a bitterness in the aftertaste that reminds her of the food she used to eat in the Tower.

'What's the magic you used to know I was coming here?' Alissa asks after a few steaming mouthfuls. 'And how did you know I'm in exile from the Tower?'

The witch puts her bowl down and taps her two forefingers on her pale blue cheeks.

'I've got two eyes, little girl, I don't need magic.' She reaches across the table between them and picks up a lock of Alissa's hair, rubbing it between her fingers.

'This is the hair of the sewing girls,' she says, and then she points behind her at her rounded, slumped shoulders. 'And that curve in your shoulder. You're young now, but if you'd have stayed there much longer you'd have ended up a hunchback. That's what you get from sitting over the silk all night and day.'

Then the witch shrugs, as if talking of something obvious. 'And you're too young to have been allowed out into the world to retire, so you must have done something to piss them off.'

The witch grins and picks up her bowl again. She slurps her soup and swings her feet gently, watching Alissa from the corner of her eye. Alissa wants to tell her what she did, she wants to ask this woman's power about the juggler, but the questions stick in her throat. Mandoré only said she shouldn't talk to the other sewing girls about the star-faced man, he didn't say anything about people out in the world, let alone witches. But she feels there must be some sort of prohibition on talking of it; you don't spend half your life embroidering the world without coming to know about secrets, even those no one calls secrets. She swallows a lump of something vaguely bitter and coughs to ease it down.

'Do you know Mandoré and the rest of them, then?'

The witch makes a gargling sound of disgust and Alissa tries not to flinch at the imagining of the phlegm rolling around her throat.

'I've met a few of them, at one time or another,' she says darkly. 'We're not friends and I can't say it was an experience I'd care to repeat. I'm for the other side, we witches always are.'

Alissa eats in silence for a few moments. She has only the vaguest idea what the witch is talking about. She has always known that the masked men in the Tower do not approve of the witches; there was always a stiff tone to Mandoré's voice whenever he called something to do with them in the pattern. But all kinds of things could make Mandoré grumpy. Whispers on the stairs. Scrapes on the floor. Slow and clumsy fingers with the needle. The witch finishes her stew in one long slurp and sets her bowl on the floating table with a bang.

'So where will you go to now, then?' the witch asks.

'I don't know.' She worries this sounds as if she is hinting at staying here with the witch, and quickly adds, 'Maybe I'll go to the city. Or the orphans' house I used to live in.'

'I could help you, you know.' The witch is rubbing one stockinged foot against the other again, the scratching hiss of the worsted the loudest sound in the room.

Alissa looks at the almost empty bowl in her hands, two bits of the bitter vegetable floating in a small puddle of broth at the bottom. Something hopeful glimmers in her chest.

'How?'

'We can scry.' She leans her chin on her hand as if she isn't so fussed, but there is a curious light in her violet eyes that tells Alissa the witch is interested in this undertaking. Why, she cannot tell. 'The Thirteen must have sent you out here for a reason.'

'I broke the rules.' Alissa lowers her voice from habit, from when Mandoré used to lurk around every corner, listening to the girls' whispers. 'I made something I shouldn't have.'

The witch shakes her head. 'No, that's not it. There's something else, something you don't know. My thumbs are itching, see?' She holds them out to show Alissa, and indeed, the pads of her thumbs are bright red, as if she has dipped them in blood. 'You should find out why they sent you out of the Tower.'

She looks at Alissa expectantly, waiting for her to say, 'Yes, tell me, I want to know.' But now Alissa feels shyly protective of her juggler, she doesn't want the witch's magic to go poking around the fragile stitches of what she made and sent out into the world, she wants to keep him safe. She has learnt that ignorance is the safest position among the Thirteen, and to let the witch do this thing would cast her out of that safety and towards all the others in the world who know something of the way it all works, but always too little to make them truly wise.

But she is being a silly little girl. The witch probably knows all about the juggler already, the way she seems to know everything else about Alissa. Perhaps the juggler is a friend of hers, the way Mandoré and the other masked men are not. Perhaps the enemies of a witch's enemies are always her friends. Alissa's mind swims with floating, glowing balls, with grinning blue faces, with narrowed eyes framed by a mask. She is mixed up in things she does not understand. What harm can a little peek in between the stitches of the world do?

Alissa gives a small, tight nod. 'Yes, please. I'd like you to scry for me.'

The witch leaps from her chair towards a shelf on the other side of the bed as if her feet have been loaded on springs. She stops at her water barrel on the way back to the floating table, which dips when she places a bronze bowl filled to the brim with water, dark like the inside of the bowl. She has a short stick with one fat end and she holds it in her hand like a spoon, letting it hover around the rim.

'You ready?' the witch says, looking up at Alissa. Her violet eyes are glinting in the firelight. Alissa wants to say no, she isn't sure what she should be ready for, she doesn't know what the witch has planned for her.

But she nods anyway. The witch taps the stick gently on the rim of her bronze bowl and it rings out, a clear, pure sound like a bell. Once, twice, three times goes the stick on the bowl and then the witch runs the stick around the rim, turning the third ding into a long, high sound like a wail. It is loud, resounding somewhere behind Alissa's head, echoing on the close walls of the cave. It gets louder and louder, gathering all the other sounds in the world towards it and folding them together in one long whine of an animal that only exists in stories.

The witch leans forward to look at the surface of the water which is rippling and spitting and steaming as though there is some monster birthing inside it. Against her better judgement, Alissa leans forward too.

What she sees in the water makes no sense, even to one who is accustomed to sewing patterns on silk that represent everything that will ever happen in the world. Patterns of whirling lines, like the grain of a plank of wood collapsed in on its knots and tangling up its life-rings. Glittery bits of rock stuck to glowing orbs which float like goat-bladder buoys on the canals. Alissa begins to feel sick with the hurdy-gurdy of it. She shuts her eyes to make it go away.

But it must make sense to the witch, because Alissa hears her sigh softly and make humming noises of satisfaction, as though the water is an old friend confiding secrets. When the witch goes quiet, Alissa opens her eyes to find the water still and the witch watching her, those violet eyes steady and unblinking.

'You have to find the juggler,' the witch says, and Alissa feels a swoop in her belly, half disappointed that the witch says his name so casually, and half glad that she doesn't have to explain to the witch all about the strange pipe music that became wordlight and wheedled its way through her needle and onto the silk.

'Do you know him, then?' she asks, trying to keep her voice even.

The witch shakes her head. 'Not personally,' she says. 'We've never met but all my sisters know of him or something that's come before like him.'

Alissa thinks about that for a moment but the sense of it floats away from her, teasingly. 'Does it say why I have to find him?'

The witch scowls. 'How would I know? That's something no scrying can help you with, it tells you what to do, not why.'

Alissa swallows. 'Right. Can you tell me where I'll find him, then?'

The witch sniffs. She glances back at the bowl, then cocks her head. 'It says you'll meet them at the Patli Bridge over the River Saman, at the cusp of spring.'

'Them?' Alissa begins to feel panicky. There are so many things she doesn't understand about what the witch has just said, she can only focus on one at a time. She remembers the way the juggler looked when she sewed him, his five-point starred face, his scarlet cape. She remembers she sewed him alone, with no connections to anything else in the world, and recently she's been thinking this must have been one of the things about him that so angered Mandoré. For nothing else in the world is separate, each thing is strung to the next with the stitches that come before and after it.

The witch shrugs. 'He's not alone. He's with a travelling circus troupe.'

The witch looks up at her, and if Alissa were thinking clearly she would see a guarded expression on her face.

'He's with a lion, a goat and a woman called Vanna. And an owl, too. They're going to Uranga and you're to meet them on the way, before they get on a spring melt boat.'

A wave of sickness passes over her and she shuts her eyes against it. She thinks of the rain, pounding out there on the earth above her; she thinks of all the nights of winter she'll have to spend out in the cold. She sees the land from above like a hawk and herself trudging across it towards the Saman, a stretch of water she knows only from the barges she's sewn on it. What will she eat, how will she know what direction to travel in, how will she get there? What will she say and do with the juggler when – if – she finds him. Why should she trust what the witch says the water said?

The witch touches Alissa's arm and her eyes fly open. There is something gentle in the witch's expression, something Alissa can't quite read but might be pity.

'It seems strange, I know. But the water doesn't lie.'

Alissa's eyes fill with tears and the witch looks away, suddenly uncomfortable.

'Look,' she says, snatching the still full bowl away from the table and placing it on the floor near the stove. 'I'll help you.'

She waves her arm across the table as though she is clearing it of some invisible load, and as her arm passes the scuffed wooden surface changes. The witch beckons Alissa around to her side of the table and she obeys, leaning over it shoulder-to-shoulder with the witch, sniffing the damp rock smell of her.

The table has become a picture.

It's mostly green, with long strips of blue that criss-cross it with a pattern Alissa feels she might almost decipher, if she stares at it for long enough. Occasionally the green bears patches of gold, and all over the map there are black smudges that become more and more frequent as they cluster towards the middle. Snaking black lines connect all the smudges, like memory knots on a string.

'Have you ever seen something like this before?'

Alissa shakes her head, mute. She hears the witch suppress a sigh, as though she is already regretting her offer of help, but when she speaks again, her voice is full of patience.

'It's not your fault. You've only seen the world in tiny stitches.'

She clears her throat. 'Alright. We call this north—' she points at the opposite side of the table to them '—and this is south.' She points at the part of the table that touches their legs. 'This part is east and this part is west. We're here.' The witch places her finger in between the south and east directions, in a patch of green. 'And Uranga, where you'll go once you meet your juggler, is here.' She points to the biggest black smudge on the map, right in the centre.

'So, the green is the land, the blue bits are the canals and rivers, and the gold patches are the labra forests. The black lines are roads, towns and cities are the black smudges, and the bigger the smudge, the bigger the city. And every time there's a bridge, there's a thick line across the blue. Understand?'

Alissa nods and reaches her finger out to the smudge that is the city. 'Where's the Saman?'

The witch traces it from west to east, sloping gently southwards across the table, stopping at one of the thick black lines that crosses it. 'Here. And here's your Patli Bridge. The river flows directly into the widdershins canal of Uranga, but slowly, so slowly some prefer to cross to the southern road using one of the bridges and ride that to the city.' She pauses. 'Maybe that's what your juggler and his friends will do.'

Alissa is too entranced by the images of her world to notice the shiftiness in the witch's voice.

'Where's the Tower of the Thirteen, then?' Alissa asks.

The witch tuts; Alissa knows she has said something stupid.

'They don't let it get painted, obviously, their mystery is part of their power. But I think it's probably somewhere about here.' The witch leans right over the table and places a long fingernail on a green patch about as far north as anyone could go.

'They keep out of the way. They don't want anyone stumbling across them.'

Alissa thinks of the silence of the Tower, how the birds that cried out as they passed always sounded muffled, like they were calling through a thick blanket of fog. Yes, mystery is part of the Thirteen's power, but only a little part. Alissa thinks she will never know the other parts of it. Perhaps she doesn't want to.

'So,' Alissa says, putting her finger back on the place where the witch lives. 'I'll go northwards, through these labra forests, past here, and here—' she points to medium-sized smudges '—and then cross this river. Then I'll turn a little west and follow the road towards the Saman.'

'Exactly. It'll take you about a moon.'

'A whole moon of walking!'

'Don't worry, you'll still get there before them. As long as you see the beech leaves unfurled from their buds and the bluebells and ramsons in the forests as you walk along the northern shore of the Saman, you'll be fine.'

Alissa gazes at the map, her eyes darting this way and that. She is trying to engrave the route on her memory, but she keeps getting distracted by the smudge the witch said was Uranga and the River Saman flowing into it.

'How will I remember where to go?'

'I'll give you a map.'

'Like this?'

'Sort of.' The witch smiles. 'But smaller, obviously.'

Alissa looks back at the table and they stand in silence for a while. The fire in the stove hisses and crackles a little, but the witch doesn't move to attend to it.

'Thank you,' Alissa whispers.

The witch makes a quiet humming noise in the back of her throat.

'You don't need to thank me,' she says. 'It's what was written.'

She turns away from the table before Alissa can think to ask what she means, and as she crosses the room to bustle around her bed, the map on the table starts to fade. Alissa stares at it long after it's gone and the wood is just wood again, thinking of the journey she has to make. There's no need to panic about what she will say to the juggler when she finds him, she has a whole moon of walking and thinking to figure that out, and it's always possible that the juggler will recognise her when he sees her. The witch makes banging sounds as she drags something out from under the bed, and Alissa warms to this theme. Yes, the juggler will know her because he has been seeking her too, his Creatrix, the girl who made him from nothing. She has to find him precisely because he is hers and this is what the witch's water scrying bowl has told her. It's the right thing to do.

'I've made you up a bed on this pallet,' the witch calls. 'I've given you extra blankets in case you get cold.'

Alissa does not remember falling asleep curled up on her side with her face close to the fleeces that cover the floor next to the witch's bed, but she remembers her dreams of that night; dreams of floating high above the land she has seen drawn on the witch's table, soaring over it like a bird, following the blue snakes of its rivers and the black snakes of its roads. After she dreams, she sleeps deeply and soundly, with total trust in her safety.

> • <

For a while the witch sits cross-legged on her bed, wrapped in a knitted blanket, watching her guest softly snoring. She cannot sleep. She is thinking about what she saw in her scrying bowl.

She was not entirely surprised to see who the juggler was travelling with, her thumbs would not have pricked so unless Alissa was connected in some way to the stitches of things that had gone before. It was their carriage that alerted her first; there's nothing else like it in all the land, so when Goat and Vanna appeared in between the ripples, she was already resigned to it. She knew Alissa was important, somehow. Nobody stumbles upon this desolate valley unless it is written somewhere that they should.

She had steeled herself for Lion's inevitable appearance, and when he came, skulking sullenly after the juggler with Owl riding his shoulder, she ignored the old flash of anger. It was done now, and there was no use in dwelling on the sense or nonsense of it. She had warned him that witches were not for wooing and he had not listened. And now he was paying the price.

When Alissa had entered the image from the centre of the ripples, the witch had experienced a curious prickling at the base of her spine. She had recognised it as the feeling she gets when she realises she has been tricked by an intelligence far greater than her own.

But no, it is not correct to call it a trick because that other thing, that maker, that creator, whatever it is, does not seek to trick her, only to summon her into its world and knot her onto its vision of a silken tapestry. Rather, call it a realisation of a pattern greater than even her own far-seeing eyes can see. The witch thinks of the stories her mother used to tell of a moon woman captured from the sky who writes in an underground cellar, bringing the world into being word by word. Be useful to her, her mother would say. Don't give her a reason to stop writing witches in the world.

She thinks back to the very first time she saw Alissa appear in her scrying bowl, at the last dark moon when she sat by her fire and asked the water what the dark stitches of winter had planned for her. She had gone out into the valley every day since, searching for the yellow-haired girl with feathers at her navel and the storm that would bring her. Offer shelter, food and scry to find out more, the water had shown her. She had obeyed, knowing the girl would bring something prickly and uncomfortable in with her but not exactly what it would be.

And now the witch sees what she herself has brought into being, following the words of the pattern, and how she herself has sown some of the seeds of all these things so long ago, heedless and ignorant. More, she has seen who is written to undo the spell she wrought of autumn leaves rustling as the fur of a lion, and how she will undo it. *One day*, the witch thinks as she stares at the yellow hair spread across the pillow below her bed, *they will speak of me and he will tell her how I ruined his life from fear and pride, and she will tell him how I saved her life from curiosity.*

The witch pulls her blankets fully over her and whispers a word to extinguish the lights in her home. She lies in the darkness tuning her ears to the subtle sounds of the storm that still rages outside, and wonders how the tapestry would have been different if she had accepted the man who is now a lion made of leaves as a lover.

> • <

In the morning, the witch wakes Alissa with a bowl of steaming porridge and points to a package lying neatly tied up in grey worsted by her other bundle and her shoes at the door.

'Your map's in there with a bit of food and some matches.' Alissa mumbles a thank you through a mouthful of porridge and wriggles her toes in her stockings.

'And I've got you a change of clothes too,' the witch says, dropping a bundle of woollen things on Alissa's feet. 'Nice to start off clean, no matter what happens next.'

Alissa gets changed into the new clothes, which are much better made than the ones she's been travelling in, she will be far warmer now. As she's pulling the tight neckline of a woollen vest over her head, the blue and bronze bird from the day before comes to sit on the unmade bed and watches her. Its eyes dart all over her body as she covers each of her limbs with the tightly woven underthings the witch has given her. She has the feeling the bird approves of something she's doing, for when she is dressed with her hair loosely braided down her back, it gives a soft cheep and goes back to its perch.

When the witch leads Alissa back through the dark rock of the tunnel, she is careful to move quietly and follow exactly where the witch treads. It seems shorter than the journey the previous night, and the light of the new day comes upon her quicker than she thought as they round a corner to find themselves out on the open hillside. Alissa blinks a little in the sudden light. She turns around to find there is no gap in the grass, nothing at all to indicate where they have come from. The witch sees her glance and grins.

'Oh, I'm almost as good at hiding as your men in the Tower,' she says.

There is a petrichor smell from the heavy rain, and the green earth is steaming as droplets of dew rise from each blade of grass.

'You need to follow the bottom of the valley that way,' the witch says, pointing towards the rising sun. 'Then you've got your map to show you the rest.'

Alissa turns to the witch, her hands fumbling with the bundles as she shifts them onto her back. 'Listen, I—'

The witch holds up a hand to stop her. 'I don't want to hear any of that, I know you're grateful. You don't need to grovel.'

Alissa looks down at her hands, embarrassed. 'But I honestly am so—'

'Enough.' The witch suddenly looks stern, and Alissa remembers meeting her on the road and cowering behind her hands.

'Fine. Just tell me, is there anything I can do for you before I go? I've given you nothing in exchange for what you've given me.'

The witch's eyes glaze and she seems to be looking far over Alissa's shoulder towards the next hill. Then she digs inside the pocket of her dress, pulling out a fistful of seeds.

'When you find a good oak by a stream, plant these.'

Alissa is bemused. She holds out her hand and the witch tips them into her palm. She rolls the tiny globes between her fingers and a rich, earthy scent drifts from them. She wonders, again, how the witch knows the things she does.

'How will I know the right place?'

'You'll know it when you see it. Now go.' She takes Alissa by the shoulders, turns her around, and gives her a little push down the hill.

Alissa follows a rocky path to the bottom of the valley, looking back every so often to see the outline of the witch standing still against the bright sky. When she reaches the road she turns back one last time to find the witch finally disappeared.

The very next day, she comes across an old oak with chicken of the woods mushrooms pouring from its bark and its lower branches dipping regally into a brook. She scatters the seeds and kicks some leaves over them and carries on walking, wondering what will grow there and if she will ever see the witch again to find out.

INTERMEDIO

Winter stays longer than anyone thinks it should, sending little flurries of snow and hail at night that carpet the frozen ground with diamond dust that still hasn't fully melted by noon. When spring finally arrives, sneaking across the land as if guilty for its prolonged absence, no one quite trusts it. All across the land, people watch the sky and wait for that sweetness in the air that will tell them they survived another year of the cold, dark days.

In the hidden Tower in the north, Mandoré calls out the patterns of a world waking up from winter, and the six yellow-haired girls embroider it on the silken mantle of the earth. Here are the golden trumpets of daffodils standing proudly on the grassy verges of the towns. Here is the froth of blackthorn blossom in the hedgerows, stitched so tightly to the thorns no one but the bees can find one without the other. The children take notice of where the most flowers are, to come back in the autumn to gather the sloes and sell them to the gin-making widows of their villages. Here are the fauns, staggering to their feet in the secluded glades of the forests as the does lick the birthing fluid from them and prepare to suckle. Here are the thrushes, singing duets with the new, soft wind as they feather their nests for their chicks.

In the Tower, the girls see none of it, they have only the gradual impression of sewing more green than white, and more warmth than frost. The Thirteen scrutinise every inch of the silk as it flows from the tower and out into the world. They do not speak of what they are looking for, but nonetheless there is a feeling among them that they are waiting for something, something that might be revealed by the changes of the coming season.

In the cold sky, the moon looks down at the shape of the earth as if she is peering at the witch's map. The moon's daughter sits, hidden in a valley no one dares to go because of the avalanches, disguised in a shape that is neither her true form, nor the one she used to take when she lived in the Tower, nor the one she takes when she goes out into the world, wandering. She sits still, hardly breathing, hardly moving, her heartbeat slowed to a hibernation speed. She thinks of what she wrote long ago which is finally coming to pass. It is the coming of this spring that will birth it all, and if she listens with that deep part of herself that was born in the sky, she can hear the voice of Five calling out her words for the girls, stitch by stitch, making the spring and unmaking the world.

The moon's daughter lets her mind drift out of the valley and up into the air. She is more comfortable there; after so many years caged inside stone walls, she yearns to be free like seeds on the wind. Fly with her; see what she sees as she casts her eye over the land she has wrought with her words, just as her mother does from her perch in the sky. Go north from that rocky, danger-ridden valley, fly over the smoke and soot of Uranga, cross the great rivers of the land to where the girl with yellow hair and feathers at her navel travels along a quiet road, on her way to find the man she thinks she made in error.

> • <

Alissa walks with a joy she did not know she could feel, a joy she has never sewn in anyone, nor imagined could exist in the world. Deep in her bones, she is remembering spring and every few steps jolts a memory from her childhood. Snowdrops peeking their buds above the frozen soil, streams gushing with snowmelt, bark teeming with beetles. Sometimes she thinks she can hear Mandoré's voice echoing in her dreams, calling the patterns of spring to the girls in the Tower, and she wakes up with her fingers twitching furiously. She wonders if all the people in the villages she passes know there is a mind directing this concert of transformation, a book that tells the trees when to bud and the lambs when to burrow their way out of the ewes and the barley when to sprout. Perhaps they think it all happens on its own. Perhaps they do not care how it happens so long as it does.

It is a joy to her to see with her own eyes something of the land the witch showed her. She walks with the witch's map before her, hovering in the air just as her table did. The map is woven of silken threads dyed to the black, green, gold and blue of the land and the water. It folds and undulates along with the contours of the ground she walks upon; and every morning, as she draws it out of her pack to set her course for the day, it revolves gently in her hands so she can follow the direction it sets, so softly she barely feels as though she is touching it.

As spring starts to blossom, Alissa walks along a black snake of a road through the greening forest, her boots splashed with the mud of the ice-melt and her fingers numb even through the gloves the witch gave her. She begins to identify the trees she passes, recognising them from all the ways she has stitched them. Here are the oaks with their roots spreading far across the road and pushing the paving stones out of tessellation with the force of their slow centuries; here are the birches standing ankle deep in the skeletons of their own shed leaves.

When she reaches a golden patch of labra groves, she slows and wanders off the road to meander through their trunks, growing straight upwards towards the sky like prayers. She puts her hand on one of the trunks and the place under her palm glows with a faint golden light. Labra sap in a living tree recognises blood. She knows that because she has stitched it. As she moves further into the groves it becomes darker and darker, the uppermost branches curving into the perfectly domed roof of an old labra forest. Alissa has stitched a man who spent his whole life making speeches about why the labra forms a roof for itself like this, declaiming them in various plazas in Uranga to a mostly indifferent public. He used to say that they made a roof to shelter their saplings from harm, like any animal might shelter its young, but now he's come to be of the opinion that their roofs serve more of a ritualistic function, seeing as only a mature labra forest that has between two and four out of every ten trees harvested each decade will make one. He says that the labra trees may well be mourning or celebrating their lost friends and family, but no one can be sure. Alissa has not thought of this man for a long time, but now she walks among the labra under their mysterious roofs and she wonders if after she has found the juggler and done whatever it is he needs her to, she could go to Uranga and find this man, maybe even help him with his research.

She comes to a river. It is not the Saman but a fast-flowing, narrow channel peppered with dark rocks that lay obstinately in the river as if dropped there from a great height. No barges can navigate this water but Alissa passes coracles of birch bark and deer hide, paddled expertly between the boulders by men with long hair slicked back over their heads and down their powerful shoulders, who shout to each other as they ferry passengers and goods along the river towards faraway destinations, throwing coral rings into the river as they paddle to pray for safe passage across the water.

She sleeps a night in a boatyard by a rickety bridge that can't hold more than two cows' weight of cargo at a time. The bridge keeper has a giant scale by the gate to weigh everything on every cart that goes past; pedestrians have to cross in between the wheeled traffic and they have last priority, so travellers sleep in the boatyard to cross first thing in the morning, before the carts rumble off the road.

Alissa is woken in the night by the snores and snorts of those walkers and wanderers she shares her temporary home with, and when she opens her eyes she is struck by a strange light pouring through the broken shutters facing the riverside. She gets up, wraps her cloak around her, and eases the shed door open slowly so it doesn't creak.

The dark water of the river is alive with sparkling lights, flowing with the current as it splashes around the rocks. There is a greenish tinge to the light, and it is so bright that when she looks to the sky the stars are eclipsed and she can see every tree on the opposite bank, the shape of each rush and reed.

The bridge keeper is awake too, standing a few steps away from her on the bank with his hat pulled right down towards his eyes, watching the weird light skitter along the water. He turns when he hears her footsteps swish through the grass.

'Phosphorescent algae,' he says, turning back to the water. 'There's a pond upstream where it blooms at this time of year, and when the current's strong like this it drags some of this stuff with it.'

Alissa sits on her haunches and watches the lights in silence, until the bridge keeper sighs, tips his hat to her, and retreats to his cottage by the giant scales. Alissa stays on the bank, watching the glowing water until the sky starts to lighten with the dawn and there are shuffles of people waking up and gathering their baggage in the boatyard. She has never even heard of anyone sewing anything like that in all her years in the Tower. She thinks of the huge books Mandoré would read from with the symbols embossed on their covers and spines, and wonders where they came from. She puts her hand inside her pocket and fingers the edges of the silken map the witch gave her. There is so much else in the world than what she has sewn, so much she knows nothing of. She starts to see the juggler as her rescuer, whatever he is and wherever he came from. When she meets him, the first thing she should do is say thank you. Thank you for releasing me from that place where I could not know what it is to be alive, thank you for exiling me from making the world so that I could live in it instead.

> • <

Now rise over the ribbons of blue rivers and snakes of black road and patches of brown fields that are beginning to turn green, and fly like one of the sparrows returning from its winter sojourn somewhere warm. Open your wings and soar away from the fast flowing river Alissa crosses in the dewy morning and go east, towards a swamp where a woman lives on her own in a cottage with a hundred or more half-made machines.

Leira sits on a low stool with a whittling knife in one hand and a block of labra wood in the other. Of course it was to be labra used for this strange task her old friend has given her; it's the only material in the world that behaves differently each time you touch it. Sometimes, as the wood writhes beneath her fingers and resists the shape she is trying to give it, wriggling into something else entirely, she wonders if Luna wrote the labra trees with their peculiar qualities for exactly this moment. Thoughts like this intrude on her more as she gets older and the memories of her girlhood stitching the world recede further and further. During all those long afternoons of sitting with the moon's daughter in that cellar room she learnt a little of how the world works, perhaps more than any other mortal alive, but still there are mysteries that she cannot solve, not even in almost thirty years of puzzling. Time, for instance. She remembers some of the symbols that were embossed on the books a masked man would read from, but she doesn't understand how they fit together. She thinks that is somehow the crux of it, the secret melting centre of the world her old friend has woven from her words, and the way she is keeping the knowledge of it from the Thirteen. Thinking about it makes her head twist and her dreams murky, though, so she keeps it all in the corner of her eye, letting the back of her brain process it as she works on this commission.

At her feet lie blocks of labra wood still to be carved, and in a basket behind her are the ones she considers finished. Plugs of different sizes, made of a labra wood base with spruce resin ringing the end. Her idea is that the resin will form the seal, and the labra will shrink or expand according to the precise hole it covers. She's got over a thousand to make before she leaves her home sometime after the May Day. The work should go quicker now she's got a prototype, but she's not worried about completing the job. Luna has written it this way.

She finishes carving a number into the wood she's holding and turns to place it in the basket of finished plugs. On each of the completed ones there is a number etched into the labra wood; this is something Luna asked of her too. It's taken her several tries to find the right tool that the labra would accept; now she's engraving each plug with a silver stylus, the only thing that doesn't make the labra turn black and rot.

Does she consider, even for a moment, what her old friend will do with these strange wooden plugs? Does she ever think about the wildness of her old friend's grey eyes, the sunken space between her cheekbones and her jaw, the hair matted with mud and a few stray feathers? *I am bound by the confidences of the star child and I request my right to go free.* She has spent many long years wondering about the moon's daughter, but she lives a free and happy life now because she has always kept her wonderings tightly to herself.

Her instructions are to make plugs from this batch of almost priceless labra wood, to number them from one to three thousand, six hundred and seventy-one, and bring them to Uranga for Midsummer. That is what she intends to do, no matter how many questions intrude upon the peace of her work.

She stretches and considers how much light there is left in the day and whether it is worth lighting a candle. She shuts her eyes for a moment and smells the fresh scent of a gentle rain tapping at her windows. Spring is almost here. Soon, her cabbages and her beans will sprout and she will hover above their tender green shoots anxiously, picking off the caterpillars and the slugs, coaxing them into a world she is less and less sure of as each day goes by.

Leave the woman with her machines – she's been so absorbed in the way the labra wood breathes and squirms under her fingers she has not noticed anyone watching – and travel westwards. Fly low like a scavenging crow towards the great northern road, until you come to a village with a public house called the Cat's Cradle. Stop at the sight of a carriage with a complex arrangement of sails and pulleys atop its painted roof and perch a little. Watch. Check they're practising their new show, for this kind of thing isn't their usual offering and there are a few differences of opinion that might cause difficulties. It all has to be straightened out before Midsummer, for nothing, nothing at all, can go wrong.

> • <

The juggler has taken charge of their rehearsals, and Lion submits to his direction as it seems he doesn't have any other choice. Every morning when the weather is fine he assembles them all on the patch of ground outside the carriage, and directs Vanna first as the water nymph, and then as the forest nymph. Each rehearsal ends with the juggler cajoling Lion into showing him something he plans for the spectacular finale of the flood, and Lion huffs and puffs for a bit before he performs a perfunctory backflip or two. Then the juggler applauds delightedly and lets him go back into the carriage to curl up on his rug. Goat watches the rehearsals from the back porch, giving his opinion on Vanna's speeches too freely for her liking. When she tells him this, in a heated exchange one evening as they all sit cramped in the carriage, sheltering from the rain, he adopts a placatory, I-know-best tone that sends her off to stay in the local inn for a few nights, a move Lion privately thinks is a slight overreaction. It is the juggler who reconciles them, with a tenderness and humour that even Lion has to admit is masterful. He brings them together outside the carriage and talks movingly of the need for old friends to be patient with each other, of the artistic boundaries they are breaking, of the creative temperament and how delicate and special it is. He gets Vanna and Goat to apologise and make promises to honour each other as artists and listen to each other's needs. When they've made up and they get back on the road there is a freshness to the atmosphere in the carriage like the clean smell of the air after rain. Even Lion is a better mood for a few days.

He still doesn't like the juggler, though. All through the winter he has watched him with suspicion every time he sips from his stupid personal carafe, and his annoyance has grown each time Vanna and Goat dismiss him.

'We can't all share everything, Lion,' said Goat. 'He's used to travelling on his own, relying on himself. I think he's entitled to some privacy.' *Like the privacy we give you and your moods*, Goat doesn't say.

'Water?' Vanna was incredulous. 'You don't like him because he doesn't drink the same water as us? Come on, be serious.'

'There's also that funny box of his. It's got this kind of mist—'

'Lion, listen. That man has completely reinvigorated us, we're incredibly lucky to have him. Do you know we've made so much money this winter we can afford to get the wheels replaced? Do you know we've got savings for the first time in however many years we've been doing this?'

Lion had shrugged and walked away then, conscious that he had contributed very little of that new money and is also contributing very little to the new show that will, everyone says, be a smash hit.

But is the new show really that good? Lion isn't sure. Goat has applied for and received the license to perform a special one-off show at the open carnival, and hopes are high that this will lead to a permanent slot in the city and they will be able to add it to their touring schedule, and with it all the acclaim and money that goes with performing for the audiences there. It's a good story, Lion will concede that, one most people know but which doesn't get performed very often, and he has to admit that the juggler has had some innovative ideas on how to stage it. Vanna has composed some beautiful tunes, she looks very lovely as both the nymphs, and the two costumes she's making herself are in a different league to anything she's made before. But still, Lion is uneasy. Have they all become so hopelessly provincial that anything they do in the capital will be seen as passé and ridiculous? And anyway, where did the juggler come from? Who was he before they saw him in that square, performing his tricks for the burghers of Janat who were so entranced they hadn't even taken off their cloak?

He thinks the juggler has some kind of magic attached to him that the others can't or don't want to see. He has not been following the juggler on purpose – and he will defend himself vigorously to anyone who suggests otherwise – but there have been occasions over the winter when he has been out in the woods, impotently chasing falling leaves to take his mind off the urge to hunt and chase and claw and kill, when he has seen the juggler moving through the trees somewhere just ahead of him. He has stopped and hidden himself each time, and perhaps in this small act of dishonesty he can be rebuked, but each time he has seen something to give him pause, something he can't explain. Once he saw him feeding a sleek, red fox at the foot of an oak, murmuring softly in a language Lion did not recognise. Another time he held out his arms to the canopy and a raven came to sit on his shoulder, accepting worms wriggling between the juggler's fingers. Yet another time Lion spotted him practising his juggling while a crow flew around and around the balls that soared in the air and a hare sat by his feet, watching dispassionately. Lion spends a lot of time thinking about these animals now, looking out for them on the road and watching the juggler for any sign there is something he recognises in him. Fox, hare, raven and crow. All animals his mother would have shooed out of her garden as nuisances. Mischief and mayhem with that lot, she would have said.

'Lion!' Vanna calls from outside the carriage. 'We need you now, we're coming to the flood bit.'

Lion thinks about pretending to be fast asleep to make Goat come inside and get him, but it feels petty. He stretches on the rug and pads outside, where the air is warmer than he expected. Vanna takes up her fiddle and starts to play the song she has composed for the flood, a tune that dips and swells like the surge in a stream after a storm.

'Hold on a second,' the juggler says, clapping his hands, and Vanna stops mid-phrase and lowers her instrument expectantly.

'I've just had a great idea.' Lion hears Goat's hooves clatter eagerly down the steps and onto the cobbles of the farmyard they're staying in, and braces himself.

'I'm thinking what Lion's doing is so great, but it needs to maybe look more water-like. Rippling, flowing. Do you know what I mean?'

Vanna and Goat nod enthusiastically but Lion stays still, hoping his majestic calm will convey something of his displeasure at what will surely be some inconvenience to him.

The juggler turns to Lion. 'I know you're going to love this,' he says. Lion still does not move.

'We can dye your leaves blue, Lion, and then you'll look more like water! What do you think of that?'

Vanna gasps and Goat stamps his front hooves on the cobbles to make a sound like clapping.

'That would be perfect!' Vanna exclaims and immediately starts chattering about some dye she has seen, something that can achieve a perfect, modulated look that might be very realistic if they were to do it right.

Lion sinks onto his front paws to stop himself from leaping at the juggler's throat and tearing out his windpipe. He shuts his eyes. It is not the human part of himself that thinks like this, he knows that; it is the wild animal the witch made of him that wants to be so violent and proud and thoroughly uncivilised and wants to solve all his problems with a quick swipe of his claws. Still, he would not like the prospect of being dyed bright blue even if he was a man again, no, it would be undignified even then.

Now they are talking about blue capes and ribbons and attaching threads to his claws to draw bits of blue silk around him as he somersaults to make it look as though water is closing in from everywhere. Lion tunes them out. He just has to bear this until Midsummer, that's all. Then the show will fail, they won't get the new license to tour to the city, and his friends will see that the juggler is a charlatan and a drifter, and he will be turned loose from their carriage.

Then everything will go back to how it was a few moons ago, miserable and grey and lonely, a state he is beginning to suspect he deserves.

> • <

It is easy to find the owl woman's house from that village. She lives only a day's soft walk north, faster, of course, if you go as the crow flies and cross the river with your wings. Land on a fence post just outside her cottage and peer in through the window to her study. The moon is waxing and the earth is awakening to spring, and Ula the Mother of Birds is drawing. As usual, she is thinking of the one child of hers who doesn't have wings.

She doesn't know she is so close to those her daughter seeks, she doesn't know anything of her daughter at all. The last time she saw her was that night Luna took the baby away, claiming she had written it this way and that was how it had to be. Since then, the years have been long and lonely. When dawn comes and she can't sleep, sometimes she walks around her cottage and stops at the places where her happy memories live. By the sink is where Luna first kissed her. On the fourth floorboard from the foot of the bed the baby smiled for the first time. By the left-hand window she and Luna laughed over a joke she can't remember now, and by the other Luna first said she loved her.

She doesn't hate Luna. Even now, as she lies on her bed already awake, watching the pink of the sunset fade as the darkness comes, she thinks about how she would welcome the love of her life into her arms if she were to come back. She is older now, perhaps less beautiful. Her feathers are greying and she can no longer see a leaf tremble in the valley from the top of the hill. Her voice is hoarse as she calls to the birds in the forest and at the river. Even so, she thinks she could be beautiful enough for Luna, if the world would only let her return.

She still loves her bird children. She still sits at her desk in the moonlight with her pen and her prism and draws feathers and wings and beaks and claws, but she is starting to worry what will become of the skies when she passes away. She wanted to ask Luna about this, back when Luna told stories about where she came from. She would speak in stuttered fragments in the pre-dawn silence just before they went to bed, and from those scattered moments the owl woman collected a whole story of her lover's life but nothing much about her own.

Then two of the masked men came. They plucked one of her wing feathers, dipped it into an inkpot and scratched at the words on the page in the threadbare book that she was called from until they thought they had made her silly with pain and terror. Then she understood that Luna would never come back for her, because she loved her too much to let her be tortured again.

'I didn't write you Ula,' Luna had whispered sleepily into the warm feathers on her back, and her voice had been full of something like delight. 'You are the only thing I've found in the world that I didn't write.'

Ula had said nothing then, but now she thinks of that moment as she looks at the white-tipped feather in her shoulder in the thin crescent moonlight. Luna did not write her, but someone did, and when she is gone from the world, like all things, will someone else write something else to make the birds?

Spring is coming, and she is drawing chicks in their speckled shells, gaping beaks rooting for worms and warm nests high in the budding branches. How many more springs will she draw? She cannot remember how many she has already drawn. She had a life before Luna came, although she does not remember it, just like she has a life now after the baby with the feathers at its navel has gone, although she does not like it. She would want to die if she knew who would make the birds when she is gone. She should have asked Luna that, all those years ago.

The owl woman glances at her prism and puts it back into line with her paper. She scratches at the paper with her pen, etching the last fluffy wing feathers of the magpie chick. She takes her pen from the paper and gives the chick a gentle push with her finger. It cheeps, then stumbles from the table and drops a little before it rights itself and makes it out of the window. Ula watches it fly north, the direction the masked men came from. She whispers a correction to the chick's course, steering it away from that dark place and towards a nest a little way away where it can rest until dawn, but she lets her own mind fly far away from her little cottage, following that northern course until her imagination reaches that tall tower.

> • <

At the very same moment the owl woman is thinking of the masked men, they happen to be thinking of her. More specifically, they are thinking of her daughter who used to live in their Tower, but whenever one of the Thirteen thinks of Alissa, her owl mother also appears at the edges of their thoughts, casting a long shadow of shame upon them.

It is council time in the cellar chamber, and the silken cloak flows over the stone mushroom table and covers the heads of all the Thirteen.

'She hasn't even found the juggler yet, let alone had any contact with the star child,' Seven says. His face is dusty; he has only just this moment returned to the Tower from a journey to the Outside. 'I'm beginning to think even sending her away was another one of the jokes in the pattern.'

'Give it time,' Thirteen says, and there is a barely concealed shudder along the cloak.

'We have precisely no time,' Three says, and although no one glances at the shelves, they all know there are only thirty-eight books left. 'If the girl is a dead end, we need to make another plan.'

Twelve, who usually takes Thirteen's side in all discussions, narrows his eyes at Three but says nothing. That is why they've come together in council, to make another plan.

There is a short silence in the room, and then Ten clears his throat.

'I wonder, gentlemen. Should we not be looking to the skies again?'

'Naturally, when the eclipse comes we'll put ourselves out of our misery,' says Eight. 'But what do you propose we do until then?'

Undeterred by Eight's sarcasm, Ten continues. 'Have we contacted the astrologers as to when the next eclipse is forecast?'

Twelve sighs. 'They don't know. They say none of their models work at the moment, that the sky is rotating in an unusual manner.'

'Another joke in the silk,' Two says.

Silence in the cellar chamber again, a silence that is coloured by a deep pessimism. They have faced crises of this kind before; the one who called herself Luna was not the first star child to go missing, nor the first to try to break the ancient contract that exists between the moon and the Tower of the earth. The world comes close to ending most days; those who pay attention to these things know this and accept it simply as the dance of life. But it is little comfort to any of the masked men that it has never ended before. Never have they got down to thirty-eight books with the star child still apparently vanished; never has a star child left such elaborate plans behind her, with years and years of glitches and missed stitches and jokes like that juggling maniac. Never have they come quite so close to the end before.

'Are we still on track to last until Midsummer?' Thirteen asks Five and Eleven, as leaders of the night and day shift respectively. They nod.

'There are enough books to last until then,' Eleven says.

'Then we have until the sun begins to wane to keep the world alive, gentlemen,' Thirteen says. He blinks, long and slow, and a pang of impotent rage flickers through each of them. They only want to keep their world alive. That is all.

'Until then, we look for the star child, we look for the eclipse, and we make sure we're following what these jokes in the silk are adding up to.'

The thirteen masked men slip the silken cloak over their heads, and let their coverings slide from their faces as their beards fall to the ground to curl into wheels. They roll out of the cellar chamber almost silently, all apart from Five, who rolls out last and turns with a sharp squeak of his wheel at the door. He has been struggling with the feeling that it is he who is responsible for all of this, and each time the Thirteen meet in council the feeling sprouts a new, barbed tentacle and hooks it into his heart. He must have done something wrong during the capture of the star child, all those years ago, to make her into this monster. He has failed his brothers and he has failed the world he swore to protect. The moon is not the only one who made a sacred oath; and more and more, he feels as though the moon's daughter is not the only one who is breaking it.

No birds fly over or around the Tower in the north, and not even a witch's scrying eyes can see something of what is happening there. So come, leave that dark Tower and watch the ripples in that pond just off the overgrown path that leads south. Follow the tiny waves as they flow towards the edge of the muddy water and dive right into the centre, the place where the stone must have plopped. The witch is scrying for news from the Tower. She has filled her golden bowl with rainwater and she's making it sing as she watches the Tower standing dark against a pink sky, so when you surface you'll emerge from between the ripples and climb out of her bowl.

She's watching the moon, rising resplendent on the eastern horizon, full and shining like a newly minted coral ring. She stands on the threshold of her cave, her bowl perched between her knees, watching the light fade from the sky. Her belly feels heavy and swollen with the power of the moon and the feeling will only grow when her sister witches arrive. It will not be long now before the night air begins to buzz with the swish and swoop of birch branches. She shivers with excitement.

The sun dips below the opposite hill, and the witch waits a little longer before she tips the water from her bowl onto the earth in a long, clear stream. She murmurs an incantation her mother taught her, one to catch the reflection of the moonlight in the water. It's a simple thing, a cantrip and nothing more, but she makes it a habit on full moon sabbats to invoke her mother in some way. Tonight she will host her tribe in her own valley and the older witches will drink to her mother and all the others passed since the Chaos, as they always do. Her mother is kept alive in these sabbat songs, and although she has always been taught the moon would curse her if she did, she hums them softly to herself sometimes, always during the day when she thinks the moon cannot hear.

A lynx cracks a twig under its soft paw, a wolf yowls at the rising moon, an owl keens as it takes off on its hunt. The witch returns her bowl to its shelf inside her cave and sits on the hillside to watch the first stars spark alight. The southern side of the valley darkens with what looks like a host of giant bats; black wings beating at the dark air. The witch lets her head fall back and she shrieks at the sky, a full-throated sound of power and joy, and as it rings out across the valley shutters slam shut, goats huddle into ditches and cows low. The host of witches turn their birch besoms towards the shriek and urge them towards the hill. The moon watches them land on the tufts of damp grass and roll out of their long cloaks and patterned dresses to begin to dance skyclad. The moon sends them fire to warm the curves of their bellies on this chilly night. The witches' sabbat has begun.

Later that night, when the witch's voice is hoarse from singing and her head fuzzy and thick from the elderberry wine, she finds herself lolling by a small fire at the foot of a wizened hawthorn, listening to one of her sister witches caress the strings on her harp and sing about a man she loves so much she cannot help but torture him. She can see others dancing in an oak clearing, thrusting their fingers towards the sky as if to draw the moon into their frenzy, and the witch thinks about going to join them, but the earth where she lays is so cool and damp and soft on her naked back that she cannot move her limbs. Instead, she listens to the song about a man mad with love and she thinks of the man she made into a lion, the man the sewing girl with the golden hair will soon meet.

The witch has been thinking of Alissa often. She fills her scrying bowl with rainwater and watches Alissa moving across the land, noting with satisfaction whenever she gets out the map to consult it. She hadn't credited the girl with any power other than that of the feathers at her navel she hadn't wanted anyone to see, but when she went to check on the seeds she had given Alissa to sow, she found them sprouted from the soil made spongy by the fungus. She picked the sprouts and ate them, although they made her belch.

She could tell her sister witches about the sewing girl released from the Tower and her juggling man. She could tell them that there is something prickling in her shoulders, some big magic crackling in the air, magic so huge it will dye all their thumbs scarlet forever and her own spells are a part of it, somehow. She takes another sip on her elderberry wine and lets her eyes drift shut. Maybe at the next sabbat, or the one after that. For the spring is not yet come, and all the signs indicate nothing will happen until then.

GALLIARD

Section 7, clause 2
All matters of mortals, including harvests and
holidays, birth and death, feast and famine shall
be left to the star child to write, the Thirteen to
call from the books, and the golden haired girls
to sew. There will be no additions or subtractions
from what the star child has written.

The river is so wide she cannot see its other bank. She stands on a ferry jetty watching the huge boat glide towards its moorings, the stevedores swirling around her like the river water around the smooth, grey rocks that make this part of the channel so hard to navigate. The sailors on the deck shout to the stevedores to catch the thick ropes, slimy with weeds, and then the stevedores heave on the iron posts to keep the ferry still. The ropes smell of musky river water and rotting wood, and every time a stevedore passes her the breeze brings the smell of his sweat to her nose.

She moves back as the gangplank fills with passengers inching their way down the steps, and they stagger past her, their arms filled with bags and coats and small children yelling from hunger and motion sickness. When the boat is steady, the stevedores form intricate chains, ant-like, along the jetty and pass boxes between their callused hands from the bank to the boat. Alissa watches silently.

If she's been following the map correctly, this river is the Saman. The light has been coming earlier every morning and there are no longer frosts when she starts walking. The blackthorn is about to flower, she passes its tight buds in the hedgerow and watches the ground for the other signs the witch told her of: the beech buds, the ramsons and the bluebells. But she sees none of them, yet.

She's been practising for the moment when she meets the juggler. She's decided she'll be honest and tell him the truth about how he came to be in the world. She'll tell him about the pipe music and the strange stitches and the way he was embroidered separately from everything else, although she knows she has to think carefully about that bit, for she doesn't want him to feel lonely, or like a mistake. If he tries to apologise for being the cause of her exile from the Tower she'll tell him she wouldn't have changed any of it. Maybe she will have hours of explaining to do, hours of telling him about her life in the Tower and the silk and the other yellow-haired girls, hours that Mandoré told her she was forbidden to spend. Maybe the juggler will know where he comes from, maybe he will tell her where and what he was before she sewed him, and what he's doing here now. She doesn't know. This is how they all live, she thinks to herself as she stands on the jetty, watching the passengers disembark. They just move through their lives blind, no idea what will come next. She is filled with fear and awe at the thought that she is one of them now.

The ferry pulls away from the jetty with a loud peal of its bell, and the stevedores stretch out their shoulders as they trudge back to the bank. Alissa stumbles as she runs to catch up.

'Excuse me!' She lunges to tap one man on the back.

'What's that you need, miss?' The man's shirt is wet and stained green where the rope was taut across his chest. He holds his jerkin loosely, dragging on the damp planks of the jetty.

'Is this river called the Saman?'

He cocks his head, takes his time about pulling his jerkin over the meat of his arms and tying the laces at his belly.

'Why do you want to know?

Alissa's belly swoops. The man has the look of a boar rootling in a cesspit, and he stares at her with an expectant leer.

She lifts her chin. 'My husband's expecting me,' she lies. 'He'll be here today. He's coming on the next boat.'

The stevedore grunts and turns away. 'Well, it's the Saman alright. Mind you don't come to any harm before he can get to you, now.'

She smiles tightly, but he doesn't look back. She stays on the jetty until all the men have disappeared into the warehouses and taverns, listening to the ferry-riled water lapping at the jetty under her feet. She was stupid. She has sewn conversations like that before.

Now she knows only what she needs; she has no idea if the Patli Bridge is up- or downriver, and when she consults the witch's map it revolves in her hands so she doesn't know which way is north, and the glimmering blue thread that shows the Saman seems to giggle at her. The bank is emptying quickly as dusk approaches. A shout comes from one of the taverns and the roar of a drunken song follows it. Alissa shudders. She should get away from here.

She treads carefully along the wet jetty until she is standing on the bank again. She has no money for a room at an inn, but maybe that's a good thing, as the inns by this river port don't look like places she should go. She pulls her hood over her head and starts to walk upriver, keeping to the path.

By the time it is fully dark, she's reached a town clustered either side of a bridge. Alissa turns down a wide avenue away from the bridge and follows the cobblestones into a large square bordered by narrow brick houses with windows framed by heavy shutters. There are no carts or barrows rumbling over the bridge or across the cobbles any more; the windows of the houses are lit with warm, orange light, and those who are still abroad have their necks shrunken into their cloaks against the cold and hurry to their waiting homes.

Alissa walks around the square more briskly than she needs to, pretending she has business in the town. She glances in each window as she passes, watching the candlelight flicker and noting the wood and clay idols on the sills. Many houses have tiny carvings of fish propped against the window frames, a sign that their masters or mistresses are fisherfolk and are trying to attract good luck on the boats. A couple have beautifully carved does with soft eyes and curved bellies, a sign that there is a woman living within who is heavy with child and praying for a safe delivery. And another, one with paint peeling from the doorway and the curtains drawn, has a still-damp clay model of a pig sitting in the window, its snout pressed to the glass. Alissa remembers that the matrons at the orphans' home would tuck a dried-out pig's trotter under the pillow of any child who had a cough or a fever, telling them a little pig would come in the night and gobble up all their illness.

She doesn't know how far she is from the place where she spent her childhood, but now she thinks maybe she is close, if the people here believe in the same kind of sprites.

By her third round the square has emptied of all but two people, who, like her, seem not to have anywhere to get back to in a hurry. One, an elderly man who is leisurely filling buckets with water, the pump squeaking with every push; and the other, a woman carrying her baby wrapped in a sling against her chest.

Alissa watches the woman for a moment, then makes up her mind. As she approaches, she hears her singing softly to her baby.

> *The daughter of the moon came to stay*
> *She swept and she sang and went on her way.*
> *The wheels they went a rolling and they took her head*
> *Placed her in the sky where the darkness fled.*

'Excuse me, is this the Patli Bridge?'

The woman stops walking but sways from foot to foot, bouncing up and down with both hands cupped around her baby's head.

'Oh no, this is Randal.' The woman glances quickly to her baby and lowers her voice. 'The Patli's the next one upriver, half a day's walk, if you go slow.'

Relief sends a shiver through her arms and sets her hands a-tingling.

'Thank you.'

The woman smiles. Alissa sees that her eyes are smudged with tiredness.

'Do you have anywhere to stay tonight, dearie?'

Alissa shakes her head. The woman turns to point at the other end of the square.

'There's a travellers' hostel down there, they'll give you a bed and a meal if you need it. Make sure you go to the back entrance.' She winks. 'The sailors tend to sleep in the porch.'

Alissa thanks her, and as she moves away across the square she hears the woman begin to sing again, her voice clearer this time now the old man is no longer making the pump squeak.

> *The daughter of the moon escaped her fate,*
> *Now heave the needle and pluck the thread, true*
> *and straight.*

> ❯ • ❮

The next morning is bright and chilly, and the path along the Saman is busy with carts and sheep and goats flowing to and from the river port in a loud, chaotic stream. None of the trees along the path are beeches, but she stops and inspects the buds anyway. The hazel catkins droop from their spindly twigs with the shy scarlet flowers turned to the sun.

Be patient, Alissa tells herself as she walks, and rehearses what she'll say to the juggler again.

The Patli is surprising. It's more of a pontoon than a bridge, made of floating rafts tied together with intricate knots. Alissa finds a sawn-off tree trunk and sits on it to watch as a team of burly men on either side of the water pull the pontoon apart like two halves of a walnut to let a boat pass through, then heave it together again. Herds of sheep wait on the bank and bleat, and when the bridge is joined again the dogs begin to edge them towards the water.

Alissa spends the day by the river, watching the boats hover for the Patli to split apart, then charge through the gap. She buys stew and mugs of steaming hawthorn tea from passing pedlars and sleeps in the traveller's hostel just off the road. Every time she ducks into the woods to squat, her heart drums a warning in her chest: *don't miss them because you're tucked away pissing!* She doesn't dare get chatting to any of the hawkers passing by, although several of them smile and ask her where she's going. She doesn't want to encounter a man like the boar-stevedore again.

She finds it hard to get to sleep at night with the sounds of the merchants coming in late and getting up early and dragging their cargo across the floor, but it is warm and sheltered from the wind. And, best of all, there is nothing that can pass in any direction she can't see from the porch as soon as it's light.

Four days pass this way.

On the fifth day, she buys a bowl of porridge from a man who tells her she looks peaky and gives her an extra ladle for free. She tries not to blush and thanks him with a smile.

She takes her usual place on the sawn-off stump and waits.

There is more bustle on the bank today. Alissa leans towards the groups of gossiping merchants standing with their hot mugs of tea. She learns that tomorrow is market day in Randal, the town downriver, and the ferry port is heaving with boats and carts and oxen, moving people and packages from land to water and back again. The wind is strong but there's something soft in it. It smells like damp, cut grass. Alissa breathes in the fresh, green scent. Spring is coming closer.

Her eyes become tired with the effort of peering into the faces of everyone who passes, watching for that blue hat and red cloak and sly smile. She sees old men and young men, rich men and poor men, men who look twice at her ribbon of yellow hair and men whose eyes slide past her as if she is another tree. But she does not see a juggler.

At midday, just as Alissa begins to feel hunger pangs, a group of girls pass her. They wear aprons with fresh green stains down the front and they hold baskets at their hips with muddy hands. As they walk past Alissa sees their baskets are filled with shiny green leaves, and a scent of pungent garlic wafts towards her.

Alissa jumps from the stump. 'Excuse me! What do you have in your basket there?'

'Ramsons.' One of the girls tips her basket so Alissa can see the long leaves with crumbling clods of earth at their base. The scent smacks her in the face and makes her stomach rumble. The girl points behind her and grins. 'They've just started coming up downriver. You better be quick if you want some, the whole village will be out there when they smell my mum's pies.'

Alissa walks back along the river path until she sees a pair of twin beeches, their smooth grey bark twisted towards each other like dancing lovers. She pulls at one of the lower branches and sees the tip of a needle-like bud bulging from a twig. Her heart rises to her throat and she runs back to her watching place by the bridge. She sits on the damp stump and holds her bundle in her lap, her feet twitching nervously.

'Just the bluebells now,' she whispers to herself as the dusk draws closer. 'Just the bluebells now.'

❯ • ❰

'Why don't we just get on this boat?' Lion says. 'It's going in the right direction.'

The mud-spattered carriage is parked by the River Saman way upstream, where the water is still sour from the sea and foggy with silt. A mizzling rain is falling but they all stand on the bank getting wet. The inside of the carriage seems far too small these days.

The juggler shakes his head. 'This one is too small. We should stay on the road until the Patli Bridge, cross, take the northern road to the River Gragan, and get on a ferry there.'

Goat digs his hoof into the mud, considering. 'There is more space at that river port,' he says. 'We could stay the night, have a good warm meal before we head off, maybe give an evening show?'

Goat is speaking with questions in his voice, but Lion knows that when he talks that way he's already made up his mind.

'Fine,' Lion says, and stretches back on his heels. Vanna yawns and pulls a shawl over her head for the drizzle. It pitter-patters into the river making tiny holes in the smooth surface of the water.

'How far is the Patli Bridge then, Juggler?' Vanna asks.

'I think only one more day. The wind looks right, we can get there quick.'

They all look up at the sky as if they expect the invisible wind to show itself. They are delaying the moment when they will have to get back into the carriage and set off again. The inside of their wheeled home is getting pokier and pokier; Goat's hooves slip into Lion's face whenever the road gets rutted and bumpy, Vanna leaps into the driver's bay just to get some time alone even though she hates to drive, and Juggler has, on occasion, hissed at Lion when his tail flicks towards the box tucked under the bench. Even Owl doesn't seem to want to be involved; she stays perched on top of the driver's bay, ignoring them all.

'One more day,' Vanna sighs. 'Then I think we need a nice break and a room at an inn. Each.'

Nobody disagrees as they climb back into the carriage.

> • <

The next morning it is market day downriver, and when the sun rises in a clear sky Alissa is the only person left in the porch. All the merchants have departed for Randal and they have left a yawning silence in their wake.

Alissa stretches and gathers her things. She hopes some hawkers have stayed behind for her to buy food from, or she'll be pulling up those raw ramsons to munch on and end up breathing garlicy fire in the juggler's face when she meets him. She combs and braids her hair and finds herself humming along to the sound of tinkling bells.

Bells.

She scrambles to her feet, her hair twisting out of its half-made braid, and rushes out of the porch to the woods behind it. The ringing becomes louder and more insistent. Alissa veers away from the pines and yews and the dead patches of darkness beneath them to the clearings of light beneath the oaks and hornbeams.

The wood is carpeted in a delicate lacework of purple flowers, each bellflower of each plant quivering on its stem. The bells become joyous as Alissa walks gingerly among them. They will keep ringing until the leaves bud and the canopy of the woods closes over them, stealing their light for another year.

Alissa stands among the trees, letting the bells shake her limbs until she remembers that now she has all the signs of spring the witch has warned of, the juggler could be here at any moment.

She flees from the woods, stops by the porch to fling her things inside her bundle, and then runs to the river. She gasps for breath as she scans the crowd for a red cloak and slumps when she sees there isn't one. *You haven't missed them*, she tells herself. *They're still coming. Just be patient.*

A kingfisher perched on a low branch of a drooping willow turns its head to look at her as she crouches by the bank. Mud squelches and seeps up around her footprints.

'Can you hear that?' she whispers to the bird. 'Can you hear the bluebells chime?' The bird flashes its blue wings in response. 'They're coming.'

The kingfisher turns back to the river to watch it flowing downstream.

> • <

By the time the carriage rattles up to the Patli at midday, all its passengers are in a foul mood. The riverbank is heaving again with the late merchants making their way downstream and the early ones returning to their homes with empty carts and full pockets. Vanna swerves and swears at the merchants getting in her way, and parks by a traveller's porch on the edge of the woods. They all tumble out to watch the chaos streaming by.

'Trust us to turn up on market day, of all days,' says Lion. He scowls and sits back on his haunches. 'I hate market day, no matter where it is. Nothing but fools and thieves.'

Vanna rubs at her temples. 'Those bluebells aren't helping. I hope the inns here have good shutters to keep that racket out.'

Goat is staring at the pontoon bridge, now being dragged apart by the stevedores. He looks worried. 'You didn't say it was a bridge like this, Juggler,' he says, with mild reproach. 'Owl will hate this. We'll have to hood her to get her across.'

Owl expresses her disgust by flying off into the woods with not even a hoot of goodbye.

'Anyone hungry?' says the juggler as he waves to a pedlar with a trayful of steaming buns. No one replies, so the juggler haggles for three and eats them each in one gulp.

Alissa watches them from her position by the bank. The kingfisher has long gone upriver, but now she is accompanied by a gaggle of geese that hop between shore and water with happy whoops. She studies the strange foursome carefully. The witch really didn't describe them properly. The goat seems ordinary enough, he's got a wispy beard hanging from his chin and strong horns, but the lion is not really a lion at all. Even from here she can see that he's made of some kind of enchantment. He is the shape of a lion, that much is true, but his body is made of thousands of golden leaves, crispy like the wind in autumn, and they slide over each other as he stretches his tail this way and that. The woman, who the witch called Vanna, is the most beautiful woman Alissa has ever seen. Her dress is a deep green velvet with a high collar that shows off the perfect curve of her throat, and her black hair is swept up in an intricate knot at the top of her head, just the way Alissa has stitched fine ladies swirling around a ballroom. There is no sign of an owl, although Alissa supposes she's probably sleeping.

The juggler she recognises as though she's been looking at his picture all her life. He is the same as when she saw him in the silk, right down to the sly grin. Maybe he will recognise her, too. Now's the time to find out.

She stands, her heart banging so hard against her ribs she fears they'll crack. She licks her dry lips and straightens her cloak. 'Wish me luck,' she whispers to the geese as she moves across the path, skipping behind a wheelbarrow full of cabbages.

She is close enough now to hear the jingling of coins in the juggler's pocket, and she's about to call out her pretend greeting when there is a commotion of flapping behind her and she spins around to see the geese lift from the water in a dark cloud of beating wings and soar upriver in their skein. She's standing right next to the lion made of leaves, and she is close enough to hear the woman called Vanna say, 'My mother used to say it was good luck, to see the first geese of spring.'

Alissa hovers for a moment, her gaze flicking between the group and the geese. Her courage is ebbing, but she knows there is no choice.

Then the juggler turns to her and smiles. 'Ah! It's you,' he says. 'I've been waiting for you. I knew you'd join us at some point.'

Four pairs of eyes stare at the juggler. Vanna and Goat frown, then turn to look at Alissa. The lion made of leaves looks suspicious, his eyes narrowed to slits.

'Do you know this girl?' Vanna says, and Alissa notes with a swoop of worry that there is a hint of jealousy in her voice.

'Yes,' says the juggler.

'No,' says Alissa at the same time.

The lion made of leaves comes to stand in front of her, and she is careful to keep her gaze on his golden eyes and not on the spaces between the leaves that make up his body. There is a rustling as he moves, like the wind through the highest branches, but when he stops Alissa can't even hear his breath.

He holds her gaze for a long moment, the corners of his mouth turned down with a sneer, but something like triumph in his eyes. *He thinks he has won something*, she thinks. *I wish the witch had told me about this bit.*

Then the leaf-lion turns to the juggler with his back arched and his tail in the air and makes a growl in the back of his throat. His voice makes Alissa flinch; it is so lion-like, such a roar that if she shut her eyes she would think the creature making it were a real beast and not an enchantment.

'I knew you couldn't be trusted,' the leaf-lion says, his leaves bristling on his back. 'I knew you were up to something. Another someone else who's going to ruin our shows, another freeloader?'

'Lion!' gasps the woman called Vanna, but the golden creature ignores her. Alissa opens her mouth to protest but the juggler puts out a hand to hush her. She obeys him, swallowing her words. This is going very badly.

'Have you been telling all your edge-dwelling mates to join the party? Free food and an all-expenses-paid trip to the city?'

'I think you're overreacting,' the goat says quietly, trying to get between the juggler and the lion. 'He's only said hello to the poor girl.'

'He said she was joining us!' the lion growled. 'You heard him, he said he'd been waiting for her! What does he have to say for himself, eh?'

But instead of turning to the juggler for an explanation, all four pairs of eyes fix on Alissa. Her face becomes hot and her bundle feels heavy in her hand. To gain time, she places it carefully at her feet.

'I can explain,' she says, trying to keep her voice steady and look more at the goat and Vanna, who are only puzzled rather than angry like the leaf-lion creature. 'I've come a long way, from the far north, and I'm very pleased to meet all of you. I was told to meet you all here as I have a message for the juggler.'

She has already decided that she will say nothing of the witch or the Tower to these other people, and seeing the leaf-lion's tail drop a little she's glad.

'Go on then,' the lion says, a little testily. 'Give him your message.'

Vanna tuts and grabs at the lion's front leg. 'Give them some privacy, idiot, you've already frightened the poor girl enough!'

And she tugs at the lion until he follows her and the goat away from their carriage and the bridge, marching off towards the wharves upriver. But as he goes he looks back over his shoulder at her with his golden eyes narrowed, and again she flinches at his anger.

Rym Kechacha

The juggler sighs. 'Don't worry about him. He's got some issues.'

She turns back to him, trying to wipe that glare from her mind.

'I didn't know if you would know me or not,' Alissa says shyly. This isn't going quite as she had expected. She had thought she would find someone a little confused, maybe a little out of place in the world. She had thought he would be travelling with the circus folk because they had taken pity on him out in the wilderness and were escorting him somewhere safe. She hadn't known if he would recognise her, or if she would have to pretend that she had come upon him by chance. Now it seems the juggler is the one taking care of his companions, not that the lion creature appreciates it; and not only does he know who she is, he's actually been waiting for her.

'Of course I would.' The juggler smiles, and pats the log he sits on for her to join him. 'That golden hair is distinctive, you girls have always had it. Can't miss you.'

Alissa sits on the log and shuffles, leaving a narrow gap between them. She frowns. Why is he talking about her hair?

'I was told I had to find you,' Alissa begins.

'Well, now you have.'

'But no one told me what I had to do when I found you, so what I've been thinking—'

The juggler slaps his hands on his thighs and gives a high peal of laughter that echoes from the trees like the clear ring of a bell. 'Can you sing?'

'What?'

'If you can sing, they'll let you stay.'

Alissa considers this. Does she even want to stay with the circus troupe? 'I don't know,' she says. 'I've never tried.'

'Try now,' the juggler says. He leaps up and disappears into the carriage. He appears a few moments later with a beautiful fiddle, and before Alissa can protest or try to get him to sit down again so she can talk to him about why he is in the world and what they're going to do about it, the juggler is drawing the bow across the strings, his eyes shut and a blissful smile on his lips, bouncing his knee with the rhythm.

Alissa recognises the tune, but the juggler is several phrases into his playing before she places it. Her heart catches and begins to thump, her palms dampen. She stands up from the log and clutches at her skirts for comfort, staring helplessly at the dancing juggler, lost in his tune.

'Sing, then!' he calls to her. 'Just sing the melody if you don't know the words.'

She shuts her eyes and the image of herself, bent over the silk mantle of the world, comes into her head. She thinks of the room in the Tower as it was the last time she heard this music, the heavy silence around the drone of Mandoré's voice calling the patterns. She starts to hum the tune the juggler is playing, then opens her mouth and sings. She doesn't know the words, she didn't even know there were any words to this song, but her voice swoops around the strings of the fiddle and ties the sound together with the lapping of the water in the river.

The juggler stops playing and she blinks her eyes open. He has the fiddle across his lap and he's looking at her with that sly look of secrets again.

'Yes, I think you'll do nicely,' he says.

'I'll do for what?'

He glances around him, then leans towards her. 'We're preparing a show,' he confides, stroking his thumb along the fiddle bow. 'We're going to perform it in Uranga at the Midsummer carnival, and it's going to be very special. It's going to put us on the map.'

'Alright—'

'And you, Alissa the sewing girl in exile, will be our secret weapon. Vanna will be the forest nymph, you can be the water nymph, and Lion will be the flood. Vanna will play the fiddle and you'll sing, and Goat will be there to sweep up the showers of coral rings. When they hear you sing they'll be crazy for it.'

Alissa feels her face become hot.

'How did you know I was a sewing girl?'

The juggler laughs. 'Oh, there're things in heaven and earth you will never know of, young lady! You can either ask and ask and make it boring, or you can dive into the mystery! That's the beauty of it all.'

'But I sewed you! I heard the music and the wordlight did something weird and it made you. Then Mandoré found out and he said I had to leave the Tower. I found the witch and she told me where to find you and now I'm here, but I don't know what to do next, none of this makes any sense!'

The juggler shrugs. 'I don't know anything about that, Alissa. I only know you were meant to be with us here, in our show, and come with us to Uranga. Are you in?'

Alissa shakes her head to clear it of the fog that listening to the juggler's riddles has made.

'Alissa, are you in?' the juggler asks. He reaches out for her chin and tips her head towards him. She stares into his black eyes and nods helplessly. It isn't as if she has anywhere else to go.

'What about the rest of your friends? They don't seem to like you very much.'

The juggler waves his hand airily. 'Oh, it's just Lion who's a pain in the arse, the others are fine, you'll see. They'll accept you no problem, once they hear you sing.'

His gaze flickers to the place over her shoulder and the sly smile widens.

'They're back,' he says. He grabs the fiddle and tucks it under his chin. 'Come on, sewing girl, show them what you can do.'

Alissa turns to see the lion, the goat and the woman called Vanna standing with trays of steaming bowls and packages of bread. She tries to smile at them but the juggler cries, 'Sing, Alissa!' and she finds herself compelled to open her mouth and let the pitch of the fiddle echo in her throat and sing that eerie song again. The market day crowd streaming around them fades and she forgets to be embarrassed about who might hear her. To her surprise, she finds she is enjoying the feeling of these sounds coming from her mouth. She does not find them pleasing on the ear; there is a quiver in the high notes that sounds wrong to her and she is too quiet, but there is a feeling of the tune on her tongue that feels like gulping water in the grip of a powerful thirst.

The lion makes a growl in the back of his throat, but the goat takes two tentative steps towards her then sits on his hind legs to listen. The woman sways along with the music, slopping the gravy from her bowls onto her tray.

The juggler finishes the song with a vibrato flourish and Alissa lets her voice fade. The bustle of the road and the bridge crashes into her again. She puts one hand to her chest. Her lungs feel airy and cool, like she's been running in the snow.

'Well, Juggler,' says Goat, rising and coming closer to them. 'You've been keeping her quiet.'

The juggler performs a sweeping courtly bow and takes a bowl from Vanna's tray. 'I like to surprise my friends.'

Vanna puts the tray on the back steps of their carriage and comes to hold Alissa by the shoulders. Alissa stares up at the beautiful woman, her rosewater scent tickling her nose. 'You've such a beautiful voice!' she says, and Alissa stammers her thanks. 'Where did you learn to sing like that?'

Alissa glances at the juggler. He licks his spoon of all the meat juices before he answers.

'She used to work in the best circus in the world,' he says. 'They travelled all over and got standing ovations every night.'

'And what circus was that?' the lion says, raising one eyebrow in a surprisingly human way.

'You won't have heard of it,' the juggler says, and he returns to his stew.

'Never mind that, Lion,' Goat says. 'She can be with us now! What do you think, Vanna?'

The woman smiles, her delicate teeth like porcelain. 'I think it's a terrific idea. She can play one of the parts in the new show, either of the gowns I'm making will look smashing with this hair.'

'Lion?' asks Goat.

The lion looks at her with a hunter's blank stare. 'Fine,' he says. 'Do whatever you want.'

He stares hard at Alissa, just to let her know he's unhappy at the way this has worked out, then drops his head and starts to groom his paw.

'Here's how it works,' Goat says, and Alissa blinks to hold his steady gaze and let him know she's reliable. 'We travel together, take turns driving the carriage, and sleep inside unless it's warm out or we're really flush and can pay for an inn. You get one coral ring a month and all other money is held in common for food and costumes and the like. Agreed?'

Alissa nods. 'Agreed.' She feels a little dizzy.

He shifts his weight so he can hold out his hoof. She reaches for it, shakes it gently.

Goat shows his teeth. 'Welcome aboard,' he says.

> • <

There are the yellow catkins of the hazel, dangling in the breeze. There is the rain, spraying on Alissa's face as she rides with her face out the window when she feels too sick from the swaying of the carriage. There are the celandines, bright patches of sun among the clanging of the bluebells on the forest floor. There is Owl, swooping ahead on the road with the tethers on her claws while the air is still.

'How long do we have until our show?' Alissa sits next to Vanna on the bench inside the carriage, every jolt of the wheels pushing their shoulders together. It is dusk and the only light is the candle inside the lantern that swings from the roof.

Vanna wipes her hands on her skirt and bites her lip as she thinks. 'Do you know, I'm not so sure. Lion always used

to take care of the dates and things like that, before he—
well, I think I'm supposed to do it now, but I haven't really
got the hang of it yet.'

Vanna leans forward to peer at Lion, asleep on the floor
with his tail twitching as he dreams. She sighs. She counts
on her fingers, shakes her head, starts to count again.

'It'll probably take us until the middle of Taurus to get to
the ferry port the juggler wants to go to. Then it'll take us
the rest of that month to travel down the river, so we should
be getting into Uranga just as Gemini begins.'

'Right,' says Alissa. She's still confused, but she sits back
on the bench and leans against the juddering wall of the
carriage. The juggler is driving and he never has much
concern for potholes or ruts or other traffic on the road;
he just swerves around all obstacles with a shout of glee.
Alissa puts one hand over her mouth and stifles a retch
of motion sickness. Vanna offers her a ginger chewing
sweet and she takes one gratefully. They nibble together
in silence, listening to the juggler's muffled whoops and
the indignant bleats from the sheep and their shepherd as
they pass.

> • <

There is the carriage, standing in a muddy ditch at the side
of the road, its sails flapping a little as the wind lifts the
young leaves from the branches. There is the juggler on the
platform of the carriage, globes of light tumbling between
his hands.

Vanna removes her fiddle from its tucked-up place under
her chin and glowers at Goat.

'I have never said I wanted the water nymph to hide!' She puts her fiddle at her feet and balls her fists. 'You always twist what I say. I *said*, I think Alissa should bow when she sees the Minstrel, *before* she unbraids her hair for the dance.'

Alissa stands between Goat and Vanna, shifting from foot to foot. In front of her Lion has a well-I'm-not-saying-a-word smirk on his face, and Alissa thinks he is pleased that, for once, it's not him arguing.

'Maybe I could—' Alissa begins before Goat stamps his hoof with a splash of mud.

'You're not in charge here, Vanna!' Goat cries. 'This is a collaborative production, you hear me? You can't just dictate what you think the rest of us should do.'

Vanna's eyes glisten and she sniffs. Very deliberately, she smooths her skirt, picks up her fiddle, and walks away from Goat.

'I need some time alone,' she says quietly as the juggler steps off the platform to let her past. 'Please don't disturb me.'

Goat bleats with frustration and turns on his hoof to stalk away into the forest.

'So,' says the juggler, turning towards Alissa, 'do you think we should practise the dance then? You need a bit more practice on that turn, you know the one I mean, where we swoop into the bow pose. You keep stumbling.'

'I think we all need a break, Juggler,' Alissa says, gathering her hair and bunching it in her hands to braid. She hates that dance. She can't do it the way the juggler wants her to, and every time she stumbles, which is often, her hair jerks out of the juggler's grip and her eyes smart. He apologises, and when Vanna isn't arguing with Goat she offers helpful tips, but still Alissa finishes most rehearsals with a headache and a leaden feeling of failure.

'But you've had less practice than the rest of us!' he says, dropping his glowing juggling balls to the ground and striding towards her. 'We can't get this wrong Alissa, it's the whole pathos of the show!'

She narrows her eyes and lowers her hands to her hips. 'No. More. Rehearsal.' *How would the witch speak to this man if she wanted him to listen?* she thinks. *What kind of terror would she put into her voice to make him fearful of crossing her?*

The juggler glares back at her. A crow caws close by, then black wings flutter in her face, feathers bristling in her nostrils. She ducks back with a splutter, but the juggler laughs and greets the crow with an answering caw and puts the bird on his shoulder.

'Fine,' he says with a shrug. 'You win.'

He turns and walks into the forest, in the opposite direction to Goat. The crow caws again and the juggler sniggers, sharing the joke.

'Why can't we all get on, Lion?' Alissa sits on the edge of the platform, rubbing at her scalp. She takes her hair in her hands again and begins to divide it for braiding.

'We used to,' he says, leaping up onto the platform to settle down on his front paws. 'Before the juggler joined us.'

'Really? You're telling me that Vanna and Goat never argued before they met the juggler?'

Lion chuckles. 'Well, they did always used to fight, that's true. But they usually made up before too long.'

Alissa's fingers twist down her hair and she ties the end off with a scrap of ribbon Vanna gave her. She doesn't notice

Lion watching the way the spring light glows along the strands as they spiral.

'Maybe it's just the stress of doing something new,' she says. 'Vanna told me you used to do your own acts so you didn't need to do all this...'

Alissa waves her hand vaguely.

'Collaboration?' Lion says with a grin.

Alissa laughs. 'Exactly.'

They hear a sound like a sniff from inside the carriage and exchange a guilty glance.

'Do you think the show will be good?' Lion asks quietly.

Alissa is surprised to be asked and not sure what to say. The truth is she hasn't seen any kind of show since she lived at the home for orphans, when a travelling troupe came by to sing and dance and pull silly faces to entertain the children for bowl of stew and a coral ring or two. She's watched this troupe's acts since she joined, handing around the hat while Lion contorts and Vanna plays her fiddle and the juggler performs his tricks with those glowing orbs he won't let anyone else touch, and they are far better than anything she's ever seen. On their best nights, they bring a sense of magic to the towns they visit, a sense that somewhere in the land there is wonder and chivalry and glamour that might be within reach, if only the music doesn't stop.

'Yes,' she says, uncertainly. 'I think people'll enjoy it. I'm just not sure if we will.'

Lion smiles. 'We probably won't.'

He swishes his tail from side to side and yawns. Alissa tries not to look at his teeth as his mouth gapes wide. Vanna told her he's self-conscious about his teeth. She waits for him to say more, but he just settles on his belly and listens to the birds singing. It occurs to her that this is the first conversation she's ever had with Lion that wasn't him moaning about the juggler or whatever Vanna brought from the market for lunch. She glances at him, his shiny wet nose twitching in the fresh air. She realises she is glad he's being nice. Being with this strange group of people feels better if Lion's being nice.

> • <

There are the rushes, whispering the secrets of the rivers all over the land. There are the boats of oak and iron and canvas, just as she used to stitch them. There are the gleaming fish in the baskets on the jetty, the eels wriggling in the nets, the cries of the fishwives flying across the dock. Alissa looks around her with unease. She recognises all of it. One night, many years ago, she heard this place and these people as a chanting drone and she stitched it on grey silk for it to flow into the world. She clenches and flexes her still-callused hands.

Goat gathers them together before he goes to the ticket booth.

'Now, can I save the coral and get us one cabin, or are you all going to kill each other before we sail?'

Vanna clamps her lips together and nods tightly. The juggler smirks. Alissa wants to look at Lion and roll her eyes but she doesn't, just in case he isn't looking back at her.

'Go on, Goat, get us all one cabin,' the juggler laughs. 'We'll play nicely, we promise.' He looks slyly to one side. 'Well, I will. I can't speak for Lion.'

Lion makes a growl in the back of his throat and Goat tuts and trots off to the ticket office.

Their ship is huge, pitching and rolling in the river like a kite in a storm. Alissa watches it straining against its moorings, each creak of the oak boards and snap of a sail makes her flinch. She looks at the railings on the deck that don't look very secure, the cubby right at the top of the mast for some unlucky soul to ride, the round windows cut into the wood suspiciously close to the water line. Maybe she could meet them in the next town.

'It's a good wind for sailing,' Vanna says as she sits on her trunk among a mound of other passengers' luggage. Alissa carries her own bundle over one shoulder. She doesn't reply. This wind doesn't seem very good to her, but she's never been on any kind of boat before, so what does she know? She has, however, embroidered shipwrecks and cargo bobbing in the waves and children reaching for their mothers' sodden skirts as they drown in unmanageable currents. She says none of this to Vanna.

Goat and the juggler oversee the stevedores hauling their carriage up the ramp into the bowels of the ship while Owl perches on Vanna's shoulder, her feathers twitching each time one of the heaving men slaps the flank of the carriage to push it through the narrow opening of the hold. Alissa is dreading the moment when the carriage finally disappears inside, for then Goat and the juggler will return and they will all go to the end of the jetty together to climb the rope ladder.

Lion comes back from the hawkers on the dock dragging a tightly wrapped parcel with grease marks. He unties the string with his teeth and Alissa takes a turnip pie and bites into it gratefully, hoping it will settle her nervous stomach.

By the time they have all clambered up the rope ladder – and helped Goat when his back hooves got stuck – found their cabin, argued about who was going to sleep on the bottom hammocks, stashed Vanna's trunk, put the juggler's box in a safe place, and made a perch by the round little window for Owl, most of Alissa's turnip pie has come back up again and is dripping in bilious strings down the outside of the ship.

Vanna rubs her back as she retches over a bucket a sailor kicked towards them.

'You poor thing, I clean forgot this might happen. It is a little rough today, I'm feeling slightly queasy myself.'

Alissa feels the ship sway under her knees and closes her eyes. There is no earth any more, nothing solid to grab onto, everything is moving and there is no up, no down, where is the sky, where are her hands, why can't everything just be still! But it is all worse if she shuts her eyes, so she opens them again to see feet streaming past her face in all directions.

'Oh look, we're leaving,' Vanna says. 'See if you can look up and say goodbye.'

Alissa thrusts her head back into the bucket and her breakfast porridge joins the stinking mess in there to a chorus of sailors' yells and passengers' cries.

As dusk falls, Alissa sways in one of the lower hammocks as the ship rolls from side to side. Owl sits on her perch by the little round window and nibbles at a rat one of the sailors gave to the juggler. Alissa hums softly to block out the sounds of Owl crunching bones and sinew. There is nothing left in her stomach but bile to bring up.

There is a knock at the door and Lion pushes it open with his nose. He drags something into the room behind him, then pads over to where she lies, swaying. Alissa quickly shoves the bucket to the other side of the hammock. It is clean; Vanna helped her sluice it out earlier, but still, she feels embarrassed at the thought of Lion seeing such a disgusting, intimate sight.

'Where are the others?'

'Up on deck,' Lion says. 'Juggler's entertaining the other passengers with his tricks.'

Alissa struggles to sit up but slides down the canvas until she's slumped. 'You can be with them,' she says. 'You don't need to keep me company, I don't mind.'

'No, no.' Lion is quiet for a moment. 'They're playing a game that I don't really like to play, so I thought I'd come down here. Vanna told me to bring you this.' He drags a tray with a teapot and a mug on it towards her. Alissa swings her legs over the hammock and pours a steaming golden liquid from the pot. She takes a sip and winces as the fire slips down her raw throat.

'She begged the ginger from one of the sailors and snuck into the kitchens to make it,' Lion says. 'I think she's got more, so don't save that for later.'

Alissa sips the tea in silence. It warms her from the belly up, and surprisingly makes her feel better. She will not know what to say to Vanna in the morning; the only time anyone else has been this kind to her was when the witch took her in on the night of the storm.

'What game are they playing up there?' She's not up to the boisterous noise of company, but she doesn't want them to feel as though she's not joining in. She remembers that from the orphans' home, the idea that you should seek to blend in with what the majority were doing, for no better reason than it was deemed strange to want to be on your own. At the Tower there was no joining anything, only the whims of the wordlight.

'Oh, it's just a drawing game,' Lion says, and Alissa thinks she can hear something deliberately unconcerned and airy in his voice. 'I never play it. I don't like drawing any more.'

Lion leaps gracefully into the other hammock and they lie swaying as darkness closes over the cabin. Alissa tries to make her hammock move with the movement of the boat rather than against it, and she finds it is actually a little bit comforting. Lion starts to snore, and she listens to his breath rustle his leaves until the sound becomes a part of her own dreams of forests and winds and silken apples falling from autumn orchards.

> • <

There are the grumpy herons, watching the ships pass by in the early morning. There are the sing-song calls of the sailors; ship ahoy, overhaul, list starboard jacks. There are the willows and alders along the eastern – port – side of the river, passing behind her before she has time to say their names. Alissa did not know that the world looks this way from the rivers. All those years, all those watery stitches making something to do with wells or rain or rivers or fountains, and never did she consider all the things in the world that count the water as their home.

They've been sailing for eleven days now and Alissa is finally able to hold down her breakfast, lunch and supper and feel cheerful about it. Some days they are becalmed in the river, the wind still and the sailors lounging lazily in the lower berths. Those are her favourite days. She likes to sit on the deck with her bare feet dangling between the railings, the river lapping at the keel, watching the coots splash and the swans gliding just beyond the ship's wake.

Sometimes, Lion joins her. He keeps his paws well away from the water line and his whiskers within the railings, sitting in silence. Alissa points out the interesting things they pass on the water but normally he just grunts in response, barely even opening an eye.

Now he comes to settle next to her and stands expectantly, making her think he wants something.

Alissa groans. 'Please don't say you've been sent to fetch me for a rehearsal?'

Lion chuckles. 'No fear, there's no rehearsals today. Juggler's playing canasta with some sailors, Goat's in the kitchens looking for some lunch for Owl, and Vanna's at her mending in the cabin. You're safe.'

'Lucky me.'

Lion turns so his hind quarters face away from her, and settles. He gives one paw a few licks, then sniffs. Alissa waits. She thinks he might be in one of his rare talkative moods but she's learnt it's best to wait for him to start a conversation in case he gets grumpy and walks away, tail raised proudly in the air.

'You're not like the juggler.'

'I know.'

'How do you know him again?'

Alissa hesitates. The juggler has never again referred to her as a sewing girl or talked about waiting for her or any of those puzzling things he said that day by the Patli Bridge. He barely even gives a hint that he and Alissa have a secret, he treats her much as he does Vanna: with polite courtesy and dry humour.

'We used to work together,' she says finally.

'In a circus?'

'Not really. It was a kind of… dressmaking shop. I used to be a seamstress.'

Lion grins. 'I bet you're itching to take over the costume making from Vanna then, aren't you?'

Alissa shudders. 'No! I've had enough of sewing.' She looks out over the railing and sees the water flowing by. It reminds her of the silk mantle flowing over her hands and out of the Tower into the world. For a second she thinks she sees farms and villages and roads embroidered on the water, a whole night's work flashing by in an instant. She blinks to clear the vision and the river is just water again.

'I wasn't very good at it anyway,' she says. She's thinking about Mandoré looming over her, his face screwed up in contempt, about the other girls on her shift, about the pipe music she heard just before the wordlight made the juggler, the song he made her sing that day when the bluebells were ringing.

Lion is tactfully silent. He knows a lot about life moving out of your grip until it has become something else altogether. They watch the river, each thinking about the transformation that has shattered their former selves into a thousand invisible pieces.

When the juggler calls them for a rehearsal, they share an exasperated smile before they stand, and Alissa is surprised to find that she doesn't want to be around the others, she was enjoying the time alone with Lion. She walks ahead of him to climb carefully down the stairs to the mess deck.

Lion follows her. He is surprised to find himself wanting to touch her hair, to run the fingers he used to have from her warm scalp to the soft curls that hang by her waist. It is not like the feelings he gets when Goat rolls onto his back and leaves his soft belly exposed, and Lion has to go outside to chew at a fibrous piece of bark to stop himself from drawing his claw from Goat's throat to his balls to get at the soft organ meat just below the skin, which makes him glad in a way he can't quite explain to himself.

No, this is like the feeling he got when the flashing eyes of the witch caught his and the sun sparkled on her azure skin. But let no one say that this lion made of leaves has not learnt his lesson. His lusts will not lead him into catastrophe again. So he climbs silently down the stairs, and when he's walking on the soft rushes below deck he lets his claws creep from his paws and contents himself with that delicious juddering feeling of release. It is enough. It must be enough, now.

> • <

The gleaming spires of Uranga appear on the first day of Gemini. The sailors give up a huge cheer and all the passengers run up the steps to see the end of their journey approach. They blink in the fierce light and stagger as the boat lurches over the wake of the other ships coming into the city. The sun shines belligerently in a cloudless sky but the deck is still slick from the rain the night before, so Vanna holds onto Goat's collar as they stand by the railings, admiring the view.

Lion stands next to Alissa in the bow, eyes squinted. The wind that buffets the sails makes his leaves rustle, but this sound is a comfort to her now. It means that Lion is somewhere nearby and is probably fixing some kind of morose joke, likely at the juggler's expense.

'Have you been here before?' asks Lion. His leaf mane flows from his head, and in this light it looks as if the air bursts into flames as it touches him. Alissa sneaks glances at him in between craning her neck over the crowd to see the city. The wind has everyone huddled in their cloaks but her face and neck are warm. She presses her cold fingers to her cheeks and hopes no one can see her blush and wonder why.

She shakes her head. 'Have you?'

'Only once.'

Smoke rises from the slate chimneys and drifts south with the wind, bringing with it the scent of murky canal water.

'I came with my mother and father when I was a child,' Lion continues. 'We came in on the ferry. When we saw the first towers, just like this, my mother told me the story of how the city came to be.'

'What happened?' Alissa asks. 'I don't know that story.'

'Really?' Lion turns to her, his golden mane aglow. Alissa feels dizzy. 'Do you want to hear it?'

'Of course.'

'Well, the grandmothers say long ago, when the moon's daughter came to our land, she wanted to make a city of water, to remind her of her home in the sky. The thirteen spirits of the earth didn't want her to, they wanted all the people to stay on the land where they could farm and look after them properly. Of course, the moon's daughter tricked them. She gathered raindrops and spun them into thread and sent them to the Tower, where the corn-haired girls obey the moon's daughter's wishes—'

Alissa looks back to the place on the horizon where the smoke rises. Could Lion have guessed? Is that why he's telling her this story? Her face flushes hotter.

'—and when they started to sew, rivers snaked across the earth, flowing from the sea into a spiral at the very centre of the land. A city started to take shape. Folk who used to hack roots out of the forests and drag their oxen across fields left their lands and came to seek their fortune. They built houses on the islands and they paved the deosil road. They made coracles to navigate the waters and ships like this one to trade grain and cloth from the world beyond. Smiths and bakers and wheelwrights and weavers moved in, then cart drivers and night-soil men. Musicians and doctors and teachers followed when they saw it was a good life. They elected burghers and seven seamstresses spent a month making a council cloak from the finest silk—'

Vanna, who is listening from the other side of Lion, interrupts.

'My grandmother told me the moon's daughter herself lay down in a spiral and made the widdershins canal with the water in her own blood.'

'Well, it's a legend,' says Lion with a hint of impatience. 'Everyone tells it differently.'

'But, you see—' Vanna is warming to her theme '—your version can't be right because we didn't have the council cloaks in the times you're talking about, they were invented after the revolution, weren't they? Don't you remember learning about it in school?'

Lion is looking annoyed but Vanna continues.

'And my grandmother remembered the revolution and she told me about it and there were no council cloaks before it, but Uranga has been here for ages, since the beginning of creation. So you shouldn't say the women made a cloak for the burghers if it can't be true.'

'Vanna,' Lion says. 'It's a story. Stop ruining it.'

He turns back to Alissa. 'Anyway, Uranga was given by the moon's daughter to everyone in the world in defiance of the thirteen earth spirits and that's why it's special. The end.'

There is a hint of a sulk around his jaws now and Alissa bites back her smile. She knows more than either of them about the way the world is made, but she's not about to add her own arguments to theirs. She has nothing to prove where she spent her youth other than the colour of her hair.

'It's a great story, whichever way you tell it,' she says, and that seems to call a truce. They all turn their faces to the wind to watch the towers coming closer, and Alissa takes a long, deep breath. The air smells like the city: woodsmoke and sawdust and shit and beer. She shuts her eyes and listens to Lion's leaves rustling beside her, the sails slackening as the sailors run to the oars and begin to sing their heaving song. The Tower feels like a distant dream. If she'd have known making a juggler would get her exiled into a world of such terrifying, exhilarating beauty, she would have done so a long time ago.

BALLADE

The witch rolls from her broomstick onto a patch of moss
and whoops with delight. The moon is bulging and full
above her and the sky in the west is only a purple glow with
the first of the stars beginning to flicker into sight. She shuts
her eyes and listens to the forest, waiting to hear the shouts
of her sister witches arriving for their sabbat. There it is: a
low humming deep in the trees. The witch grins. From a
pocket inside her blue and gold dress she takes out her pot
of vision ointment. She lets her cloak and her dress and her
stockings fall from her body and stands naked as she rubs it
in. The smell of henbane and wolf fat makes her swoon but
she wallows in it, there is no more seductive scent to her.
She rubs the grease all over, dipping her fingers into every
crease; at the backs of her knees, her elbows, the hollows
at her armpits, under her breasts, her vulva, the rolls of
her stomach that appear when she reaches for the spaces
between her toes. Her nipples become hard and her flesh

pimples like a chicken skin as the night breeze caresses her body. She shivers with delight. The forest starts to sing to her, the call of her sister witches the bass notes in the chorus. She flings the pot of ointment onto the pile of her clothes that lie by her besom and plunges into the trees. The moonlight makes her blue skin glow like a sapphire.

The elderberry wine is already flowing in the small meadow between willows by a gurgling stream. The moon is reflected in the ripples and the gathered witches take turns to float towards it and bathe in its beauty in the water. Some of the witches greet her with her mother's name and others shriek in gleeful welcome, flicking a finger to send her a mug of wine. Others come to kiss her on the mouth and twist locks of her scarlet hair around their fingers to test her strength. She grins, swigs at her wine, and slips into the cool stream. A film of the vision ointment rises from her skin and is borne away by the flowing water. Magic thrums in her belly. There is nothing as delicious as a sabbat with her sisters.

The night becomes darker, the sky drawing from indigo to black, and the witch is idling in a pool with bulrushes tickling her neck and eels lazing along her legs when there is a shriek from the bank.

'Look to your thumbs, sisters!' comes the cry, and the witch struggles to open her eyes and focus on the shadow of the drooping willows across the moon. 'There is something afoot!'

The witch pulls her hands out of the water and the eels slink away. She squints. Even in this darkness she can see there is something fire-like about her thumbs, like embers flaming in the wind.

A shrieked command comes from the meadow: 'Sisters! Gather on the bank!'

The witch hauls herself out of the water, still staring at her thumbs. There is an excitement building in her. She half expected something like this on this night. She knows why her thumbs blush so: this is the full moon of Gemini, and whatever the girl Alissa is mixed up in is coming to pass now.

The mother of the coven stands at the centre of the circle with her silver staff held to the sky, her legs spread wide and her shoulders quivering with the power of the moon as it flows through her. The witch takes her place in the circle and holds out her thumbs alongside her sister witches. She sees now that while her sister witches look as if they have dipped their thumbs in blood, hers are alight, and there are murmurs of surprise among the other witches at the brightness of her skin. There is no doubt that whatever is coming, is coming for her.

The mother of the coven turns to face the witch and points the silver staff right at her face. The witch begins to feel a frantic buzzing in her belly. She swallows hard, and when the mother of the coven gestures to her to speak, she begins to tell her sisters what happened one night in the winter when she gave an exiled sewing girl shelter in a storm.

'You're right, sisters,' she says as the other witches listen quietly, their thumbs burning vermilion. 'There is something huge afoot, something I know only a strand of. I will tell you what I know and then we will ask Mother Moon for her guidance.

'I had a vision, in my singing bowl, of a yellow-haired girl with feathers at her navel who would walk along my valley in a midwinter storm. When she came, I gave her shelter and I scried for her.'

The mother of the coven keeps the silver staff pointed steadily at the witch's eyes. It gleams in the moonlight and gives the witch courage to speak the truth to her sisters.

'The threads tangled around her were many, and they shone brightly. She was to fall in love with a lion made of leaves, a creature I myself made when, as a man, he attempted to seduce me. She had embroidered the Trickster in an earthbound form when she was prisoner of the Thirteen in their Tower, and she was bound to meet him by the shores of the Saman River, in the company of the lion made of leaves and his circus troupe. Then I saw them sailing for the spiral city, with its waters roiling. The visions tasted of Mother Moon. I don't know what she means to tell me.'

When she has finished, there is silence in the meadow. The mother of the coven whistles, then looks up at the sky.

'Mother Moon,' she says softly, 'your daughter is a-tricking us.' She pinches her scarlet thumb and her forefinger together and pulls a black silk ribbon from the air. She holds it aloft so all the witches in the circle can see that their vision game is about to begin, then throws it onto the ground where it forms a perfect circle that the witches gather around.

'I will go first,' she says, 'and then the staff will choose.'

She stands frozen in the moonlight, pointing the silver staff at the moon, gripping its handle. It begins to shake like a dowsing stick and move towards the earth. The mother of the coven follows it, allowing it to fall onto the damp earth by the stream, where it starts to move, without her directing it, drawing lines that form a picture in the mud.

The staff glows, the signal that it wants to seek another player, and it hurls itself towards a sister witch, who catches it with two strong hands and lets it judder back to the earth. The staff starts to sketch another part of the picture.

On the outside of the circle the witches sway and sing. Their thumbs drip with blood.

They call it the exquisite corpse, but no one can remember why. The elders used to say that the game was a gift from the moon to the witches at the time of creation, a way of peeking between the threads of the tapestry to see what is written. The game, and anything revealed in it, exists in the ancient contract as a link between earth and sky, like the sisters themselves, and as such is bound by the same rules that constrain those in the Tower and she who writes the world.

And although all the sisters know they should remain poised in the middle between them, those old enemies and collaborators in creation, the earth below and the sky above, it is known that this is not how it always happens. There are stories about the sisters leaving that middle place and entering the tapestry on one side or the other, but the witch knows they are really warnings. The tales speak of witches who turned their allegiance firmly to the sky and plotted with the moon's daughter to release her from the Tower, or cast spells on the sewing girls to alter their stitches. Then there were those who did the bidding of the earth, entrapping the moon's daughter somewhere on the land to return her to the Thirteen, or selling talismans to the masked men to protect them from whatever she wrote. The stories were stark and violent and little told because it was not the sisters' task to keep the world or lose it. They were to remain exquisitely balanced in between, worshipping the moon but living upon the earth and dependent on the Thirteen's guardianship of everything in it for sustenance. As far as the contract went they were neither dead nor alive, a corpse that never rotted nor breathed.

The blue-skinned women take their turn with the silver staff, letting its power shiver through them to etch some still-murky picture of the future onto the muddy bank. As the witch suspected it would, the staff chooses her last. It drops its weight into her palm, draws a squiggle in the mud, and then hurls itself into the sky to join its forger. The mother of the coven watches it fly until it is only a speck in the darkness, then gestures to the sister witches to make a circle around the picture their silver staff has drawn. Each witch holds up her fading thumbs and whispers incantations to make light. Now the glade starts to blaze, the reflections of the sisters' thumbs flickering in the stream like fire. The eels and the frogs are scared away and they slip off downstream to let the eldritch creatures complete their magic.

There is silence while the sisters examine the message in the mud, each pair of violet eyes scanning the picture drawn inside the confines of the black ribbon.

Their silver staff has drawn something no one present, not even the ancient mother of the coven, has ever seen before. Drawn on the mud beneath their feet, they see the spires and masts of Uranga with its winding canal and broad plazas. They see the sun at its highest point, blistering the Gemini sky with its heat. They see a black-haired woman dressed as a forest nymph and a yellow-haired girl with her hair stretched behind her like the strings of a bow. They see a juggler diving into the black canal without making a single ripple. They see a woman with streaks of white in the faded shine of her yellow hair carrying a basket of thrumming labra wood, and a tall, hooded figure following her. They see a lion made of leaves dyed bright blue flip over, drawing water from the canal. The water comes and comes in a greedy black flood, rising like a wave over the city, drowning the plazas and flowing through the shutters and rising above the roofs, making islands of the spires. Then the water starts to seep across the fields and forests, turning everything slimy and black in its wake. It mixes with the rivers and poisons them, distorting their flow until the water reaches the sour sea and merges with the waves. Everything is dead, everyone is drowned, the world as they know it is ended, Mother Moon shining mutely on an endless, gleaming ocean.

And then they see their sister witch in the drawing too, the one who stands among them with her thumbs burning brightest of all. They see her holding the hand of a grey-haired woman with her palms scarred by labra wood, singing. In the background are more sister witches, and they are singing too.

The mother of the coven is swaying on her feet. Her eyes are squeezed tightly shut and tears follow salty tracks down her face.

'We are called, sisters,' she whispers, and there is a keening note of grief in her voice. 'The daughter of the moon has called the Trickster and moved against the earth spirits, and like everything else in creation, we must decide where we stand. I will not pronounce, I will not force anyone to turn a certain way, but turn one way each of you certainly must. If you see fit you may respect the star child's wishes and offer your sorrows to her mother the moon as the world expires and the contract is broken. Or, if you cannot let this world go, you may turn to the Thirteen and aid them in whichever way they seem to need.'

Fearful eyes turn to the witch with the brightest thumbs, whose heart is hammering like a woodpecker on an oak. There is no doubt in her mind which way she will turn. She has no choice, she has had no choice since that man first laid his eyes upon her.

'I will come to the earth, coven mother,' she says, and there are murmurs of surprise. 'I will go to the city and find the players and the sewing girl and try to stop the star child's flood. And if there is any help from my sisters, I will gladly take it.'

The mother of the coven smiles sadly. 'I cannot tell if this is what Mother Moon wishes or not, daughter. You go with my blessing, and I will offer my help if you call.'

Two more sisters come to the witch and touch her back to offer their help too. They are shocked, their eyes glazed. The witch bows to them and murmurs her thanks.

Another group of sisters stand in a huddle and shake their heads fearfully. 'I won't disobey the star child,' one of them says. 'I am afraid of dying but I am more afraid of her wrath. We're sorry, sister.'

The witch inclines her head respectfully and the group leave the meadow by the stream.

One of the older sisters, who may be the next mother of the coven, sighs heavily. 'I'll scry more on this. I cannot decide yet.'

The witch bows again. Her head is spinning, she is struggling to stay on her feet. What would her mother say if she could see her now? Would she have offered her help as her daughter stepped to the earth to tip the scales, or would she have turned to the sky? The witch swallows a lump in her throat. There is nothing to say her mother would be angry with her. None of her sisters seem angry. They look sad. And relieved it wasn't them with visions of the earth spirits in their Tower.

The other sisters pronounce their allegiances, one by one, and then they leave the meadow sadly. The flasks of elderberry wine are tipped into the stream and the fires of the thumbs are pinched out. The sisters return to their robes and broomsticks and mumble their farewells. Usually they would speak of where to meet on the full moon of Cancer, each sister offering her own forest glade or hill with a bawdy joke and a promise of cakes and wine and unsuspecting young men roaming the woods looking for adventure. But this night they are not sure if the world will survive to see another cycle of the moon. It is an unstoried situation, there is no way of knowing if the pictures in the mud will come to pass or not. One by one they fly off weeping, and when their tears fall from their faces they drop to the earth as hemlock seeds, which burrow into the earth to be hidden from the light before the sun rises.

By dawn, only the witch and the mother of the coven are left in the meadow, looking at the fading drawing of how the world ends.

'Do you think there's something else?' the mother of the coven asks. 'Something we're missing?'

The witch shrugs. 'There's always things we don't know.'

'Will you go to the city now, then?'

The witch gestures to her still-naked body with a wry smile, streaked with the grease from her vision ointment. 'Well, I was thinking of getting dressed first.'

And the coven mother cackles, startling the wrens from their song. She puts her muddy palm tenderly to the witch's face for a moment, and then she walks out of the meadow back into the forest. The witch stands alone, listening to the birds singing up the sun, thinking about how unlikely it is that she – moon-worshipping, human-shunning, poison-stewing hag – is now the being tasked with saving the world.

CANTUS FIRMUS

Section 1, clause 15(a)
The Earth spirits shall move around the land
freely, from the spiral city to the sour seas. They
shall take note of the seasons, the weathers, the
plants, and the beasts, and shall endeavour to aid
the star child in crafting all of creation accurately.

Here is a ship on the widdershins canal of the spiral city, Uranga, its sails slack as it rolls in the headwind. Here are the jetties and the stone bays and the sweating stevedores who haul barrels and crates from the boats and into the warehouses that line the canals. Here are the fishermen sailing in from the eastern sea, their holds packed with ice. Here are the jackdaws, strutting greedily along the canal sides eager for scraps from the merchants and hawkers, cawing their displeasure when they are chased away by tiny, giggling boys.

High in the silent Tower, Mandoré calls the patterns for the wordlight to snake around him and into the needles of the sewing girls. His voice is hoarse as he calls each moment of the city into being. He does not think of what will happen to the city when the books run out; he is disciplined and concentrated on the task at hand. The moment for that grief came this morning, just before dawn, when he descended the stairs to the cellar room. He took the next book on the shelf, glancing only briefly at its time signature before counting the rest of the books. Sixteen left. They have been running through them quicker and quicker in the past months; the council agrees it is part of the mess the star child left behind her.

He held the heavy book in his arms and leaned against the stone wall, dizzy. Shame prickled in his throat. He loosened his mask and wiped away the sweat from his upper lip. There is an unsaid and unsayable blame in the council these days, and the heaviness of his masked brothers' silence is beginning to choke him. Mandoré knows they think this is his fault because it was he who captured her, all those years ago. Maybe, he can see them thinking, he ruined something in her as he coaxed her into the cage. Or it could have been as he brought her out of the sky; did he take the proper precautions as he entered the Earth's atmosphere? He can feel the blame burning in their eyes as he moves around the Tower, and he's beginning to wonder if they're right. Maybe he did fuck it all up. Maybe the world really is ending because of him.

He gripped the seventeenth-to-last book to his chest and shook himself. Then he tied his mask again, climbed the stairs to the dormitory of the day shift, and shouted their wake-up call. When the girls heard that hoarse harshness in his throat they hurried to dress and comb their hair, even more silent than usual. All the masked men of the Tower have worn dark looks and heavy brows for months now. The older girls shrug when the younger ask them why. 'It's probably nothing to do with us,' they say. 'They get like this sometimes when they don't like what the pattern's making.'

Now he stands in the sewing room and calls the city, its thick smoke and its cart rumbles and the waste offal that gets flattened into the spaces between the cobbles. He has not told his masked brothers this, but he thinks the star child is there, in the city he is creating with her words. There are no clues in the books or the wordlight or the silk, just an intuition born of the connection between captor and captive, and the words of an old rhyme about a star child dripping her blood onto the land to make a spiral city.

He should go to Uranga himself to find her.

The conviction builds in him throughout the shift, even when the wordlight moves to form May blossom and elderflowers budding in the hedgerows and a village of badgers who decide to use a council cloak made of moss to govern themselves. Yes, he is sure of it. Whatever the star child is planning for the day when the books run out – Midsummer, the last day of Gemini – it will be in Uranga, the navel of the world. And she will be there to see it.

At sunset, he guides the day shift out of the Tower and back to their dormitory. On the other set of stairs he hears Eight taking the night shift up. Mandoré left the seventeenth-to-last book up there for Eight to call from, there's enough written to last at least until dawn.

He hangs around in the corridor outside the dormitory until Three and Ten come along with the day shift's dinner tray. He waits while they ladle out the bowls of soup, pour the tea, then clears his throat as they shut the door to the sewing room gently behind them.

'I'm thinking of going to the mountains for a few days. To Tristaane.'

Ten glances at him sharply. 'Was there a clue in the silk? Do you think she's there?'

Mandoré shakes his head, making his face look glum. It isn't too difficult. 'No,' he says. 'But I want to talk to the granite, see if they know anything.'

'Well, don't let the spring up there know what you're about,' says Three. 'You know what the water's like.'

Mandoré nods. Ten starts to load up the trolley with the emptied bins of the day shift. 'It's worth a shot,' he says. 'We haven't involved granite before and I think it's probably about time. To be honest, any ideas at this point are better than none.'

Three says, 'I'll take the day shift until you come back,' and Mandoré thanks him. They wheel the trolley away and let it clatter as they drag it down the stairs.

Mandoré leaves the Tower at midnight. At first, while he is within the perimeter of his brothers' influence, he walks west, towards Tristaane; but as soon as he feels the tug of the Tower lessen and the silk of creation steadier beneath his feet, he pulls his power around him to make a kind of suction space. He will be nowhere on the silk now, he is a negative stitch, a space that appears only on the ugly underside of the silk that no one looks at.

Then he turns directly south – to Uranga, to the middle of the world – to try to stop its ending.

ESTAMPIE

Section 6, clause 2
Uranga, as the navel of the world, shall be the
centre of all mortal activities and governed
by mortal laws as the star child has seen fit to
write. The widdershins and deosil canals shall be
trafficked upon according to the age and revered
according to custom.

Alissa has a headache. The noises in this city are too much for her. They never stop. From dawn the cockerels start, followed by yowling cats who try to get into the yards to invade the chicken runs and wander off with a feathered meal, but are thwarted by the honking guard geese and the furious barking of dogs. Then the merchants set up their market stalls, and unlike in the towns Alissa's been travelling through for the past months, there seems to be no logic here to where people sell their wares; she's seen no evidence of licenses or permits. The merchants shout until they're hoarse: 'Best wool to be had in the region, get your may blossom medicines before they go, freshly baked buns for your family.' Gangs of children zigzag through the legs of striding shoppers, chasing the geese and the pigeons and the crows, which occasionally take their revenge and chomp off a finger. Girls wander with their spinning tangling in cartwheels and boys duck down alleys with wheelbarrows while goodwives shriek at them to get out of the way. Foxes in bow ties strut along the deosil road, daring anyone to ask after what they've got in their pockets, and the bridges are almost always blocked with polecats that stink of musk trying to hitch a ride on the delivery boats winding their way into the centre of the city. Every so often the great bells of the city clang with a cacophony of voices, and then the streets teem with people trying to get where they were supposed to be, shoving at ambling idiots like Alissa who get in their way.

After dark, the thrum of the city starts to roar with mischief, and it gets louder each night as Carnival comes closer. The inns are full until past midnight, riots break out at closing time, and every night in one quarter of the city or another illegal fireworks are set off and whizz around the rooftops until they fall into the canal with a splutter and a hiss. The next morning, the city guards stomp down the streets and hammer at doors to arrest the firestarter for disrupting the peace of the realm, and the whole thing starts all over again with the cockerels.

The plaza where they've parked the carriage is probably the noisiest part of the city because that's where all the performers for the carnival are staying. The cobbles are covered with tents and carriages and carts; some magicians are even sleeping in upside-down coracles that everybody trips over in the dark. It's relatively quiet until noon, apart from the snores and occasional giggles when the performers stumble, bleary eyed, from their tents. Then the brewers' boys arrive with their barrels, someone will start playing arpeggios on an accordion, and the singing begins. All afternoon the plaza fills up with players at their rehearsals, weeping one moment and laughing the next, never a moment with a dull face. The acrobats make pyramids seven people tall then tumble from them in a fluid heap, and the singers flubber their lips and flex their voices with screams and gargles. The dancers stretch their bodies and practise their turns, and the drummers bounce their hands off the skins, competing to play faster and louder than the musicians in the pitch next to them.

When the sun sets there is a momentarily lull in the players' plaza, as the troupes spread across the city to seek out food and drink. But before the moon has risen over the rooftops everyone is back and merry and setting up their parties. Gone are the segregated groups of players glancing at other rehearsals from the corners of their eyes; now they all sprawl on stools and upturned empty barrels, and share beer, mead and stories of the road.

Every day, Goat tries to persuade Alissa and Lion to go and spy on a different troupe to see what shows are being prepared, but they laugh and wander off into the city together to buy honey cakes and get swept along with the throngs of people and animals lining the deosil road. Goat becomes increasingly tense as the days of Gemini creep on. Now he's registered them for a slot, he has nothing better to do than wait for the performance schedules to be announced, chase them all for rehearsals, and criticise the dresses Vanna is making.

The juggler disappeared into the city as soon as they disembarked from the boat, and since then has only been seen once. That was four days ago, when they came back from dinner to see him surrounded by a cheering, stamping crowd, his distinctive glowing balls arcing in the air.

Goat had made a panicked, squealing sound. 'Where has he been? We haven't done a rehearsal since we got here, I'm furious with him.'

Alissa glanced at Lion, who looked smug. It was the first time she had ever heard Goat say anything bad about the juggler.

They followed Goat as he pushed through the crowd, and spread out across the front row. Alissa was pleased when she saw the juggler wasn't doing his absolute best tricks, just some ordinary six- or seven-ball cascades that she knew cost him no effort.

Vanna leant over to her and whispered in her ear, 'Goat shouldn't worry we'll lose him.'

Alissa grinned, Lion made a facetious coughing noise, and the juggler caught all the balls and turned to them with mock surprise and a bow.

'And now, players, I have to leave it there. My troupe are back!'

The juggler ducked into the carriage to a storm of cheers and offers of drinks, and Goat shut the door behind them. Owl hooted with annoyance at being woken up and turned to the wall.

'Right, when's our next rehearsal,' Goat said. 'I've been watching some of what these other troupes are getting ready, and honestly, the competition's stiff.'

'Relax!' The juggler patted Goat on the head, which would have made Goat gnash his teeth with frustration had anyone else but the juggler been so condescending. 'We've been rehearsing for ages, we're ready.'

Goat nodded mutely and Alissa and Lion exchanged smiles. The juggler yawned and stretched his arms to the ceiling, brushing against the two dresses hanging there.

'Are these the costumes you've been making, Vanna?' He took them off their hangers and held them against his body, his face a painting of delight.

Vanna beamed and shivered with pleasure. 'They're almost finished,' she said. 'Do you like them?'

'Oh, I think they're perfect. You're a genius.' He held the blue one up against Alissa, humming appreciatively. 'I think that'll go perfectly with her hair, you've got the colour exactly right.'

Then he held the green one against Vanna and smiled. 'Clever you,' he said, 'weaving that golden brown thread through the green. I feel as if the forest itself has come to greet me.'

Vanna took them from him, her eyes shining with tears, and hung them gently back on the hanger.

After that, Goat said nothing more to Vanna about the costumes.

Now it is five days until the Midsummer carnival, and today is the day when the performance schedules and venues are announced. Goat wakes them up with fierce bleats and chivvies them out of the carriage while the rest of the performers in the plaza are still sleeping.

'We need an advantage on them,' he yips as Alissa and Vanna sleepily braid their hair and Lion grooms his flanks. 'Knowledge is power!'

'Is this a competition, then?' Alissa murmurs. 'I've never heard that before.'

Goat yelps and barges out of the carriage cursing everyone's stupidity.

Lion licks his lips. 'No one wins, but if the crowds don't like us we won't be given a slot next year. This year is our shot, we're an unknown quantity, we could be terrible or amazing and no one knows yet. That's why he's so stressed.'

Vanna holds the door open for Alissa and Lion to hop out of the carriage, and locks it behind her to a soft, appreciative hoot from Owl. She isn't so keen on the city. There's plenty of food for her – mice in the kitchen gardens and rats along the gutters of dock warehouses – but there is altogether too much commotion for her to be at peace.

They follow Goat as he weaves through the carriages and upside-down coracles and skips over the almost-invisible guy ropes securing the tents to the cobbles. There's already a small crowd around a man standing atop an upturned bucket wearing a grey hat to mark him out as an envoy from the city council.

'The Poortown Players, sunset on Midsummer Eve,' the man calls. 'Slick Jims, moonrise on Midsummer Eve. Magical Mayhem, midnight on Midsummer Eve.'

Clearly there is no one from those troupes present yet as the small crowd remain still, leaning towards the council man, nodding for him to continue. He goes on to announce the players for the next day, droning through all six bells. Still, they have not been called. She knows that Goat wants to perform sometime in the evening as those are the best slots, but secretly she would have been content to go first. Then they could have got it out of the way and she could enjoy the rest of the carnival without worrying she'll forget her lines, or having to keep her hair clean and untangled.

'Fire and Ice—'

Goat, Lion and Vanna lean forward eagerly. Vanna holds Goat's hoof with one hand and Lion's paw with the other.

Alissa feels apart from it all, for the first time since she met them at the Patli Bridge. She sees them now as they must have been before the juggler turned up, a strange collection of souls, but three who knew each other better than they knew themselves. She is surprised to find herself jealous.

'—sunset on Midsummer Day,' he calls. Lion grins and turns away with his tail high. Vanna muffles her excited squeal and they all drop out of the circle pressing around the council man, to let a woman with a green and gold parrot on her shoulder take their place.

'Wait until the juggler hears about this!' Alissa whispers excitedly as they meander back across the square to their carriage. She is trying to keep her voice down so as not to wake the other performers and cause a stampede.

Goat looks pained. 'It's not the best slot of them all,' he says. 'The night-time slots are really better, the crowds are warmed up and ready to enjoy themselves.'

'Stop it,' says Vanna. 'You have to be proud at some point and this is that moment. It's our first time here and we've got the sunset slot! This is thrilling!'

Goat shifts from hoof to hoof and bites his lip nervously. 'But we might not have any audience. People have their dinner at sunset, it's when the inns get their refills of beer. We might play to an empty crowd.'

Vanna unlocks the door to their carriage and shoos them inside.

'She's right,' says Lion, as he settles onto his haunches and starts to groom. 'I never thought I'd say this, but this is working out well. If we don't fuck it up we'll be back here next year, and then maybe we'll have a shot at one of the night-time shows.'

Alissa smiles at him but doesn't catch his eye. She sees now that he is so much softer than he pretends; she imagines him as the kind of little boy who cries hot tears of frustration when he gets in trouble or hurts someone. She doesn't know why he was transformed, although Vanna has hinted at a love affair gone wrong. She has never asked him herself. She has seen over these past months that he likes her, and is starting to count her among his friends as surely as he does Goat or Vanna or Owl, and she has discovered that his friendship matters to her.

Later that day, just after the fifth bell, Alissa sees the juggler at an inn by the docks. Alissa has her hands cupped around a mug of mead, that she's pouring onto a plate for Lion to lap at, when she sees the distinctive crest of his blue hat and the two long sections of his beard pointing at his feet. She calls out to him, and waves, and although Alissa knows Lion definitely doesn't want to spend his free time with the juggler, she gives a loud whistle to try and attract his attention in the jostling crowd of stevedores, sailors and tired travellers.

But the juggler either doesn't see them or completely ignores their calls. He walks out of the inn and along the street with a long, purposeful stride and an absent frown, as though he is late for an unpleasant task. Alissa presses her nose against the thin, dirty window of the inn to watch him go. She notices that his trousers are soaked up to the thighs and he carries his red cloak in a sopping wet bundle over his arm.

'What do you think he's been doing all this time we've been here?' Alissa turns back to Lion to find his mead finished and him holding out the plate for some more. She laughs, and pours for him.

'He's all wet,' she says. 'Do you think he's been in the canal?'

Lion rolls his eyes. He's a little bit drunk. 'Crescent only knows what he's been up to, and to be honest, I don't care as long as he turns up for the show.'

He could tell her that he saw the juggler talking to crows and hares and ravens, but it doesn't seem important now. Likewise, Alissa could tell him the truth about how she knows that star-faced man and how he turned her life upside down before she'd even met him, but now doesn't seem to be the time.

Lion balances precariously on his hind legs and holds up his plate with a puddle of mead on it. 'To us,' he says, clinking his plate against her mug. 'To Fire and Ice, their friendship and their shows.'

'To Fire and Ice,' Alissa giggles, and takes a long gulp of her mead. She would like to stay here forever, here in this cosy inn with Lion by her side, the smell of freshly baked bread wafting from the kitchen and a sunny breeze tickling her neck from the open door. The mead is making her a little woozy, too. She shifts on the bench to be closer to Lion and breathe in the smell of him: autumn and wind, and that musky, territorial smell. She wonders what it would feel like to kiss him, whether his lips would feel dry or meaty or soft.

Then she takes another gulp of her mead and closes her eyes. *Don't*, she tells herself sternly. *You'll make a fool of yourself. He's your friend, he loves another. He'll never love you back.*

ORGANUM

Section 6, clause 8(g)
Midsummer and Midwinter, as the fulcrums of
the year, will result in a laxity of this contract.
This is not the fault of the artist, nor the Moon
nor the Earth, but it behoves all signatories to
honour their commitments.

There are four days left of the month of Gemini, and three nights until Carnival starts, when Leira arrives in Uranga. She arrives on a ship, like so many of the other summer pilgrims, as the roads into the city are now thick with laden carts and muddy carriages and visitors pitching threadbare tents along the wild banks of the widdershins canal, to the despair of the city council.

She travels with a box as tall as her, that she's nailed shut and fixed tough iron wheels onto the bottom. She could hear the labra plugs cooing to each other as she waited on the jetty to embark on the boat, and she worried that it would do something unexpected and eldritch, as labra wood is wont to do. She had expected the captain of the ship to smell the cargo somehow and make a fuss, but he barely glanced at it as he stamped it and shouted to the dockworkers to get it in the hold.

'It's kind of important, that box,' Leira tried to say as he counted out her fare and dropped it into his bag.

He rolled his eyes. 'Everyone's luggage is important, mistress, and I've never lost a parcel yet.'

Leira bristled and pursed her lips. *If only you knew what and who you were messing with*, she thought, *you wouldn't be so cavalier.* But she relinquished the box anyway and climbed the ladder to the top deck. She knew she would hear the labra over the sound of the river as they sailed, singing and wriggling away, and sure enough every night as she swayed in her hammock on the ladies deck there it was, humming a steady tune for all the world to hear. She wondered if anyone else could hear it or if it was only her because of all the time she'd spent whittling it, rubbing its sap all over her hands and breathing in its dust. *That stuff is driving me half mad*, she thought. *I can't wait to give it to Luna and get it out of my mind.*

The captain had been as good as his word, and the box had rolled off the gangplank as if it had been newly made. Now she's wheeling it through the city, looking for a place to stay, cursing when the wheels get stuck in the cobbles and she has to kick them into alignment, fouling her boots with whatever unspeakable filth gathers in the crevices of this city.

Leira hates Uranga. She lived in an orphans' home here until she was taken away by Mandoré, and although she doesn't remember where she was born and lived with her mother in the early part of her life, she knows it was peaceful and green and far away from the noises of other people. There was a hedgerow of hawthorn and elder right by their house, she recalls, and blackberries in the summer. She doesn't know how she ended up in the city after her mother died, but she remembers being scared of the bells and the smoke and the dark water of the canal. Mandoré had rescued her from this place, but she doesn't think of that because it gives her a heavy feeling in her chest, still. To be glad to have gone from being an urchin to a slave, what does that say about her life? When Luna told her what she would give up by helping her to escape the Tower, she had laughed when she came to the bit about being banned from the spiral city. But now she is here regardless, flouting an old restriction from an ancient contract. She pulls at the box and the labra squeals inside. 'Shut up,' she whispers. 'Don't start that here.'

The reputable inns are full. The girls lean on their mops and wipe their cheeks with their slimy aprons as they frown at the sight of the wheeled box and shake their heads.

'They're four to a bed up there,' one says. 'You'll have to find somewhere else.'

She finds a disreputable inn on the inner western canal bank and gets a small room, with a straw mattress and low beams with scars in the dark oak from knife fights and crescent knows what else. The toilet is a shed in the yard that empties directly into the water even though she knows that's illegal.

The girl sighs when she sees the wheeled box, blowing her greasy fringe away from her face. There's nobody else about but the stains of last night's spills and a left over miasma of beery breath.

'Can't you just leave that down here? Won't nobody touch it, we're an honest lot.'

Leira counts out the coral rings the girl asked – an eye-wateringly inflated price, but that's what happens at Carnival – and then adds four more.

'I'll keep the box in my room, thanks.'

She girl shrugs and pockets the extra corals. She moves a couple of steps up the staircase and wipes her hands on her skirts ready to pull the box.

'What's inside, anyway?'

'A flying machine.'

The girl's eyes goggle and she laughs nervously.

'Only joking. It's a present for a friend.'

The girl ducks behind the box and gives it a sharp tug. She grunts when it tips towards her.

'It's actually quite light,' Leira says, grabbing for the corners of the box to stop it falling on top of the girl. 'We should be able to take it up the stairs just the two of us.'

They manoeuvre it up the staircase and around the corner, the girl huffing and panting, Leira with a grim, stolid set to her mouth and the labra chuckling. The girl scarpers back down the stairs as soon as the box is over the threshold and Leira shuts the door behind her, shoving the rusty bolt across the doorframe.

She sprays the mattress with a decoction of her own recipe to kill the fleas and lice, and then she sits by the window. The labra is humming a tune and trying to get her to join in, but she keeps her mouth clamped shut and her eyes on the street outside. She keeps expecting to recognise people from her childhood: maybe the beaked nose of the night matron on one of the old women shuffling along arm in arm by the flower stall, or the ruddy cheeks of the boy who once cut her hair for a dare or the red face of the fish hawker.

She shuts her eyes and leans on the damp wall. Luna will arrive soon. There is a prickle of something at the back of her neck and she wonders, again, what this is all for. She has an unpleasant feeling of being compelled, a sensation she hasn't had since the first days of being exiled from the Tower. She knew it then and she knows it now: she is not making choices, she is not being herself. She is being led by the stitches of yellow-haired girls kept as slaves, and the wordlight that flows from the books Luna once wrote.

As darkness falls, her stomach begin to complain of hunger. The labra is silent, for once, but the underworld of Uranga has announced its arrival for a night of merriment downstairs with the sound of glass breaking and shouted curses, so she decides it's a good time to go out. She locks the room and wanders along the quayside towards what she thinks is the main plaza. Her feet have not trod these cobbles for thirty years or more, but still they recognise something in the stones and that old feeling of panic rises along her spine. She wants to look into the eyes of every woman who passes her, just as she did when she was a little girl, asking each one, desperate to find her mother again.

This close to Carnival the streets heave and throb with noise and colour. All but the most essential work has stopped; all but the most business-savvy and the cooks have shut up their shops and come out onto the streets in their best clothes. Leira weaves between one crowd gathered around a crier reciting lists of the performances on Midsummer Eve, and another forming a tight circle around two foxes waltzing on their hind legs.

She turns a corner onto the deosil road and hears a faint drumming. The crowd is flowing along the road in the direction of the main plaza, and Leira is swept along with the songs and the drumbeats. All around her are young women with their hair loose and long down their backs, cornflower, honeysuckle and meadowsweet braided through it making everyone sneeze; and young men with crowns of oak leaves and lavender perched on their hats. They all walk hand-in-hand with their lovers. The goodwives hanging out of their windows above the road shriek lewd insults, and the lovers shout back the crudest things they can think of to the delight of the crowd around them.

Leira feels her face redden and ducks down an alley and presses her back against the brick. She remembers watching the lovers' parades as a girl, holding onto the rope that corralled the children so she didn't get lost, the matron's stern ears listening out for any rude comments that would, as matron put it, disgrace the name of their noble founder and put the offending mouth straight to bed with no pudding. In the days after Carnival the talk in the dormitory after lantern-out would turn to what kind of lover the children all wanted to walk the deosil road with when they were grown: a tall one, a rich one, one who was kind to donkeys, one who could sing sweetly. Leira had always listened, interested, but never taken part. She wonders now if there was a part of her – perhaps the part that Luna or some other star child had already written – that knew she would have neither beau nor belle, and would never walk hand-in-hand with a lover towards the silver-cloaked burghers to jump over the fire at the main plaza, declaring her marriage to the citizens of the spiral city.

She watches two young men pass her, their hands entwined. One holds a fist of pink dog roses up to his scraggly beard and then presses it into the face of his fiancé, who pulls off his lavender-crowned hat and kisses him. A woman dressed in mourning leans out of the window directly above her and whistles with glee. The lovers break apart to blow kisses up at her and the widow pretends to swoon.

A beer-seller approaches her with a foaming pewter mug and she swaps a coral ring for it gratefully, slurping it down before he has a chance to move away.

'Do you know where I can get some food?' Leira asks him as she puts the empty mug on his tray. 'Somewhere quiet.'

The beer-seller smiles and gestures down the alley. 'My cousin does a good fish pie. Follow this alley until it opens out and turn left.'

Leira thanks him and strides off along the flower-strewn cobbles. The drums and screams of the parade fade as she turns the corner. Only four more days of this madness, then she can return home.

> • <

She returns to the inn with a full belly and a clearer mind, relieved to have been away from the labra for the first time in months. The bar is filled with pipe smoke and leery laughter that swells in waves from the huddle around the fireplace. Leira pulls her hood over her head and dodges the staggers of a drunken stevedore to pass up the stairs to her room unnoticed.

The lock has not been tampered with but there is a metallic smell lingering in the corridor. She opens the door and the smell becomes stronger, like the iron dust clinging to a smith's blackened apron. She strikes a match, lights the lantern, and holds it up to the place where she left the box of labra plugs. It has gone. She holds the lantern above her head to lengthen its light. There is a dark, thin shadow on the bed. Leira puts the lantern on a stool and reaches for whatever has been left for her. Her fingers tingle as she touches it.

It's Luna's pipe, still as smooth and shiny as the day Three brought it to the cellar, the grain of the labra twisting around the reed like a secret language. Leira puts it to her mouth, blows softly, and listens to the faint whistle. She doesn't know how to play this thing, she never has, and she wonders now why Luna has left it for her. Is it in thanks, or does she want her to do something with it?

Leira sits by the window with her lantern and watches the quayside below as she turns the pipe over in her hands. Pairs of lovers are starting to stumble back from the weddings, their happy, drunken parents following behind them haphazardly throwing confetti and singing bawdy songs. Leira extinguishes the lantern so she doesn't have to watch them.

She wishes she had seen Luna. She wishes Luna had wanted to see her. She had thought there would be time together, after she'd delivered the labra plugs, to talk about what they've been doing all these years and be effortlessly close the way they used to be.

She can leave tomorrow, if she wants to. There is no reason for her to stay in Uranga now. She feels the stitches tugging at her, making her imagine packing up her things, finding a boat, sailing out on the widdershins canal and getting home in time to rescue her salad leaves from the rabbits and her strawberries from the squirrels.

But she doesn't want to obey the stitches. She wants to see Luna.

She sits in the darkness, feeling for the stitches that bind her. In her mind, she cuts them, one by one. Here is the desire for the half-made machines in her workshop, *snip*. Here is the southerly wind in her face as the boat winds along the widdershins canal, *snip*. Here are the quiet forests of the western roads, the sailors passing around a bottle of cowslip wine on Midsummer Eve, the herons greeting the boat as it passes in the dawn: *snip snip snip*. She waits, unstitched, in the darkness, letting the cut threads unravel around her and remake themselves into a tapestry in which she is doing exactly as she pleases.

When the first glow of the morning starts to lighten the eastern horizon, she brings the pipe to her lips and blows. The sound drifts between the cracks in the shutters and out onto the quayside below, around the oars of the moored dinghies and across the water. Leira keeps playing notes that sound interesting to her, even though she knows no tunes, imagining the music floating high over the chimneys and spires of Uranga and away to the Tower in the north, where as surely as the gibbous moon rises in the corner of her eye, new stitches are being sewed to bind her.

FANTASIA

It is almost dawn on Midsummer Day in the Tower, and Three is sweating as he calls out the patterns. It is the last book left in the cellar and its time signature is a simple one that even the sewing girls understand. It is a straight line up and down, with a sort of horizontal tail that hovers just under it. It means that the words in the book will be evenly split between things to happen right now as the fattening moon hangs low in the western sky, as soon as the stitches are secure on the silk; and those things that will take a little more time to flow from the silk into the world, that won't happen until the sun has risen, or maybe tomorrow night. Although it is simple, it is also a difficult time signature, one the Thirteen dread. There is no time to ponder the star child's words and no time to fix any mistakes the girls might make. They have known for a long time this night would come, the book has been sitting on the shelf with its sinister sign for years. Now it lies open in Three's hands, its words ending the world before their own eyes.

One, Seven and Thirteen stand behind the sewing girls, examining the silk, looking for signs of the chaos to come. They see Carnival everywhere, bursting from the canals and the hedgerows all over the land: flowers frothing from elder and hawthorn and dripping off the drunken heads of the merrymakers swinging around the oaks; wine and mead and beer pouring from barrel to jug to mug to mouth.

Here is a laughing man with a wooden leg lying in the lap of a woman holding onto the crown of ivy on her black hair. Here is a dancing line of revellers, flowers wilted and soggy in their hair, singing as they wind along the deosil road. Here is a juggler, standing in a plaza in Uranga among a mess of tents, making balls of light dance in the air.

'He's here!' Seven cries, making the sewing girls of the night shift jump. 'I've found the Trickster, he's in Uranga!'

Three carries on calling the night while Thirteen rushes to Seven's side. One goes to the door and calls down the stairs to his masked brothers.

Here is a carriage with three sails lying flat in the wind; here is a lion made of leaves, watching the juggler with a scowl; here is a hooded figure slipping into a black canal, swimming like an eel to its depths; here is a girl with loose yellow hair wearing a fine green dress.

'Three, stop calling from the book!' Thirteen shouts. The fingers of the sewing girls falter. The eldest of them looks up from the silk, glancing between the masked faces. Nothing like this has ever happened before.

'We need more time,' he says. 'Something's happening in the city.'

'What shall I say?' Three asks. 'I don't know what they should sew.'

'Make it up!' Thirteen hisses, and Three looks shocked. 'It's Carnival, it doesn't matter. Make the people drunk and happy so we can give them something to wake up to tomorrow.'

Three starts to call. He sings of potent wine, bawdy rhymes, and crowds clapping and chanting as they watch the travelling players cavort. There is a desperation in his voice, a tumbling edge of despair that cracks his words and makes his voice stumble. The wordlight becomes sludgy; now it looks like strings of mud as it flows through the needles. On the silk the stitches form bottomless barrels of grog; hard, high-pitched laughter; fiddle music that screeches off the strings like a death whine; breathless, spinning dancing that ignores the skittering heartbeats of the dancers and pushes the feet harder and faster.

The Tower begins to fill with the other masked men, and although the girls are hunched over the silk, obeying what Three calls with no time to wonder at what he's saying or what the other masked men are doing, their hands quiver with fear. Don't look up, don't let your fingers slow, don't let them know you're scared or you'll feel the crack of a staff across your back.

'Nine, get the day girls up,' Thirteen commands. 'We need all of them here.'

Nine disappears back down the corridor as his brothers rush to the silk, breathless from their dash up the stairs.

Here is a girl stumbling on the cobbles as she dances, lilac blossoms falling from her hair; here are a couple rutting in the shadow of a docked ship; here is a white-bearded man dressed in mourning, vomiting his sadness and regret into the dark water of the canal.

Three's made-up calls mix with what the girls embroidered overnight and make a mess of the silk. The wordlight shivers like it has a fever as it pours through the needles.

'Look at this!' Eleven calls. He points to a collection of stitches that make up a river, flowing into the widdershins canal and then to Uranga. The water isn't flowing in the right direction. It's rising over the bank, creeping among the reeds and sneaking across the grass like a thief.

'What the fuck is happening to all that water?' Eleven says. 'Where's it coming from?'

Two places his finger on a black stitch that is still growing from the needle of the girl who cowers beside him, and traces it as it spreads across a road.

'It's coming from the spiral city,' he says. 'It's a leak. That blasted time signature, she must have slipped it in somewhere earlier.'

The masked men cross the room to look at the place on the silk where Two has his hand. They watch as the black water spreads from the canal over the ankles of the revellers.

'It's not a leak,' Thirteen says quietly. 'It's a flood. We need to go to Uranga, now.'

There is a short silence as they contemplate the enormity of what is happening. Even Three stops calling and the girls suppress their breaths of relief.

'I'll stay to keep the wordlight going,' he says.

Thirteen shakes his head. 'We'll have to be together. We'll leave the repeat on.'

Twelve looks panicked. He pulls at his mask as though it itches him. 'But to leave the Tower, all of us at the same time? Thirteen, we can't do it. We've *never* done it.'

Thirteen grips his silvery staff, and if any of the girls had been looking at him they would have flinched. 'We'll have to,' he says. 'We'll need the full circle. We'll invoke council privileges and leave the repeat mechanism on.'

Twelve takes a step towards his elder brother. 'But the contract—'

'I don't give a fuck about the contract!' Thirteen shouts, slamming his silvery staff into the floor. 'Why should we play by the rules when she's been tearing up the old agreements without a care for years now?'

Twelve turns away. He smooths his cloak over his stomach and clenches his fists.

'If we're all here,' Ten says, 'let's go.'

Nine appears at the doorway with six bleary-eyed girls behind him. Before anyone can open their mouth to tell him what's happening, he holds up his hand to silence his brothers.

'I heard,' he says. 'Let me get them settled and I'll be coming.'

The night shift yawn as they move over on their benches to make way for the day shift. The new girls have dressed in a hurry and their hair is wispy, escaping from their braids and glowing in the new dawn light. The day shift pick up their needles from where they left them at sunset last night and try not to look at the night shift, who seem terrified.

Nine looks around the room, his eyes narrowing as he takes in the grimy wordlight.

'Hold on,' he says. 'Where's Five?'

The masked men start to look around, count themselves, check which pairs of eyes stare back. One of them is missing.

'Did you see Five down there?' Thirteen asks.

Three breaks off from calling drunkenness and debauchery to say, 'Has he come back from Tristaane yet?'

'What?' Thirteen tugs at his mask and frowns. 'Why did he go there?'

'He said he wanted to talk to granite,' Ten says. 'A few days ago. I thought he'd come back.'

Slowly, with horror, the Thirteen turn to the silk. Three shuts the book and leaves it on the lectern, twisting his hands around the air in front of the wordlight urn to turn on the repeat.

Seven makes a choked noise as he leans over a part of the silk that is almost out of the window. His brothers rush to peer over his shoulder.

Here is a man who wears a mask tied tightly over the lower half of his face, striding along the wide deosil road of Uranga. He sticks to the shadows and moves his fingers continuously by his thigh, turning the memories of those who see him to slurry. Here is a hooded woman whose face glows with an unearthly light. Her cloak is soaking wet, as though she's been swimming. Here is a juggler, boots wet to the ankles, holding the hair of a yellow-haired girl and playing it like a fiddle.

Thirteen lets the silk flow out of the Tower and steps back, his eyes grim and hard. He holds out his staff and each of his brothers, except for the missing one who has defied all the rules, touches their gloved hand to it. A fierce, hot wind rushes through the stone arches of the Tower and the sewing girls drop the fistfuls of the silk to cower under the tables, gagging on the smell of singed hair.

When the air is cool again, the girls push the stools out of the way and sit back at the desks. They do not pick up their needles again. They never do when the repeat is on. The eldest of the night shift hurries down the stairs to fill a kettle. She puts loaves of bread and thin slabs of butter on a tray and carries them up for the others.

As the sun climbs up the sky in the eastern windows of the Tower, they eat their bread and butter and chat about the lives they used to lead. They let the murky wordlight flow over the silk unstitched, making messy splotches of whatever chaos it wants, and they do not care.

FUGUE

Section 9, clause 5
*While the Trickster is counted as neutral between
Earth and Moon, he obeys laws unto his own
devising and knowledge, and shall never be
counted as an ally to either.*

A slanted ray of sun protruding through the shutters wakes
Leira on Midsummer morning. Dust hangs in the shaft of
light, frozen like dead fish in a winter lake. Immediately, she
knows that whatever Luna has been planning has begun.

She opens the window. A group of dishevelled men sit on
the cobbles of the quayside, singing old sailors' songs with
hoarse throats. Their shirts have wine stains and grease
marks at their fronts, their trousers are ripped at the knees,
their hair is slick with spilled mead. They see Leira at the
window and wave at her. She ducks back into the window
before they start climbing towards her.

She dresses, tucking Luna's pipe into her pocket, and goes
out to the illegal toilet in the yard. The landlady is slumped
beside it, curled lovingly around a puddle of vomit. Leira
hears her snores and steps gingerly into the shed, bolting the
splintered door behind her. She hears the scurrying feet of rats
in the dark and leans forward to hold the ankles of her trousers
tight. She will leave this place as soon as she's seen Luna.

It isn't only at the inn that the citizens of Uranga have spent
the night overindulging and wreaking havoc on their home.

There are lampposts tumbled across the street; washing lines fallen from windows with their white shirts streaked with mud; shards of broken pots crunching underfoot. But still the party carries on. Nobody is working now, even the innkeepers have opened their barrels to everyone and the mead and beer never seem to run out, no matter how long the stevedores and night-soil men lie under the taps with their mouths open. The musicians play their fiddles with broken strings, their trumpets with dents, their drums with loose skins; but still the tunes drift over the rooftops, mingling with the smoke to make a haze over the city that hangs like a cloud. Children sneak under tables to sit and race grasshoppers, their faces sticky with honey. Was it like this when she was a girl? She has no memory of the matrons at the orphans' home drinking until they fell down, she can't remember being left to run down the streets stealing meat pies from the hawkers while they slept, nor the older ones pushing the younger ones into the canal and making bets on who could swim. A little boy with holes in his shorts brushes past her and lifts the pipe from her pocket, tucking it into his waistband as he darts away. She catches him by his collar and takes the pipe back.

'Get out of here,' she whispers. 'Before I call for the guards.'

The boy smirks but he backs away. 'Call them,' he says. 'See if they come. The last guards I saw were flashing on the Southern Bridge.'

He runs away, the sole of his shoe flapping.

Leira walks towards the heart of the city. She keeps a friendly smile fixed on her face but moves with purpose, hoping it will deter anyone from thrusting a drink at her, pulling her into their dance or leering for a kiss, but she needn't have worried. Not one person meets her gaze, their reddened eyes slide off her as she passes, moving like a scent through the crowds.

She takes short cuts across the canal whenever there's a bridge and finds the debauchery continuing on delivery boats and dinghy taxis – it's a wonder the city still has beer left. She avoids the dirty puddles and the places where the rats compete for the leftovers of someone's feast, steps around the crushed flowers from the lovers' parade and dodges the limbs slumped in the shadows.

She comes to a plaza full of tents and carriages and walks among them, baffled. It's different here, there's more of an atmosphere of concentration, although still no one looks at her. The people here are not so drunk as the rest, there is the feeling that – perhaps uniquely in the city – they still have a job to do. A drummer tugs at the skin of his instrument to repair it, a woman dressed all in white stirs a pot hanging from a makeshift tripod bubbling over a smoky fire, and a clutch of pigeons march towards a spilled sack of grain.

She sees an owl sitting atop a carriage, blinking in the light. The owl turns its head and stares directly at her. Leira feels a shiver creep along her skin and knows that the creature has recognised her. This bird knows she is unstitched from the silk. Leira weaves around the tents towards it.

At the back of the carriage where the owl sits is a strange gathering. A goat chews on a mouthful of hay and nods while a black-haired woman talks, waving her arms and pointing towards the central plaza just a few streets away. A lion who rustles like a pile of autumn leaves lies still while a yellow-haired girl kneels before him with a paintbrush in her hand.

Leira looks closer at the girl wielding the paint. She looks back at the owl, who blinks and turns away. Leira feels her heart start to skip. Perhaps surprisingly, this is the first time this has ever happened to her. Her life since leaving the Tower has been empty of people and their problems, she hasn't seen another girl with the yellow hair favoured by the Thirteen since the day the masked man sent her to the cellar to be Luna's companion. But this girl can't be like everyone else, she'll know the Tower as Leira does, she'll have spent hours of her days and nights hunched over the silk, her fingers loose over the needle; she'll have felt that cold burn of the wordlight. Leira's past is rushing at her with a roar – here, in the city where she spent her unhappy childhood; here, looking at a girl who was taken out of time too.

Leira creeps forward. She wants to say hello, introduce herself and ask questions of the girl. She has never felt this yearning to be with another person before, she usually scoffs at anyone who cries for loneliness, but before she can say anything a man in a red cloak bounds in front of the girl. He throws seven glowing balls into the air in an intricate pattern and catches them easily.

'Are we all ready?' he says, and Leira shrinks back to hide herself behind another carriage. Her stomach flips over as she recognises the newcomer. 'Why aren't you painted yet, Lion? We should be ready by now.'

The yellow-haired girl calmly puts her paintbrush back in the pot. 'I notice you're not in your costume either, Juggler, so I'd calm down if I were you.'

The lion made of leaves gives her a wicked grin and the goat clears his throat with annoyance. The juggler tucks his handfuls of balls back into his cloak and adjusts the blue hat on his head.

Leira shuts her eyes with a sigh. 'Oh Luna,' she breathes, her voice a husk that barely moves the air. 'Why have you brought him here? What have you written?'

Leira watches as the players – for now she realises that is what they are – take their places and start to practise their show. She watches as the yellow-haired girl unwinds her braid and offers it to the juggler, who grips it with one hand, and with the other draws the bow of a fiddle across it. They start to dance, the juggler holding the threads of hair tenderly as they gracefully swoop and turn around each other. The yellow-haired girl sings a love song as they dance. She has a pretty voice.

Now the black-haired woman enters and starts her own dance. She plays the fiddle as she moves around the juggler, tempting him with the sway of her hips and the curve of her shoulders. Leira is quite entranced by the beauty of her movements and it's a jolt when the juggler pounces on her and the music stops with a screech, mid-melody. The black-haired woman laughs, and the yellow-haired girl wails. She is not quite as convincing as her friend, and the rehearsal stops for a moment for the goat, who is watching every single movement with narrowed eyes, to comment and make her practise the wail again.

And when the rehearsal starts again the lion, with only his front paws painted blue, leaps over the black-haired woman, who falls to the ground with a shriek. He leaps over the juggler's head in one bound and runs around the perimeter of the rehearsal area, the suggestion of muscles in the leaves of his flank rippling as he moves.

Leira sneaks a look at the juggler, who is watching the lion perform his leaps and flips while the yellow-haired girl waves her arms vaguely beside him. There is a look of satisfaction in his eyes as he tugs on the two points of his beard and watches while the lion leaps in a circle, hissing and roaring and spreading his limbs as far as he can.

Leira watches the lion too, puzzled. Why would he be painted blue? This is the story of the Minstrel, she's figured that out, but what part is he playing?

She glances at the juggler, sees that his trousers are wet up to the knees. She looks back to the lion and his blue paws.

Oh.

Leira looks up at the owl, still perched atop the carriage. Bile rises in her throat. The owl confirms with a single nod, stretches her wings and flies away from the plaza. Leira turns away from the players and stumbles down an alleyway with upturned stools strewn across it, and leans against the warm bricks. This is why Luna would not see her, this is why she wrote telling her to go back to her cottage after she brought the labra plugs. She feels inside her pocket for the pipe, presses her fingers to the holes.

She shuts her eyes, and etched on her dark eyelids she sees thirteen masked men standing in a cellar, surrounding her with their righteous certainty that she was the evil one. It did not trouble her conscience, the last time Luna wrote chaos into the world, even though she knew what was going to happen. She had helped it come to pass. She sat in the cellar and listened as Luna spelled out her plan and coached her on the contract. She told her what kind of cottage she wanted, and she practised hauling Luna up out of the window frame over and over again until her shoulders ached.

But this will not be the same. She knows that. Before, Luna assured her everything she was writing was only to help her get away from the Tower, and that the world would sort itself out again soon. She had said she was writing good things for the years after the wars and the famines and the plagues. She had said it was like throwing everything rotten in the world away to let the good, new things grow in their composted remains.

This time, there will be no good things after. In the story of the Minstrel, the water spirit floods the world until there is nothing but the sour sea, undulating as the wind caresses it, mourning for the lost earth. For heartbreak, because a man did not love her, the water spirit destroyed everything that anyone could love.

Leira raises the pipe to her lips and blows. She does not know Luna's tune, the one she uses to call the wind, but she plays the notes she knows. Her eyes itch with tears. She doesn't expect Luna to come but she plays anyway. Maybe the moon, invisible behind her brother's light, will hear anyway, and then she'll know it wasn't Leira, not this time.

The alleyway becomes cold, like a gust of icy air has rushed into a tightly sealed room and extinguished the fire with one gulp. There is a swish of a cloak, a smell like hot metal. Leira opens her eyes to see a dark shape looming at the end of the alleyway.

'I don't have time for this, Leira!' Luna glances behind her at the plaza and comes to hide her face in the shadows. Her hood is pulled far over her head but Leira can see the shine of her skin. She is agitated, her eyes darting this way and that. She is forgetting to cover the pale glow of her face with the illusion of human sallowness.

'You should be far away from here, you should have left days ago.'

Leira lowers the pipe, clutching at it tightly. 'I saw a juggler, Luna. He's here, in this city. What have you called him for?'

'You weren't supposed to be here, you weren't supposed to see him. You should go home.'

'The contract says — and you told me this, Luna, remember?'

'I should never have told you about that stuff, it wasn't your problem to—'

Leira interrupts, 'The contract says that "if the star child calls the Trickster she will forfeit her rights to a constellation". Do you really think he's doing your bidding? Do you really think you can trust a spirit your own mother couldn't?'

'Don't talk to me about my mother.' Leira flinches, a shard of fear splintering from Luna's hard, quiet voice and piercing her skin.

'It's already gone wrong,' Luna says softly. 'The Thirteen aren't calling what I wrote, they're fucking it all up.'

Her voice is flat with despair, a tone Leira has never heard before.

'But it doesn't matter,' Luna says, looking away from the filthy alley floor and into Leira's eyes. Leira wants to reach out and wrap her arms around her, the way she used to after a long day at the writing desk, or after one of the masked men had complained about something in the silk. 'It'll be over soon.'

'Please, Luna. You should stop it. You're the only one who can. The Thirteen are bastards, but all these people—' Leira waves her hand desperately in the direction of the players' plaza '—they don't deserve to die. They don't deserve for their world to end for good.'

The moon's daughter is silent.

'I want to take back the plugs,' Leira says. 'I don't want this.'

'It's too late for that.'

Leira's knees buckle and she clenches her fists to press them against the wall to keep herself steady. Luna is staring at her but she isn't seeing her, she is staring into the past or the future, or perhaps into the present, where thirteen masked men panic as they watch the silk of the world they adore warp and tear.

'Even if you stop it, which you can't, there are no more books in the cellar. They've run out and they know it. Now the water will be a mercy, Leira.'

Leira slumps. The pipe is loose in her fingers. 'When will it happen?' she asks.

Luna doesn't answer. Instead, she pulls her hood back to expose her shining face and comes to stand against the wall with Leira.

'I thought you'd understand. That's why I wrote you to help me.'

'But this is suicide for me, Luna. You get to live in the sky again, or you would have done if you hadn't called in the juggler. But me, I'm just human. I'll die with the rest of them.'

Luna is quiet. 'That's not what you said to them as you left. You tore away from the stitches. You said a world that was based on lies and slavery wasn't any kind of world at all and it should end.'

Leira swallows. She remembers saying that. She had disobeyed Luna's instructions to say nothing but the formula she had her practise over and over again. She remembers the rush of power it gave her, to wrench her tongue away from what her friend had written for her and tell the Thirteen exactly what. She'd been so young, and so stupid. She'd thought she could wound them on her way out the door, shame them into leaving Luna alone. Of course, she was wrong.

And now she's changed her mind. She isn't a slave any more, she's not been a slave for many years. She's low and stupid and selfish for it, but now she wants to live.

'How can you move around this city, watching all these thousands of people, and know they're going to die? Look at them, Luna! You wrote them, you made them, and now they want to live!'

Luna pushes herself off the wall and flicks her hood back over her head. She walks towards the alley and Leira finds her arms reaching out after her. There is a roaring in her ears that gets louder and louder as the dark shape that is Luna comes to the end of the alley.

'Well,' Luna says coldly over her shoulder, 'they've got until sunset. Let them make the most of it.'

Leira lets her knees soften and she slides down the wall until she is crouching in the shadows. In the plaza a drum starts. She listens, tracking the beat until it synchronises with her own heart. They don't know how few heartbeats they have, she thinks. They think they'll wake up tomorrow, tongues furred and heads thick from mead, and grin ruefully at their friends. The children think they'll be able to scrounge broken things to make toys from, the young men and women who got married think they'll wake up entwined in the arms of their lover.

Leira places the pipe on her knees and watches the grain of the labra shiver as it feels her breath. She thinks of all the plugs she carved, now hidden somewhere in the bowels of this city. The labra knew, all the time she was carving it, and it tricked her each day. It knew what its destiny was, and because it belongs to the moon it didn't mind at all.

ANTIPHON

Section 9, clause 6
Neither shall the Earth nor the Moon have reason
to trust the spirits of music, as they have been
created fickle and can be turned to any being's
desire as they choose.

Here is the sun, bowing to the oncoming darkness in a blaze of violet as if it is his last time. Here are the sparse, wispy clouds, dyed pink on their undersides and changing every minute. Here are the gleaming rooftops of Uranga, the thick waters of the canal, the weary cobbles pounded with staggering dancing feet. Here is the moon, hovering anxiously below the horizon, mourning for the daughter she lost.

Leira sits on one of the benches arranged in an amphitheatre around the raised stage. She has a feeling of floating above the braying, drunken crowd. There is a lightness to her step, a sense she has that she is dreaming and so nothing she says or touches can really be heard or felt in the world. The laughter and the shouts and the sucking, slurping noises of drinking and kissing are dimmed.

She can see the juggler's blue pointed hat on the stage. He is doing tricks with those glowing balls as the lion made of leaves and the black-haired woman fuss with the yellow-haired girl's costume at one side of the stage. The crowd gasps and oohs with each revolution of the balls, punctuating each trick with applause that thunders like rain on a lake.

Leira feels the tension in the crowd shift. Although everyone in the city is stitched into the drunken frenzy Luna wrote for them, there is, for a moment, a single point of focus. It concentrates to a point like sunlight in a convex lens, and the mass of bodies ripples and frightened murmurs flitter to her underwater ears. Leira looks up to the place where the noise is strongest, a shiver of fear and wonder. She grips the pipe. Here it is, the beginning of the end. Luna is showing herself to the people who think she is nothing more than a myth, a kind of gremlin to scare children into going to bed, just before she ends their world.

But when the bodies part, it is not Luna she sees. It is a blue-skinned, scarlet-haired witch with a long golden cloak covering her body. She is staring straight at Leira. The witch cocks her head and narrows her eyes.

'So this is where it's happening, then?' the witch asks. She has a strange accent Leira has never heard before, there is something hard on the vowels and rolling on the tongue.

Leira cannot speak, her throat is stoppered with shock. She has never actually met a witch before, although she used to embroider them. She remembers Luna groaning as she wrote witches into the chaos that would hide her escape. 'Why do you write witches into the silk if they make you anxious?' Leira had asked. Luna had made a face. 'I don't write them in,' she'd said. 'They're already there. The contract says there's things they're here to do, so I have no choice.'

Leira stares as the witch bares her teeth. She realises the witch is trying to smile at her.

'I think you're scaring them,' Leira says finally. 'Can you come away from the silk, like me?'

The witch glances at the ever-widening circle around them, the tight faces shrinking from her outlandish waves of blood-coloured hair.

'You're right. Careless of me.'

She makes a gesture with her left hand, like twisting a key in a lock. The tension slackens. They are pressed by bodies again, invisible to all the ordinary people of the world who are lucky enough not to know that they will not live to see another morning. The spirit of chaos floods back into the crowd with the sweaty smell of ferment and sex and days-unwashed men and women. The witch gags theatrically and sits on the bench next to Leira.

'Tell me,' the witch says, 'what do you have to do with all this?'

She crackles. It is unsettling to sit too close to her, like trying to picnic in a patch of stinging nettles, but Leira swallows and turns to her, holding the pipe on her lap like a talisman.

'I made her plugs of labra wood and brought them here. She's enchanted them to close up the drainage of the city spring, so the sour sea floods the city. In a couple of days the entire land will be under water.'

'Is that still what you want?'

Leira feels her eyes flush with tears. 'No. I never wanted that.'

The witch looks up at the stage where the juggler is performing tricks with nine balls, making them cross over each other with their tails of light streaming behind them like shooting stars.

'And them?' the witch asks.

'They're a cover. I think. Apart from *him*, who comes from a place in the sky none of us can go and can't be trusted.'

The witch twitches her nose, following the patterns of the balls with her gaze. 'When does the play start?'

'Any time now.'

The witch looks back at Leira. She has eyes the colour of violets, kin to the fading purple of the sun as it subsides into the horizon. Leira thinks of the way Mandoré used to call anything to do with a witch, the way his voice would suddenly drip with contempt until the blue-skinned figure was off the needle, onto the silk and out into the world. She wonders why she isn't more scared. Years ago, when she had just left the Tower, she might have been, but now there seems to be nothing in the world worse than her oldest friend. Leira finds her eyes itching as she looks at the witch, so she gazes around the plaza. There is a wild energy building in the crowd, people are staggering and floppy, their movements uncoordinated and jerky. The spaces between the bricks of the buildings are wobbling, there are strange surges in the conversations around her, and the air is hazy with more than just smoke and dust. She blinks, and time seems to stutter. She thinks the repeat must be on inside the Tower. Perhaps the Thirteen are trying to trick some time from the last book Luna wrote.

'You know my sisters and I are not bound by the silk?'

Leira looks back into the witch's violet eyes and nods.

'We worship Mother Moon, but I've decided to side with the earth this time.' Leira feels her palms begin to sweat. The labra pipe wriggles in her hands. 'But I need some help.

Can I have your hand?' the witch asks. Leira grips the pipe in one hand and offers the other.

On the stage, the juggler takes a bow and there are sharp cracks of palms as the drunken citizens of Uranga applaud him.

'I need you to think of the labra you carved,' the witch says, raising her voice against the swelling noise of the rabble. 'Pretend like you're still touching it.'

Leira tucks the pipe inside her pocket and flexes her fingers. 'I'm ready,' she says. She obeys the witch because she crackles and it would hurt her not to do as she says. She is a coward, really. She's only just learning that about herself. She doesn't understand why the witch wants her hand, or to think of the labra. There is nothing anyone can do to halt what Luna has put in motion. Not a witch, not the earth spirits, not even the moon or sun themselves.

'Then I want to you to call to it. Ask it to obey you until it listens.'

The crowd stills and the applause fades. There are only sounds of shuffling feet and rustling skirts. This is Luna's doing, this attentive listening. Midsummer plays in the city are never so quiet; these people have been written silent so they will not struggle as they drown. From the corner of her eye, Leira sees the yellow-haired girl step onto the stage. She wears a green dress with gold threads sparkling at the seams and a crown of oak and ivy sits upon her head.

The witch takes Leira's hand and she has to clamp her teeth together not to cry out with the jolt of it. It is not painful, not quite, but it makes her skin feel as though it is melting from her bones. A kind of burning, itching fire creeping invisibly along her flesh.

The juggler steps onto the stage and bows a deep, chivalrous greeting to the yellow-haired girl.

The witch begins to hum. Softly at first, no louder than a bee at the nectar of a primrose in spring, but then louder and louder until it has become the purr of a cat. No one around them hears, no one notices them. The citizens of Uranga sitting in this plaza, watching this play, are all stitched into the spell by now. When the water comes, they will not feel a thing.

Leira shuts her eyes. She calls to the labra. She feels ridiculous; she has no power. Silently, she says, 'Labra?' Nothing. For moons it hissed and giggled at her in its baskets in her workshop, and now it is stubbornly, insolently silent.

'Talk to me!' she whispers fiercely. She feels the witch squeeze her hand and a surge of exquisite power flows across her skin. Now she hears more voices in the humming and the purring, harmonising and swooping over and under the note. She feels the warm breath of hundreds of voices at the nape of her neck, hundreds of witches who have come to the side of the earth to sing with their sister. The witch beside her lets out a long, loud whoop that soars into a stream of light curling in upon itself like the widdershins canal, spiralling deeper down in ever tightening circles right into the belly of the earth.

And then, underneath the chorus of far-away witches, the tiny chuckle of the labra. Leira opens the palm of her hand not clamped around the witch's and imagines the weight of it, the places where she pressed her silver knife along its grain, the curve of its knots at the base of her thumb.

She hears the labra sigh, and the witch squeezes her hand again. 'Come to me,' Leira croons. 'Come, goldwood, sit in my hand and let us play again.'

The labra writhes a little. She feels the stitches of the world shift, tear, fray.

Under the city, a plug pops from its pipe, leaving a tiny ring of space around it for water to dribble through.

Leira grins.

CADENZA

Section 3, clause 8(e)
It shall be prohibited in the strongest terms for
the fleshly bodies of the Thirteen to contact the
earthly manifestation of the star child.

Fuck, Luna thinks. *There's a witch here.*

She can smell her hot, sweet blood under her fingernails and gushing through her body, the woodsmoke from her hair. She looks around the bodies pressed into the plaza, her eyes flicking between gurning faces, seeking out the periwinkle skin of the traitor who's come to ruin it all. She can feel the labra wriggling deep under the city. On her hooded forehead cold droplets of sweat pop from her skin. She brushes them away and tiny diamonds fall from her fingers and tinkle on the cobbles.

She can hear humming, like the clouds are singing from far away. It gets louder and louder as other witches add their power, building to a painful screech at the base of her skull. She begins to push her way through the crowd, her nostrils flaring, hunting down the witch. On the stage, the juggler dances with Ula's daughter, holding her hair like the strings of a violin. She had hoped to be able to watch her, to see the curve of her mother's jaw in her face. She had wanted that to be the last thing she saw on the earth.

The witch is near, Luna can feel her heartbeat. She shoves past a tall man wearing a long brown cloak; he won't sense her, he's under the spell of the play she wrote long ago, his veins thick and dull with beer and his legs heavy with lust.

But then the man turns. His body moves quicker than it should and there is a soft sound of triumph that echoes in the silence of the crowd as they watch the juggler and the yellow-haired girl waltzing around the stage. It makes Luna hesitate. She looks at the man, sees the faded green rag that covers his mouth and nose, the thick eyebrows that protrude over the black eyes like a cliff. The man's eyes narrow with malicious delight. She has seen this expression before. Those black slits are the first thing she ever saw on earth, the memory that began everything.

She cannot run, he will catch her. She cannot beg the chiselled stones of the plaza to let her sink through them, for they belong to the earth and will surely give her up. She cannot ask for shelter in the flames that leap atop the lantern posts, for fire has always been neutral and she has broken too many rules and promises now to make bargains. She could leap into the widdershins canal, the water will always be of the moon; but the canals are filthy with mud and wrecked coracles and the shit of a thousand different animals. That water is more his than hers now, she cannot be safe there.

There is only one place left to go.

She lets her body swell. Her stomach, breasts, hips and face become engorged and round; now she has no sharp planes or straight lines on her body, now she resembles her mother. It is a relief to finally let herself flow into something like her true form. She almost weeps from the pleasure of it. Her skin starts to shimmer, now she could no longer be said to look anything like human. The place where her feet used to be no longer touches the stones. She drifts into the air like a wisp of smoke, and in an instant she clears the heads of the silent crowd.

There are creases of panic scrawled on Mandoré's masked face and she wants to laugh with the glee of it. It has all failed; all her years of plotting have come to nothing, but at least they won't catch her. No, the earth will not be swallowed by the waters of the sour sea as she'd hoped, but never again will she sit in a skyless cellar. They won't find the other books, she reminds herself as she climbs higher. Their precious blob of rock and mud is done for.

Below, the black-haired woman has begun her fiddle dance and the witches' song has become a roar, a humming bass note under the fiddle that makes her heart itch. Below that, there are labra plugs floating free in the canal. Luna turns her attention away from the bobbing goldwood and towards the sky.

But then she feels something tugging at the place where her feet used to be, something constricting what she used to call her ankles. She looks down, screams a silent curse. There he is, holding on to her with his claw-like fingers, scrabbling for any purchase on her true body. There is a bloody smell of fear like a rotting carcass on him. She knows he has never left the surface of the earth before without the protection of the lottery. Luna laughs, a wild shriek.

'Do you think that'll do it, earthling?' she calls. 'Do you think you're coming to the sky again?'

There is no net in his hands like before, nothing he could possible tie her with, but still he clutches at her. She is not scared of him, not this time. She will not let herself be captured again.

'Oath-breaking bitch!' he cries.

In reply, she soars higher and tumbles over to make him spin. He moans with rage, but his grip on her becomes even tighter. She drifts to the south, towards the water. The canal is polluted but she will be stronger there. He is heavy and doesn't seem to be losing his grip.

'I won't go back to the Tower!' she shouts down at him. 'Don't think you're going to get a single more book out of me.'

'I don't want you back there!' he shouts back. She can see his feet flailing, she thinks he won't hold on for much longer now.

Luna drags them higher and higher. Her body is straining with the effort; the power that keeps him tethered seems to be almost as strong as that which lets her fly. They drift through a cloud bank and she opens her mouth to drink in the cold droplets of water. They fortify her, and she rises higher into the air. Uranga is far below them now, she can see the spiral of the widdershins canal gleaming like a coiled snake on the land, the rivers beyond winding across the forests and fields. It galls her that the blasted place is still green as an emerald.

'I want you dead,' he continues. 'I want your body lying broken in some crater in a valley. Then I'm going to have the girls stitch all your worshippers come to mine your flesh with pickaxes. They're going to chip bits off you to make jewellery.'

Luna kicks at him but she doesn't connect. 'Fuck you, Mandoré. You and I both know your girls have nothing more to stitch. I'm going back to the sky, and if you come too I'm going to take you to the dark side of my mother where you'll never be able to see your precious lump of rock or your brothers, and I'm going to torture you like you did to Ula.'

Mandoré laughs.

'You don't know anything, star child. You're not going anywhere. You broke the contract, the sky won't have you and the earth will tear you apart.'

Now she can see the sour sea encircling the land, they are so high up she can see the horizon curving at each side. The air is thin and delicious, she puts out her tongue to taste its purity. She remembers it now, the feeling of it clear at the back of her throat. Tears prickle; a ridiculous human habit she picked up from that body. She will see her mother soon. She will feel nothing else but this cleanness for the rest of eternity.

'You sure you don't want to let go, earthling?' Luna calls. She revels in the terror she can smell from him. 'You sure you don't want to change your mind?'

Mandoré is silent. Her courage falters. Why does he not beg her for mercy? Why does he not let go and return to his brothers? They are almost at the earth's limit now, the darkness of her mother's realm is closing on them. She is almost free.

But the border looks wrong. It is not porous and welcoming to her as she remembers from her infancy, the way the contract described it. It is hard, diamond-like, shimmering silver as they approach. Mandoré tugs at her feet. She looks down at him, feels her stomach twist to see the ugly, righteous smirk in his eyes. He is wrong, this is her home. Her mother will save her. She'll be welcomed back with joy.

Her head bumps against the border. It is only a small jolt – on earth it wouldn't even dislodge a leaf skeleton from a wintry twig – but here creation obeys different rules. The diamantine crust of the atmosphere trembles and creaks, there is an almighty crack of a roar like shards of ice on a lake and the force of it sends her reeling backwards. In the silence, she hears Mandoré cackling. It sounds like birds twittering and snakes slithering and a million intestines convulsing: all the revolting things of the earth.

And then they are falling, both of them, plunging towards the earth again like hawks diving for the same prey. Luna howls, and high above, her mother the moon shudders. She turns her face away from the plummeting bodies and hides her tears. She has to rise soon, she will have to watch it all, impassive, from her perch in the sky. She has shed too many tears over that curse of a contract in these long centuries, every time one of her daughters chafes at the rules and breaks them. The moon reaches out to the obedient ones who created and wrote and sat still in the Tower until they were called back, those who now sit behind her in the sky as Ursa, Lyra, Auriga, Cassiopeia. They coo wordlessly back at her, offering comfort as mindless as a caress from a suckling baby.

Fuck the earthlings, she thinks, borrowing from the daughter who calls herself Luna. *Fuck the Thirteen who take my children and give me back bright, shining idiots. I hope she ruins you all.*

SEQUENCE

Section 4, clause 9
The star child must concern herself with writing
love stories over any other kind of tale, for these
are the type that keep the mortals happiest of all.

The applause is deafening; it rises like a wave from their feet, breaking over her head. Alissa stands between Vanna and Lion, bowing over and over again. Her cheeks feel tight from smiling and her bottom lip is starting to twitch with the effort of it. From the corner of her eye she can see Goat, stamping his front hooves on the cobbles and sobbing deliriously. It was a good show, even she can tell that.

There is a flash of a blue face at the back of the crowd and Alissa blinks, looks back at the place where she thought she saw it. She scans the plaza. She is sure she saw the witch, no one else could possibly look like that. Alissa would love to see her again. She wants to introduce her to Lion, Vanna and Goat. Maybe Juggler too, but she has a feeling the witch would have something to say about him. She wants to tell the witch that she has fallen in love, and to ask her to fill her singing bowl to see if there is any chance, any chance at all, that he might love her too.

But she can't get another glimpse of that blue face. Instead, her attention is stolen by an orb falling through the now-dark sky. It looks like one of the juggler's balls, it glows in that same way and makes the same kind of strange loops.

She cannot tear her eyes away from it. It feels familiar, as though it is something she saw once in a dream. Perhaps she stitched it, or perhaps Mandoré called it on one of her shifts, and the girl next to her stitched it and she saw it on the silk as it flowed past her and out of the Tower.

The applause is finally fading and Vanna jumps off the stage to throw her arms around Goat.

Alissa follows her, taking her eyes off the floating ball for a moment as she climbs off the platform, but then she looks up in the sky again and there it still is, lower now. It is hanging over the rooftops of the city, pretending to be balanced atop a spire. Now it drifts to the east. She knows it will fall, somewhere in this city, and she has a curious feeling that she must rescue it, or at least see what it really is when it falls. She lets Vanna, Goat and the juggler go ahead, and instead of following them she ducks between the pungent citizens of Uranga who are drinking raucously again, her gaze moving quickly between the sky and the ground. She murmurs apologies as she pushes out of the central plaza and turns towards the canal, breaking into a trot as the thing falls faster and faster towards the city. She is breathless, mindless. She does not know why she has to find what is falling but she doesn't question it. This is the spiral city, so much happens here she cannot account for.

> • <

Lion watches Alissa watching the moon-shaped thing in the sky as he follows her out of the plaza and along the canal. He is drawn towards her as if she holds him by a leash, he barely sees where they are going as she darts out of the plaza and down a side alley. He can tell she hasn't noticed him padding behind her, and he is surprised to find this provokes in him a kind of noble chivalry. He wants only to protect her from the rabble of the city at Carnival, only to make sure she comes to no harm.

There is a helpless, swooping feeling in his stomach that he observes with dread. He knows what this is, he has felt it before. It is akin to the feeling he had when the witch issued her first rejection; only this is more hollow, more bitter, more melancholy.

Her hair is still loose and it streams behind her as she rounds the corner. Lion tries not to look at the way it catches the lantern light like a ribbon of flame as she moves. *She is not yours, she will never be yours*, he reminds himself. *Keep your longings to yourself, for once.*

OSTINATO

Section 9, clause 11(b)
There shall be no mercy for an Earth spirit or a
star child who disobeys the terms of this contract.

The impact, when it comes, is more painful than anything Luna has ever felt. Her bones shatter as they hit the cobbles, the shards splintering into her flesh with a thousand tiny tears. It is worse than the blinding pain of being dragged through the border in Mandoré's net, worse than climbing through the window in the cellar room, worse than leaving Ula all those times. She has always thought pain like this would kill you.

But she is not dead, not yet. Probably because the ancient powers that wrote the contract are trying to figure out what to do with the spirit of a star child that can neither stay on earth nor return to the sky. In a tiny place in her battered heart, she is proud of that. She has caused them all trouble. She has not got most of what she wanted, but she's got that.

She opens her human eyes. The lanterns in the plaza flicker. She can see her sister stars in the sky but no Mother Moon, and this is the biggest wrench. She wants to catch a glimpse of the moon before this body dies, she wants to know if her mother forgives her.

An excruciating throb drums in her shattered skull and she lets her eyes sink closed. Someone will come, soon, and kill her somehow. They won't let her live. She's got their attention now.

The dank soil smell of the Thirteen fills her nostrils. Her heart starts to skitter, the pain rumbles through her body. They'll take her back to the Tower, she should have known. It's the only place in creation she can be now. Hot, desperate tears leak from her useless eyes and track down the skin she can't stop from glimmering.

She opens her eyes again. She can see the shapes of their heads silhouetted against the sky, she can feel the warmth from their breath seeping out from under the masks. She tries to roll over to crawl away from them, but her legs don't work and her back screams and she cannot move anything but her face and two fingers on her left hand.

'Lift her up, I want her to see what she's done.' She recognises the imperious voice, she used to know it as Thirteen. She feels rough hands on her shoulders and neck and arms dragging her upright and backwards. She shrieks, but they ignore her. She can't struggle, nothing on her body works. She is left to slump against some damp, cold wooden post. She can't see their faces, the light is too dim and they are still masked. But she knows there are twelve of them. She can smell twelve meaty hearts, twelve puffs of sour breath, twelve variations of clammy sweat.

The spirit she knows as Thirteen comes to crouch in front of her. She can tell it is him because the lines around his eyes are deeply carved into his temples, like rocky valleys that once sheltered powerful rivers.

'Are you happy now you've ended the world?' he says softly, his voice muffled as always by the grey mask tied around his mouth and nose.

'That's where you're wrong, Malanii,' she says. Her voice is nothing more than a whisper. It rasps at her sticky throat as she struggles for breath.

She sees that he tries not to flinch at the way she spits out his name, but there is a flicker of anger in his eyes that he cannot hide.

'You all think the world has a beginning and an end, but really it goes round and round.' Luna tries to lean towards him but her back is severed from her head, she can only make her mouth hang open. 'There are no straight lines in heaven or earth, Malanii. Only circles.'

Malanii – who she used to call Thirteen, but fuck the politeness and respect due by the contract – shuffles on his knees to one side so she can see beyond him to where the other earth spirits stand in a silent circle around some glowing thing lying on the cobbles.

'Look,' he says, taking her chin between his thumb and forefinger to pull it forward. 'Look at why your mother can't bear to have you back in her realm.'

Mandoré's bones glimmer, just like Luna's skin, now that he is not alive to keep their shine hidden by flesh and skin and hair. There is none of that left now; it could not survive the thin air so close to the border and he knew it. There is only a skeleton lying in a pool of congealing blood in the place where the fifth spirit of the earth fell to his beloved. Luna lets her eyes trace over the concave planes of the skull, the sharp scapulae, the symmetrical wings of the pelvis bone. She looks at the curved vertebrae of his wheel, the beard that once lovingly oiled it gone, burned up in the fire of the atmosphere as he fell, leaving behind only a hint of singed hair lingering in the air.

Luna looks back at Malanii, who is watching her with an expression of hatred in his eyes. His mask has slipped a little; she can see a thatch of greasy dark hair on his upper lip.

'What do I care if he's dead?' she says. Each word sends a jolt of agony along her spine. 'He killed me a million times over.'

One of the masked men breaks from the circle around the wheeled skeleton and flings himself to the ground beside Thirteen. She recognises him by the ring of green threaded through the black irises of his eyes, eyes she saw several times a day for many years.

'Is this really what you want, child?'

Luna can tell Three is close to tears. She turns her eyes away from him in disgust. He will beg her now, with the same voice that used to comfort her during her nightmares, and it will scrape at her heart until it bleeds. She wishes she could cover her ears.

'Do you know we've run out of books? You killed so many people the last time, but you saw fit to salvage something as I knew you would. It is not the earth's place to question what the sky brings it to sew. But now? Luna, child, you are going to lose your eternal life. So many innocents will die.'

Luna says nothing. She clamps her lips shut, ignoring her old nursemaid as he starts to weep. Thirteen gently pushes him back to the circle around Mandoré's skeleton and comes back to Luna.

'But why all this show, star child?' Thirteen says. 'Why plan this carnival of chaos if you knew we had nothing beyond today? You could have just let everything end.'

Luna stares at a house over Thirteen's shoulder. It has a blue door and a lantern sways gently. The handle makes a creaking sound in the hook as the wind takes it, and the flames make the shadows on the cobbles dance. There are closed shutters above the door, and then above that shutters again, before the brick turns into slate and slants backwards into a roof. There are no lights within the house. Luna wonders how quickly the family that lives there would have died, if the witch hadn't betrayed her and the waters had come. Where would they have drowned? In their beds or in a tavern somewhere, dancing to fiddle music with sweat flying across the room? Or perhaps one of them would have died across the city, lying drowsily with their lover on a bed of crushed flowers from the parade. Romantic, Luna thinks, to drown in the arms of your lover. She'd like to ask them to let her die like that, but she can't bear the thought of them going near Ula again.

Thirteen takes her chin again and a shriek of pain echoes in her skull, but she refuses to look at him. The earth spirits are silent. She can't tell if it is grief or anger and she no longer cares.

A pigeon struts on a rooftop, some rodent scurries along a gutter. In an opening to this small yard in this big city, behind Luna where she cannot see, a yellow-haired girl and a lion made of leaves stand and watch the curious scene. Alissa has a fistful of her fine blue skirt thrust into her mouth. Her body quivers and she drags silently at the air through the cloth. The lion doesn't understand why she shakes so but he stands close to her, close enough for her to lean gratefully on him to stand upright. They watch as the twelve masked men surround the skeleton and the glittering, paralysed woman, but they cannot hear a word.

Thirteen makes a strangled sound in his throat and Luna knows instantly that she has lost, the eldest spirit of the earth has found her out and every single dream and scheme she's been laying for years is gone, lost to the earth's insatiable appetite.

'There are more books, aren't there?' He seizes her face with both hands and presses her cheeks together. Luna wails with pain and the light that radiates from her skin pulses with her weakening heartbeat.

Blasts of pain fire all over her body. For the earth to touch her skin this way is madness, she will die. Malanii is melting her right here in the city of her sisters, and he will never be punished, for it is she who broke the first rules – and besides, she is almost dead. It won't be long. What's this pain now, compared to the pain of her eternal exile?

'Tell us where!' Thirteen shouts. There is restlessness among the remaining masked men. They leave the skeleton in its pool of blood and creep closer to their brother and the star child. They lean in, blocking out the lantern and the starlight, making Luna gag with their sudden, rotten smell.

'You're monsters!' Luna screams back. Flecks of spit fly from her teeth and land on his loosened grey mask.

'You are the monster,' Thirteen says, squeezing her face even harder.

'It's not my oath!' Luna moans. She can barely breathe now. 'The contract is older than anything else in the world. I didn't make it, I didn't choose it!'

'But you have no life without it, it is what you were born for.'

'No life?' She gurgles, a twisted laughing sound. 'I lived just fine when I wasn't with you. I had my magic, I had love, I had the whole world I had written. I could have lived with my family, I could have been with my own kind. Without that cursed contract, I would have had everything.'

Thirteen narrows his eyes. 'Where are the texts, star child. There's no solace for you in the heavens now.'

'I don't care. I'm dying. You got what you wanted, I'll never leave the earth now. I'm going to fade here and leave a stain on this goodwife's yard that she'll never be able to scrub out.'

Thirteen squeezes Luna's face again, and again she screams.

Behind her, Alissa flinches. She puts one hand on Lion's warm head and pulls him closer towards her.

'Where are the books, star child?' Three says. He is cajoling, as if he is trying to persuade her to get into bed without her toys. It is this that wrenches something loose inside her.

'Call me Luna!' she shrieks. 'My name is Luna!'

'Where are the books, Luna?' Three says patiently.

She shuts her eyes. The silver light of her skin throbs a little, flickering like a candle flame.

'I wrote these last books long ago,' she says, 'when I first began to think of this.'

She opens her eyes and looks around the masked men. She holds the gaze of Seven and lets her lip curl a little with contempt. He never showed her the slightest kindness, she remembers, never came to sit on her bed to keep her company while she was writing, never brought her a present to brighten her imprisonment.

Her face is blank as her gaze moves on to Three, who is wringing his hands in misery, tears leaking from his eyes. He whispers her name but she ignores him and carries on looking, past Nine, who she used to sit with to show him her time signatures; past Ten, who brought her the rug which she foolishly played with as a child; past Six, who made her the window she escaped from.

Last of all, her gaze comes to rest on Five's corpse, twice her captor, lying in his pool of blood.

'You've got them.' She looks back at Thirteen. She tries to smile, because this is the last thing she's going to have to smile about, her last and only triumph. 'You've got one, and he's got one, and him and him. They're wrapped around your wheels.'

None of the masked men move. They look first at the ground, at the illusion of their two feet, and then they look at Thirteen.

'Look in him,' Luna says, 'if you don't believe me.' She looks at Five's bones, lying glittering on the cobbles. 'He's not using his any more.'

The masked men are very still, waiting for a signal. Slowly, Thirteen nods. Luna can feel the silent tussle between them over who will go to the corpse. A web of ancient favours and slights dredged, considered and mapped until all eyes are finally turned to One. He swallows. Luna can see the lump on his throat quiver as he fumbles inside his cloak and pulls out a knife.

He kneels by Five and slices at the joint where his spine meets the wheel. Ten and Eight turn away, Four raises a hand to his mouth as if to hold back vomit. Three sobs loudly.

One's hands becomes bloodied to the elbow and his cloak is soaked as he hacks at the bone. The squeaking sound of the knife sawing at the cartilage makes Luna smile softly. She didn't want to get to this point, it was only ever a backup plan. But here she is, watching her enemies dismembering her captor, and she finds some pleasure, at last, in how it's all turned out.

One's knife breaks through the bone. He holds the wheel with one hand, and with the other gingerly reaches into the soft marrow. His brothers cannot look away from his probing fingers, they are fascinated by their own horror. Luna hopes they are imagining the pain. She hopes it is as great as her own.

He begins to pull something from the skeleton wheel. It rasps as it slides across the bone. He holds a long, white tube up to his brothers, slimy with grey spinal fluid. They frown, squint at what he holds, leaning towards him. One starts to unroll the tube. Now they see it is a tattered scroll in One's bloodied hands, creased in the middle from where it has been curved.

'Don't you like my new work?' Luna shuts her eyes. She is tired now, and it is just as delicious to imagine their faces as to look at them. 'Or is it only me that should be mutilated in the service of ancient treaties?'

Thirteen releases his grip on Luna and she swallows her gasp from the jolt to her neck. He stands and walks to One, taking the scroll gently from him. Luna opens one eye, just a crack, to see him turning the scroll over. On the back, just as she has written, there is a sticky blob of Five's congealed blood. It makes a star with five points. Thirteen holds it up to his brothers for them to see. They all recognise it as a time signature and they shudder.

Thirteen sways on the illusion of his feet. Luna hopes their fear of the pain they know they will have to endure to keep their precious earth is turning their hearts to ice. She hopes they can already feel the shock of a cold blade slicing into their spines.

'Leave me to die now,' Luna whispers. 'You got what you want.' It is as if all the fight and hatred has gone out of her, her voice is mellow and far away.

Thirteen shoves the scroll into Ten's arms and comes to stand in front of her, blocking the light from the lanterns in the plaza. His hands are shaking, so he hides them inside his robes. 'When will a new star child come?'

'Soon.'

'Tell me when!' Thirteen shouts.

'I don't know, I didn't write it.' She smiles, lets her head loll to one side. His voice feels far away, her mind is drifting just beyond. 'You'll need all the scrolls, though. I know that much. Don't think you'll get away with keeping yours, Malanii.'

> • <

Alissa does not understand what the masked men are about to do, but she knows that the slumped, glowing creature has won. She watches as they surround the bloodied, wheeled skeleton and take turns to reach out and touch it with the tip of one finger. They rear back when the skeleton bursts into flames and stand in a circle, watching it burn with a cold, white heat that lights up the yard, the windows reflecting its pale, flickering fire. She wonders which of them it is, dead and burning to ashes. She hopes it is Mandoré. She would like him to be punished more than the others; there was a cold meanness in him that made her think he enjoyed his cruelty.

Now they have let the illusion of their feet fade and their masks are loose around their necks, it is clear to see the hair that flows from their faces to curl around the wheels where the feet should be. Alissa feels Lion glance at her with puzzlement, but she doesn't return his gaze. She is not surprised. She has never seen any of the Thirteen move on their wheels, not with her own eyes, but rumours hummed in the stones of her dormitory from generations of sewing girls who had chanced to see the earth spirits' true form and had passed whispers from bed to bed. *They roll on a single wheel just like a cart, they have beards as long as a staircase that wraps around their wheels and tells them where to go, when we see their feet it's only a trick.*

They stand, perfectly balanced on the rim, as they fumble inside their cloaks. Each pulls out a knife that glints in the light of their brother's pyre. They hold the blades high and there is no hesitation as they swing them towards the bottom of their spines, the tender place just before the wheel curves backwards, at exactly the same place where their brother sliced open the corpse. There are hard, thumping noises as they hack at themselves over and over again, pulling at their wheels to crack open the vertebrae. Alissa feels Lion cringe beside her and he turns his face away from the blood starting to trickle onto the ground. It flows between the cobbles, making islands of the stones. But she is not frightened. It is only justice, she thinks. They are only asking of themselves what they have taken from so many for so long.

The earth spirits do not make the expected noises of agony as they pull the jagged pieces of flesh from their sawn bodies. One by one, they break through and hold their wheels aloft, floating off the ground like geese skimming the water. They touch the pulpy mass at the bottom of their spines gingerly, reaching in with careful fingers to tease out the scroll hidden there. Alissa counts the scrolls as they are extracted and given to the tallest masked man. Thirteen rolls of bloodied paper. How many days on the earth is that? Alissa wonders. How many moments of wordlight, how many stitches?

Now the Thirteen hold their wheels with distaste, like rotting lumps of meat. None of them seem to be in pain. Alissa is disappointed about that. The hair and muscle and sinew fall from the wheeled bones like the shank of a lamb tenderised in a bubbling cauldron. The Thirteen float forward and feed their flesh to the white fire consuming the corpse of their brother. As it swallows each wheel it hisses and spurts green, and then the white flames jump even higher. From her hidden place in the shadowed alley, Alissa can smell singed hair and charred pig. She covers her nose with the sleeve of her dress. Lion's whiskers quiver.

The masked man who holds the scrolls points to the sky to attract his brothers' attention. The others look up into the darkness, and what they see there clearly frightens them. There is a flurry of whispered discussion, each of them moving awkwardly, bumping into each other as they float about without their wheels. Then the one who has the scrolls holds up his hand and the others fall silent. They look to the sky as if they have been called, and then they are gone. Alissa blinks, shakes her head. All twelve of them have disappeared.

Now the plaza is empty, aside from the cold fire and the cloaked figure slumped by the lantern post which has been still and quiet for so long. Whoever it is is surely dead by now. Alissa waits for a moment, then creeps out of the shadows. The cobblestones are slick and slippery with blood, and she picks up the hem of her skirt to stop it dragging in the muck. The white fire is only as tall as her knees now, running out of flesh and bone to burn.

'What are you doing?' Lion whispers. 'Let's go. This is too weird, let's get out of here.'

Alissa ignores him. She steps carefully in the clean patches of stone towards the slumped figure. She turns back every few steps to look up at the sky. She sees nothing; then nothing again; and then the moon, rising full and bright between two chimneys. So bright and big that Alissa can see the dark shadows of her dry valleys and dusty mountains. A wind blows into Alissa's face, and it brings with it a soft keening noise that is almost too faint to hear. It is coming from the moon. Alissa isn't sure how she knows it, but there is no doubt in her mind that the moon is watching the fire and the newly dead figure in the plaza of her spiral city, and she is weeping for what has come to pass.

Alissa looks back at the cloaked figure only a few steps away from her. Quiet voices from the stones of the Tower sigh in her ear. *There's a woman in the cellar who writes the books, she comes from the stars, she's the daughter of the moon, she's a spirit as old as the world.*

The figure doesn't move as Alissa approaches. She hears Lion's paws padding softly behind her, and she is glad to feel him close. She kneels before the still person and reaches out to draw the hood back from their face. It's a woman, but unlike any Alissa has seen before. Her skin glitters and her features are too sharp, too perfect to be entirely human.

'Do you know her?' Lion whispers, his tail high and tense, his flanks ready to leap in front of Alissa in case this woman is one of those urban dangers he is desperate to protect her from.

Alissa puts one finger to the woman's neck and feels a tiny flutter of life still pulsing there.

'She's the moon's daughter,' Alissa says quietly.

Lion makes a soft growl of shock in the back of his throat but he says nothing. Alissa is grateful for that. She knows she will have to account for so much that they've witnessed tonight, but not now, not yet.

'My lady?' Alissa says. 'Can you hear me?'

The woman's eyelids flutter and Lion flinches, takes a step backwards. A tiny moan escapes her and then her eyes blink open. They are black, with white pupils like tiny moons. Alissa wonders who would ever be fooled as to who and what this woman really is, if they ever saw eyes like that.

The moon's daughter takes a few moments to focus on Alissa. She stares for a while longer, and then her whole face lifts into a sweet smile of joy that drenches Alissa with warmth. No one has ever looked at her that way. She feels tears prickling at the bridge of her nose.

'It's you,' the moon's daughter murmurs. 'I'm glad. I've been so longing to see you.'

RITORNELLO

Section 9, clause 14
If all these conditions are followed by all
signatories, it is clear that the world may keep
going, renewing itself over and over again in a
perfect cycle forever more.

Leira and the witch stay on their bench long after the darkness has settled like a cloak around their shoulders. The plaza is almost empty; there are only a few pairs of groping lovers scattered in the shadows and three small children crawling under the benches, examining what has fallen out of pockets to see if it can be saved or sold. The merrymakers have moved on to find more mead and beer and elderberry wine in other parts of their still-dry city. Leira watches each of the entrances to the plaza, waiting for Luna. The bricks are still and solid again, the air soft with night, the sounds of the city smooth and continuous. Luna has lost and the Thirteen have won, but Leira does not know how, nor what is keeping the world she can see and touch stable now. She fingers the labra pipe in her pocket, lying suspiciously still and quiet. She could play a few notes, summon her, ask her for forgiveness and offer to help her escape, again. She presses her forefinger to each of the holes, tentatively asking the wood each time, *where is she?* It refuses to answer.

Neither the witch nor Leira speak. Leira would quite like to talk; questions are bubbling on her tongue and threatening to burst out from behind her teeth, but she keeps them tightly clamped. The witch sits with her eyes closed, swaying gently. Her face moves as though she is miming a conversation with someone invisible to Leira. Now her face screws up in disgust, now she smiles wanly, now she raises one eyebrow as if to say, *really?* Perhaps she's communicating with her sister witches. Leira wishes she could still hear that song. That's one of the things she'd like to ask the witch: where that song comes from and how she can hear it again. She'd like to make an instrument that might sound like that, something like a harp that will chime with a chorus of voices every time it is plucked. She knows very little about music so it will take her a long time, but she doesn't mind.

'Well, that was a close one.' The witch pulls her golden cloak around her and cracks her knuckles. 'I don't mind telling you, there were a few moments there when I thought it was over.'

Leira smiles. 'I thought you weren't scared at all. When you pulled your sisters towards you I thought you were all fearless.'

The witch shrugs. 'I'm good at pretending.' She stretches her arms over her head and bends to each side.

'Crescent, I'm starving,' she says. 'Where do you go in this place to get something to eat?'

Leira winces. 'Just the taverns and inns. They'll be full of drunken louts, but I suppose you can keep us discreet enough.'

The witch frowns. 'The earth spirits are here, in the city. I can smell them.' She sniffs the air theatrically, then wrinkles her nose. 'They stink like a compost heap.'

'All of them? They're here together?'

The witch nods.

Leira shakes her head slowly. 'They never do that. Sometimes they have council and leave the sewing room. They have a device they leave behind, something that repeats elements of what's been written in the past few days. I didn't think they were all allowed to leave the Tower at the same time, Luna told me there was something in the contract about that.'

The witch sweeps her cloak across her shoulder and picks up the hem of her dress to move delicately around the benches, trying not to step in the accumulated filth of the city.

'We're a bit beyond the terms of the contract now, don't you think?'

Leira follows the witch past the benches and towards the voices spilling from the tavern around the corner. Of course they're beyond the contract. They're beyond the books stacked in the cellar, beyond the stitches on the silk, beyond all the legends about stars being dragged in nets from the sky. Now the world is floating through the darkness of the night, untethered from its words, its spirits either silent or screaming, its bodies spiralling between drunkenness and madness as the sun hovers under the world, trying to decide if he will come back or not.

And it is only the witch, uniquely in the entire world, who seems not to care.

PAVANE

Section 2, clause 4
Upon their ascension to the skies to take the form of a constellation, the star children shall lose all memory of being upon the Earth.

Alissa cannot look anywhere else but into those strange, moon-shaped eyes. She is falling endlessly into them, drifting into their blinding light, but there is no fear, no sense that she is unsafe. She can feel Lion breathing heavily beside her, but he does not touch her or try to draw her away from the shimmering woman. She loves him more for that.

The moon's daughter lets her eyes sweep over Alissa's face as though she is searching it for clues of something, or trying to carve it into her memory.

'I want to tell you that I'm sorry,' the moon's daughter whispers. Her voice is hoarse, her tongue so swollen it is forming tiny canyons of blood in her cracked lips. 'I wrote you into the Tower, even though it was torture for you and torture for your mother.'

A rock settles in Alissa's stomach. 'My mother?'

The moon's daughter smiles and a speck of bloodstained spittle runs down her chin. 'The love of my life,' she says. She tries to swallow her slug of a tongue but chokes and coughs.

Alissa cannot speak. A cavern has opened in her mind, black with all the things she doesn't know about herself, the world, who and why she is. She blinks to dislodge the stars crowding the edge of her vision, tries to focus on the moon's daughter again. She can see the woman is slipping away, that she will die in the next few moments, but where does a star go when she dies on the earth? Why isn't she up in the sky with her own mother?

'Go to Magdra,' the moon's daughter breathes. 'Ask for the owl woman's cottage. She'll know you.'

Alissa opens her mouth to ask more, trying to choose one of the many questions that buzz on her tongue, but she is too late. The glittering light on the skin of the pained, dying woman flickers, flares, and then the moon's daughter shatters in a silent explosion of white light. There is not so much as a breath of air displaced, nor a spark of heat in the burst; only the dazzle of the light. Alissa screws her eyes shut and slaps her hands over her eyes but the blaze is imprinted on her eyelids, she cannot escape that light. Beside her, Lion moans with the sudden blinding. He ducks his head and presses his whiskers to the ground. The darkness behind his eyelids, too, has been replaced with the diamond brilliance of the blast.

Moments later, they hear tinkling sounds, like a soft rain falling onto a thin slate roof. Alissa opens her eyes, her vision watery and wobbly as her pupils adjust to the darkness of the square. Falling all around her, onto her hair, her shoulders, her feet, are tiny pieces of something like glass. They sparkle with reflected moonlight and lantern flame. They fall gently, like snowflakes, and when one lands on her nose it is so slight she hardly feels it at all.

Lion looks at the place where the moon's daughter was only a few moments ago, slumped against the lamppost, then gazes around him at the drifting flecks of solid light. He whistles.

'This has been the strangest night of my life,' he says quietly. 'And I have lived through a revolution, contortionist school, an unrequited love affair with a witch, and a magical metamorphosis.'

Alissa reaches out to touch his mane, and for a moment he thinks she is going to stroke his head, but instead she picks out a large piece of the light. She turns it in her fingers. Most of it is transparent, but there are trapped flecks of solid silvery threads inside them. They remind Alissa of the wordlight in the Tower.

'Will you help me collect all the pieces of her?' she asks. Lion nods.

'What will we do with them?'

'I don't know yet. I just don't feel right leaving her lying here.'

She places the shard by her feet, on top of a scatter of tiny pieces no bigger than a mote of dust. Lion nudges another few shards towards her and turns to gather more. The cobbles are dusted with the silvery glass which crunches under their careful feet, but the flow of the falling pieces is slowing now. Alissa works quickly, sweeping the glittering pieces towards a heaping pile at the foot of the lamppost, trying not to crack them under her tread. Lion, with his delicate paws and elegant stride, is lighter.

The moon, poised high in the east, sighs for her baby. She watches as the yellow-haired girl and the lion made of leaves gather up the body that will never return to the sky. Gleams of her light shine onto the pile of shards. Although she wants to turn away and leave her daughter in the darkness she craved, she cannot. Her light shines on all, it obeys rules other than her will. For there are other, even older contracts between the moon and the earth and all the other forces of creation, and not even a clever daughter with a flute and a devious imagination and a deal with the Trickster can break them all.

CAROL

Section 1, clause 13
The Thirteen of the Earth shall take measures
to heal themselves when they are sick or injured
such as the land takes, and within a similar
time signature as the Earth takes to heal, that is
to say a thousand years. This shall be separate
and outside what is written in the star children's
books.

Leira puts her hand on the chimney-warm brick of the
house to steady herself. She leans over, watches the cobbles
writhe like the eels in the canal. She knows she's being
irresponsible, getting drunk with a witch, but she can't help
herself. She's floating deliciously on the fermented tide of
booze that laps at her brain and she wants to find another
tavern, another barrel, another set of stomping songs to
sing.

'You said we should have a few drinks to celebrate saving
the world!' she says between hiccups. 'You never said you
were going to charm him into giving us his ten-years-aged,
special-strength moonshine heather mead!'

The witch laughs. She is carrying her wine particularly
well, Leira notices. She won't be found staggering down
Uranga alleyways to retch.

'I didn't know I was going to ask for it until I smelt it in
his cellar.' The witch tosses her red hair over her shoulder.

'Really, I was doing him a favour. The guards would have got it at the next raid.'

'Let's go and find some more!' Leira stands up straighter and the shadows of the alleyway come to rest lazily in their proper places. Her eyelids feel heavy.

'I think we've had enough,' the witch says.

'We saved the world! We deserve it.'

The witch hooks her arm through Leira's and tugs her towards the street. The witch's body is warm and it bumps against hers as they wander, waving to the merrymakers with drums and lily garlands and half empty bottles of wine dangling from their grubby fingers.

'Well, it was really you who saved the world,' Leira continues. 'Not me.'

'Don't tell anyone!' the witch laughs. 'I'll never live it down.'

'I won't tell,' Leira says, whispering theatrically. 'I'm good at keeping secrets.'

She doesn't want the night to end, and not only because she knows there are no more books and the sun may decide not to bother with rising tomorrow. She misses her workshop and her half-finished projects and her deep copper bath, but her home is so silent, so still. No one moves things in the kitchen when she's spent the day among her machines, no one sings while they wash up their lunch dishes, the only smells are those of her own cooking, her own laundry, her own sweat. Being with the witch reminds her of being with Luna, a simple companionship. *Was there anything in the contract that forbade me from having friends after Luna?* she wonders. She can't remember. All those afternoons Luna spent coaching her on the contract, explaining the archaic clauses and the conditions and the precise language, and she never thought to ask.

The sloppy, boozy part of her wants to ask the witch to be her friend, but even as she thinks it she cringes from it. *There's nothing special about me*, Leira thinks. *Nothing magical that would make a being like this one want to spend time with me. Even Luna had no choice.*

Leira blinks away the unexpected tears. She is just about to open her mouth to ask the witch, as casually as she can, what her plans are for the next few weeks, when the witch wrenches her arm away from Leira and hisses. They stop dead in the street and Leira sways a little and the witch stares at her hands. Her thumbs are scarlet red. She looks up, glances around the now-empty street and shuts her eyes. She sniffs at the air while Leira watches her, her happy feelings fizzing out like bubbles in the rain.

'Ah,' the witch says. 'I forgot about them.'

She makes a face and strides away, turning off the main street into the narrow gap between a house with a white awning and a greengrocers. Leira stumbles to catch up with her, the aftertaste of the mead burning in her throat.

She did not have any expectations of what she would see when the alley opened out into a lantern-lit, cobbled yard; there is no one calling the world, time is slipping past unstitched and so anything can happen. Still, she has to admit she's surprised to see the yellow-haired sewing girl from the play and that enchanted lion made of leaves, standing in the middle of the yard next to a pile of glittering, broken glass.

At the sight of the witch, whose hair looks like a burning bonfire even in the dim lantern light of the yard, and Leira, lurching out of the shadows towards them, the girl and the lion fumble guiltily, moving to hide the pile of glass. As the witch walks towards them, Leira watches their whole bodies change. The yellow-haired girl's eyes become round with delight, she rushes towards the witch, throwing her arms around her with a huge whoop. Leira feels a twinge of jealousy.

But the lion is retreating, his belly low to the ground, his tail thick and high and his mane standing puffed around his face. He is growling, a low throaty rumble that makes the glittering glass vibrate and tinkle, and even from where she stands Leira can see the terror in his eyes.

The witch gently disentangles herself from the girl's embrace and points to the black puddle staining the cobbles.

'What's that?'

'It's the blood of the Thirteen,' the girl says. 'Mainly the dead one, I think, but they all bled there.'

The witch raises her eyebrows. She points to the pile of glass.

'And that?'

The yellow-haired girl sighs. Leira creeps forward to stand just behind the witch's shoulder, glancing at the cowering lion. Soberness rushes through her stomach and her chest, making her head pound and her mouth dry. She needs another drink. She will never drink again.

'It's the moon's daughter,' the girl says. 'She killed one of the Thirteen, so they killed her.'

Leira finds a keening sound erupting from her. She claps her hands over her mouth to stop it but its echo soars around the dirty yard like a hawk swooping in the night. She sinks to her knees, noticing the sparkling dust that coats the cobbles. *I killed her,* she thinks. *I betrayed her to those who I swore I would never betray her to, and now she is dead.*

'She was her friend,' Leira hears the witch explaining to the girl. 'They were very close.'

The witch puts her hands carefully on the cobbles, glistening with a million tiny specks of silvery dust. She murmurs something in lilting words that neither of the sewing girls understand. She leans forward until the periwinkle skin of her forehead touches the dust and she stays there for a few long moments, muttering so quietly in that ancient language only the ants can hear.

When she sits up, she doesn't wipe the dust off her forehead, leaving her skin shimmering like Luna's did in her unguarded moments, like a holy mark. Leira watches that sparkling place on the witch's forehead, that piece of Luna held on her. She would like to press her head to the dust of Luna's body too, she would like to think a tiny fragment of her only friend could burrow its way inside her skin and stay a part of her forever.

'What will you do with her?' the witch asks.

The girl frowns. 'I hadn't thought of that yet. I just didn't want her to be scattered here for any old person to sweep up.'

The witch nods thoughtfully. 'Do you want to keep her, Leira?'

Leira blinks so that her tears tumble over her eyelids and onto her cheeks. Luna used to scoff at the prohibition on touching her. 'It's only for *them*,' she'd say, pointing to the ceiling where Leira imagined the masked men relaxing with cups of comfrey tea on embroidered chaise longues after a long day with the wordlight. 'The contract doesn't say anything about *you* touching me.'

But Leira took the side of the earth when it really mattered, and now the shattered fragments of the star child are not hers to touch, not with her forehead like a benediction nor with her hands like a death rite.

'No,' she says, and she is surprised to find her voice is normal, not like that screeching hawk any more. 'It's not what she would have wanted.' She looks at the yellow-haired girl. 'Did you speak to her before she died?'

The girl nods.

'Did she mention anyone?' There is a tiny crocus of hope flowering in Leira's heart. Maybe it was she who was last on Luna's lips.

The girl looks at her feet. 'She talked about an owl woman,' she says quietly. 'She said the owl woman was my mother.'

Leira glances at the witch to see if this means anything to her, but her expression is inscrutable.

'Then you should take her to the owl woman,' Leira says, and she is proud that her voice doesn't crack, that she has managed to fully clamp that wail of grief she let escape earlier. But there is a sharp, itching kind of pain, as if she has swallowed one of these glass shards, stabbing at her throat. She welcomes it, swallows it down and lets it burrow under the fibrous muscles of her lonely heart to root there.

'We could do with a broom and a few jars,' she says. She looks at the witch. 'Can you sort that out?'

The witch whistles and makes shooing motions for Leira and Alissa to stand back. Moments later, a dark shape hurtles out of the sky. The witch thrusts her hand out to catch it, but it slips through her fingers and crashes to the floor. She bends to pick it up and holds it out to Leira. Then she reaches inside that blue and gold cloak and pulls out a jar that she sets on the cobbles at her feet.

'You sweep and we'll pick her up,' the witch says. 'You don't have to touch her if you don't want to.'

Leira's hand is white around the besom. Its handle is chilly from the night air. She shuts her eyes, but her mind is swamped with visions of her dead friend. Luna, sitting on her bed and gazing at her mother through that enchanted window; sitting at the chair Leira made for her; hunched over her manuscripts to mutter them aloud. She looks back at the witch and nods, mutely, touching the broom to a crystalline pile of stardust.

> • <

The fragments of the moon's daughter fill three large jars with sparkling light. Lion stands in the doorway of an abandoned house and watches the three women at their sweeping. He is paralysed by the bizarre sight of the witch he used to love talking to the woman he now loves, while picking up pieces of a mythical creature being swept up by a woman wearing the same kind of patchwork dress his mother used to make and sell at the spring fairs all over the eastern swamp. His claws feel brittle with tension, his fur bristles like a pine tree. The lion in him wants to take Alissa's gold-embroidered collar between his teeth and drag her away from this dark yard, but the man in him wants to slip away, find a dark hole and climb into it until the blue-skinned hag is gone.

He knows the witch knows he is here. He knows she's waiting, toying with him like captive prey. He knows

Alissa will find out who it was that cast this spell and that will be the end of their friendship, let alone any kind of love. Somehow, although he cannot imagine how such a wretched coincidence came to be and he would like to tear at something's flesh until it is shredded into mincemeat, Alissa knows the witch. It seems that she thinks the witch is her friend. She put out her hands to embrace the witch when she has never done such a thing to him. Lion shuts his eyes and leans against the stone wall of the building. The dark and the cool soothes him.

But then there are footsteps approaching and he springs forward, out of the shadow of the doorway and onto the swept cobbles. Alissa is coming towards him, reaching out like she wants to take his hand in hers. Her muscles have forgotten, at least in this moment, that she has never seen him with hands before.

'Lion, come and meet my friend,' she calls. There is a brightness in her voice that hurts him, like facing a sunny day with a hangover.

He follows her meekly, his tail swishing this way and that as it tests the air. How will he get out of the way if the witch raises her hands to him? Could he cover his ears so he can't hear her spells? His brain fizzes with fleeting plans of escape, but a few moments later he is standing in front of all his heart-hammering, sheet-drenching, lung-bursting nightmares and he can't hear anything but the waves of blood pulsing in his ears.

'This witch saved my life,' Alissa announces proudly. 'And this is Lion, who is my best friend.'

He has to look up at her, exposing his tender throat. Her features are still and expressionless, but there is something glinting in her violet eyes that makes him think she is about to start laughing. Again, he thinks of how his feline cousins toy with their weak, furred prey before they crunch into its bones.

'We've met,' the witch says.

There is a long silence while the older woman in the patchwork dress with hair like Alissa's joins them. She stands awkwardly by the witch, her eyes rimmed red like she's been crying or drinking.

Lion looks at Alissa. The lion in him thinks again about taking her by the collar and dragging her back to the caravan, and the man in him searches desperately for something to say that will end this before it has begun and let him get out of this yard with both his life and his dignity. But he is still and mute, undone by the progression of emotions through her face. First joy at her friends knowing each other, then puzzlement at how that might have happened, then concern. The silence drifts on, becoming a lingering bad smell no one can quite account for.

'Oh,' she says, turning to the witch. 'It was you!'

The witch folds her arms across her chest. 'He was bothering me! I used no glamour, I didn't hide who I was, he knew all the risks of courting me.'

Lion thinks he can hear a defensive tone in the witch's voice, but he doesn't want to get too hopeful. He looks down at the cobbles. He had thought there were no lower shames than those he has endured these past moons in his new form, but he was wrong.

Alissa glances at him, then back at the witch. 'Can you turn him back? He's no trouble to you now.'

The witch lets her hands fall to her sides with a sigh. 'I can't. That's not how this spell works.'

'How does it work, then?'

'It's the usual kind of boring thing,' the witch says. Her voice is full of scorn, but as she turns to Lion and sweeps her eyes over him like he's a smear of shit on her shoe, he could swear she almost smiles. 'The only way to undo a spell like this is with the power of true love.'

She turns to the straw-haired woman holding the broom with its bristly birch sticks facing upwards, and holds out her hand.

'Can I have that?'

The woman hands it over, and the witch turns it horizontal and mutters something that sounds like a command. She hoists her leg over the handle and wriggles on it, settling herself comfortably. She tries a few variants of her grip on the handle, settles on having her right hand in front of her left, blue thumbs facing up.

'You coming?' the witch says to the straw-haired woman. 'I can drop you back at your house, if you want.'

The woman scrambles awkwardly onto the broom and wraps her arms around the witch's waist. The broom rises a little off the ground and the woman stifles a little shriek. The witch turns the broom around to face Alissa and it bucks a little, prompting a moan from the woman behind her. The witch tuts, taps a finger on the disobedient broom, then smiles broadly at Alissa.

'Take care,' she says as the broom keeps rising into the air. 'You know where to find me if you need anything.'

'What shall we do with that blood?' Alissa calls out, reaching up to the sky as if she wants to catch it and hang on as it drifts away.

The witch shrugs. 'Leave it. It's where it belongs.'

> • <

And then they are gone, past the thatched houses of this yard, past the tiled rooftops of the towers and turrets, past the highest branches of the oaks and the beeches planted for shade and beauty in the plazas of Uranga. Past the owl heading home to her nest, past the fluttering midges that hover in the air, waiting for the dawn.

The witch turns the broom and then they are flying directly towards the moon. Its white light fills Leira's vision with a searing cold and her eyes begin to stream with tears.

'I'm sorry,' she whispers, over and over again, clutching at the witch's cloak and letting her tears tumble into the fur to make them damp as rain.

The witch reaches back to squeeze her hand and the broom slows a little.

'Don't worry,' she says. Leira tries to swallow the sharp shard of guilt in her throat but it catches and slices at her. 'Mother Moon knows you had no choice. None of us did. It was all written a long time ago.'

> • <

Far below them, tethered to the earth by a different contract, Alissa and the lion watch their silhouette soar across the bright moon for a moment and then plunge into darkness. They stand a little apart from each other, so that no part of their bodies will accidentally touch.

Alissa is thinking about the power of true love. She is wondering how the spell will measure it, and how much of it is enough. Yes, she loves Lion, but is it true love? She starts to walk and she feels Lion moving alongside her. She breathes in the musk of his fur and breath. She doesn't want to go anywhere he isn't, she wants to walk beside him for the rest of her life. Is that what the witch meant? Is that enough?

Lion is also thinking about the power of true love. He is wondering if it counts as true love if it's only one of the loving pair who would die for the other, or if one lover's desire should hobble itself to match the other of more reluctant affections. He waits for Alissa to say something, but she is quiet as they walk out of the yard and back towards the square where the performers are camped. He doesn't mind her silence so much, he's in no hurry. He would rather stay a lion and be with her than leave to go and search for someone who might just be another one of that witch's dirty tricks. He will stay a lion until his leaves dry out and drift from his hide and become food for worms on the forest floor, or until Alissa says she loves him. Whichever comes first.

SCHERZO

Section 2, clause 1
And the Moon shall reign as Queen of the Skies
and she shall have dominion over all that occurs
past the air border.

The merriment and revelry is beginning to taper off. Here are the stragglers, stumbling home as the taverns finally run dry of wine and whisky, beer and mead. Here are the last puffs on a flute, bangs on a drum and plucks of a fiddle, as the instruments are abandoned on the tables of the inns for their musicians to attend to in the morning. Here are the sighs of the newlyweds, reaching for warm flesh in the stillness before dawn, their beds strewn with crushed daisies and forget-me-nots. Here are the wrens and the blackbirds, calling up the sun with their songs.

Alissa and Lion arrive at the performers' camp without having said a word or touched since the witch and her friend left them. The silence between them is thick, treacly with a sweetness that is entirely new to them both. They walk, suspended in it like flies in amber, afraid to utter a single sound that might crystallise it and make it shatter, flinging all their secret hopes to the wind.

They can see their caravan from across the plaza and pick their way through the tents and the debris of torn costumes and abandoned headdresses. They determinedly do not look at each other as they pass tents shaking gently with the rustling of lovers, neither do they catch each other's eye as they pass tents thick with snores and snuffles. There is an intimacy to their silent witnessing of the sleeping sounds of strangers that reminds them they have shared four walls as they sleep, and this makes both their faces flush, even in the chill air of the dawn.

Vanna and Goat are sitting on the platform at the back of the caravan, dozing lightly. Goat opens his eyes a crack as they approach and gently nudges Vanna awake.

She yawns and squints at them. 'Where have you two been? We were looking everywhere for you. We got you some breakfast, we thought you'd be hungry.'

She points to two covered plates nestled under the wheel, and Lion nudges them out from under the platform. They sit down to eat, mouths itching at the sight of food.

'Is the juggler with you?' Goat asks.

Alissa shakes her head. 'No. We haven't seen him since the show.'

Vanna stretches and smooths her hand over her hair. She watches as Lion delicately picks up a slice of bread between his teeth and drops it on Alissa's plate, while she puts her two sausages onto his. *So that's what they've been doing*, Vanna thinks. She bites her lip to stop herself from smiling; she told Goat she thought that might happen on the second day of them getting on that boat from the Patli Bridge, and he had looked dolefully at her and told her she should respect the depth of Lion's grief for his old form and shouldn't seek to matchmake him out of it. She wants to elbow Goat now and say, 'Look at them, I was right, they're in love'; but because it would embarrass Alissa, annoy Lion, and perhaps tear something of this new, fragile bond, she keeps her peace and her congratulations to herself.

A shadow briefly blots out the sun and then there is the swish of wings and the rustle of feathers. Owl lands on the roof of the caravan, then hops down to the platform, where she pecks a lump of meat from Lion's plate and swallows it with one gulp. There is a hint of disgust about her beak at the lack of a crunch. She stares at Alissa for a moment, then hops off the platform to skim the ground towards the glowing jars. Owl nudges them with her beak, making a tapping sound on the glass.

Vanna follows Owl's movements. She cranes her neck to see the jars better, and Alissa thinks about trying to move them out of the way or hide them under the fabric of her dress, but it is too late.

'What've you got in those jars?' Vanna asks.

Alissa pauses, takes a bite of her bread. 'The moon's daughter.'

Vanna starts to laugh. 'Good one,' she says. 'Lion's sense of humour is rubbing off on you, and I like it.'

Alissa and Lion share a glance and a throb of complicity, an almost unbearably sweet feeling of a secret shared that threatens to burst out of her skin. Alissa drops her eyes quickly to her plate and tears off another crust of bread to shove into her mouth. She chews and chews at it but it doesn't seem to be disappearing into her belly. Lion buries his head in his paws, pretending to doze.

Vanna notices the surge in the air. She ducks her head to hide her grin and asks no more about the jars, busying herself imagining what exactly the pair of them got up to.

Goat yawns and gets to his feet. 'Well, there's no sense in waiting up for the juggler any more, he knows where to find us.'

He turns with a clatter of his hooves and nudges aside the curtain with his nose. He steps forward until he is halfway through the doorway, his hindquarters sticking out from the curtain, and then he bleats with a desperate kind of shock.

'His box is gone!'

Vanna clambers to her feet and pulls the curtain fully aside, flooding the caravan with light to expose the leaking stuffing from the cushions, the scuffs on the floor, the glaze of dust on the shelves. Alissa climbs onto the platform to peer over Vanna's shoulder, Lion stands next to Goat with Owl on his shoulder. They are all looking at the place in their home where the juggler used to keep his mysterious box and his carafe of water. There are clean patches in the dust where they once stood; this is the only indication that something is missing.

Goat lets out a pitiful sob. 'But they've invited us to perform at the mayor's show!' He wails and drums his front hooves on the floor, raising a drift of dust that makes Alissa's nose twitch. The acrid tang reminds her of the way the moon's daughter smelt when she shattered. She turns to the jars, standing abandoned on the cobbles by her grease-smeared plate. They don't so much glow, she realises, as suck in the light around them and reflect it again with a white glare. She retrieves them, kicks the plate under the wheel to deal with later, and steps up into the carriage.

Goat is inconsolable. 'But I thought he liked us! We said a year and a day, but he must have known that's just a convention. He must have known we liked him!'

Vanna has a comforting hand on his shoulder, rubbing his fur this way and that. Owl stands on her perch, her eyes closed and her wings folded and still, but Alissa can tell she's not asleep. She listens; probably not to Goat's meandering complaints but to something else, something beyond the plaza filled with tents and caravans, something far away in the sky that only a bird can hear.

Alissa sits on the bench and tucks the jars away inside the cloak she brought from the Tower last winter. It was the juggler who invited her to join this troupe, who more or less told them all that she would be joining, and still she doesn't understand why. She probably won't find out now, either. She wonders if she will have to leave them, or if Lion will become the thread that binds her to them. *He wouldn't like that*, she thinks, *replacing the juggler in any way*. The witch's words ring in her head. *Can one person decide it's true love?* she thinks. *And if they can, which of us will it be?*

'Alissa?' Goat asks tearfully, trying to sniff his snot away. 'Do you know where he's gone? Did he tell you anything?'

She shakes her head. 'He's always been a mystery to me,' she says, truthfully. 'I don't know anything.'

Vanna fluffs up the pad of straw for Goat to sleep on. 'You're exhausted,' she says soothingly. 'We all are. Time to get some sleep. Maybe he's just gone to see a friend. We'll probably hear something from him later.'

Goat sniffs again and lies on his bed. 'You're right. He won't have abandoned us. He'll be back soon.' He buries his chin in the straw and sighs.

Lion turns around on the rug and settles on his paws. He has said nothing since they arrived back at the caravan, and now he lies so that his face is towards the driving bay. She waits for him to say something sarcastic about the juggler, to say *good riddance* or *I told you so* or *I never liked him anyway*. But he is silent. His tail sways gently, moving across the rug with the rustle of a breeze through a beech. Alissa watches his tail move and then she knows he is not thinking about the juggler at all. That's the way Lion's tail moves when he is afraid of something.

Vanna pulls the curtain across and the door shut, lying down on the opposite bench in a nest of her knitted blankets. She wriggles with a sigh of satisfaction and reaches up to close the shutters, leaving the caravan black with only a few lines of light around the door and window.

Alissa lies with her eyes wide open in the darkness. She listens to Goat's tired snuffles and Vanna's soft snores, but even though she knows she's tired, her eyelids will not droop. She listens for the deep, rasping breath that means Lion is asleep, but she cannot hear it.

'Lion?' Alissa whispers after losing count of Vanna's snores. 'Are you asleep?'

'No.'

She hesitates, then says, 'Do you want to go for a walk?' For a second there is only the exchange of hot, stale air in the carriage, but then Alissa hears his mane rustling and feels the caravan sway gently as he stands up. He pads to the door, nudges it open to let the light pour in through the crack. Vanna sighs and turns over. Alissa pushes her blankets gently onto the floor and follows Lion out, letting the door to the caravan shut gently behind her.

Owl opens one eye. She turns her head towards the door and listens to their footsteps winding across the cobbles. In the cellar of the inn on the corner of this plaza, she hears a family of mice skitter in between the sacks of barley.

Alissa and the lion made of leaves walk aimlessly through the city; now along the widdershins canal, now through the alleys that connect the different spirals of the waterway, now along the curving avenue of the deosil road. Everywhere is deserted, the only bodies around are still, their minds drifting in the clumsy dreams of the drunk. They see a man propped up in a doorway, his sky-blue suit vividly stained with purple splotches of elderberry wine; two young women with flower crowns curled around each other under a table outside an inn; and a little boy sleeping in a wheelbarrow, clutching a snoring kitten in his arms. The taverns are shut, the musicians are silent, the markets are empty. Everyone is asleep at last.

Alissa imagines the day shift in the sewing tower, letting the wordlight flow onto the silk to weave this peaceful slumber. One day she will tell Lion that she used to live in the Tower. She will tell him of all the things in the world she has seen stitched on the silk: the villages she has made of brown and green and grey; the boats she has sent along choppy rivers; the complex roofs of the labra forests she has constructed. She will tell him of the music that made her stitch the juggler, and who the masked men they watched hack off their wheels really were. She will take him to meet the woman the moon's daughter said was her mother.

They turn into a plaza with phantoms of a fruit market. Little green caps of strawberries, squashed gooseberries, and the twin stems of cherries litter the cobbles. The air smells of fermenting sugar. Lion pads his way in between the empty crates to the fountain and sits on the shady side. The water trickles slowly but clear from the stone lips of a large fish that leaps directly upwards, as if twisting away from the hungry mouth of a dolphin. Its scales are etched into the stone, and where the water trickles down its belly the carving is worn faint.

'I don't feel anything for the witch any more,' Lion says quietly. 'I want you to know that.'

Alissa doesn't know what to say. She would like to touch him but he seems too distant from her. She stuffs her hands inside the folds of her green dress. It feels so long ago that she put it on and combed her hair in preparation for the show. She can barely remember a thing about it now. Everything important in her life has happened since it ended.

'Now I think that I never did really love her, and she knew it,' he says.

Alissa looks at him, staring out across the silent square. In the curve of his profile she can see an echo of the man he used to be. *I would want him even if he couldn't change back*, she realises in that moment, and the force of her longing takes her by surprise. She reaches out, her hand quivering like the wings of a butterfly landing on a flower, and puts her palm tenderly on the side of his face, just underneath his whiskers.

He nuzzles into her hand and her belly melts into a silvery, tingling liquid and flows out through her sex. Her hand grows hot and then, just as the heat is beginning to sear her, a shaft of golden light shoots from beneath her palm. She cries out and snatches her hand away, Lion yowls softly. She examines her palm; there is no burn or singe or scald. The sudden pain of that golden light has disappeared as quickly as it came. When she looks back at Lion, she swallows a gasp. On his face, where she touched him, is a patch of skin the colour of a chestnut.

'Lion—'

'I know,' he murmurs, and his voice is different, laboured and rasping. 'I can feel it. Don't stop, please.'

She puts her fingers on his snout, runs them down to his nose and then along the other side of his face. Light explodes in all directions, bouncing off the stone steps of the fountain and darting off at another angle. Her hand throbs with the pain of the heat, but in the wake of her caresses she can see that chestnut skin appearing and it makes her go faster, moving her hands all over his face to stroke away the enchantment of leaves.

'Is this hurting you too?' he asks her. Lion is holding his whole body rigid with tension, she can feel the pain radiating from him just like the light.

'No,' she says, and it is almost true. This is not a pain, but it is not so comfortable either. But she doesn't care. She moves to kneel in front of him, so she can run both her hands down his forelegs. Light shoots out of the gaps between her fingers like blasting arrows, and she dodges them as they launch towards her. She runs her hands along his shoulder, his chest, his side; moves her hands to the place above his head to stroke all the way down his back, his neck, the sides of his ribs, his hips. She pauses before she reaches back to run her hands over his flank, feeling the skin become smooth and warm under her fingertips as the enchanted light pings off the fish fountain, leaving a little singed patch on the stone.

Lion presses his new, old face into Alissa's shoulder as she touches his back. His weight grows with every stroke but she braces her legs against the steps and leans into him. She feels as though she would like to disappear into him, dive into the pores these shafts of light are exploding from and live inside him for the rest of her days.

He groans, but there is something intimate and helpless about the sound. He is in pain, but there is an edge of delight in it and this makes her brave. Heart pounding, she grasps the leaves hanging between his legs and under her hands it becomes warm and hard. She strokes, light pouring from between her fingers, and she can feel Lion's hot breath on her ear.

'Keep going,' he murmurs.

She runs her hands down his hind legs, being sure not to miss a patch; on the outside, on the inside, in the places on his inner thigh where the skin folds. She comes to his hind paws and strokes downwards towards the claws, but what she leaves behind her is fur instead of skin, golden fur the same colour as the leaves that carpeted his body before. No golden light sprays from his feet.

'Leave them,' he says, and his voice is similar to the one she knows but more in his throat. 'I thought she'd leave me with something changed.'

He pushes away from her and stands, stretching his back upright with a grimace of effort. He is naked, his skin glistening in the late morning light. Alissa cannot stop her eyes from roaming all over his body, taking in the tight curls of black hair on his chest, his legs and the nest around his sex. His limbs are lean with taut, defined ropes of muscle. There is a shadow of a beard on his face and twin hollows at the base of his throat and the centre of his chest. At his ankles the skin fades into fur where he is left with great paws instead of feet, but it doesn't seem to affect his balance. He is standing upright now, as if the time he has spent on all fours was nothing but a dream.

She watches him flex his fingers without looking at them, balling his hands into fists and then releasing them. He lifts his hands to his face, running his fingers over the skin covering the line of his jaw, and then he looks at them, turning them over to examine the lines that criss-cross his palms.

Then he looks back at her, and he smiles. She sways a little towards him. She is dazzled by him now, the sight of his chestnut-coloured skin still glowing from the light is making her vision swim.

'What was your name?' she asks this stranger standing in front of her. 'Before you were Lion?'

'It doesn't matter now. I want you to call me Lion still.'

He takes her hand and pulls her towards him. She stumbles into his warm arms, her face pressed against his shoulder with the sharp edge of his collarbone pressing into her cheek. She is melting, liquifying, her limbs are dissolving into the ground. There is a miasma of heat around them from the arrows of light. The air smells like smoke, like the inside of the witch's cave.

Lions puts his lips to hers and she opens her mouth to kiss him back. Time falls away as her mind wheels, and her skin drips away from her bones where he touches her and there is no past and no future, nowhere else apart from this dribbling fountain in the spiral city and these steps where her true love holds her against him as though they were the only two beings in the whole world.

> • <

They leave Uranga that night, joining the long lines of empty carts driven by dishevelled, yawning men, following the roads out to the farms to restock the city with the grain, meat and wine that it has eaten empty and drunk dry in the past days of Carnival. There is no wind, so Owl's feet are strapped to the caravan to tug it along, the sails slack and lying against the roof in a heap.

The glowing jars filled with the pieces of the moon's daughter sit where the juggler's box and carafe used to be. Whenever the caravan swings to follow the meander of the road, the light of the gibbous waning moon beams in through the open shutters and the jar flares with brilliant white light that makes Goat, Lion and Alissa, bumping along inside the caravan, squint to protect their eyes.

Soon they are outside the city limits, and instead of houses squashed together lining the deosil road there are tall hedges of hawthorn and elder, with dustings of cow parsley and dog rose. Vanna steers the caravan to the side of the road and unclips Owl from the tethers. She flies off across the fields, the wheat glowing silver in the moonlight, hunting for her dinner. Vanna climbs into the back and settles on her bench with a yawn. They are all still tired and could do with more sleep before they start on the long journey towards the village of Magdra. Alissa had said there was someone she wanted to see there, and Goat, too astonished to see his friend back to his old form, albeit with two golden lion's feet to show for his adventures, had not troubled her with any more questions than what direction they should take first.

Here is an owl swooping for her dinner of fresh mouse among the labra trees, her keen eyes fixed on the embrace between a girl with hair the colour of buttercups and a man who was once a lion made of leaves. Here is the pale road, wandering like a thief through the land, eating up the footsteps and wheel-rolls of its travellers. Here is the night sky, clear as a pool of ink with no clouds. Here are Lyra, Cassiopeia, Ursa, Aquila; gleaming with tears for their dead sister from their tombs in the night sky. They know that no one looks at the heavens that way, as a graveyard of Mother Moon's daughters, but that's what it is. The place where things go to die when they have made their worlds.

Soon, when everything in creation begins to be called from words scribbled on a scroll with a time signature that loops and swirls like the flight path of a starling, the sun will start to slide across the moon. He will smile gently at her, encouraging her as the birthing pains begin. When his fiery bulk is fully hiding her from the curious gaze of the earth, she will begin to labour with her next child.

CODA

Section 9, clause 3
Do not look for the Trickster, he will not come, or
he will come only when there is another force at
play which is beyond the scope of this contract.

MEXICO CITY, 1960

The light in her studio is fading to a coral glow as the sun
sinks over the bowl of the hills that enclose this city like a
womb. She can hear the clink of crockery as Walter moves
around downstairs, trying to find the coffee press he likes
best. He will boil the kettle for both of them and let the water
meant for her sit in the steel, waiting for her footsteps on the
stairs. She will make a pot of tea with some of the tender leaves
of one of her potted herbs that sit on the sunny landing, and
they will sit at the table for a while, letting chatter about their
respective days weave around tender silences.

She has long stopped work for the day but a fine brush
dangles between her forefinger and thumb as she sits at
the window, watching the sunset drench the wispy clouds
with its brash kind of pink. For a moment she wonders if
Leo would like to paint with that colour, but rejects it as
too harshly feminine. The canvas she's been working on lies
abandoned on the easel, sulking at her for her inattention.
She rebukes it for failing to interest her and she fancies that
it shrinks away in shame.

She leaves the brush on the windowsill and reaches behind her for a biscuit from her tin. She has dreams that her paintings rearrange themselves while she is not looking; that the carefully proportioned archways of her buildings and the shadowed folds of her characters' robes and cloaks become twisted into another realm. She is not worried by this thought, only vaguely regretful that they don't trust her enough to do it in front of her.

She reaches for the tarot cards that sit in a snarled pile behind the dusty curtain. A present from Kati, who said the first pack should always be a gift. Remedios shuffles them slowly, watching a black cat pick its way along the sloping roof of the building across the street. She greets the cat silently, for you must never ignore a black cat crossing your path, then pulls a card from the bottom of the pack.

She turns it over to see a figure in a green tunic decorated with yellow stars, boots the colour of sunshine with a bag tied on a stick slung over his shoulder. One foot is out, ready to step off the cliff into the unknown world of whatever lies beneath, ignoring the little white dog that pulls at his ankle. She feels a satisfied smile spread on her face. She loves this card. She feels it is her own talisman, speaking to her across all the times she has leapt into the dark in her life. She draws it whenever she has a decision to make, whenever she is feeling restless in her work, whenever she longs for Spain. Number zero. The Fool.

It reminds her of what she wrote that day when Leo brought the *toloache* from the *mercado* Sonora, that contract between the moon, the sun and the earth. She remembers she had written in a wildcard, a kind of juggling gleeman. She had imagined him wandering the world just like this trickster of the tarot, warping beginnings and endings into his own cryptic pattern, and she realises now that the Fool was the character she had in her mind the whole time. She will tell Leo, someday, how the images of the cards are sliding from the deck and into her imagination.

But where is that piece of paper? she wonders, half-heartedly moving a pile of books from a chair and kicking at a wastepaper basket. She would like to find it again, to read that contract and see if there is anything in it worth kindling. Perhaps it will have changed behind her back, like her paintings. Or perhaps it will have dissolved already, the ink evaporating from the paper and drifting into the dusty air of her studio, the paper crumbling into little specks of carbon that will one day, far in the future, float off into the sky where who knows what will become of it, for who knows what will become of any of us on this wide, wild earth where nothing but the wind is free.

ACKNOWLEDGEMENTS

My heartfelt thanks to:

George, Dan and Vince, for bringing this novel into the world and making it look wonderful.

Anne and Dave; for everything.

Djamel Eddine for his support.

Lorna; who read early parts of this book and said keep going.

Ashley and workshop friends at the Unthank School for the encouragement to stagger over the finish line.

Janet Kaplan, whose book *Unexpected Journeys* was an invaluable resource to me on the life and work of Remedios Varo.

Eden; for all the ways she lights up the days and nights.

Ed; the structure, the space and the steel that girds it all.

And my eternal gratitude to Remedios herself. Though she passed to another world over half a century ago, I will always be thankful for the simple fact that her paintings exist, as well as the example of her artistry. I am humbled to be able to pay my own homage with this novel.

ABOUT THE AUTHOR

Rym Kechacha is a writer and teacher living in Norwich. Her debut novel, *Dark River*, was shortlisted for two British Fantasy Awards.

DARK RIVER

RYM KECHACHA

> "A tender and lyrical novel with mythological power. Kechacha's work is full of care for a broken world."
> **Naomi Booth, author of *Sealed***

☆ **British Fantasy Awards Best Novel finalist**
☆ **British Fantasy Awards Best Newcomer finalist**

Doggerland, 6200 BC. As rivers rise, young mother Shaye follows her family to a sacred oak grove, hoping that an ancient ritual will save their way of life.

London, AD 2156. In a city ravaged by the rising Thames, Shante hopes for a visa that will allow her to flee with her four-year-old son to the more prosperous north.

Two mothers, more than 8,000 years apart, struggle to save their children from a bleak future as the odds stack against them.

At the sacred oak grove, Shaye faces a revelation that cuts to the core of who she is; in the wilderness of the edgelands, Shante finds herself unprepared for the challenges and dangers that confront them at every turn.

As Shaye and Shante desperately try to hold their families together in the face of disaster, these two young mothers uncover a terrifying truth: that it is impossible to protect the ones they love.

www.unsungstories.co.uk/darkriver

Follow Rym @RymKechacha

THREADING THE LABYRINTH

TIFFANI ANGUS

"A poignant and elegant
meditation on time and identity"
M. R. Carey, author of *The Girl With All the Gifts*

☆ BSFA Best Novel Award finalist
☆ British Fantasy Awards Best Novel finalist
☆ British Fantasy Awards Best Newcomer finalist

Toni, the American owner of a failing gallery, is called to England unexpectedly when she inherits a manor house in Hertfordshire from a mysterious lost relative.

What she really needs is something valuable to sell, so she can save her business. But, leaving the New Mexico desert behind, all she finds is a crumbling building, overgrown gardens, and a wealth of historical paperwork that needs cataloguing.

Soon she is immersed in the history of the house, and all the people who tended the grounds over the centuries: the gardens that seem to change in the twilight; the ghost of a fighter plane from World War Two; the figures she sees from the corner of her eye.

A beautiful testament to the power of memory and space, Threading the Labyrinth tells the stories of those who loved this garden across the centuries, and how those lives still touch us today.

www.unsungstories.co.uk/threading

Follow Tiffani @tiffaniangus

GIGANTIC

ASHLEY STOKES

Kevin Stubbs is a Knower. He knows life hasn't always treated him fairly. He knows he wants to be allowed access to his son again. But most of all, he knows that the London Borough of Sutton is being stalked by a nine-foot-tall, red-eyed, hairy relict hominid – the North Surrey Gigantopithecus.

Armed with a thermal imaging camera (aka the Heat Ray) and a Trifield 100XE electromagnetic field reader (aka the Tractor Beam), Kevin and his trusty comrades in the GIT (aka the Gigantopithecus Intelligence Team) set out to investigate a new sighting on the outskirts of Sutton. If real, it will finally prove to the world that the infamous Gartree-Hogg footage was genuine, and a British Bigfoot is living in suburban London: FACT.

But what he discovers undermines everything he believes in – and forces Kevin to face up to his own failures, and the very real, very scary prospect that he might have got it all terribly wrong.

www.unsungstories.co.uk/gigantic
Follow Ashley 🐦 @AshleyJStokes

ALWAYS NORTH

VICKI JARRETT

> "Compelling, beautifully estranging and wonderfully urgent in its imaginative passion."
> Adam Roberts, author of *The Thing Itself* and many more

★ 2019 KITSCHIES AWARD FINALIST
★ THE GUARDIAN'S AND FINANCIAL TIMES' BEST SCIENCE FICTION OF 2019

We all have to work to live, even if it is an illegal survey for oil in the rapidly melting arctic.

Isabel is part of a weathered crew of sailors, scientists and corporate officers she sails into the Arctic. A great icebreaker carves into the brutal environment, and the days grow longer, time ever more detached, as they pass through the endless white expanse of the ice.

But they are not alone. They have attracted the attention of seals, gulls and a hungry, dedicated polar bear. The journey to plunder one of the few remaining resources the planet has to offer must endure the ravages of the ice, the bear and time itself.

This is what we find when we travel – Always North.

www.unsungstories.co.uk/alwaysnorth
Follow Vicki @Vicki_Jarrett

GREENSMITH

ALIYA WHITELEY

Penelope Greensmith is a bio-librarian, responsible for a vast seed bank made possible by the mysterious Vice she inherited from her father.

She lives a small, dedicated life until the day the enigmatic and charming Horticulturalist arrives in her garden, asking to see her collection. He thinks it could hold the key to stopping a terrible plague sweeping the universe.

Soon Penelope is whisked away on an intergalactic adventure by the Horticulturalist, experiencing the vast and bizarre mysteries that lie among the stars.

But as this gentle woman searches for a way to save the universe, her daughter Lily is still on Earth, trying to track her down, and struggling to survive the terrible events unfolding there...

www.unsungstories.co.uk/greensmith
Follow Aliya 🐦 @AliyaWhiteley